THE WORLD IS MADE OF GLASS

'The reader can be entirely ignorant of Jung and his work to enjoy and be informed by this extraordinary book'

Bookseller

'An enthralling story'

Spectator

'A gripping account . . . Jung would have loved it'

New Society

'A riveting, solid, well researched novel'
Daily Telegraph

'West has spun a psycho-sexual web and unfolds a tale both exciting and important'
NANCY FRIDAY, author of
MY MOTHER, MY SELF

'Forceful narrative drive . . . West's theme is undeniably fascinating'

Newsday

THE WORLD IS MADE OF GLASS

THE WORLD IS MADE OF GLASS

I know that I am very close to madness and I am desperately afraid. At night I lurch, panic stricken, through nightmare landscapes; seas of blood and ravines between saw-toothed mountains and dead cities white under the moon. I hear the thunder of hooves and the baying of hounds and I do not know whether I am the hunter or the hunted.

When I wake, I see in the mirror a stranger, wild-eyed and hostile. I cannot read a text-book; the words jumble themselves into gibberish. I slide into dumb depressions, explode into irrational rages which terrify my children and reduce my wife to tears or bitter recriminations. She nags me to seek medical advice or psychiatric treatment; but I know that this malady cannot be cured by a bottle of physic or the inquisitions of an analyst.

So, to affirm my sanity, I have devised a ritual. To the stranger in the mirror I recite the litany of my life . . .

THE WORLD IS MADE OF GLASS

'With riveting narrative skills West reconstructs a razor's edge folie à deux, rich in theme and lavish in the ambience of prewar Europe'
Publishers Weekly

'His most interesting book up to now'
Sunday Telegraph

'A triumph of the imagination and Morris West's best book'
The Plain Dealer

'A haunting story, full of sexual aberrations and the darker mysteries of the mind'
Eastern Daily Press

About the author

Morris West was born in Melbourne, Australia in 1916, the eldest of six children. After completing secondary studies in Melbourne he joined the Order of Christian Brothers, took his vows and spent eight years as a teaching monk. In 1941 he left the Order just before taking his final vows. He joined the army, then worked as a publicist and radio producer. His first bestseller was CHILDREN OF THE SUN. Other famous books include THE SHOES OF THE FISHERMAN and THE CLOWNS OF GOD. After many years in Europe, he has now returned to Australia where he has been appointed Chairman of the Council of the National Library of Australia.

THE WORLD IS MADE OF GLASS

MORRIS WEST

CORONET BOOKS
Hodder and Stoughton

First published in Great Britain in
1983 by Hodder and Stoughton
Limited

Coronet edition 1984
Fifth impression 1989

Printed and bound in Great
Britain for Hodder and Stoughton
Paperbacks, a division of Hodder
and Stoughton Ltd., Mill Road,
Dunton Green, Sevenoaks, Kent.
TN13 2YA. (Editorial Office: 47
Bedford Square, London WC1B
3DP) by Richard Clay Ltd,
Bungay, Suffolk. Photoset by
Rowland Phototypesetting Ltd.

British Library C.I.P.

West, Morris
  The world is made of glass.
  I. Title
823[F]   PR9619.3.W4

ISBN 0-340-34710-4

For
JOY,
with love,
to celebrate a homecoming.

Author's Note

This is a work of fiction based upon a case recorded, very briefly, by Carl Gustav Jung in his autobiographical work, *Memories, Dreams, Reflections*. The case history is undated and curiously incomplete. I have always felt that Jung, writing in his later years, was still troubled by the episode and disposed to edit rather than to record it in detail.

I have chosen to set this story in the year 1913, the period of Jung's historic quarrel with Freud, the beginning of his lifetime love affair with Antonia Wolff and the onset of his own protracted breakdown.

The character of the unnamed woman is a novelist's creation; but it conforms with the limited information provided in Jung's version of the encounter.

The character of Jung, his personal relationships, his professional attitudes and practices are all based on the voluminous records available. The interpretation of this material and its verbal expression are, of course, my own.

For the rest, every novelist is a myth-maker, explained and justified by Jung himself in his Prologue to *Memories, Dreams, Reflections*: "I can only make direct statements, only 'tell stories', whether or not the stories are 'true' is not the problem. The only question is whether what I tell is *my* fable, *my* truth."

M.L.W.

Commit a crime, and the earth is made of glass. Some damning circumstance always transpires.

(Ralph Waldo Emerson: *Emerson's Essays*, first series, "Compensation", 1841)

Jung was always very well aware of the danger of mental contagion; of the adverse effect that one personality might have upon another . . . Anyone who has practised psychotherapy with psychotics will confirm that delusional systems, and other features of the psychotic's world, are indeed contagious and may have a very disturbing effect upon the mind of the therapist.

(Anthony Storr: *Jung* – Ch. 2)

MAGDA
Berlin

At midnight yesterday, my whole life became a fiction: a dark Teutonic fairy tale of trolls and hob-goblins and star-crossed lovers in ruined castles full of creaks and cobwebs.

Now I must travel, veiled like a mourning wife, because my face is known to too many people in too many places. I must register in hotels under an assumed name. At frontiers I must use a set of forged documents for which I have paid a royal ransom to Gräfin Bette – who, of course, is not a Gräfin at all, but has been bawd and pander to the Hohenzollerns and their court for twenty-five years.

For emergency disguise – and for certain sexual encounters which still interest me – I shall carry a small wardrobe of male attire, tailored for me in a more cheerful time, by Poiret in Paris. Even this record, written for myself alone, must contain inventions and pseudonyms to protect my secrets from the prying eyes of chambermaids and male escorts.

But the truth is here – as much of it as I can distinguish or bear to tell – and the tale begins with a sour joke. Yesterday was my birthday and I celebrated it in Gräfin Bette's house of appointment, with a man near to death in my bed.

The event was distressing for me, but not unusual for Gräfin Bette. Middle-aged gentlemen who indulge in violent sexual exercise are prone to heart attacks. Every brothel of quality has the means to deal promptly with such matters. The house doctor provides emergency treatment. Dead or alive, the victim is dressed and transported with all decent speed to his house, his club or a hospital. If he has no coachman or chauffeur of his own, Gräfin Bette supplies one: a

17

close-mouthed fellow with a catalogue of convincing lies to explain his passenger's condition. Police enquiries are rare – and police discretion is a highly negotiable commodity.

This case, however, was not so simple. My companion and I were paying guests in the Gräfin's establishment. He was a man of title, a colonel in the Kaiser's Military Household. I am a known personage in society. I am also a physician and it was clear to me that the colonel had suffered a coronary occlusion and that a second incident during the night – always a possibility in such cases – would certainly kill him.

He was married – none too happily – to a niece of the Kaiserin and he had told his wife that he was attending a conference of staff officers. That story – thank God and the Junker code! – would hold good. But finally, my colonel, living or dead, would be delivered to his spouse and there was no way of concealing either his cardiac condition or his other injuries: lacerations of the lumbar region, two cracked vertebrae and probable kidney damage.

Gräfin Bette summed up the situation, click-clack, in the accents of a Berlin gutter girl:

"I'll clean up the mess. You'll pay for it. But understand me! You're not welcome here any more. You used to be amusing. Now you're dangerous. There'll be a wife and a son and the Kaiser himself and a whole regiment of cavalry baying for blood over this affair. If you take my advice, you'll be a clever vixen and go to earth for a while. Now I need money – lots of it."

When I asked how much, she named exactly the sum I had been paid for the six hunters I had sold that morning to Prince Eulenberg. I didn't ask how she knew the amount or how she had calculated the bill. I had the cash in my reticule and I paid it over without a murmur. She left me then to pack my clothes and to watch over the patient, who was fibrillating badly. Forty-five minutes later she was back with a set of personal documents in the name of Magda Hirschfeld and a first-class ticket on the midnight express to Paris. She also brought me an outer coat of shabby black serge and a black felt hat with a veil. I made a joke of it and said I looked like an English nanny. Gräfin Bette was not amused.

"I'm doing you a favour you don't deserve. Every time I've heard about you lately, it's been a little crazier, a little nastier. Now I understand why . . ."

I asked her what she proposed to do about the colonel. She snapped at me:

"That's my affair. What you don't know can't hurt you or me. I don't like you; but I keep my bargains. Now get to hell out of here."

My colonel was unconscious but still alive when Bette hurried me out of the house and through the kitchen garden to a postern gate where a taxi-cab was waiting to take me to the station. I arrived with three minutes to spare, and paid the conductor handsomely to find me an empty compartment. Then I locked myself in and made ready for bed.

That night, for the first time, I had the nightmare: the dream of the hunt through the black valley, the fall from my horse and then being locked naked in a glass ball which rolled over and over in a desert of blood-red sand.

I woke tangled in the sheets, sweating with horror and shouting for Papa. But Papa was long dead and

19

my cry was drowned by the wail of the train whistle, echoing over the farmlands of Hanover.

JUNG
Zurich

I know that I am very close to madness and I am desperately afraid. At night I lurch, panic stricken, through nightmare landscapes; seas of blood and ravines between saw-toothed mountains and dead cities white under the moon. I hear the thunder of hooves and the baying of hounds and I do not know whether I am the hunter or the hunted.

When I wake, I see in the mirror a stranger, wild-eyed and hostile. I cannot read a text-book; the words jumble themselves into gibberish. I slide into dumb depressions, explode into irrational rages which terrify my children and reduce my wife to tears or bitter recriminations. She nags me to seek medical advice or psychiatric treatment; but I know that this malady cannot be cured by a bottle of physic or the inquisitions of an analyst.

So, to affirm my sanity, I have devised a ritual. To the stranger in the mirror I recite the litany of my life, thus:

"My name is Carl Gustav Jung. I am a physician, a lecturer in psychiatric medicine, an analyst. I am thirty-eight years of age. I was born in the village of Kesswil, Switzerland, on the twenty-sixth day of July, 1875. My father, Paul, was a Protestant pastor. My mother was a local girl, Emilie Preiswerk. I am married, with four children and a fifth on the way. My wife's maiden name is Emma Rauschenbach. She was born near Lake Constance – which sometimes she seems to believe is the navel of the world."

The recitation continues all the time that I am shaving. Its purpose is to hold me fixed in space, time and circumstance, lest I dissolve into nonentity. I breakfast alone and in silence, because I am still trailing the cobwebs of my dreams.

After breakfast, I walk by the lake, gathering stones and pebbles to build the model village which is beginning to take shape at the bottom of my garden. It is a childish pastime; but it anchors my vagrant mind to simple physical realities: the chill water, the form and texture of the stones, the sound of the wind in the branches, the dapple of sunlight on the lawn. As this part of the ritual continues, I hear voices, and sometimes see personages from the past. Occasionally, I hear my father's voice expounding Christian doctrine from his pulpit in Kesswil:

"A sacrament, my dear brethren, is an outward and visible sign of an inward grace. Grace signifies a free gift from God."

I have long since rejected the religion my father preached. His God has no place in my life; but the grace, the free gift – oh, yes! This is given to me every morning when my ritual is completed and, promptly on the stroke of ten, my Antonia walks into my life.

My Antonia! Yes, I can say that, even though my possession is neither complete nor perpetual, as I would wish it to be. We are lovers, but more than lovers. Sometimes I think we have celebrated a marriage more complete than the legal one which unites Emma and me. Toni has given me her body so generously, so passionately, that even when I hear her footfall or the sound of her voice, I am alive and erect with desire. My gift to her is of herself, a singleness of spirit, a health of emotion, a wholeness, a harmony between the conscious and the subconscious. When she came to me, as a patient, she was like the princess sleeping in the enchanted forest, imprisoned by brambles and vines. I awakened her. I swept away the nightmares and confusions of her long slumber. When she was cured, I made her my pupil. Then she became my companion and collaborator.

Now, in my own time of terror, our roles are reversed. I am the patient. She is the beloved physician whose voice calms me, whose touch transmits the healing gift.

I grow lyrical, I know; but it is only in private that I can be so: for this secret journal, during the hours Antonia and I spend together, locked in my tower room, where no one else may enter uninvited. But, even here, our communion is not complete. We flirt, we fondle, we caress – we work, too, believe me! – but we never make love, because Toni refuses to surrender herself to climax in another woman's house. I regret that; but I have to admit the wisdom of it. Already Emma is rabidly jealous and we dare not risk being discovered in the sexual act.

Of course, this forced deferment of release adds to my emotional tension; but there are compensations, in that Toni is forced to observe a certain detachment which is valuable in our clinical relationship. For my part – much as I desire it – I cannot demand to stifle all my perplexities in her abundant womanhood. As well drink myself silly or stupefy myself with opiates and fall asleep mumbling that all's well with the world.

So, each morning we greet tenderly. She makes coffee for us both. We deal with the mail. Then we work together to analyse the psychic conflicts that are tearing me asunder.

In spite of our clinical relationship in these sessions, I am alive, every instant, to her sexual presence. I study the curve of her breasts, the fall of the skirt about her thighs, the wisp of hair that trails at her temple. I am in high sexual excitement; but she sits calm and cool as the Snow Queen, just as I have taught her to do, and puts her questions:

"What did you dream last night? Was it related to symbols we have discussed?"

Today we were discussing a new sequence, unrelated, or so it seemed, to any others I had experienced. I was in a town in Italy. I knew it was somewhere in the north, because it reminded me of Basel; but definitely it was Italy and the present. The people were in modern dress. There were bicycles and autobuses and even a tramway. I was strolling down the street when I saw before me a knight in full armour – armour of the twelfth century – with a red Crusader's cross upon his breast. He was armed with a great sword and he strode forward like a conqueror, looking neither to right nor left. The extraordinary thing was that no one took any notice. It was as if I were the only one who saw him. I felt the enormous power of his presence, a sense of impending revelation, if only I could follow him; yet I could not.

The interpretation of the dream brought Toni and me very close to a quarrel. I was – and am – convinced that it contained magical and alchemical allegories connected with old folk lore: the Knights of the Round Table and the search for the Holy Grail – which symbolised my own search for meaning in the midst of confusion.

Toni disagreed emphatically. The knight was Freud, she said. Freud was the lonely crusader unrecognised by the heedless. She claimed that I recognised his worth and his power but could not follow him because I could not accept the fundamental thrust of his ideas – and because my affection for him had turned to hostility.

I began to be tense, as I am always at the onset of another irrational rage. Then she broke off the argument and came to me and held my throbbing head against her breast and crooned over me.

"There now! There! We'll have no arguments this beautiful morning. We're both frayed and tired. I lay awake half the night thinking about you and wanting you. Please, will you walk me home this evening and make love to me?"

Had she been combative or timid, I might have raged at her for hours, as I do sometimes with Emma; but her tenderness disarms me totally and sometimes brings me close to tears.

Even so, she surrenders no ground in clinical debate. She is convinced that my problems with Freud contribute to my psychosis. I admit that to myself; but I cannot yet admit it to her. I have never told her of the homosexual rape to which I was submitted in my youth, nor of the consequent homosexual element in my affection for Freud and how hard it is to free myself from his domination.

Sooner or later the truth must come out as we continue my analysis together. But, please God, not yet! I am a middle-aged, married fool in love with a twenty-five-year-old girl. I want to enjoy the experience as long as I can. I see battles looming with Emma; and if my dark Doppelgänger ever takes control of me, I shall be lost to all joy and all hope. Rather than endure that despair, I shall follow the example of my old friend, Honegger, and put myself to sleep for ever.

MAGDA
Paris

For the first time in twenty years I am not staying at the Crillon but in a modest pension near the Étoile. I take my meals in the house and my promenades in those quarters of the city where I am least likely to meet friends or acquaintances. There is a kiosk nearby where foreign newspapers are on sale and I have ordered a daily copy of the *Berliner Tageblatt*.

So far, I have seen no mention of my colonel or of his fate. The only reference to my presence in Berlin has been a brief item announcing that: "Prince Eulenberg has bought, from a well known stud, a string of six hunters which are being schooled on his Baltic estate for the coming season."

So, I consider the logic of the situation. My colonel is alive or he is dead. If he is dead, they will announce the news in the obituary column. They will bury him with full military honours: muffled drums, a riderless horse with empty boots in the stirrups, reversed cannon, the whole panoply of military nonsense. If he is alive, he must be at least temporarily crippled and he will have had to find some plausible explanation for his wife. I know him for an epic liar in erotic affairs; but this episode will really stretch his talent.

There is, however, a more sinister possibility: that my colonel is in convalescence but plotting my downfall. He has no reason to love me. He may well be afraid of blackmail – one of the few games I have never played. However, there is much talk lately of new struggles between the Great Powers. Bulgaria has attacked Serbia and Greece. Here in the West there are tales of spies, anarchists and assassins. Only three months ago there was an attempt on the life of King Alfonso of Spain. If the Kaiser and his colonel want to get rid of me, they can arrange it very simply. It is stale news that the Kaiser is very sensitive these days about the honour of his court. Even his royal cousin in England once remarked: "Really, Willy is so clumsy!" And I was nearly ruined by rumours which identified me – quite wrongly for once! – as "the equestrian beauty with whom the Kaiserin is reputed to be in love".

So, for the present, I sit demurely in my pension near the Étoile. I read the morning papers, shop a little, take a ladylike stroll and pray that Gräfin Bette in Berlin gives value for money! I make a joke of it, but truly it is not funny at all. I am scared, shocked to the marrow of my bones – not because of what any-one may do to me but of what I have done to myself. Suddenly, a black pit has opened at my feet and I am tottering on the brink of destruction.

The only way I can explain it is to recall what happened twenty years ago, when I had just finished my studies. Papa took Lily and me on a cruise to the Far East. We travelled on the flagship of the old Royal Dutch Line calling at Hong Kong, Shanghai, the East Indies, Siam and Singapore. One day we were ashore in Surabaja, walking through the market, when sud-denly there was panic. People scattered in all direc-tions, shouting and screaming. We looked up and saw a Malay running towards us, slashing and stabbing right and left with a big, curved kris. He was quite close to us – ten metres perhaps – when a Dutch policeman shot him dead. It was, Papa explained, the only way to stop him. The man was amok, in the grip of a murderous manic rage against which no reason could prevail.

"So, you kill him," said Papa, in that cool, smiling fashion of his. "It's a mercy to him and an act necessary to the public order. That kind of madness communicates itself like the plague among these people."

I wonder what he would have said if he had seen his daughter amok in the bedroom of Gräfin Bette's house of appointment. It began as a common sexual game – albeit a somewhat violent one. My colonel, a big stalwart fellow, a martinet with his troops, liked to abase himself to women. He demanded to be abused, humiliated and punished for fictional faults. I was the perfect companion for his fantasy. I am tall, athletic, a good horsewoman and well known in hunting circles. I enjoyed the game, too – as indeed I enjoy most sexual experiences. But suddenly it was not a game any more. I was a shouting fury full of vengeful angers that welled up from nowhere. I wanted to kill the man. I lashed him and battered at him with the handle of my riding crop. And it was only the sight of his cardiac seizure – his chest caving in, his mouth contorted in a breathless rictus of agony – that shocked me back to reality. It was hard to believe how close I had come to murder – and how much I had enjoyed the experience.

Looking back now, from my discreet refuge in Paris, it is very easy to believe that the experience may repeat itself and that next time I may not be so fortunate. Something is happening to me – has been happening over a long period – which I cannot explain.

Every night before I go to bed, I study myself naked in the mirror. I have every reason to be pleased with what I see. I am forty-five years old. I have borne a child, but my breasts are firm, my skin is clear, my muscles are strong as a young girl's. My hair is still its natural russet brown. There are a few telltale lines round my eyes, but in a kind light and with careful maquillage, even these are hardly visible. My menstruation is still regular and I have not yet begun to experience any of the discomforts of menopause. If I go tonight, as I am tempted to do, to Dorian's club or to visit Nathalie Barney, I shall have my choice of the flower basket, man or woman.

The change, whatever it is, is taking place inside me. It is as if – how shall I explain? – as if a door has opened in my brain and all manner of strange and freakish creatures have been set free. They are out of control now. I cannot recapture them. They are not all cruel and angry, like the one which possessed me in Gräfin Bette's. Others are fantastic, witty, bawdy, full of wild and brilliant speculations; but it is their own caprice which they follow and not my direction. I could as easily turn cartwheels in the Tuileries Gardens as make lesbian love with Nathalie Barney at a tango tea.

But this is precisely what troubles me. I hate to be out of control. With men, horses and dogs I have always been the mistress; with women, either a tender friend or a most subtle enemy. I have never depended on alcohol or on drugs, though I have used them both.

It was Papa who taught me that lesson in his offhand, agreeable fashion:

"Never fall in love with a bottle or an opium pipe. There's no fun and no future in either. Never have sex with a stranger. Syphilis plays hell with the system. Remember that the only lover who can break your heart is the one you depend on."

I wish he were here now, so that I could ask him the questions that are plaguing me.

"What do you do when you can't depend on yourself? Where do you turn when you can't read the street signs? What do I do about all these strangers capering inside my brain-box?"

But this is foolishness. Wishes are beggars' horses. Papa is long, long gone and I cannot spend the rest of my life talking banalities with the widow of a deputy and defending my non-existent virtue against a wine salesman from Bordeaux who pats my knee under the table. Whatever the risks, I have to get out of this place. So, tonight it is Dorian's and whatever befalls in that freak show.

Freak show? Who am I to talk? I have been a member of Dorian's club for longer than I care to remember. According to Papa – usually a most reliable chronicler of the demi-monde – it was founded by Liane de Pougy, who was the poule de luxe of her day. The King of Portugal lavished a fortune on her. Baron Bleichroder and Lord Carnarvon and Prince Strozzi and Maurice de Rothschild all paid tribute in passion and money. The passion she exploited ruthlessly. The money she spent like water on girl lovers and wrestlers and oddities from the dives of Montmartre.

The club was to be her own private raree-show,

where she could milk a little more from her complaisant clients. Her manager was Dorian, a little humpbacked gnome from Corsica who looked like Polichinelle, had a sputtering temper, a fine disdain for most of the human race and a heart as big as the hump on his back.

Papa used to visit both Pougy and Dorian whenever he came to Paris. She consulted him about the ailments of her trade. Dorian he treated for the arthritic pains that racked his twisted frame. When Pougy wanted to sell out her share of the club, it was Papa who financed Dorian to buy it. So, one fine day I inherited a life membership.

When my husband died and my small daughter went to live with her aunt, I was left with a large fortune and a variety of urgent appetites which – unless I, too, wanted to set myself up as a poule de luxe – could only be satisfied in secret. Dorian's became my Paris rendezvous. When I introduced myself and presented Papa's old card, Dorian embraced me and instantly appointed me his personal physician. I remember vividly his crooked grin and how he laid his index finger against his nose and told me:

"Fair exchange, eh? You'll keep me healthy. I'll keep you out of trouble. I liked your Papa. He was a bold one; but he had healing hands – and oh such style! The English milords couldn't snub him. The Germans never dared to bully him. And the French never quite understood him! I'm not certain I did either. I was never sure what he was up to with you. He had very strange ideas about bringing up a young daughter . . . But that's none of my business! Some like fish and some like fowl and how do you know till you taste 'em, eh?"

Dorian is older now, by more than a decade. His hair is white. His bones creak as he moves. He has the dusty pallor of a cave creature. He keeps body servants always at call: a sinister silent fellow from Ajaccio and a barmaid from Calvi who looks as though she could strangle an ox with her bare hands. The barmaid runs the household. The man from Ajaccio is Dorian's shadow: close, scarcely visible, but dangerous as a viper.

When I visit Dorian, I go first to his house on the Quai des Orfèvres. It is a ritual courtesy. I am his physician. I am expected to examine him. Afterwards, with the big, silent fellow in attendance, we step across the cobbled courtyard to the club, where Dorian's exotics display themselves.

Tonight I decided to wear my Poiret suit – black trousers, black smoking, white ruffled jabot, with a cloak lined in midnight-blue silk to cover it all. As I dressed I wondered how much I dared tell Dorian of my predicament. We are good friends, but in our circus of the absurd, malice is always an element in the love play.

However, I need not have troubled myself. Dorian knew everything – more than I, in fact. My colonel was alive and recuperating on his estate in East Prussia. He had recovered from his heart attack, but his back was still in plaster. He had resigned from the Kaiser's household to take a post on the General Staff. As for me, there would be no reprisals, but I would be well advised never again to set foot in Berlin.

"You got off lightly!" Dorian was terse about the whole affair. "If you can't control yourself, don't play these games. I promise you the Prussians can get very rough . . . Now, take a look at me and tell me how long *I've* got to live."

As I examined his grotesque little body, listening to the râles in his lungs, feeling the bony spurs in his spine, the chalky nodules in every joint, he lectured me like a schoolmaster.

"Women! You're fools, every one of you! You never understand that you're playing against the house – and the house wins in the end. Take you, chérie! You're tough and you're rich and you're intelligent, but even your hide's rubbing thin. Soon you'll be galled down to the raw nerves. That's when the screaming starts. Except you won't be yelling for help; you'll be shouting murder. Next thing you know the flics will be hustling you off to gaol."

He reached up and stroked my cheek with a tiny arthritic hand, clenched like a bird's claw. The gesture was at once tender and threatening.

"You worry me, chérie. Most of the women who come in here I can read like a child's catechism. A man's done 'em wrong. They've got the middle-age miseries. They're lesbians – or loners looking for a new kind of thrill. They're on drink, drugs or both. But you're different. One minute you're a madonna with a honey smile and breasts full of child milk for all the world; the next you're Medusa with poison in your mouth and a wig made of snakes."

"Do I frighten you, too, Dorian?"

"Frighten me?" He laughed, an odd, furry chuckle that ended in a coughing fit. "Not at all! I know you too well. Besides, nobody dares frighten a hunchback. They rub his hump for good luck. You can rub me too, if you want. You need some good fortune."

The word "rub" was a code word tacitly agreed between us. It was his cry for sexual comfort from a friend who would not laugh at him or tell outside the secrets of his twisted body. I was happy to oblige him. It was, God knows, a brief enough exercise, but I felt neither resentment nor distaste in performing it. Instead I experienced a curious surge of tenderness. I wanted to give him pleasure, make him feel a man, watch him afterwards, drowsy and content as we sipped a cognac together. It was then that he faced me with the blunt question:

"Why do you do this . . . this lion tamer act?"

"Lion tamer?" The idea was so incongruous that I burst out laughing. Dorian was instantly angry.

"Don't joke. That's your name now on the whole European circuit: La Dompteuse de Lions."

"That's not funny."

"It's not meant to be. It's a risky reputation to have. What do you get out of this crazy exercise?"

"Nothing."

"So why indulge in it?"

"I don't know, little friend; truly I don't. When it happens, it's a rage, a firestorm. I hardly know who I am any more."

"Where are you living now?"

"In a mousehole with other grey mice. It's a pension near the Étoile."

"Can you entertain there?"

"No."

"So, stay here tonight. Use my guest room. I'll introduce you to someone who'll leave you tranquil as a nun at vespers."

"Thanks, but no! I couldn't cope with any man just now."

"Who said anything about a man?" He combed my hair with his little talon fingers. "This is a girl like the one Sappho sang for on Mitylene. I think you need someone like her just now. Besides, what do you have to lose? If you sleep happy and wake friends, you'll both be better off than you are now."

He was right. I lost nothing. I gained something – I think. She nuzzled at my breast like a child and then cried out, "Love me, little mother! Love me! Take me inside you again."

I thought of my lost daughter and was gentle to her. Then I, in my turn, burrowed at the mouth of her womb, but found it too small and too tight to admit me. Still, I was not angry because she wanted so much to welcome me. It was not her fault that the house was too small and had never yet been lived in. We fell asleep in each other's arms, not happy, perhaps, but tender and quiet.

Somewhere around three in the morning I woke. She was sleeping in the crook of my arm with her lips against my breast. The moonlight lay on her face and I saw with a small shock of surprise that she was almost as old as I, with the same crow's feet at the corners of the eyes, the same furrows downturned from her lips. I felt no regret, no disappointment. I had only the sudden poignant memory of my father grinning at me across the breakfast table after my first all-night adventure. He said:

"It's a hell of a problem, isn't it?"

"I beg your pardon, Papa." God, how prim I was! "But I have no problem."

"You're lucky, then!" He was still grinning at me like Til Eulenspiegel. "When I was young I never knew what to say to them afterwards."

"But you've learned now?" Two could play this teasing game.

"Oh yes. I always say the same thing: Thanks and, with a thousand regrets, goodbye."

"That must really bring tears to their eyes."

"No." He laughed and waved a croissant at me. "But it leaves the situation fluid. One doesn't make an enemy. One may be lucky enough to keep a friend for a cold winter night."

I didn't want to keep my girl-woman. I withdrew without waking her and left money on the pillow. I crept out into the grey of the false dawn and hailed a fiacre to drive me back to the pension. The driver was surly, the horse too spavined to raise a trot; but over the slow clip-clop of his hooves on the cobbles, I could hear Lily singing the bedtime song of my childhood.

Ride a cock horse to Banbury Cross
To see a fine lady upon a white horse,
With rings on her fingers and bells on her toes
She shall have music wherever she goes.

JUNG
Zurich

I am committed now to a voyage more dangerous than any made by the ancient navigators – a voyage to the centre of myself. I must discover who I am, why I am. I must make terms with the daimon who lives inside my skin. I must reason with my father, long dead, about the God he preached and I rejected. I must talk with my mother, gone too, whom I never learned to love. I must encounter the man who raped me when I was a boy and the dark gods who

35

haunt my adult dreams. I must cut the cords that bind me to Freud and that, believe me, is no easy bill of divorcement! I must push out from the last known shore into the wild ocean of my own subconscious.

There is a terror in this. I wrestle with it in the small dark hours after midnight. I am like a mariner staring at an ancient map where, just beyond the Pillars of Hercules, the cartographer has drawn terrible fire-breathing beasts and the legend: "Sailor, beware! Here be monsters and the edge of the world." I am familiar with monsters. I have dreamed a whole menagerie of them: the giant one-eyed phallus in the cave, the dove that speaks with a human voice, the living corpses of Alyscamps, the black scarab and the rocks that spurt blood! One or another of these beauties always keeps watch by my pillow.

I reach out in the dark to touch Emma, draw her close to me for comfort and reassurance. She gives a little moan of displeasure and rolls away from me, clasping her hand over her pubis. This defensive gesture angers me. I have never forced myself upon her. I understand that, two months pregnant, she may be disinclined for sex; but she does not know how solitary I feel in this marriage bed, how naked to all my ghostly enemies. If I had not Toni in my life at this moment I might well be reduced to impotence.

Of course there is more involved than a seasonal aversion to sex. Emma has always been somewhat auto-erotic. Indeed she confessed as much to Freud in her last correspondence with him. So, she has less physical need of me than I of her. My illness has changed me and changed my role in the family. I have become a liability and not an asset. I am no longer working at the clinic. I have given up lecturing, because I cannot concentrate on the simplest text. My list of private patients is pitifully small. I am no longer the breadwinner and we are subsisting on Emma's inheritance. She has become "matrona victrix", the victorious matron, secure in her role as childbearer, safe in her self-respect, while mine is diminished by illness and financial dependence. Thus, she is able to exact, at last, a subtle vengeance for my infidelities, real and imagined.

I make no claims to sexual virtue. I am not promiscuous; but I am not by nature monogamous either. I think the Greeks had the right combination: a wife for the house and the children, the courtesan or the boy comrade for companionship, and the bawdy house for rough-and-tumble fun if you wanted it. Our stolid Swiss Calvinist society imposes intolerable restraints on men and women. In a good marriage one needs a licence to wander a little.

Of course, Emma doesn't see it that way and I try not to make an issue of it. We are already having scenes about Toni, and Emma does not hesitate to rehearse, very loudly, certain of my indiscretions in the past – like the Spielrein woman who wanted at all costs to bear my child!

This business of analytic psychology is strewn with temptations. Even if you are as virtuous as a hermit in a hair shirt you cannot resist them all. When a woman bares her soul to you, she is much more dangerous than when she simply slips off her blouse and skirt. The ones you reject spread scandal. The ones to whom you yield so much as a gesture of affection become as voracious as maenads.

So, you're damned if you do and damned if you don't. And your wife compounds the problem by turning away from you in bed and covering her sex with her hand like a Botticelli virgin. To hell with it! Better to be up and working than lying here in the dark, nursing old fears and an itch in the crotch.

The study is cold and quiet as the grave. I wish Toni were here to put warmth and fire into it. I am tempted to telephone her; but even I am not selfish enough to wake her at two in the morning! I pour myself a large measure of brandy. I load my pipe. I open, on the lectern, the black book in which I record each step of my pilgrimage to what I pray will be a final illumination. I set down on my desk the file of dream analyses which Toni and I have worked up together. Beside it I place a notepad, a sketch book, my pencils and my coloured crayons. I light my pipe. I inhale the first smoke gratefully. I take a long, slow sip of brandy. "Now," I tell myself. "Now," I tell my dark Doppel-gänger. "Let's begin. Let's see if we can make sense to one another."

I pick up the black pencil – the soft one – and try to write. Immediately I am blocked. I simply cannot translate my fantasies into linear script. It is only with the greatest effort that I can write down the simple ritual questions: "Who am I? Where do I live? What is my profession?"

After a few minutes I abandon the pointless exercise. I drink. I inhale the sedative smoke. I fall into reverie. I pick up the pencil again and begin to draw my dreaming. As I draw, I lapse into a wonderful calm. The walls of my study fall away. My clothes disappear. I am standing naked in front of a great cliff of ochre rock, drawing on it with a charred stick.

I make first a great circle, confident and perfect as Giotto's "O". Inside the circle I draw a girl and a man.

She is young, just matured to womanhood. He is old and venerable, with long white hair and a flowing beard. He carries a staff. He has an air of serene authority. I emphasise the smile that twitches at the corners of his mouth. Behind me a deep voice utters a commendation: "Better! Much better!"

I whirl to face the speaker. There, standing before me, are the old man and the girl. I am dumb with wonderment. I look from the drawing to the reality. The girl laughs at my discomfiture. The old man smiles and says:

"It is really very simple. I am Elijah. This is Salome. You dream us and paint us on a wall. But who are you?"

I cannot answer him. I look down at my nakedness and am ashamed. I shake my head.

"I do not know who I am."

The old man says, "It does not matter. We know who you are."

The girl stretches out her hand. I take it, diffidently. She draws me close to her and to the old man. I am calm again. I remember that my name is Carl Gustav Jung and I am proud to tell it to them. We sit down together on a flat rock. I ask, respectfully:

"Elijah, sir, is this young lady your daughter?"

"Tell him, child." The old man is amused by the question, but he does not answer it directly. "Tell him what you are to me."

"I am everything – daughter, wife, lover and protector."

"Are you satisfied, Carl Gustav Jung?"

"I am amazed. I am not satisfied."

"You have no claim to be satisfied. Face the wall again and finish the drawing."

When I turn, I am back in my study. My pipe is smoking in the ashtray. The brandy is spilled and I wipe it up with my handkerchief. But there is indeed a drawing in my sketch book. The circle is perfect as Giotto's "O". The old man and the girl are just as I have dreamed them and drawn them on the rock wall. What does it mean? How can I come to terms with this phenomenon?

Then I remember something. I spend an hour scrabbling through my bookshelves. I write notes furiously. No difficulty now with linear script. By four in the morning I have come up with three small snippets of history. Simon the Magician, one of the early Gnostics, travelled with a girl from a bawdy house. Lao Tzu, the Chinese sage, fell in love with a dancing girl. Paul the Apostle, so says the legend, was tenderly attached to the virgin Thecla . . .

Ancient tales all of them! But what cosmic magic planted them in my subconscious? Elijah and Salome are as present to me now as if I could reach out and touch them. If they were not real – in some special mode of reality! – how could I have dreamed them? Is all our history thus buried within us, forgotten but available, waiting only to be conjured up like will o' the wisps from dark bog water?

I cannot face the question now. I close the sketch book. I walk out into the misty grey of the false dawn. I stand on the beach tossing pebbles into the lake and crying over and over:

"Elijah! Elijah! Salome, my love!"

My only answer is a flutter of wings as a moorhen skitters through the shallows.

MAGDA
Paris

This morning I saw a sad and silly spectacle. I was strolling down the Champs-Élysées, thinking about my night at Dorian's and looking for a suitable café to take my morning coffee. A fruit vendor – one of those who serve the local restaurants – crossed in front of me, carrying a basket of oranges on his head.

He stubbed his toe on a paving stone and lurched forward. The basket slipped off his head and the oranges went rolling in all directions. Some of them split; some were gathered up on the run by a trio of schoolboys; some were kicked into the gutter by passing pedestrians.

For a moment the vendor stood, hypnotised and helpless, staring at the cascade of golden fruit. Then, since I was the nearest witness, he whirled on me in fury and shouted in Italian:

"It's all your fault! Your fault!"

He raised his hand and made the sign of the horns at me, tossed the basket at my feet and stalked off. His rage was so childish, his accusation so ridiculous that I burst out laughing. But, when I sat down to coffee, I found that I was trembling. The incident was no longer comical, but magical and sinister. Suddenly I was back in the landscape of my dream. The oranges were balls of glass and a naked Magda was sealed inside each one, and none of the Magdas could talk to the others.

It was a moment of pure horror: the same horror that seized me the day my best hunter went berserk under me and I had to thrash and gallop him into exhaustion. There was the same eerie prickle of evil that I had felt when I found Alexander, my wolf-

41

hound, dead outside my door, with a bloody foam around his muzzle – and three days later, my rose-arbour devastated by some vandal with an axe!

The gesture of the horns, the primitive sign of exorcism, was no mere vulgarity. Did I look like a witch? Had I indeed the evil eye? Was there the mark of Cain on my forehead? I fumbled in my reticule for a mirror and peered into it. The mirror told me only that I was pale and that the man at the table behind me was trying to decide whether I was an early working whore or an indiscreet lady out for an airing.

That didn't help either. It convinced me that there was only a very bleak future for a middle-aged widow crying into her coffee on the Champs-Élysées and making midnight love with strangers in houses of appointment. I felt as if a trapdoor had opened under my feet and I was falling over and over into darkness.

The man at my back stood up and approached me. He asked, politely enough:

"Madame is unwell? Perhaps I can help?"

"Thank you, but I am perfectly well."

"If Madame is sure?"

I was perfectly sure. I was equally sure that I needed help from someone. The problem was where to go and what to say when I got there. I speak six languages, including Hungarian, but none of them is adequate to express the life I have led since I was a little girl.

Sex is easy to talk about. No matter how bizarre your tastes, you can always find an attentive audience. But the rest of it – my childhood in the enchanted castle, the primitive but strangely beautiful rites of my initiation into womanhood, my years at the university and in hospital residence – these are tales from a far country, from another planet even! I am not sure I can make them intelligible to anyone else.

Besides, the same shadow falls across them all – the shadow of a gallows tree – and there is no way to explain that over coffee and croissants! Even Papa, who could shrug off most human aberrations, would never discuss this subject with me. He knew what I had done and why; but the nearest he ever came to an admission of his knowledge was a single dry comment:

"I hope, dear daughter, you don't talk in your sleep!"

Since Papa died and the husband I adored was snatched away before his time, I have slept in many strange beds, with a whole gallery of men and women. Several of them have been quite capable of blackmail; but none has ever hinted that I tell secrets in my sleep.

So far, so good; but, as Dorian warned me, my endurance is wearing thin. I cannot tolerate for ever these wild swings from manic debauchery to deepest depression. I need a steady lover, a friend, a confidant – perhaps even a confessor . . .

The thought intrigues me. It represents the oddest of all solutions for a woman who has never had any religious convictions at all. Papa was an old fashioned rationalist who taught me that life begins and ends here and that we have to reach out and grab the best of it. He used to say:

"I've cut 'em living and I've carved 'em dead; and I've never caught any glimpse of God or of a soul."

I loved Papa so much it would never have occurred to me to question any one of his opinions. I do not question them now; but I toy with the idea that it might be pleasant to turn Roman Catholic and then be able to walk into a little box every Saturday, recite my sins and come out clean as a new handkerchief.

It's an idle thought and, of course, quite illogical. If you don't believe in God and you don't believe in sin, why worry? The fact is that you do worry. You blanch at the sign of the horns and you make doll magic out of fallen oranges.

I feel guilty – no, I feel ridiculous and ashamed – because I am tossing myself away, piece by little piece, like confetti at a wedding. Even a whore has better sense than that. She sells what she has. The funny thing is that part of me is very careful indeed. Peasant-frugal was Papa's word for it.

I run my estate like any business. My accounts are meticulously kept; and they always show a profit! I buy the best clothes – but I get them at discount because I wear them well and in fashionable places. When I trade bloodstock, I drive hard bargains. At an auction I can smell a bidding ring a hundred paces away.

In polite society I am demure and discreet. Most of my friends would be shocked if they knew how profligate I am in my pleasures, how foul tongued in my pillow talk. Time was when this double life seemed a heady and exciting game. Now it is a perilous experience: a night walk down a foetid alley full of menacing shadows.

I paid for my coffee and set off for the banking house of Ysambard Frères to draw money against my letter of credit. I hoped that Joachim Ysambard, the elder of the two brothers, would invite me to luncheon. Joachim is in his sixties now, white haired, witty and wise in women's ways. Ten years ago we had a summer loving in Amalfi. Then he came back to marry his second wife – a marriage of great convenience – a dynastic alliance with an old Alsatian banking family. Miraculously we remained friends, probably because, even in bed, he reminded me very much of Papa.

He was in conference when I arrived, but his secretary brought me a message begging me to wait and have luncheon with him. Meantime, brother Manfred would like a few words with me. Manfred is in his early fifties, dapper as a mannequin, impeccably polite but oddly bloodless. He has never married. He has, at least to my knowledge, no permanent lover, male or female. There is a monkish aura about him which I find disconcerting and sometimes repellent. On the other hand, Joachim speaks of him with awe and admiration:

"Manfred is a genius. He understands trade in a way no one else does. You can start him with a mountain of tea bricks in Tibet and very soon he will deliver you wool in Bradford, gold in Florence, pig iron in the Ruhr and a profit in our books in Paris."

With all of which I am forced to agree. Manfred's management of my French funds has made me a second fortune; but he shrugs off my thanks with fastidious disdain:

"There's no magic in it, Madame. It's simply barter on a slightly larger scale than the town market. The real skill is in the timing. Which brings me to your affairs. Joachim and I advise that you now invest at least half your capital outside Europe."

"For any special reason?"

"A spread of risk. There is fighting in the Balkans. The rest of Europe will be at war within a year."

"How can you be so certain?"

He permitted himself a faint patronising smile.

"The ancient augurs studied the entrails of birds. We're much more evolved. We watch the movements of coal and ore and chemicals and money. For example, at this moment, every cavalry regiment in Europe is looking for remounts and places to stable them. It's a madness, of course – a folly of senile generals. One year of modern warfare and the horse will be as obsolete as the broadsword. However, this would be an excellent time to sell your stud." He paused and then added a barbed comment: "Your reputation, as a breeder, is still high. The property is in prime condition. Our advice would be to sell now at the top of the market and invest the proceeds with Morgan in New York. This would give you a secure base in the New World, should circumstances ever force you to leave Europe."

I told him I could not imagine any circumstances that would force me to leave Europe. He chided me:

"Dear lady, war is a most unseemly affair. It rouses man's basest passions and provides excuses and opportunity to indulge them. You are – how shall I say it? – well known, but not everywhere well regarded, in society. You are vulnerable to gossip and to manipulation."

"Manipulation? That's an odd word to use."

"It is nonetheless accurate. Let me show you something."

My file was lying on his desk. He opened it, picked out a letter and passed it to me. The notepaper was headed, "Société Vickers et Maxim". The letter, addressed to Manfred Ysambard, was written in an emphatic, sprawling hand.

Dear Colleague,

I am happy to tell you that, by unanimous decision of our directors, Ysambard Frères have been appointed bankers to La Société Vickers et Maxim and to La Société Française des Torpilles Whitehead. We look forward to a long and profitable association with you and your esteemed brother.

Perhaps we may begin it with a supper party at my house, to which you will invite that very special and beautiful client whom we discussed last week and to whom I now beg to be presented.

A bientôt,

Z.Z.

The signature was a bold double "Z". Who, I asked, was the writer? Manfred was embarrassed. It was the first time I had ever seen him blush.

"His name is Zaharoff, Basil Zaharoff. He's in everything – steel, arms, shipping, newspapers, banking."

"And how did he hear of me?"

"Not from us, I promise you, Madame. Joachim will verify that. It was Zaharoff who mentioned your name to us. We were surprised at the amount of information he possessed about you and your affairs; but that's the kind of man he is. He deals at the highest level of politics – with kings, emperors, presidents. He has the best private intelligence service in the world."

"And why should he be interested in me?"

I had expected an evasive answer; but no, Manfred was eager for confession.

"Zaharoff uses women as allies in his affairs. He pays well and willingly for service and information.

47

He has your history at his fingertips. He knows your father's story as well. He hints at other matters of which we have no knowledge. In short, he has done Ysambard Frères a big service. He asks a modest favour in return – an introduction to you."

"And if I decline to meet him?"

"He will find another way to arrange the encounter. He is a very determined man."

"I can be determined, too."

"Please!" There was a note of desperation in Manfred's voice. "Let me try to explain this Zaharoff. He deals, on a huge scale, in military armaments. He represents, for example, the British company, Vickers. He would like very much to gain control of our French company, Schneider-Creusot. So what does he do? Very quietly, he starts buying up shares in the Banque de l'Union Parisienne, an institution owned by Schneider-Creusot, which raises finance for them and for other French industries. Already Zaharoff is on the board; nevertheless he brings us big accounts to make us, too, his allies. In the end, mark my words, he will run Schneider-Creusot. If he wants to meet you, he will – one way or another. So, why not do it the graceful way? Let us bring together two of our distinguished clients. Well?"

"What does Joachim think of all this?"

"Ask him yourself at lunch."

The answer Joachim gave me was as clear as a church bell in frost-time.

"If half the gossip I hear is true, you need a protector. Who better than Zaharoff, the most powerful man in Europe?"

"Why do I need a protector, Joachim?"

"Your age." Joachim gave me a thin smile. "And a growing tendency to sexual indiscretions."

"And how would you know about those, dear Joachim?"

"Some of it I hear from my own gossips."

"And some, no doubt, from this Basil Zaharoff."

"Correct."

"What's he like in bed, Joachim?"

"How should I know?" Joachim was only a little amused. "My guess is that he doesn't want you in his own bed at all."

"You make him sound like a pimp."

"Rumour has it that's how he started – as a runner for the whore houses in Tatavla."

"That sounds like the end of the earth."

"It's the old Greek quarter of Istanbul."

"And now this Greek, this Turk, whatever he is, has Joachim Ysambard pimping for him!"

It was a calculated cruelty; but I couldn't resist it. Joachim digested the insult in silence. His answer was mild, almost apologetic.

"I wish I could tell you bankers have cleaner hands than brothel touts. We don't. We're putting up millions for guns and explosives and poison gas. We're lending money across the map, so, whichever side wins, we can't lose. I should be ashamed. I find I'm not. I work for money, I married for money. You were one of the few indulgences that cost me money."

"And now you'd like to call in the debt?"

"Don't be vulgar! Besides, I'm doing you a favour. Zaharoff needs a woman to run his salons and cultivate his clients. He'll set you up like a duchess."

"And throw me out like a pregnant parlourmaid when the party's over? No, thanks."

49

"As you wish, of course." Joachim was studiously formal. "Now, as to your financial affairs . . ."

"I'll take your advice. We'll sell the property and the bloodstock and invest the proceeds in the United States. What else should be liquidated?"

"Manfred and I will prepare a list. We'll discuss it before you leave Paris. Where can we get in touch with you?"

"As from tomorrow, at the Crillon. I've decided to put myself back into circulation."

"Please think about Zaharoff."

"I will, Joachim. Thank you for your care of my interests."

"Our pleasure always, my dear."

And that was another chapter closed, another friendship dead and buried. As I walked out into the afternoon bustle of the rue St. Honoré, I felt, once more, ridiculous and ashamed. A man who had been my lover was treating me like a chattel, an object of barter in the market place. Worse still was his bland assumption that I ought to be very happy in the transaction.

What was happening to me? What did others read in my face that I could not see in my own mirror? Why should they assume that I, the most independent of women, was suddenly in need of a protector? And even if I were, how dared they offer me a jumped-up gun peddler from Tatavla?

I didn't see the humour of it until I was back in my bedroom at the pension. I was paying good money for worse company every night of the week. I was paying, not to be protected, but to be exploited; and, instead of being set up like a duchess, I was a target for every policeman and pimp in the game. I threw myself

50

on the bed and laughed until I cried and cried and cried.

JUNG
Zurich

It is hot today and excessively humid. Dark thunder clouds pile up over the lake. We shall have a storm before midday. I have been working since dawn, collecting stones from the lakeside, piling them beside my model village, sorting them by size and texture. I am stripped to the waist like a labourer. My face and my body are streaked with sweat and dust; but I feel relaxed and content.

Emma and the children are spending the day with friends who have a villa near the peak of the Sonnenberg. Toni has set up a card table under the big apple tree and is writing up her notes. She has made a pitcher of lemonade and has brought out clean towels so that we can bathe before lunch and change in the boathouse.

We do not talk much. There is no need. We are content to be together, each carried forward by the current of a private musing, like two streams in confluence. As I build my toy village, it is as if I am rebuilding my childhood out of the scraps and shards of memory: like the legend of my mother's father, Pastor Preiswerk, who, every Wednesday, entertained the ghost of his first wife, much to the chagrin of his second, who bore him thirteen children!

My father, too, was a Protestant pastor – an intelligent and kind man hopelessly frustrated by the restrictions of a small country parish and an outmoded theology which he never found the courage to examine. So, he took refuge in reminiscence: the good old days, the romantic student years, the laurels he had won as a graduate in Oriental Languages, which he never read any more! He quarrelled often with my mother, a big, jolly woman, warm as new bread, who loved company and chatter. Later experience leads me to believe that the quarrels had a sexual basis as well. I cannot say where the fault lay. The hypocrisy of the Swiss about sexual matters is sometimes beyond belief. The fact is that my mother lapsed deeper and deeper into depression and was for a long period under hospital care.

I have strangely ambivalent feelings about her. Behind that warm, fat, comfortable persona lurked another, powerful, dark, commanding, who would brook no contradiction. This one, I believed, could look into my eyes and see what was going on inside my skull. My feelings about her have coloured all my later relations with women. For many years, my response to the word "love" was always one of doubt and distrust. My earliest, and in some ways my most profound, dream experience relates to my relationship with my parents and theirs with one another.

In this dream I discovered, in a meadow behind our house, the entrance to an underground passage. I went in. I found myself in a vast chamber in which there was a royal throne. On the throne stood a phallus as big as a tree. Its single blind eye stared at the ceiling. I heard my mother's voice calling, "Look at it! That's the man eater!" The dream repeated itself night after night. I was too terrified to go to bed and that caused arguments with my father to whom I dared not communicate what I had seen.

The dream, as any analyst will tell you, is open to a

whole gamut of interpretations, and I have continued every year to find new meanings to it. But recalling it now in this summer garden, I am moved, not to terror, but to desire for the beautiful creature who sits only a hand's reach away.

I go to her. She pours me lemonade and holds the glass to my lips. Then she dries the sweat from my face and my body. The touch of her hands is like a charge of electricity – and like Galvani's frog, I jump to it. I plead with her: "I want you." She tells me: "I want you, too." Then – a gift from the elder gods! – the first raindrops fall and the first lightning crackles across the ridges. Toni gathers up her notebooks and we rush to the shelter of the boathouse.

There is no pleading now, no protest. While Toni undresses, I make a bed out of the cushions and sails from my boat. We tumble into it as the storm bursts into full fury outside, with lightning and thunder and hailstones as big as bullets slamming against the roof. It rages for an hour and more, up and down the lake. No one can intrude on us. Emma will not leave the Sonnenberg until the storm is over. Our servants are penned inside the house. Toni and I are free and happy as children. Our love making is wilder and more passionate than we have ever before enjoyed. When all our passion is spent, we lie breast to breast, wrapped in the white sails, listening to the whine of the wind and the drumming of the rain, and the creak of the apple tree bowed under its load of young fruit.

Then, as always, the slow sadness of the aftermath envelops us. Toni clings to me desperately and murmurs the old refrain:

"Wouldn't it be wonderful to be like this all the

time? Wouldn't it be beautiful not to have to take precautions? I hate to be the one who gets up and goes home. Why didn't we meet before Emma came along? Don't you wish we could be married?"

I dare not tell her that a wedding ring changes everything; that there is no better recipe for boredom than year-round sex with a legal wife; that half the excitement we share comes from the risks of discovery. Still less can I explain to her how swiftly the dream symbols transmute themselves for me: how the womb cavern where the phallus reigns, erect and triumphant, becomes a burial chamber where an ugly white worm is the only vestige of life.

Toni, herself, is magically transfigured in this misty post-coital country. One moment she is Salome, sister, wife, lover and protector. The next instant, she is the servant girl who kept house for my father and me while my mother was in hospital. She has the same lustrous black hair, the same matt skin, the same woman smell, and she, too, giggles when I tickle her ears with my tongue.

When the rain stops, the magic stops, too. Toni leaps up and dresses hurriedly. She asks all the usual questions: "Is my hair tidy? My lips aren't bruised, are they? Is my hemline straight?" I button her blouse, give her one last kiss and send her back to work in the house. She will be there when Emma comes home with the children. I stuff the sails back into their canvas bags, pile the cushions tidily, lock the boatshed and resume my mason's work on the model village.

Among the pebbles I found this morning is a curious, conical fragment of crystal. It will make a splendid spire for the church. The church makes me think of God, the Trinity, Jesus Christ and my father, their official representative. My father conducted funerals. The dead were screwed into black boxes, carried on the shoulders of men in black frockcoats and black boots, then buried in holes in the ground. Father would say at the service, "God has taken them to himself. Jesus, the Saviour, has welcomed them into his Kingdom."

So, to my childish mind, Jesus Christ became a black and menacing figure whose kingdom was the dark underworld, home of blind moles and chirping crickets and one-eyed monsters.

Of course, the one-eyed monster can turn up anywhere. For instance, this house, quite near the church which I am building, is for me a sinister place. The man who used to live here was a friend of my father's and a friend of mine, too. He used to lend me books. He nurtured my childhood passion for painting and sketching. He took me fishing and swimming. He taught me the rudiments of archaeology. He gave me my first look at the erotic symbols of the Greeks and the Romans and the courtly scholars of the Renaissance. Then, one summer's day, while we were bathing in a secluded corner of the lake, he tried first to seduce me to have oral sex with him. When I drew back in fear and disgust, he seized me, thrust my face against a tree trunk and raped me.

It was a painful and humiliating experience, the more so because, mixed up with my sense of moral outrage, was the conviction that I had somehow failed the friend who had turned to me for comfort. The element of pleasure in the copulation confused me still further. I had come to climax, I had ejaculated, and the older man was quick to use these pleasant

55

sensations to justify his invasion of me and my enforced cooperation in the sodomy.

Even now, in my middle years, brief minutes after my passionate union with Toni, the memory of that other encounter still haunts and confuses me. It colours my whole situation with Freud, for whom I have entertained a great affection, the sentiment of a son for his father, of a pupil for a beloved master. But the situation has always been more complex than that – very Greek, very Platonic. I am the comrade-in-arms, who has shared his blanket on bivouac and who now deserts him to fight under another banner, for a different cause.

Still, I must say that, for all his finical Viennese manners and his Hebraic subtlety, there is in Freud, too, a touch of the bully – just as there is in me a touch of the female who desires to be dominated and in Toni the latent male who desires to dominate me.

There is a pattern in all this which I begin slowly to understand and which I am trying to codify. The problem is that I lack the vocabulary. When I was younger, I used to complain loudly that philosophers and theologians created great gob-stopping words for the most elementary propositions. Now I understand why. The bigger the word, the more magic it holds, the better cover it makes for human ignorance. But once you establish it in the ritual, the magical word becomes the sacred word. To challenge it is heresy and, worse still, blasphemy!

I put the capstone on the steeple of my toy church and step back to admire the effect. I ask aloud, a question of the dead:

"What do you think, Father? Will your God like the house I have built for him?"

My question is a challenge to my dear parent, whose formulae of faith are no longer valid for me. It is also a deliberate recall of a boyhood dream. In the dream I saw God the Father, ancient and powerful, enthroned in the blue sky, exactly above the spire of our cathedral. As I watched awe-struck, God gave a thunderous fart and a big, divine turd fell – plop! – on the roof and flattened the cathedral to the ground.

It was for me a dream of liberation – God rejecting man's attempt to enclose him in systems and rituals. Yet here am I in my own garden, rebuilding my childhood prison-house. Why? My father cannot tell me. He is locked in his black box far under the earth where everything is different.

In the secret kingdom of the unconscious, nothing is quite what it seems to be. The dead talk and the living are dumb. The phallus is a cannibal god gorged with blood. The moist womb solicits the rapist. The rapist violates for a love he cannot experience. Janus, the two-faced guardian at the gate, sees the past and the future, but is blind to the present and unconscious of the eternity which includes them all.

Suddenly, Elijah and Salome are present to me. I show them my village. I tell them the memories it evokes. I ask them:

"Does any of that make sense to you, Elijah? To you, Salome, my sister, my love?"

For the first time I am aware that Salome is blind and that, now, there is a third personage with them: a big black snake with eyes that shine like obsidian. The snake draws close to me and twines its body round my leg. He is clearly a friendly creature, but I am afraid. Salome reaches out a hand to reassure me. I withdraw from her touch. Elijah smiles in his slow, wise fashion and teases me.

"You are more afraid of Salome than of the serpent."

I admit that I am; because today she reminds me of my mother in her sombre moods when she seemed to look right into my head. I sense that Salome's blind eyes see more than the eyes of the serpent. Then, as suddenly as they have come, they are gone. The only other living creature in the garden is a brown thrush pecking for worms in the damp earth.

MAGDA
Paris

At ten o'clock this morning, while I was taking breakfast in my old suite at the Crillon, a page brought me a note. He told me that a uniformed chauffeur was waiting downstairs for an answer. The note was from Basil Zaharoff.

Dear Madame,

Our mutual friends, the brothers Ysambard, are excellent bankers; but, in the diplomacy of the heart, they are children. I gave them a commission to arrange an informal meeting with you at a supper party in my house. They bungled the commission. I can only hope they have not damaged my credit with you.

I desire, most earnestly, to meet you. I have long admired your beauty, your sense of style and your independence of spirit.

Will you do me the great honour of dining with

me tonight? If you consent, I shall come myself to fetch you at eight o'clock.

I am not, believe me, the ogre I am sometimes painted. I have a healthy mistrust of my fellow-men but a most ardent admiration for womankind.

Please say you will come.

Z.Z.

The double "Z" was scrawled with imperial disdain across the whole width of the page. He knew that I would accept. How could I not? I felt like Eve, with the old serpent winking at her and offering her a second bite at the apple from the tree of knowledge. I had been a long time out of Eden. What did I have to lose? I scribbled a note accepting his invitation to dinner and inviting him to take champagne in my salon beforehand.

I telephoned my couturier and asked him to display some gowns for me at midday. I then arranged for André to do my hair and help me with my toilette at five-thirty. Both were delighted to hear from me. Life had been dull of late. They hoped I would set off some fireworks in Paris.

The arrival of Basil Zaharoff was heralded by gifts and explanatory notes: a vast arrangement of summer flowers, "because this is a festive occasion"; a crystal phial of perfume, "blended in my own parfumerie at Grasse", a bowl of caviar, iced and garnished, "to accompany the champagne". By contrast with this opulence, the man, himself, was a model of discreet charm. In spite of his Levantine origins, Basil Zaharoff was the very image of a traditional European aristocrat. He was tall with strong, aquiline features, white hair and a small goatee, immaculately trimmed.

His eyes were grey with a humorous twinkle in them. His manners were cool and courtly. His first words were a compliment.

"Madame, you are even more beautiful than I expected."

"And you, sir, are an extravagant but welcome guest."

"What did you expect?"

"Someone rather more formidable."

That seemed to please him. I sensed that he needed flattery, liked people to be in awe of him. I saw now that the grey eyes were restless. They appraised everything. They lingered only on sensual detail. They could, I thought, turn hard and frightening. I asked him:

"Why were you so anxious to meet me?"

He did not answer immediately. That was another of his tricks I noticed. He always gave himself time to think before he answered even a simple question. He opened the champagne carefully, poured two glasses and handed one to me. He announced:

"Let's toast the meeting before we try to explain it. To a new friendship and a long one!"

We drank. He made a canapé of caviar, offered it to me and waited for my approval. Only then was he prepared to answer the question.

"Why did I want to meet you? You are agreeably notorious. You have beauty, style and a certain recklessness which I admire. You are old enough to spell all the words and I am also old enough to be bored by young virgins just out of finishing school. Then, of course . . ." The hesitation was just long enough to be intriguing. ". . . There is the fact that many years ago I knew your mother. I felt I owed myself the pleasure of meeting the daughter who is so much like her."

I felt a brief, poignant shock, then a sudden surge of anger that my defences had been so quickly breached. I explained, coolly, that I knew nothing about my mother, not even her name. Zaharoff showed no surprise and no emotion.

"There were reasons for that. I'm not sure they were good reasons, but humans are stupid animals. Your father was a brilliant man; but he could be stupid, too – like all Hungarians!"

"Did you know Papa, too?"

"For a while, yes. Then, as happens in life, we lost touch with each other. But let's leave reminiscence until after dinner. It is only when people know one another that the past makes sense and the future arranges itself comfortably. . . . To begin, may I call you Magda?"

"Of course."

"And you may call me Zed-Zed. All my friends do."

Once again, instinct warned me to make no comment. I was supposed to be able to spell the words. It was clear that Zaharoff was setting the ground rules for any relationship that might develop. In such a relationship, everything would be done by rescript over that imperious double "Z". Zed-Zed would sign bankers' orders; Zed-Zed would order breakfast in bed or love at the lift of an eyebrow; Zed-Zed might equally order a banishment or an execution – but he did write graceful letters!

He was a gracious host, too. We dined à deux in his house. The servants were in livery, the porcelain was antique Sèvres; the cutlery gold, the napery embroidered in Florence. Zaharoff treated all this finery with studied indifference; but he lavished great attention on the menu and his own part in its preparation. The pâté was made to his private recipe; the soup was seasoned with his own bouquet of herbs. He had a set of personal carvers for the roast. He also had a little *mot* for the occasion: to the world he was a maître de forges, an old fashioned iron master like Krupp or Schneider; but here at home he was a maître chef who could still teach his own chef a lesson or two. He made a great ceremony of the wines, instructed me, pedantically, on each one, and watched carefully to see how I reacted to the drink. I wondered whether I was being tested as a candidate for bed or for the catering staff of Torpilles Whitehead.

I guessed his age at somewhere in the mid-sixties. I also guessed that he was still vigorous, or at least ambitious, in bed – what the French call "très vert". His body was trim. His hand clasp was firm and dry. He used every opportunity to make a physical contact, however fleeting.

For my part, I had no objection to his little stratagems. I am always curious in sexual encounters and I have had some very pleasant surprises with men of Zaharoff's age. Even so, I was disposed to be cautious with this one. I wanted no more opera scenes that might suddenly run out of control; and, besides, there was a whiff of danger in the air. So, when we went into the drawing room for coffee, I prompted him, quietly:

"You were saying you knew my parents."

He smiled and patted my hand, as if to commend my patience.

"Let me see now. I met your father first, in the early eighteen-sixties. I was in Athens, a young immigrant from the Levant trying to scratch a living in the capital. I hung around the Hôtel Grande Bretagne, paying a daily tax to the concierge, who permitted me to tout for the souvenir shops and act as guide to the tourists. Your father was staying at the hotel. I remember him as a handsome and obviously wealthy young bachelor who was being stalked by every female of marriageable age in the hotel.

"The concierge identified him as Count Kardoss, scion of an old Hungarian family, resident in Vienna, by profession a surgeon and physician. He was, the concierge told me, an ardent collector of antiques and sexual experiences. If I could manage him, I could have him. I did just that. He tipped me generously. I kept him out of trouble and saw that he got value for money. By the time he left, we were as near to being friends as was possible for a titled Hungarian and a little tout from Tatavla.

"The next time I saw him was a year later in London. I was there trying to start an import business on a small amount of capital I had borrowed from an uncle. Your father was working as assistant to a famous London surgeon who specialised in gynaecology. We met by chance one Sunday morning in St. James's Park. Your father was walking with one of the most beautiful women I had ever seen. He did not offer to introduce me. Clearly, he wanted me gone as quickly as possible. We exchanged cards and arranged to meet later in the week for luncheon at a modest Greek restaurant in Soho.

"At this lunch your father explained the situation. The young lady was the wife of a titled personage on the staff of the Viceroy of India. Her husband still had twelve months to serve. She had returned early because the rigours of the Indian climate had proved too

63

much for her frail constitution. The famous surgeon was her medical advisor. His assistant, your father, became her lover. I ventured the opinion that she looked as healthy as a prize filly. Your father laughed and said she was both healthy and newly pregnant to him.

"I pointed out that both he and the lady would be ruined if that little item became public and that a safe and discreet abortion seemed to be the answer. Your father told me they were considering another solution. He would return immediately to Europe and set up practice in Baden-Baden. The lady would follow, after a short interval, on the pretext of visiting friends abroad. From a safe distance, she could compose matters quietly with her husband, arrange a divorce, have her baby and live happily ever after with her beloved physician. However . . ." Zaharoff gave a small theatrical sigh of regret. "That's not quite the way it turned out."

"Obviously. But what happened?"

"Your father left London and went to Baden. He was personable and well recommended. He soon had a thriving practice in the spa. The lady dallied in London as long as her condition permitted. Then, accompanied by her maid, Lily Mostyn, she set off on a much publicised visit to friends on the Continent. She would be home, she said, in time to greet her husband as he stepped off the ship from India. And indeed she was!"

I gaped at him in shock. He gave a little regretful shrug.

"She lived with your father until you were born and she had recovered from the delivery. Then, one day, she left the house alone and never came back. You were suckled by a local wet nurse. Lily Mostyn stayed on to help your father rear you."

"And my mother?"

"Went back to her husband, who shortly afterwards inherited the title to a duchy in the West of England. She gave him an heir, lived out her virtuous days between London and their country seat and was buried beside her husband in the local cathedral."

"No wonder my father hated her!"

"I think your mother had her own bill of complaints," Zaharoff chided me, gently. "Your father was an incurable womaniser. He was on the prowl, day and night. He would take anything in skirts anywhere. As you, yourself, have reason to know."

I do not blush easily, but that last mocking phrase sent the blood rushing to my cheeks. I challenged him, angrily:

"How can you possibly know all this?"

"My whole business depends on accurate information. My researchers are well paid and very thorough."

Too late I remembered Manfred Ysambard's warning that Basil Zaharoff had the best private intelligence service in the world. I wondered how much more he knew about me. I put the question to him, directly. His answer was mild but devastating.

"I have, I think, an authentic biography. Your academic history, for instance: for a woman to do as well as you in medicine was something quite phenomenal. I know about your marriage and your husband's untimely death. I know your financial status, which is sound but could be improved. I am aware of your problems with your daughter. I have a complete record of your sexual adventures." I opened my mouth to protest. He silenced me with upraised hand. "Please! Let's be calm! There is no shame, no great mystery. I own a number of the houses where you play: Gräfin Bette's, for instance, the Orangery in Nice, Dorian's here in Paris. A lot of my business comes from these places. Pillow talk sells a very wide range of commodities: mortars, field guns, submarines, high-tensile steel . . . You'd be surprised."

"Not any longer." I surrendered with as good a grace as possible. "You're a very formidable personage."

"I might say the same thing of you, dear lady. We should work well together."

"Work together?" I had not expected so blunt a proposition.

"Why not? We have everything to gain and nothing to lose. Let me be frank. You and I are both outsiders – outlaws, too, come to that. Oh yes, I know the tale of the fox hunt and the poor woman who fell at the brush fence and died as you were trying to revive her. A sad story which can never, never be disproved. I have created fictions in my own life, dozens of them, and documents to prove they're facts. We outsiders have to invent lives for ourselves, temporary identities, cover names, all that nonsense; but after a certain point that play becomes unnecessary. Once you hold power in your hands – and I do, believe me! – nobody cares whether you're iron master, brothel keeper or the Dalai Lama."

"Aren't you risking a lot telling me this?"

"The knowledge puts you at risk, Madame, not me. So be quiet! Listen to me!" He was harsh now, and threatening. His cold eyes watched my every reaction

66

to his words. "There is a war coming to Europe. I can even give you the approximate starting date: summer next year. I'm going to be sitting here in Paris running that war – with Vickers guns and Whitehead torpedoes and Krupp steel and French nickel and Skoda vehicles and Clyde ships and Swiss precision instruments. I'm the merchant they'll all have to come to – iron master to the world's armies and brothel master to the generals and the politicians."

"And where do I fit into that grand design?"

He grinned at me over the rim of his brandy glass. Suddenly, he was the young imp with the sly smile, who milked the tourists at the Grande Bretagne.

"You'll be the madam of the biggest brothel in the world, with branches in every capital and clients from every court and cabinet. You'll be my hostess when I need you and the lover of any man or woman I nominate. Whatever you pick up on the side is your own affair; but you'll have a guaranteed income of a hundred thousand pounds sterling a year, paid monthly into a Swiss bank. Clothes, transport, lodging and – how shall I call it? – the necessary *mise en scène* will be charges against my enterprises."

"It's a generous offer."

"You'll earn every penny of it."

"And afterwards?"

"What about afterwards?"

"I'll need provision for my retirement, insurance, call it what you like."

"There will, of course, be a substantial retirement bonus. But insurance? I will be very open with you, my dear Magda. The best insurance you have is my continued goodwill. Lose that and you are on Route Zero, a one-way street to nowhere."

I would not argue that point. I believed him implicitly. I asked, instead:

"What makes you think I'm qualified for this métier?"

He had that answer, too, worked out in his head. He recited it like a grocery list.

"Item: you are a beautiful and intelligent woman with a mania for sexual experiment. Your indulgence will be my profit. Item: you are financially independent and therefore beyond bribery. Item: you are a physician; you have a knowledge of drugs, poisons and their application in personal and political situations. Item: you are vulnerable to your own vices. Your loyalty is guaranteed by your need of protection. Item: you can only flourish in an artificial environment and I am the best man in the world to provide it. Does that make sense?"

"As you explain it now, yes. You're a very persuasive man, Zed-Zed. However, I'd like to think about it for a few days."

"Of course. One should not make this kind of contract lightly. It is not at all easy to break."

"Thank you for being so considerate."

"Please, my dear! The best business is done calmly and deliberately. On the other hand, the best loving is done on impulse. I'd like to go to bed with you – now!"

"Nothing would please me more; but I beg you, my friend, not tonight." Once again I saw the sudden anger in his eyes. I hastened to explain: "You wouldn't like me very much. It's the wrong time of the month. But next time, I promise. May I call you tomorrow?"

"Whenever you wish, my dear. I'm sure we'll

68

be seeing a great deal more of each other."

He lifted me to my feet and embraced me. He kissed me with open mouth and stroked me with practised hands. I responded warmly enough to persuade him of my interest; but I felt nothing. That was strange for me and rather frightening. I can be wakened so easily – even by a smile or a waft of perfume or a touch on my cheek. With this man, I felt dry and dead, like a winter leaf tossed in the storm wind.

J UNG
Zurich Today Toni has the grippe and must stay in bed. Emma is delighted to have me to herself and urges me to take her and the children sailing on the lake. It is a beautiful day, with a light breeze blowing, and I am easily tempted out of my fusty isolation. While Emma packs a picnic hamper, I go down with the children to rig the boat.

I have a momentary pang of guilt as I handle the sails and the cushions on which Toni and I have made love. The guilt evokes a physical memory of our mating and I hold the coarse fabric against my cheek as if it were a handkerchief or a scarf. Agatha, my eldest child, a precocious nine year old, asks:

"Why do you do that, Papa?"

I stammer the excuse that it is simply to feel whether the sailcloth is damp. She and Anna help me clip the sails to the halyards and thread the main to the boom. The little ones, Franz and Marianne, fold the cockpit covers and lay out the cushions. Their childish chatter gladdens me and recalls me to a simpler world from which I have been absent too long.

When Emma comes down, dressed in summer muslin, I feel another pang of regret for a lost and distant time. She is thirty years old now and pregnant with our fifth child. I saw her first when she was only sixteen years old and I remember saying to myself, "That's the girl I'm going to marry!" I loved her then; I love her now; but love is a chameleon word and we humans change colour more quickly than the words we speak.

Emma is old Basel, old burgher class, old merchant money. I am small country folk, a poor pastor's son clawing his way out of the muck of the cow byre. Our first quarrels were over money. She had it. I didn't. Our next fights were over precedence. When I began to make my reputation as a clinician, an analyst, a lecturer, Emma felt deprived of the social attention which she had hitherto accepted as her due. So, the harness of marriage galls us both. We love each other, but we are often constrained to be less than lovers with each other.

The wind fills the mainsail. I push off from the jetty and we head out on a broad reach across the lake. The children squeal with delight as the boat heels; Emma takes the tiller while I cleat down the jib and mainsheets and coil the mooring lines. Emma's cheeks are flushed, her eyes are bright with pleasure. As I scramble past her, I deliberately brush her breast with my hand and try to plant a kiss on her lips. She does not refuse the caress, but there is still that first hurried glance at the children, the first instinctive withdrawal, as if I have done something indecent. To mask my irritation, I make a broader gesture and nuzzle at her neck like a bumpkin lover. Now she thrusts me away, and the boat luffs up as she pushes too violently on the tiller. The children are frightened. Emma is irritated. The small sweetness of the moment is lost for ever. Emma is aware of it; but she makes no gesture to me. She turns her attention to the children. I feel guilty again because I am jealous of my own offspring. I am reminded of Freud's remark: "I have paid off the mortgage on my marriage!" At the time, I did not understand what he meant, but I have begun to see how unrequited gestures can mount up like entries in a ledger until the whole equity of a marriage is consumed.

Just at this moment, a neighbour's boat, much faster than mine, draws abeam and robs us of our wind. It is a common prank among sailors. Our neighbour laughs and we exchange friendly insults. His boat is called *Pegasus* and carries, stencilled on the sail, the image of a winged horse. The horse reminds me of the dream sequence which I recorded in *The Psychology of Dementia Praecox*. A horse in a harness of straps is hauled in the air. The straps break. The horse falls; but then gallops off, dragging behind it a huge log. The horse is myself, elevated in my profession, but constrained by family and professional ties. I break out of the harness – but I am still hampered by the log, which is, like the tree phallus, an image of my own burdensome sexuality. Freud wrote to me about this dream and said that it had to refer to the failure of a wealthy matrimony. That was a long time ago. My marriage to Emma is still intact; though sometimes, God knows, I wish I were free of its miscellany of obligations – and I wish that my sexual needs were assuaged by corresponding sexual satisfactions!

The wind freshens a little and I am forced to

concentrate on my sailing, rather than on the analysis of old dreams and situations already too rigid for change. Emma passes cake and cordial to the children and pours a glass of beer for me. We clink our mugs and shout together: old rhymes in dialect, student songs my father taught me, snatches of lieder that Emma sings in her clear sweet voice. The countryman in me delights in this simple open-air fun. The other daimon-haunted self rejects such rustic simplicity and burrows deeper and deeper into the who and the whence and the dark why of things.

I have to confess – at least to myself – that this new discipline of analysis puts its practitioners greatly at risk. When I was working at the Burgholzli Psychiatric Hospital in Zurich, I dealt with hundreds and hundreds of patients. Bleuler ran the place with almost monastic efficiency. We weren't allowed to drink. We rose at six-thirty in the morning and had to be ready for a staff meeting at eight-thirty. We typed our own case histories and junior residents had to be in at 10 p.m.; after that the gates were locked and we juniors had no key. It was rough discipline, and there were many gaps in our knowledge – but our attention was directed outside ourselves, focused on the patient.

In my present state, all my attention is on myself. I am the patient. I am the clinic. I wonder if this is why our group of pioneers – Freud, Adler, myself, Ferenczi, all the rest – is as inbred as a hill tribe in the Atlas Mountains. We bitch like women. We nurse grudges. We read slights into every random word.

At our conference in Bremen, we were talking about the bog men, whose mummified corpses, some of them clearly the victims of ritual execution, are often discovered in the peat lands of Germany and Denmark. Freud got furious. It was almost as though he felt himself to be a possible victim – and he literally fainted away! My point is that it was impossible for him to be objective even about a matter of local archaeology.

"You're miles away, Carl!" Emma cuts across my musings with the old trite question. "What are you thinking about?"

"Bremen. How Freud fainted away while we were talking about the bog men. What was it he said?"

"I remember very well. He was quite snappish. He said, 'Why do you always have to talk about corpses?' You made a joke of it and said, 'Not always, dear friend; quite often I talk about pretty women.' "

She reminds me of something else, too. After the incident, my dreaming did become obsessed with the dead. I dreamed, for example, that I was in Alyscamps, near the French town of Arles, walking down an avenue of sarcophagi. They are there in actuality. They date back to the Merovingians. In the dream, as I passed by each coffin, the mummified body inside it stirred and came to life.

I put the grim fantasy out of my mind and concentrate on tacking into a little cove where we shall drop anchor and have lunch. The children want to go swimming. Emma says the water is too cold. I will not contradict her orders. So, I get out a box of tackle and a jar of bait and set them fishing from the boat. Emma and I drink white wine and munch on chicken legs and young celery and crisp homebaked bread. I make a toast to her and tell her she is the best wife in the canton. She gives me an odd sidelong smile and tells me:

"That's nice to hear, Carl; but my talents aren't limited to the kitchen and the nursery."

I pat her belly and tell her that her other talents have never been in dispute. She is mollified, but only a little. She has sometimes remarked that although Europeans do not practise female circumcision, they do everything else to discourage women from pleasurable pursuits outside of marriage. It is a thorny subject and I have no intention of discussing it while we are bobbing at anchor in a windy lake. I unbutton my trousers and pee over the stern. Behind me, I hear young Franz announcing in his piping voice:

"See! I told you! Daddy's is enormous."

Emma and the girls burst into giggles. I laugh, too; but inside my head it is as if a fire has flared up. I remember another inlet on another lake and a deep, friendly voice urging me:

"You see how big it gets and hard. Take it in your hands, feel it. In the old days every Roman garden had its priapic Pan and young and old touched him for good luck."

This memory always recurs when I think about Freud and the difficulty of escaping from his influence and authority. One of the lessons I must teach my son is that you can never piss against the wind, especially when it blows out of the deep, dark caverns of memory.

MAGDA
Paris

Tonight, with all the casual cruelty of a caliph, Basil Zaharoff violated me. He debased me, stripped off every shred of self-respect and then offered to buy me like a brood mare at auction.

He did more. He barbarised something that was beautiful to me. He marched through my private Eden, trampling down the illusion of my childhood, the cherished images of Papa and Lily. He heaped mockery on us all. I wish to God I could have given him the lie; but I could not. So, from now to eternity, he can blackmail me with what he knows about my origins, suspects about my marriage, its prelude and its aftermath – and what every madam in the business will be happy to report to him on my sexual needs and aberrations.

On the way back to the Crillon, I felt physically sick. I wanted to stop the car and vomit in the gutter; but I would not make Zaharoff's chauffeur the witness of my humiliation. I fought down the nausea until I was locked in my room; then I voided Basil Zaharoff's fine food and classic vintages into the toilet. Afterwards, still in my evening clothes I flung myself on the bed and stared unseeing at the painted pastoral on the ceiling.

Whoever had contrived the pattern of my life, the life of Magda Liliane Kardoss von Gamsfeld, was a master of all the ironies. I, who had ridden so high, was tumbled in the dust. I, the lion tamer, was subdued by a single flick of the whip. I, who knew every trick of the tart's trade, was more bruised than any country virgin at her first encounter with the brothel-master.

The strange thing was that I couldn't blame Zaharoff. I could even envy the cool genius of his contrivance. He knew that I would not be shocked by anything he might ask of me. I had done it all before – often in less than the Zaharoff style. I was, in a sense, the perfect partner for him. We were King and Queen from the same suit of cards. So long as I served the King's interest, he would maintain me in my proper status.

If we lasted together – no estrangement, no divorce, no treachery of rivals – we might even become friends of a sort. There is a kind of comfort in low-life society, where everyone knows how to spell the same dirty words! But – this was the fear I gagged on! – from the moment I made a pact with Basil Zaharoff, I would never again own any part of myself. The terms would be non-negotiable and eternal: no rebate of interest, no remission of the final debt. When Mephistopheles came to collect payment, Faust – or Fausta now! – must surrender her soul.

But why worry? Papa had assured me I had no soul. I, too, had probed for one in vain in the dissecting rooms of a dozen hospitals. So why hesitate? The money was good, the working conditions first rate, the insurance total. What was this precious self that I was, suddenly, so unwilling to surrender?

The room began to spin and I was sick again. After the spasm and the vomiting I stripped off my soiled clothes, soaked a long time in a hot bath, then curled up in bed with the companion of my solitary nights: a rag doll called Humpty Dumpty. Lily had made him for me – God, how many years ago! She had sewed black threads across his face to make him look like a cracked egg. She had taught me the nursery rhyme that English children sang about him.

Humpty Dumpty sat on a wall,
Humpty Dumpty had a great fall.
All the King's horses and all the King's men,
Couldn't put Humpty together again.

I felt myself sliding into darkness. I heard myself whispering in a child's voice: "Lily, where are you? Lily!" Then I heard the baying of hounds and the thunder of galloping hooves, and once again I was back in the nightmare.

I am riding to hounds with the old crowd. It is spring; the whole countryside is in flower. We have flushed a fox, he is heading for the hills. The hounds are after him in full cry. I am leading the hunt, just behind the pack. The fox leads us into a defile between high black cliffs. I gallop ahead; but when I come out on the other side I am alone. There are no hounds, no huntsmen, only the small bloodied carcass of the fox. The land has changed. All around me is a flat wilderness of red sand, above which the sun glows like a great crimson eye. My horse rears and throws me. When I look up he has disappeared. I am alone in the wilderness. I am naked and my head is shaven like a nun's. I am imprisoned in a big ball of glass which rolls over and over displaying all my private parts, while the red eye stares at me and a terrible silence mocks me.

When I woke, I was curled up in the foetal position, clutching my Humpty Dumpty between my legs as if I, still unborn, had just given birth to him. I had to force myself to straighten out in the bed and look at my watch. It was still only three in the morning; but I felt an urge to write down the dream, its prelude and its aftermath.

It was almost as if Papa were talking to me, repeating his old refrain: "Write every case history, girl! Get the symptoms clear. Make sure you've set down the whole clinical sequence, or if you haven't, that you know at least where the gaps are. Then you can look at the logic. That's what diagnosis is: logic and probabilities. But if your first record is unorganised, you confuse yourself and put your patient at risk. Write it down; write it."

So, still obedient to the first man I ever loved, I propped Humpty Dumpty in front of me and began, disjointedly at first, then with greater fluency, to write my own case history, thus:

My earliest memories are of woman smell and milk taste and the big smooth breasts of my wet nurse. I recall kitchen things: roasting meat, baked parsnips, nutmeg, cinnamon, stewed apples, floury hands pounding the dough for country bread.

I hear women's voices, singing, laughter, chattering; men's voices greeting and growling. Heavy boots clomp on stone tiles. Friendly fellows who smell of cows and cut grass and sour beer and tobacco snatch me up and toss me towards the ceiling. Afterwards they hold me in their laps and feed me warm strudel with whipped cream.

There is a whole kaleidoscope of other images: rooks cawing in the elm trees along the drive, cattle with heavy udders ambling slowly home at milking time, Lily and I dancing through a meadow golden with dandelions and buttercups. There is a geography to all this, but it makes small matter beside the fact that these were happy times and places. For the first two years of my childhood we lived, Lily and I, on a farming estate just south of Stuttgart. Papa was working at the Klinik in Tübingen and doing two days a week private practice in Stuttgart. Sometimes he joined us at weekends; sometimes he didn't. When he did come, his pockets were full of gifts and he laughed a lot and smelt of lavender water.

Later, when I was four or five, we moved to Silbersee in Land Salzburg. Papa had sold his estates in Hungary and bought a small baroque castle with a dependency of tenant farmers who raised dairy cattle and pigs and bred farm horses and cut timber on the upland slopes. The castle also drew revenue from the lease of a guest house and a Stüberl in the local village.

At this time Papa was senior surgeon at the charity hospital in Salzburg and had as well a large private practice in that city. He took what he called his "social diversions" in Vienna, where also he was occasionally asked to operate. Zaharoff's portrait of him as a wealthy womaniser with small interest in his profession is a patent falsehood. His visits to Schloss Silbersee tended to be sporadic. Sometimes we did not see him for three or four weeks at a stretch. His factor ran the estate. Lily ran my life: traditional governess, little mother, big sister to a child who could have been intolerably lonely but was, for those few years at least, blissfully happy.

How can I describe this Lily Mostyn whom I loved so much? By contrast with the peasant women of our household, blonde, big busted, broad of back and buttocks, Lily looked like a Dresden doll. But under all the sober trimmings, the modest blouse, the bombazine and the petticoats, there was the body of an athlete.

She could run, skip, stand on her head, do handsprings and cartwheels, swim like a seal. When I asked her how she had learned all these things she cocked her head like a quizzical parrot and told me in a broad Lancashire accent:

"When you get bigger, luv, and your bones firm up, I'll show you. We'll do exercises in our room and find a quiet meadow where these Salzburg bum-slappers can't see us. That's another secret we'll have."

Everything was a secret with Lily. She taught me English "so we can say what we like in front of the servants". She made Papa teach us both Hungarian "because, lassie, when he's in bed, he prefers to talk in his native tongue. Every man does; but he can't talk to the wall, can he? Besides, if I can talk the bloody language, maybe folk will take me for the Countess Kardoss – which I wouldn't mind being; but I'll never get the offer."

I asked her why not. She squatted in front of me and explained with a cheerful grin:

"Because your Papa's never going to marry anyone. I don't blame him after his experience with your mother. Besides, you know the old saying, the more women you've known, the less you want to settle for one. As for me, even if I did marry, how could I get a better bargain than this one? Me, daughter of a country parson in Lancashire! I live in a castle. I'm paid three times as much as I could earn in England. I've got a baby to love – which is you, my sweet lassie. I've got a man to love me – which your Papa doesn't do often enough because he's off chasing expensive tarts and wealthy widows in Vienna. But when he's here it's wonderful and he makes sure I don't get pregnant – and he doesn't bring home the clap. At home, I'd be sighing my heart out to marry a bank clerk or a schoolmaster. Now, let's get undressed and we'll have a hot bath together and then take supper in our dressing gowns."

Of course I didn't understand half the things she said to me; but then, I didn't have to; it was enough that she talked, touched, kissed and cherished me. This is my tenderest memory of Lily and my father. They were wholly sensuous. They embraced the world through every sense. They touched it, tasted it, heard it like music, inhaled it like a perfume. When Lily brushed my hair, and plaited it, she communicated pleasure. It was as if she were handling filaments of gold. When she offered me a flower to smell, she cupped her hands round it so that no whiff of the perfume would escape. When she taught me a song, she would say, "Listen to this, it's *beautiful*!" Or, "It's so *dancy*!" When she bathed me, every touch in every place was a caress and an awakening.

This was, I think, what made my father such a good surgeon – and so desirable a lover! He handled human skin as if it were the most precious fabric in the world. His constant complaint about his colleagues was: "They hack into tissue like pork butchers. They stitch it like cobblers, leaving traumas everywhere." To see him cleansing and binding a cut in a farmboy's hand was a lesson in fastidious care and a quite gratuitous gentleness. Every time he came home, he would examine me with clinical care from top to toe and the experience was like being kissed by butterflies. He liked food, he liked drink; but he never guzzled. He savoured every mouthful. To watch Lily and Papa, curled up on the big ottoman in front of the fire, was like watching a pair of beautiful sleek cats and being proud to be the kitten of such a pair.

81

The three of us had no shame with each other – and no fear of intrusion. Our quarters in the Schloss – my nursery, Lily's bedroom, our bathroom, the big living room and Papa's quarters beyond – could be entered only through a single ante-chamber, past which no servant was permitted without a summons.

Once inside the suite, however, one could pass freely from room to room. We could stand naked at the window and watch the sunset-glow over the far peaks of the Tauern Alps; or we could draw the drapes and huddle into the sensuous security of a fairy tale kingdom. What happened in that kingdom was the biggest and most jealously guarded secret of all.

When Papa was at home, he belonged completely to us. We entertained guests – at dinners and to feasts and hunts; but no outsider, man or woman, ever lodged at the Schloss. Equally, I have to admit that neither Lily nor I ever saw the inside of Papa's lodgings in Salzburg or Vienna. I do not know how many other lives he led; but in Silbersee he had only one and we were the centre of it.

We were, in all but legality, a family. Papa slept with Lily. When he was away she moved back into her own room next to my nursery. I snuggled with them, like any child with any parents. Lily was my first teacher – my only one until I was old enough to be sent to a boarding academy for girls. She taught me reading, writing, mathematics, languages and the rudiments of music and the pianoforte.

Papa always examined me quite carefully on the work I had done since his last visit. He insisted also that I learned to ride; so the studmaster schooled both Lily and me in the elements of horsemanship. All this was normal enough for the girl child of a wealthy physician – a nobleman and a Hungarian to boot! – but the rest of my education was decidedly unorthodox. It was, I suppose, what the French used to call "une éducation sentimentale". Later, much too late indeed, I began to understand it as Papa's effort to complete, by fantasy, the shortcomings of his own sentimental career. I believe, for instance, that he was madly in love with my mother, that he truly wanted to marry her and found a family with her. Certainly he wanted a son. What he got instead was a girl child born on the wrong side of the blanket and a wound from which his male pride never recovered.

In spite of the fact that women doctors were rare, and regarded, if not as witches, most certainly as eccentrics, he manipulated me carefully to choose medicine as a career. He encouraged me to ask questions about his work. He told me colourful tales of medical history: of Cos, the healing island, of the arts of the old Egyptians and the magical herbs like digitalis and hellebore. Slowly he turned my attention to his text-books. He used his own body and Lily's and mine to teach me physiology and anatomy and the glandular functions. Patiently, over many years, he sought out those schools of medicine which accepted women, and established friendships with important members of their faculties. It was only after he died, when I was going through his correspondence, that I realised how much time and labour he had spent to find a school to accept me.

He was obsessed in other odd ways with continuity. When I was quite small I remember his explaining that when a woman married she took her husband's name. Then he added, "But of course the woman can keep her own name as well. That's what I want you to do: always keep a Kardoss in the name. You'll promise me that, won't you?"

I swore my biggest, most sacred promise. I told him that I would one day give him a grandson. In that, finally, I failed him. But he failed me, too. No! It was not failure. It was something else: misdirection, malfeasance, a lie fed into my childish life. He and Lily changed the signposts; and by the time I was able to read them, I was already far down a one-way street with no exit at the other end. Strange, isn't it? Zaharoff told me the same thing in other words; but I hated him for it.

It's very late and I am very tired, but I must try to set down this thought. It has been with me too long, coiled like a black snake just at the threshold of dreaming. Papa was trying to contrive an impossible creature: a son who would continue his name and his imprint on the planet and a daughter in whom he could possess the woman who had deserted him, enjoy her and, in strange and subtle fashion, exact revenge on her.

He accomplished his end not by cruelty but by indulgence. My sentimental education was carried out in the isolation of a hothouse. I was coaxed into sexual life, as I am told the Orientals coax their child whores, by serene seduction. Papa was too good a doctor to submit me to trauma, but every year he drew me more intimately to himself, brought me closer to the moment when he would initiate me – tenderly and beautifully, oh yes! oh yes! – and bind me to him more closely than any young lover could possibly do. My whole life gives testimony to how well he succeeded.

And Lily? My Lily whom I still love and miss at

times so terribly? She was my first madam! Why did she do it? At first I think she saw little harm. She was a healthy lusty girl, to whom a tumble in bed was as natural as dancing. But later, when I began to replace her as Papa's bedfellow, she had to know what she had done. She had tried to use me to hold him. In the end she lost him and we all lost each other.

Now I find myself at the end of that one-way street, with my nose rammed hard up against a brick wall. I cannot go forward. If I turn back, I walk straight into the arms of Basil Zaharoff. Perhaps the only solution is to jump right over the wall.

There now! The thought is out, written in my own physician's hand. I have released others from life's prison-house. It would not be too hard to contrive a tidy and painless exit for myself. What say you, Papa? Lily, what say you?

JUNG
Zurich

I am bedevilled now, haunted day and night by my conflicts with Freud over the interpretation of the incest taboo. I dread what will happen at our Munich Congress in September, when this and all our related disagreements will be chewed over in the most partisan fashion and when our personal relationship will be finally and publicly destroyed.

Freud sees the incest wish, as he sees every other psychic phenomenon, as rooted in the sexual impulse. I see it as a symbol of something deeper and more primal, related to the sun myths. It is not intercourse which is desired, but rebirth, which can only be accomplished by re-entry into the mother's womb . . .

Similarly, I disagree totally with Freud's concept of infantile sexuality. It seems to me . . . But why go over old ground? Freud is obdurate. He is wedded to authority and not to truth. The respect I had for him has been eroded. I can no longer sustain our relationship.

And there precisely is the personal problem. I cannot sustain the relationship – but I cannot destroy it either. It is too strong, too complex. It is like a tropical vine whose roots spread everywhere and whose tendrils thrust and twine though every crevice of my psyche.

First he was my mentor; then, very quickly and very easily, I adopted him as the father figure in the construct of my adult life. I was flattered by his slightest word of praise. He was flattered too, I think, though he would never admit it in so many words. He liked the deference of a man who had many more years of clinical experience than he. After all, Freud's institutional experience was minimal; while I had worked years in the Burgholzli, with a thousand or more patients under daily observation. I had devised and applied clinical tests and procured valuable statistical evidence which still stands.

But our relationship went further. I developed a "crush" on him – a strongly erotic attachment – coloured by my youthful experience of homosexual rape by an older man. I was open with Freud about this. He confessed to similar feelings for me and for another colleague. This made our relationship more open, but no less difficult.

When we began to diverge radically on matters of theory, Freud begged for my support to preserve his authority as leader of our circle and to provide at least a visible doctrinal consensus for our infant science. But when he invoked our friendship, I felt put upon. It was almost as if he were blackmailing me with confessional material. I felt – and I still feel – that the only remedy is the biblical one: lay the axe to the root of the tree and chop it down.

I wish to God it were as easy to do as to say! Whom do I kill first? The teacher, the father, the lover? And when, if ever, I have extirpated them all from my psychic life, what will be left? With whom can I share the experience of shame and loss?

Emma understands something of what ails me. She has become a reasonably good analyst – though not as acute or brilliant as Toni. She has also maintained a friendship and a correspondence with Freud; I deprecate this, but I cannot forbid it. However, Emma knows nothing of the homosexual element in my relations with Freud and is much more concerned with our family situation. My rages upset her and the children. She is still resentful about early episodes with women patients. She is jealous of Toni and is plagued by her constant presence in our house. She finds that my new existence as a scholarly consultant is very hard to explain to our neighbours and friends. It was much easier when she could use my titles: Clinical Director at the Burgholzli and Senior Lecturer at the university. We Swiss need very precise categories if we are to live comfortably together!

I am in an even greater dilemma with Toni. She is very well aware of the father-son aspect of my attachment to Freud. She knows my need of a strong parent figure to replace that of my father, whom I loved but could never wholly respect because he would not confront with me the issues of faith and doubt. All this

I can discuss freely with Toni. But the other, no! Our sexual relationship is rich and passionate. I shudder to think of what would happen if suddenly I confronted her with the base and brutal image of rape *per anum*.

So, I am left alone with this demon. I must grapple with him in secret. As my self-disgust grows, so does my resentment of Freud. My resentment extends to that little circle of lick-spittle cronies who cluck and cavort around him like courtiers around King Sun. "The master disagrees. The master is offended. The master this, the master that!" You'd think sometimes he was the Lord Buddha himself, instead of a Viennese Jew whose best ideas are tainted by delusions of grandeur!

This is another issue between us, which for obvious reasons, neither of us wants to put into words. Freud is a Jew who has been able, quite comfortably, to dispense with the religion of his race. For him all religion is man-created myth – a crutch for the ailing psyche which must be thrown away before a final cure is pronounced. I am a Swiss German, bred in the Lutheran Church. I have abandoned the religion of my father, but never my search for a deity who makes sense to me and to whom I can pledge myself as a rational man. I do not see man's myths and fairy tales and diverse religions as a crutch. I see them rather as sacraments of healing, as symbols by which man expresses his perception of mystery and adjusts his psyche to its burden.

I know that certain of Freud's diehards dismiss me as a mystic or some kind of failed poet dabbling in the science of the mind. Some of them have even spread malicious rumours that I show symptoms of dementia praecox! They forget that my clinical experience is much longer than theirs and that I have written what is, so far, the most authoritative work on the subject.

But these rumourmongers have done me much harm. My practice has fallen off. A number of patients have deserted me. I am forced to indulge in the sordid little game of exploiting rich patients who are not neurotics at all but who are simply bored or at odds with their circumstances.

I am ashamed of this. I am angry that I am forced to degrade myself for money. I know that I am reaching far beyond Freud's frontiers, and I am convinced that one day I shall touch a truth beyond the stretch of his imagination. I am being drawn to it as the moth is drawn to the candle flame; though I cannot yet see the light or plot the way towards it.

Toni arrives late, still pale and coughing from the grippe. I scold her and tell her she should have stayed in bed. She protests.

"I'm better working. In bed I get myself into a fever, wanting you, hoping you'll come to see me."

I explain a little impatiently that Emma and the children wanted to go sailing and I cannot refuse these simple family requests. Toni accepts the argument with reluctance. This is where the shoe pinches. Her standing in this affair is always one step lower than mine. Professionally she is still an apprentice. As a mistress she takes second place to the wife and the family. When I assure her that she is first in my heart always, she reminds me that my heart is a strange country, sometimes harsh and unfriendly. There is a brief bitter moment when it seems as if we will quarrel again; then she surrenders. We kiss and the bitter taste is gone. She tells me of a dream she had during her afternoon nap.

"My head was full of you and my body was aching with the need of you. I fell asleep and dreamed that I was a seagull flying over the lake. I saw you sitting on the beach, crosslegged like an Oriental. You were naked and alone. I flew down to join you; but when I came closer there was another man with you. He was embracing you and fondling you in a sexual way – the same way as I do. When he saw me he waved his arms and motioned me away. I flew off, but I hovered in circles high above, watching the love-play. Then Emma came down to the beach and began hitting the man with her umbrella. I flew away because I didn't want her to see me."

As I listen to Toni unfolding the dream, I feel a surge of emotion, like a rush of floodwaters, muddy, turbulent, full of strange debris. Has she guessed the dark secret that plagues me? Have I, by some mechanism of the unconscious, communicated it to her? This dream came to her while I was in reverie about the same matters, on the boat anchored in the quiet cove. This is a situation which presents itself more and more often: coincidence, synchronicity, things happening at the same moment in time, without causal connection, but still closely related in nature. The connection merits a closer examination in the context of psychic experience. I do not trust myself to comment on the dream immediately. I sit down at my desk, make brief notes of its content and then, in the formal fashion we adopt for clinical discussion, I question Toni.

"Before you fell asleep, did you know I was going sailing?"

"No. But it was such a beautiful day I thought you might take the boat out."

"Was there any other trigger to the dream?"

"Oh yes. A white bird dipped past my window and I thought 'Lucky you! I wish I could fly like that.' Then I must have dozed off."

"Tell me now." I take a peremptory tone. "Tell me, without reflection, what the dream signifies to you."

"Oh it is very clear!" She answers with that limpid innocence which so easily disarms me. "It was clear even while I was dreaming it. We have talked so much of the *anima* and the *animus*: the female element in every male, the male element in every woman. Well, the you I saw on the beach was your *anima*, the female part of you. The Buddha in meditation never displays any male sex organ. The male who was soliciting you was the male me, my *animus*. We were loving each other like that because in real life our roles are reversed. Because of our situation, I have to pursue you. You are passive and female until I present myself to excite you. Then, of course, you are wholly male. But whichever role we assume, Emma always comes to separate us. It's really quite a banal dream, no mystery in it at all."

"Let's not dismiss it so lightly. Were you excited by the female me?"

"Oh yes."

"Could you in real life tolerate such a reversal of roles?"

"That's what the dream says, Carl: I have to tolerate it all the time. You don't pursue me like a courting lover. I have to pursue you, grasp at every moment of your company. Oh yes, you desire me; but you wait here until I come to you. Of course you're the active one when we make love, but before and after – yes –

the roles do reverse themselves. I'm not complaining. I'm stating a fact, interpreting my dream."

"Suppose I tell you, Toni Wolff, that you're lying to me, that you never had such a dream, that you're playing games and inventing clinical evidence. What's your answer?"

"There are three answers, you grouchy old bear! I'm lying. I'm telling the truth. I'm offering a dream construct that fits our situation. You make the choice!"

I am very tempted to accuse her of lying and vent all my fears and frustrations in anger. In the same instant I am aware that Toni expects just that. She is looking at me with the same expression, half amused, half threatening that I used to see on my mother's face when she looked inside my head. I know that if we quarrel I shall end by having to apologise, to explain myself – and this time the cat will pop out of the bag! I shall have to reveal the sordid little story of my rape and my erotic attachment to Freud. Toni senses the truth. The dream is her strategy to force me to reveal it.

So, I do what I always do. I lie. I take her hands and draw her to me. I kiss her on the lips and fondle her breasts and tell her:

"I make bad jokes because I've missed you so much. Of course I believe the dream. It tells the exact truth about you and me. We're so close that we're one person – all our parts are mixed up together like fruit in a pie."

The words are hardly spoken when we hear Emma calling the children in the garden. We draw apart hastily. Toni retreats to her desk, I to mine. I am angry because I feel ridiculous. Toni is still in her teasing mood. She smooths the blouse over her out-thrust nipples and giggles at me: "I wonder if Emma's carrying her umbrella."

MAGDA
Paris

I woke this morning in a quite suicidal depression, convinced that I must either mend my life or end it. Clearly there was no way to mend it in an association with Basil Zaharoff; so I must deal with that situation immediately. But how? It could only be by yea or nay. Zaharoff would tolerate no games. He was too practised a pimp to be deceived by feminine by-play. If I wanted to refuse, I had to confront him and convince him of my unfitness for the role he had written for me.

I forced myself to bathe, bundled up my soiled clothes, locked away the material I had written during the night, then summoned the maid to bring me camomile tea and an ice pack. I had a blinding headache, against which even the new German aspirin tablets gave little relief. When I looked at myself in the mirror I was shocked. My skin was pale as milk; my lips were bloodless; the crow's feet were etched deep around my eyes, and the fear I read in my face – a fear of imminent disaster and future threat – was plain for all the world to see.

At ten I called Basil Zaharoff. His manservant told me he was sleeping and could not be disturbed. He had become ill during the night and his doctor had only just left. I told the servant that I, too, had been ill. He was instantly in panic. Mr. Zaharoff had suspected a bad oyster at last night's meal. Now there could be no doubt. Please would I stay in the hotel? Mr. Zaharoff himself would most certainly telephone as soon as he was recuperated. Meantime, please dear lady, the greatest care! I am sending immediately for the physician!

He came like a heavenly visitor, so that I gaped in wonderment. This was Giancarlo di Malvasia, colleague of my student days in Padua and intern service in Vienna. He was in his mid-forties now, but still as handsome as Lucifer, still the same fastidious Florentine who had once declared his ambition to be the greatest diagnostician in the world and then be co-opted as a noble celibate with the Sovereign Order of the Knights of Malta.

We had always been amiable colleagues, but somehow the chemistry of sex had never worked between us. I was too much the tomboy for him. He was too much the Tuscan snob to trust with my outlandish history. But somehow we had succeeded in a cautious friendship and a professional respect. We had worked together on ward rounds, in anatomy classes, in occasional correspondence on difficult cases. Then, when I gave up medicine we had lost contact. I understood from Papa that Giancarlo was building a lucrative practice among the internationals who made the annual European circuit. I hoped that he was not too closely acquainted with my raffish reputation.

He was discreetly delighted to see me – still that damned Florentine condescension! – and politely interested in my association with Basil Zaharoff. He examined me thoroughly, then relaxed enough to pay me a barbed compliment.

"My dear Magda, you look ten years younger than you have any right to do. My compliments."

"And mine to you, Gianni. Clearly you've realised all your ambitions."

"Not all." He shrugged and made a small grimace of distaste. "I am no longer a candidate for the Sovereign Order of the Knights of Malta."

"Does that worry you?"

"My marriage worries me more. It is a childless union, neither loving nor convenient."

"I'm sorry."

"Please!" He held up a deprecating hand. "One learns to accommodate to the inevitable. And how are things with you? I know you're a widow and that you have a varied and diverting life. This – er – affair with Zaharoff, is it new?"

"This 'affair', as you call it, my dear Gianni, has been limited to one dinner with bad oysters. Zaharoff has made certain proposals which at this moment I view with great reserve."

"I hope you can keep matters like that." Giancarlo frowned and fidgeted uncomfortably. "He's a dangerous man. I'm his personal physician and he pays me like a prince; but he would as quickly have my head if I crossed him. However, I mustn't meddle in your affairs. Stay in bed today. Take only lemon tea and dry toast. You won't be able to face oysters again for a long time."

He made as though to take his leave. I begged him to stay awhile and talk with me. I told him I was in desperate need of advice – clinical advice under the Hippocratic oath. He gave me a long searching look, and then asked dubiously:

"Are you sure that's wise? I'm not your regular

physician. I know nothing of your medical history. Besides I've never specialised in gynaecology. I could recommend you to a good man . . ."

"Let's decide that when you've heard what I have to say. Please, Gianni! I need a sound opinion, but I don't want to discuss this with a complete stranger."

"Very well then." He settled himself on the edge of the bed and took my hand between his own. "Tell me!"

Then it was a question of the words, and suddenly I was struck dumb. I burst into tears and finally managed to stammer out:

"Gianni, I'm a mess! My whole life's a mess! I don't know what to do about it."

"Neither do I, until you explain the mess!" He gave me his pocket handkerchief to dry my eyes. "Now that you've had your cry, let's try to be professional, shall we?"

I fumbled again for the words and finally found them.

"Vienna, Professor Richard von Krafft-Ebing. Remember him? Remember his book *Sexual Psychopathology* and the big debates we all used to have about it?"

"I remember. So?"

"There was a phrase he used to use in his lectures on the forensic aspects of sexuality. 'Il faut toujours avoir pitié de ceux qui ont le diable au corps. One must always have pity on those who have the devil in their bodies.' Well, I'm one of those, Gianni. I've seen everything, done everything – but nothing puts out the fire. I'm known to the police and the professionals on the underground circuits. That's why Zaharoff wants me to work for him. He wants me to run his European brothel circuit. If I accept, I get protection and make a fortune. If I refuse, I'm left with the devil who lives in my skin! Before you walked in this morning I was ready to end it all. Where do I turn, Gianni? Who helps people like me? Don't despise me, please!"

I despised myself. I was abject, grovelling to a man I hadn't seen for years, crying maudlin tears into his silk handkerchief. He did not answer me. He got up abruptly, strode to the window and stood a long time looking out at the flowers on the sunlit terrace. When he turned back to me his face was in shadow. He asked me an oddly irrelevant question.

"Are you a believer? Do you belong to any communion – Catholic, Lutheran, Waldensian?"

"No. Sometimes I've thought I'd like to be a croyante – I've never had the real urge or the aptitude for religion. Why do you ask?"

"If you have a faith, it can sometimes help. It helped me. In fact I'm sure I could never have endured without it."

"Endured what?"

He sat down and took my hands again. He was smiling now, a wintry ironic smile that transfigured those pinched aristocratic features with an extraordinary pathos.

"You used to call me a snob. I wasn't really. I was trying to create an identity for myself. I would be a Renaissance man, one of those young gallants from the court of Lorenzo the Magnificent. The fact is I am incurably homosexual. My mother nagged me into marriage. My wife's parents urged her into a union with a wealthy and noble family. It was a ghastly mistake for both of us. We're trying to have it annulled by the Roman Rota, but it's a tedious business and ruinously expensive. Meantime my wife has taken a lover – for which I don't blame her. And I . . ."

He broke off. I waited out a longish silence and then prompted him.

"I've made my peace with God. I've gone back to the Church and joined the Third Order of Saint Francis. I dedicate part of my time to charitable work among the poor."

He announced it so simply that it took my breath away. It was the first time in my life I had heard a profession of faith and I was not sure whether to smile or weep. I asked cautiously:

"And you find that changes things for you?"

"It doesn't change them. I am still drawn to men rather than to women. But I do live celibate and I believe there's merit and purpose in the sacrifice. I find I think less about my own problems and more about other people's. When the desperate days come – and believe me, my dear Magda, I do have many of those – I pray and I feel I am not alone."

"You're lucky. I don't have a talent for piety!"

He shook his head. His face was sombre again.

"It isn't a talent. It's a grace, a gift. Why God gives it to some and withholds it from others is a mystery – perhaps the most troubling mystery of all."

"That doesn't help me, does it? And, forgive me, it doesn't say much for your God either!"

"That's what faith is about – living with paradox. I understand your scepticism, but I wonder if you would not at least take some religious counsel. For people like us, my dear Magda, the doctrine of forgiveness, of new beginnings, holds much consolation. Instead of seeing ourselves as freaks and oddities we perceive ourselves as in some sense the chosen, bearing a heavier cross, to fulfil a greater destiny. I know I sound like a village missionary, but I, too, was very near to despair. Then an old priest, who used to be chaplain to our family, persuaded me to make a retreat with the Camaldoli, who have a big monastery near Florence. Outside it is a grim place, but inside I found so much serenity, so much compassion for the afflicted . . . I wish I could share it with you, explain it in better words than I have."

He was so solemn about it all, I thought I would burst out laughing. I remembered myself mooning around him in the lecture halls, wondering why I couldn't raise a spark of sexual response! All those wonderful looks wasted on a finocchio! Then I had the crazy impulse to drag him into bed and play wild games and teach him how to enjoy himself. A retreat with the Camaldoli, prayers to cure the Venus itch? Dear God! I was glad Papa wasn't there to listen to such claptrap. Fortunately I was able to control myself. I sat modestly in bed, eyes downcast, hands folded in my lap, waiting for this aristocratic sobersides to finish his little sermon. His next question surprised me.

"How long is it since you gave up medical practice?"

"Oh, more than a dozen years. My husband died of cancer. I treated him during his illness. That was my last case."

"Have you kept up with your reading – the latest journals, the new texts?"

"No. Why do you ask?"

"I've been following the psychoanalytic work of Freud and Jung and their associates. I went two years ago to their conference in Weimar. The papers they presented were of high quality and full of new insights into psychotic and neurotic disorders. Their analyses of dreams, their examination of familial and ancestral relationships – these I found most valuable in coping with my own problems and treating those of my patients. But of course I'm not trained and not skilled enough to go into full-time analytic practice. One day perhaps. However, my dear Magda, it occurs to me that you might do worse than consult with one of the experts in this field. Analysis doesn't necessarily solve the problem, but it does reduce it to human size. It is no longer a giant shadow cast on the wall."

"How has it helped you?" I still wanted to tease him. "It can't be more potent than God – although it might be more tolerable than a month's solitary confinement in a monastery."

For the first time he laughed and there was a ring of genuine amusement in the sound.

"I know! You still think I'm a stuffy Florentine snob tied to his mother's rosary beads. But I've made my own journey through hell – and by a singular mercy I've survived it. The same staff that served me won't necessarily support you. But, like Dante, you need a guide, someone to talk to in the wild country. Otherwise you'll really go crazy."

Suddenly I was ashamed of myself. I was a self-destructive bitch mocking a good man because he probed too close to the truth. I offered an awkward apology. He waved it away with a grin.

"Let's consider which of these people could help you most. Freud is the most obvious choice. He is the most daring and illuminating exponent of human sexuality in all its aspects. Where Krafft-Ebing dealt

100

with symptoms and manifestations, Freud deals with origins and determinant factors. On the other hand I, personally, developed a certain antipathy to the man. He is Jewish of course – and I admit to a historic prejudice against the race. He is brilliant, but inclined to arrogance." Giancarlo had the grace to blush as he said it. "I know! I'm arrogant, too! But one thing does bother me about Freud. He excludes altogether any religious concept of man, any belief in God or divine intervention in human affairs. That to me is a very drastic negative to his system. Jung on the other hand is exploring the historic symbols which recur in our conscious and unconscious life. He embraces the religious experience even though he does not always define it in orthodox terms. Then there are people like Bleuler, a very experienced clinician, the Americans Putnam and Brill and a young disciple of Freud's, very ardent and very clever, called Jones. However, on balance I would recommend Jung. He's in Zurich, quite close, and I do know that he takes private patients. In fact they all do. Psychoanalysis is much talked about as a new science, but it's not yet as profitable as normal medicine." He reached out and tilted my chin up so that I was forced to face him. "Don't take this too lightly. Menopause is a bad time anyway. You'll need help if you're going to get through yours without some nasty traumas. What do you say? Would you like me to drop a note to Jung and ask him to see you?"

"Let me think about it, Gianni. If I decide to go, I'll write to him myself. If I don't, maybe you can find me a nice comfortable convent in Tuscany."

"I could find you a dozen. They'd all welcome a rich penitent!" He added a grim little afterthought:

"You'd certainly be safer in a convent than with Basil Zaharoff."

"I know. Perhaps you can help me handle him."

"How?"

"He knows you're visiting me. You could tell him I'm recovered from the oysters, but demonstrating acute hysterical symptoms."

"Take my advice, Magda. Deal with Zaharoff simply and bluntly. Believe me, he won't want to reason about it. That isn't his way. If you reject this offer the matter will be closed – but pray God you never have to turn to him for help in the future!" He bent and kissed me lightly on the forehead, told me to call him if I had any recurrence of the nausea, then left without further ceremony. I lay a long time staring at the painted nymphs on the ceiling and wishing there were a man or woman to share my solitude.

I dozed through the afternoon until, at six o'clock, Basil Zaharoff was announced. He looked a little washed out, but elegant as ever. He came, he said, to make honourable amends for any discomfort and for the incredible carelessness of his kitchen staff. The "amends" took the shape of a bracelet of antique gold with a clasp of diamonds and rubies. I protested that I could not accept the gift.

Zaharoff was adamant. He put the bracelet on my wrist and locked the safety clasp. It was only then that he permitted me to speak. I told him my decision. I could not accept his offer. I hurried into my explanation, humbling myself to appease the vanity of the caliph who hid behind the mask of the gentleman.

"I was flattered and tempted by your offer. It would solve a lot of problems for me, but it might also create many for you. You're the kind of man I admire very much. Your esteem and your patronage would mean much to me, but I have to be very honest. I am not sure I can count on my stability. Things are happening inside myself that I don't yet understand. I'm a physician. I recognise the signs of stress, the erosion of self-control. I am not yet in menopause, but that could prove to be a bad time for me. You will be involved in great affairs. You need a more reliable consort than I."

I found myself tearful again, from sheer relief that the words were out. Zaharoff was sedulous to comfort me.

"Please, dear lady! Don't cry, I beg you. I regret the loss of your talents of course, but I value your honesty and I trust we may remain good friends."

"I do want that, believe me."

He took me in his arms. He told me I was beautiful and desirable. He reminded me of my promise. What better time than now to divert ourselves together? What better time indeed? If I wanted to get off the tiger, I had first to make sure that the beast was drowsy and friendly.

This may be the only testimony that will ever be given in defence of Basil Zaharoff, boy-pimp from Tatavla, who peddled death around Europe and never saw a spot of blood on his own hands. He was a skilful lover and, for his age, surprisingly vigorous.

He paid me a compliment too. He was dressing to go home and I was helping to adjust his silk cravat. He cupped my face in his smooth old hands and said, with smiling regret, "My dear Magda, I wish you'd reconsider my offer. If you turned professional you'd be the greatest in the game!"

That night I had again the nightmare of the glass

103

ball. This time, however, it was not the eye of the sun which mocked me. It was Basil Zaharoff. He was turning the ball over and over with the tip of his cane, tapping on the glass shell until great cracks appeared, like the cracks on the face of Humpty Dumpty. I huddled naked inside, a foetus-woman, wondering in what monster form I would come to birth, when the shell burst open and spilled me on the blood-red sand.

J UNG
Zurich

As I re-read the material I have written in this private journal I am surprised at its simplicity and directness. In my published work I am often prolix, always self-conscious, overly literate, as if everything I say is loaded with Delphic mystery. Here I write as I feel, in the blunt fashion of a countryman.

In public, in the company of my peers, I conform to the ritual, use the magic language, rattle my beads and baubles a little louder to prove how potent a shaman I really am. I lie, too, when it serves my purposes; but then we all lie in one fashion or another, because we are not scientists always; we are sooth-sayers – dealing with arcane symbols and the stuff of dreams.

I had a new dream last night; I want to set it down in outline before Toni comes. I want to study it before we analyse it together. I must not be caught unaware as I was by her dream of the seagull.

I was on a train. I knew that I was coming back to Switzerland from somewhere in the North. Suddenly I looked out of the window and saw that all the land, as far as the eye could see, was under water. It was not

104

still water, but a vast yellow wave rolling southward towards the Alps, which reared themselves up like a wall against the torrent. Then I saw that the wave was full of debris: trees, animals, fragments of houses, clothing and human corpses, thousands and thousands of them. Even as I watched, the colour of the flood changed. It was red . . . blood-red. Next I began to distinguish, among the dead, people I knew. Freud was there and Honegger and Emma and the children and my own father. I was oppressed with fear and shame because they were dead and I was alive and I did not want to leave the warm carriage and risk being drowned.

Then Emma was prodding and shaking me. I had frightened her with my shouting and bruised her as I flailed about in the nightmare. I settled her back to sleep and then came down to spend the rest of the night in my study.

Let me write down now what I dare not say to Emma or even to Toni. This dream has frightened the hell out of me. In my clinical work at the Burgholzli Clinic, I noted that chaos dreams, visions of world disorder and destruction, are almost always a symptom of the schizoid state associated with dementia praecox.

The patient is aware that his personality is fragmenting itself, exploding into pieces as a circular saw will do when it is driven too long and too fast; but he cannot define the experience in words. He dreams it. Gradually the borderline between dream and reality becomes blurred. Finally he cannot distinguish one from the other. He abandons himself to a state of permanent delusion, which nevertheless has its own logic – the logic of schizophrenic insanity.

The mere fact that I am writing these lines tells me that I can still distinguish dream from reality; but the warning is there. It may not always be so – witness my dialogues in the garden with Elijah and Salome, who are figments of my unconscious, but who are sometimes as real to me as Emma and Toni. I cannot face this fear alone in my study in the cold hours between midnight and dawn. So I begin to dissect the dream, phrase by phrase, like a grammarian:

I am travelling in a train.

A traveller is mobile, rootless. He has no anchorhold in time and space. He is isolated, in his own conveyance, from which he sees the world but can make no contact with it. This is exactly my case, since I gave up my appointment at the clinic, my lectureship at the university. I have travelled much, in Europe and abroad. I have attended many conferences, but I am deprived of daily contact with my peers.

Outside the land is engulfed in a great flood.

Ever since Bulgaria invaded Serbia and Greece in June this year, all Europe has been haunted by the fear of hostilities between the Great Powers. Switzerland would of course remain neutral; hence the dream image of the Alps heaved up as a barrier against the flood. So, in contrast with my journey backwards to meet Elijah and Salome, perhaps this dream is a prophetic experience, a clairvoyant glimpse of the future. Even as I toy with this thought I am uneasy again. This is exactly the kind of spurious logic which the schizoid patient constructs for himself in dementia praecox. I pass quickly to the next image:

I see dead bodies of people I know.

This is a less frightening symbol. It expresses desire

but not intention. Like every married man who has ever embarked on a love affair I have fantasies about being single and free again. My wife, my family, are obstacles to that freedom. My unconscious harbours the thought that, if they were to die, all my problems would be solved. Freud and my father are conjoined in another context. Father is dead. I am freed from his dominion. If Freud were dead I should inherit his mantle of authority.

I am oppressed with shame because I do not want to leave the warm carriage.

This is almost a mirror image of the moment, only a few days ago, when Emma, driven to desperation by one of my rages, accused me bitterly.

"You think of no one but yourself, Carl. It is always what you want, never what we may need of love and care and simple kindness. You lock yourself in your study like an ogre in his cave. You share your secrets with your mistress and not your wife. Perhaps you think you're achieving something that will make it all worthwhile – but not for us, Carl! Not for us! Children live for today, not for tomorrow. I want today as much as they do. Most times I feel as though I'm waving you goodbye at a railway station, and I'm not certain you'll ever be back."

I made all sorts of protestations, but in my heart I knew she was right. I am a selfish man – the more so because I am frightened of the cracks and divisions in myself. I need the reassurance Toni gives me. I flee the responsibilities family life lays on me because I am so far from the fulfilment of my personal ambitions. I am loud and disputatious because I have so many uncertainties. So, however glib my analysis of the nightmare, I know it is a chaos dream and sooner or later I shall have to recognise its secret warnings.

I fill my pipe and bring out the brandy bottle. I see a certain risk in this habit of tippling in the small hours of the morning, so I limit myself to one, generous measure. If Toni were here, or if Emma were more eager sexually, I wouldn't need to drink at all. I'm still only thirty-eight, and I'm damned if I'm going to live like Simon Stylites.

The image of that old curmudgeon, perched on his pillar in the desert, living on bread and water and dried dates, performing all his natural functions in full view of his devotees, intrigues me. I see his strange existence as a parody of my own. I want to withdraw from the commerce of people. I need to exhibit myself, to have the merits of my work recognised. The two needs never quite reconcile themselves. My colleagues regard me as an arrogant eccentric. My patients – some of them at least – make gossip about my lecheries.

Simon Stylites reminds me of our own Swiss hermit, the Blessed Klaus of Flühli. When I was a boy, I visited his shrine with my father, and that same day met a young girl who haunted my dreams for a long time. Brother Klaus the Blessed seems to have discovered the formula for beatitude in his life and the next. He was married. He had children, but he spent only half his life with his family and the other half happily communing with himself and his Creator in a hermitage.

Perhaps this is the answer for me. Find a piece of land, build myself a hermitage and go into retreat whenever home life becomes intolerable. Toni could join me there. I don't think Emma would raise too many objections – especially if it took Toni out from under her feet at Küsnacht.

I open my sketch pad and begin to draw a stone tower, set foursquare on the lakeshore. I surround it with a wall, inside which I can live my hermit life. There will be a well in the courtyard and wood, cut and corded for the winter, a stele upon which I will carve the cryptic record of my works and days. The furniture I shall make myself, with simple country tools – an adze, a spokeshave, a bow saw, a wooden mallet and a plane honed on a whetstone. There will be flowers and a spice garden and onions hung from the rafters in my kitchen. There will be lamplight and candlelight and an iron stove to bake bread and country meats.

When I draw the ground plan for the whole edifice, I notice that it consists of two geometric figures: a square enclosed within a circle. I remember that it was from a circle that Elijah and Salome stepped into my conscious life. I invoke them, but they do not answer.

Nevertheless I sense a presence in the room. It is more powerful, yet somehow much simpler, than theirs. I invoke this one too. There is no answer, but the silence seems to intensify around me, as if the presence is becoming more solid.

Involuntarily I pick up the pencil and retrace the outline of the square – one, two, three, four. In the same automatic fashion I write a letter by each side of the figure, as if I am setting out a problem in geometry. The letters in sequence are Y H W H. I stare at them a long time. Then, in an instant, their meaning is plain. What I have written is the Tetragrammaton, the four-letter Hebrew symbol for the unspeakable name of God.

Once again, my unconscious has yielded up material from its store of myth and symbol. The circle and the square are perfect figures. The Tetragrammaton is the symbol of the ultimate perfection we call God. The silence, the solid silence, envelops me as the Creator envelops his whole creation.

I look again at the figure. I remember having seen it in many variations and with sundry embellishments in Oriental texts. It is the mandala, the symbol of completion, of the quiet of ultimate arrival. The tower I have dreamed will be for me a place of quiet repose. I am sure now that I shall build it, and that, bidden or unbidden, God will there present himself to me.

He will not be the God of my father – a narrow jurist, counting the delinquencies of his creatures on some divine abacus. He will not be the God of the Romans who insists on putting his castrated priests in shovel hats and black skirts. On the contrary, he will be the deity written on every heart, hidden in the collective unconscious of the whole race, whom the old Gnostics perceived, whom the canonists and theologians obscured behind their formulae.

In this bleak hour before cockcrow I have stumbled upon an important truth. For me, Carl Gustav Jung, there is no royal road to wisdom. To arrive at the future I must journey into the past. To reach the sun I must penetrate the dark kingdom of the unconscious. To attain the sanity of oneness with the One, I must risk the whirling madness of the possessed.

Like old Martin Luther, I have come to the moment of decision. "Hier stehe ich; ich kann nicht anders. Gott hilfe mir! Here I stand, I cannot do otherwise. God help me!" The haunted silence weighs on me like a leaden cope.

MAGDA
Paris

I am calmer today. I have appeased Basil Zaharoff. I am free to address myself to some personal decisions. The Brothers Ysambard suggest I re-invest part of my capital in the United States. After my talks with Zaharoff, I am convinced they are right. There will be war in Europe. A stake in the New World will be a comforting insurance. Next, they suggest I sell my estates with their valuable bloodstock. The market is high. I can spread the proceeds over a broader base and reduce my risk in the aftermath of war. I am in two minds about this proposal.

The union of Papa's property in Silbersee with my late husband's estate in nearby Gamsfeld gave me one of the richest holdings in Land Salzburg. All my roots are there, my sweetest memories of Papa and Lily and the only other man I have ever loved, my husband Johann, Ritter von Gamsfeld.

I know this country like the palm of my hand. I can recite the history of every Schloss and shrine. I speak the dialect. I know all the old songs and dances. I grew up with the sons and daughters of the local farmers. To give up my inheritance would be like cutting off my right hand and yet the matter is, in a sense, already decided because I am no longer welcome in my home place.

The night before I left for Berlin to deliver the horses I had sold to Prince Eulenberg, my studmaster came to see me. His name is Hans Hemeling. He is sixty years old, a Tiroler, a lion of a man with a mane of white hair and a weather-scored face, the very image of his country's hero, Andreas Hofer. When I came to Silbersee as a child, he was one of the grooms. It was he who sat me on my first pony, dusted me off

111

and dried my tears when I took my first tumble. Together he and I built up some of the best bloodlines in European horse breeding. Now he was my accuser, grim as a hanging judge.

"You take Apollo, our best stallion. You deliberately ride him past the mares. Then, when he gets restive you thrash him and rowel him bloody and gallop him into exhaustion. You break the heart of a beautiful beast! Why for God's sake? Why? Your own hound comes up to you to be patted. His muzzle stains your riding habit. You beat him half to death; so I have to shoot him and bury him in the rose garden. Then you get up at midnight and chop down the roses! Oh yes! You swore you didn't do it. Maybe you even believed it. But you were seen! How do you think our people take these things? I'll tell you, Madame! They think you're a *Hexe*, a witch! If you don't go away from here, they'll all leave – and I'll go with them! If you think you can run this place with foreigners, don't try it! Your stock will be stolen, your farms will be burned. The only reason it hasn't happened already is because I've told them you're going to Berlin to get medical attention and I'm going to be in charge here. Don't argue! Just do as I say! At least you know I'm honest. You won't be out one Pfennig! But if you stay, you'll lose everything."

I knew he was right. Ever since those days of madness I had felt the hostility building around me like a wall of fire. I appealed to Hans to explain me to myself. He shrugged wearily.

"I don't know. I wish I did. You were always a wild one. Your husband – God rest him! – tamed you for a while. After he died you went wild again. I used to think all you needed was another lusty fellow to breed

112

sons out of you. If I'd been younger and single I'd have bid for you myself. But that's all in the past. Now you act as if you're bewitched and even the animals sense it. I don't know whether you need a doctor to look into your head or a priest to drive the devils out of you!"

That was old country talk; but it hit me harder than any rhetoric. We have a church on every hill and a shrine at every crossroads; yet the ancient Germanic gods and demons live on in the black forests and the high crags and the dark tarns. They have always been more real to me than any plaster saints. I know them from fireside yarns and kitchen gossip and old wives' tales about spells and counter-spells. After my murderous rages I could well believe that a whole legion of evil spirits had taken up residence in my skull-case. So, I didn't fight Hans any more. I bowed my head like a penitent child and told him I would stay away until the devil was driven out. Then I would come home again.

He was not mollified. He warned me bluntly:

"Don't hurry! And write to me before you even think of coming back. Our people have long memories!"

The message was plain. They would never forgive or forget what I had done. So, this morning in Paris I telephoned Joachim Ysambard and told him I agreed with his recommendations. He should sell the property, disperse the stock, make due provision for my staff and invest the residue in equities in the United States. Joachim was gratified by my good sense. He asked about my future plans. I asked him whether he would like to take another vacation with me in Amalfi. He laughed and hung up.

For me it is no laughing matter. I am, now, desperately alone. Before I can make any plans, I must be cured of the madness that afflicts me. Hans Hemeling's words still haunt me. "Find a doctor to look into your head, or a priest to drive out the devils." It is Giancarlo's advice in different words. But both, it seems to me, are prescribing a strong dose of magic: the magic of old religion, or the magic of a new breed of faith healers, working without anatomical charts, with no patterns of clinical procedure and certainly no promise of cure.

I remember Papa telling me how, in the ancient world, patients suffering from mental disorders were taken to the sacred island of Cos. There, after ritual preparation, they were submitted to the "experience of the God", which seems to have been a combination of hypnotic ecstasy and a primitive therapy by shock and terror. It was, Papa explained, a profound piece of curative wisdom. The patient was renewed, reborn. The "experience of the God" was like baptism for the Christian, the datum point from which his new life began. But first he had to pay the price: the long rituals, the magical lustrations, the infusions of soothing drugs. Finally, in the innermost shrine, in darkness and dread, he had to make a leap into mystery.

I have to make the same leap, in the darkness of some confessional or in an analyst's consulting room. It is not the mystery which terrifies me. It is the simple, brutal risk. How far can I trust the man, priest or physician, who takes my confession? I know all about professional ethics and the Hippocratic oath; but I've been in too many common rooms and too many beds to trust my life to the discretion of my peers. Yet, if I do not make the confession, the whole exercise is pointless. I shall be like the patient who reports a migraine while all the time there is a cancer growing in her belly.

So Magda, my dear, what are you going to do? You can't stay locked in a suite at the Crillon all your life. You can't go trotting round the fashionable houses of assignation, knowing that every escapade will finally be reported to Basil Zaharoff or to the police. You can't make any plans at all; because, without a radical cure, the future for you is demon country. It is not guilt which haunts you. It is something far more sinister. You have learned that there is no greater excitement than to hold a life in your hands, knowing that you can snuff it out like a candle flame. There is no orgasm more potent than that produced by the act of execution. You have experienced it. You are obsessed to repeat it – and sooner or later, you will.

There now! I've said it, written it; the truth about Magda Liliane Kardoss von Gamsfeld. You see, I understand myself. Why do I need the intervention of an analyst? And certainly a priest can't help because I'm not at all sure I'm repentant. But I am afraid. My hands tremble so that I cannot hold the pen. I cannot be alone. I reach for the telephone and ask the operator to connect me with Doctor Giancarlo di Malvasia.

He was very gentle, very concerned. He took me to lunch at a quiet restaurant on the Ile. He told me that he had got up early and attended a mass to pray for me. I was so touched that I was ready to blurt out the whole sorry tale then and there; but he forestalled me.

"I confess that I was tempted to accept you as a patient, and treat you here in Paris with the assistance

115

perhaps of someone like Flournoy or Janet. Then, while I was at prayer, it became clear to me that this would be a great mistake. We are too vulnerable to each other. We could compound each other's risks. On the other hand, it would be dangerous for you just to tell me your history in fragments. It must be all or nothing."

"That's precisely my problem, Gianni – all or nothing! You don't know, you can't know, how vulnerable I am to blackmail. How many of your colleagues can you really trust to keep their mouths shut about their patients?"

"Some – but I admit, not all!"

"How many priests then?"

"With the priest it is different. The situation is anonymous. You can confess in any church you like, to any priest you choose. The confessional is dark. You are nothing but a disembodied voice. Your narrative is a matter of substance, not of circumstance. You don't have to write a novel about your theft or adultery. You come to the priest as to Christ. He absolves you from your sins in Christ's name. By Christ's merit you are restored to grace."

"It sounds wonderful! Adultery on Saturday, absolution on Sunday! A real conjuror's trick. Now you see it, now you don't!"

I was mocking him and he knew it; but he was shrewd enough to understand and forgive me.

"You've got it wrong, my dear. It isn't innocence which is restored, but the relationship between Creator and creature. The child says, I'm sorry! The Father embraces him back into the family. But we carry the scars of our follies until we die. I think perhaps the real value of analytic psychology may be

116

that it makes us intelligible to ourselves and therefore tolerable to ourselves."

That at least made sense. I know from bitter experience that my worst excesses were committed when my self-esteem was at its lowest point. I repeated my first question.

"How far can I rely on professional secrecy with Freud or Jung?"

Gianni shrugged resignedly.

"Who's to say? At Weimar one heard the usual backstairs gossip about both men. Jung apparently has had a number of tricky episodes with women. But they are the leaders in their field. The risk of their indiscretion has to be weighed against the risk of your own death wish. You're near the breakpoint now. Take my advice. Leave Paris tomorrow and go and talk to Carl Jung. Use another name if it makes you feel more comfortable."

He took a prescription pad from his pocket, scribbled a few lines on it and thrust it at me. The note was superscribed to Dr. Carl Gustav Jung, Zurich. It read:

Dear Colleague,

You will remember that we met briefly at Weimar. The bearer is a distinguished lady whom I have known for many years. It is on my recommendation that she presents herself to you. For personal reasons she desires to remain anonymous, at least for the moment. I beg you to see her and offer her what counsel you can.

With most respectful salutations,
Giancarlo di Malvasia, M.D.

"Take it!" said Gianni earnestly. "In God's name take it and talk to the man! It may be your last hope."

It was not his eloquence which persuaded me; not even my own sense of need. It was the note from Basil Zaharoff, which I found waiting for me at the hotel.

My dearest Magda,

I have known many women in my life, but never one who has given me such a generous variety of pleasures. I cannot bear the thought of losing you after a single so beautiful encounter. I leave tonight for London to meet with Lloyd George. As soon as I get back, let us dine and renew our passion together.

I want also to discuss another idea with you. I see now that the arrangement I proposed was much too rigid and burdensome for a spirited woman like yourself. I am sure we can work out another association more flexible, but no less profitable to us both.

I kiss your hand. I kiss your sweet lips. I carry you in my heart on my travels.

Lovingly,
Z.Z.

I tore the letter into shreds and flushed it down the water closet. Then I called the concierge and asked him to send me up a set of railway timetables and a Thomas Cook guide to the hotels of Europe. Afterwards I walked down to the little pharmacy where my signature is known and my prescriptions are accepted. The old pharmacist raised a cautious query when he read my recipe.

"Madame understands this stuff is deadly? I shall put a wax seal on the bottle for safety."

I thanked him for his solicitude and explained that one of my hounds had an incurable canker and must be destroyed. I loved him so much that I wanted to put him to sleep myself.

"Ah Madame!" The old man was immediately reassured. "You remind me so much of your father. He was a beautiful man – of great heart, great tenderness!"

Oh Papa! If only you knew what kind of woman your daughter turned out to be. But then you did know, didn't you? You never admitted it; but you knew. And the only comment you ever made sounded like a line from a Schnitzler play: "I hope, my dear, you don't talk in your sleep!" Be assured, Papa, if this last desperate magic doesn't work, I shall sleep long and soundly and never breathe another word of my secrets or yours. I am quite calm now. See! I can even smile at myself in the mirror. I remember one of Lily's history lessons about the execution of the English king, Charles the First, and myself saying how much it must have hurt the poor fellow.

"Don't you believe it, lassie," said Lily in her happiest voice. "It looks messy but it's very quick. Once your head's off, you don't have a worry in the world!"

JUNG
Zurich

The chaos dream, about the great flood, has now become a matter of earnest and sometimes acerbic debate between Toni and me. She insists that my analysis is too glib, that I am wrong to read the dream as prophecy and that the death-wish symbols have many more sinister undertones than I will admit.

I argue that she is falling into Freud's error. He tends to see the unconscious as engaged in a kind of mischievous hide-and-seek with the conscious. The dream images it harbours are, for him, a smokescreen thrown up to obscure an unbearable reality. I don't agree with that at all. To dream is as natural as to breathe.

The unconscious is like an attic where all the unused or unusable material of our personal and tribal experience is tossed, higgledy-piggledy: old wedding photographs, grandmother's shawl, great-grandfather's diaries. They pop out of the clutter by accident, as when children play there or an inquisitive housemaid begins turning over the dusty relics. Nature doesn't set out to deceive us. We don't even set out to deceive ourselves. It is simply that we cannot cope, all at once, with the clutter of information and emotion that is delivered to us. So we consign it to the attic of the unconscious.

I am writing about this very calmly. But today's debate with Toni was anything but calm. It was complicated by an embarrassing letter, which Toni opened with the rest of the morning mail. The letter was from Sabina Spielrein, who not so long ago was pleading with me to give her a child . . . our little Siegfried! Christ! How I am beset by these women! I cannot live without them. I cannot live with them. If I had the money I would pack my bags and be off to Africa tomorrow!

A new chain of disasters begins, as it always seems to do nowadays, in the small hours of the morning. I have the chaos dream again; but this time new elements appear in it.

Elijah is on the train. He is dressed as a conductor. He settles me into my compartment. Salome is already there. She is naked. She stretches out a hand to touch me. There is a large straw basket on the seat beside her. The snake is inside it. I hear the rustle of his body against the straw.

Again I am uneasy with Salome. I am expecting Toni. I do not want to have sex with a blind girl who carries a snake. The train starts, and once again I see the flood – yellow at first, then blood-red – rolling across the land. I recognise the same bodies tossed in the waves. This time, however, there is one living creature: a beautiful black stallion. I see his noble head and forequarters as he struggles to leap from the water. As he comes closer I see his wild eyes and his flaming nostrils and the great muscles on his neck. Now I really try to get out and rescue him. I batter vainly on the window until I see the stallion swallowed up by the blood-red water. I cry out in despair and wake up.

Mercifully Emma is still asleep. I creep down to my study, prepare my pipe and my drink and begin to record the new elements in the dream. I am very lucid. What I write contains a number of fresh and stimulating ideas. The next thing I remember is Emma's voice calling me and the morning sun flooding into the room. Emma is standing by Toni's desk pouring coffee. I am startled and I yell at her:

"Emma! What the hell! Haven't I told you never, never to interrupt me here?"

She answers in that bland, controlled fashion which is her usual response to my boorishness.

"Don't bully me, Carl! It's tiresome. I brought you breakfast. Would you like to wash before I serve it? There's a clean smock on the chair."

It is only then that I become aware of my condition. My face is sticky from lying in ash and spilled drink. My hands are filthy. My sleeves are sodden with brandy. My papers are stained. There is a large burn scar on the leather surface of the desk. I lurch to the wash basin and look at myself in the mirror. Emma's comment is apt but redundant.

"You really are a mess."

I mumble an apology through the soapsuds.

"I'm sorry. I must have . . ."

"You were dead tired and dead drunk. One of these nights you'll burn the house down with that confounded pipe!"

I strip off my soiled shirt, sponge and dry myself and put on the peasant's smock which is my working garb. Then I go to offer Emma a good morning kiss. She turns a cool cheek to me, hands me the coffee and moves two paces away from my contaminated presence. As I stuff a piece of pastry in my mouth and gulp a mouthful of coffee she attacks.

"This is crazy, Carl! Five times in a row you've been up all night. You smoke like a chimney. You're drinking too much. You'll kill yourself!"

I choke on my coffee, which entirely ruins the effect of my reply.

"For God's sake, Emma! You exaggerate everything. I woke at two in the morning out of a terrible nightmare. I couldn't get back to sleep. I didn't want to disturb you. I came down here to record the dream and have my notes ready for a proper analysis. I had one glass of brandy. I never have more. I was weary. I fell asleep. Is that a crime? Besides I got through a lot of work — good work! Look, I'll show you!"

I go to my desk, pick up the stained sheets of notepaper and hold them out to her. She takes them, glances at the first page. Her expression changes. She leafs through the rest of the material — three sheets in all — then stares at me, horrified. I ask her what is the matter. She tells me, very quietly.

"Carl, this is gibberish. Utter nonsense! And the handwriting. It's just a scrawl!"

I snatch the pages from her. The words I can decipher make no sense at all. They are a garble of German and Latin and Greek and no language at all. I make feeble excuses.

"I must have been more exhausted than I thought. You know, the body wastes build up and you get a temporary narcosis. The thought patterns become confused. The handwriting drifts."

She comes to me, and lays a gentle hand on my shoulder. She seems suddenly invested with authority. I am glad to have her by me. She admonishes me tenderly.

"Please, Carl! Sit down. We have to talk."

She leads me to my desk. I slump in my chair. She pulls up another chair and sits facing me. She takes my hands and caresses them as she talks. It seems an age since we have had contact, skin to skin, like this.

"Carl, I want you to listen to me very carefully. You're a sick man! Everything points to it: the nightmares, the insomnia, the depressions, the rages that

123

scare the children so. Be honest with yourself. What would you say if one of your patients at the clinic had produced those pages of nonsense!"

"Clinically that material's irrelevant." I was immediately irritated. "Extreme fatigue or simple anoxia will produce the same effect!"

"All right! Let's admit they're irrelevant; but the rest of it is very much to the point. Please, my darling! Can't you understand we're all desperately worried about you?"

"I'm worried about myself."

"Tell me then – after all you trained me! – suppose I were the patient and I came to you with all the symptoms you have, what would be your diagnosis?"

It would only make matters worse to tell her that the rumourmongers accuse me of suffering from dementia praecox, that I recognise at least primary schizoid symptoms and manic-depressive cycles. Instead I try to hedge my answer.

"I wouldn't be prepared to offer a diagnosis yet. It's too early. The symptoms are too varied. I would recommend a complete physical examination. Then if there is no physical pathology I would like to put the patient into analysis for a trial period."

"Then, my dear physician;" she strokes my stubbled cheek and coaxes me tenderly, "why don't you follow your own prescription?"

We are on easier ground here. She knows I've seen Lansberg for a physical check-up. She knows his verdict. I am sound as a prize bull, except for an occasional labile blood pressure, which is associated with emotional stress. But that does not satisfy her. She presses me.

"But you know the problem isn't a physical one."

124

"True. On the other hand . . ."

"So, why don't you put yourself into analysis?"

"With whom, for God's sake? Bleuler, Ferenczi, Jones? These are not my peers!"

This is an old frayed question between us. I know she corresponds with Freud. I know she thinks my disagreements with him are overstated and inflamed by my ill humours. As I expected, she walks head first into the trap.

"Freud then! I know you and he have disagreed over a lot of things but . . ."

"Disagreed? I don't believe in him any more. I can't trust him any more. The man's a hopeless dogmatist. He faints when he's confronted with an unpleasing thought! Faints clean away like a woman with the vapours!"

I am determined to end the discussion. I get up from my desk and walk to the window, where I stand, silent and hostile, looking out at the garden. Emma refuses to abandon the argument. She challenges me again.

"What do you see out there, Carl? Elijah? Salome?"

I am shocked and angry. I have never discussed these personages with her. I confront her harshly.

"How do you know about them? Have you been going through my papers?"

"You know I never do that, Carl. You talk in your sleep. You talk to yourself, loudly, as you stride up and down the lawn. Who are these people, Carl? What do they mean in your life?"

Suddenly I am not angry any more. I am tired and fearful like a stricken child. I answer wearily:

"I don't know who they are. They are personifications from my subconscious. All I know is that when Elijah's there I feel safe and content. I don't like Salome; but it seems I can't have one without the other."

"Can you see them now?"

"No. I can't."

Emma stares at me for a long silent moment; then with a strange wintry sadness she pleads with me.

"I'll tell you what I see, Carl. I see a great man far advanced towards a mental breakdown. I see the one-time clinical director of the Burgholzli, the most brilliant lecturer in his subject at the university, babbling to himself like one of his own patients. I say to myself, that's my husband. I love him. I'm carrying his fifth child . . . and I wonder if he'll be rational enough to recognise the baby when it's born!"

She bursts into tears and buries her face in her hands. I am ashamed to have hurt her so much. I hurry to her and try to comfort her, but her grief pours out in a torrent of broken words.

"You don't know, you don't care, how bad it is! I wake in a cold bed. The children don't know you any more. They're scared to be near you. You lock yourself in here like . . . like a monster in a cave. I can't bear it any more! I just can't bear it!"

I put my arms around her and rock her wordlessly from side to side like a child. Then, as gently as I know how, I try to reason with her:

"Emma, my love, I'm sorry. From the bottom of my heart I'm sorry. But I have no words to explain what it's like when these black storms start inside me. The only thing I know is that I can't fight them. I just have to ride out the fury and hope I'll be sane afterwards. That's why I hide down here – to spare you the spectacle."

"You can't go on hiding for ever. You need help!"

"I know . . . but I know how little real help is to be had."

"How can you say that, you, of all people?"

"Because this science of ours, this medicine of the mind, is still in its infancy. The methods are tentative. The procedures are incomplete. So, I ask myself whether I am not being prompted – called even! – to make a journey beyond the charted limits. Perhaps that's what Elijah means: a prophet from the Old Testament, who was swept up to heaven in a fiery chariot!"

"It's not heaven I see in your eyes, Carl. Sometimes it's the suffering of the damned. And I can do nothing about it."

"Neither can I. I'm like a leaf tossed in the wind. So, I have no choice but to let myself be swept along by these storms of the subconscious and see where, finally, they drive me."

"You're taking a terrible risk."

"It's not such a big risk, truly."

"For us it is."

"You are the anchor that holds me to reality. You, the children, our life in this house."

"Just so the anchor holds! I'm not sure how much we can take, Carl. We're human, too. We need a little laughter in our lives."

Her vehemence shocks me. I have always presumed so much on her stability. I try to calm her with soft words.

"Of course you do. So, until I'm through this crisis,

I want you to forget me. Ignore my moods. Let me come and go as I please. Treat me like . . . like a piece of furniture. Concentrate your thoughts on the new baby. Build your life round the children."

"And leave you to fight your devils alone?"

"I won't be alone. Toni Wolff will record the experience, and help me to analyse it. She's been through her own crisis. She understands in a way that no one else can."

I am a fool with a big mouth. The words were hardly out before the storm burst around my ears.

"I can't believe what I'm hearing, Carl! Let me be sure I have it right. You admit you're in a situation of psychic crisis. You don't trust Freud. You say Bleuler and Ferenczi are not your peers. You find me inadequate. But you put yourself in the hands of a twenty-five-year-old girl who was once your patient. Does that really make sense?"

"It makes sense to me. She's young but she's brilliant. I've trained her myself and . . ."

"And what, Carl? Let's have the truth!"

Now it is my turn to rage. This is the way the game goes. It is easier to abuse one another than to disabuse ourselves of illusions. I shout at her:

"The truth is you make a scene about every goddamned woman who steps into my office . . . and I'm sick of your pathological jealousy!"

"And why shouldn't I be jealous? Look at the scandals we've had. You're a fool with women! You turn on that great tender charm, and they all think it's an invitation to bed. Sometimes it is, sometimes it isn't; but it gets you a bad name and damages the practice. But with Toni it's way beyond that. You want to make her a member of the family!"

128

"She has a legitimate place in my life – just as you have."

"Legitimate place! Do, please, tell me about that!"

"You are my wife, the mother of my children, the mistress of my house." As I mouth the pompous phrases I have a sudden comic vision of my father acting out his Sunday sermon. Like my father I ignore the comedy and plough on: "You have my love, my respect and my unswerving loyalty. Toni began as my patient. Her personal experience of mental illness and her natural intelligence make her a most valuable collaborator."

"And in bed, Carl? How is she? What do you do? Read case histories to each other?"

Before I have the chance to reply, the door opens and Toni comes in. She carries the morning mail and a new summer hat that dangles from a pink ribbon. She greets us both cheerfully, tosses the mail on the table and displays the hat to Emma.

"How do you like this? I trimmed it myself."

"Charming!" Emma is frigid but meticulously polite. Not for nothing was she bred among the good burghers of Basel. Toni looks to each of us for some explanation of this moment of suspended animation. Finally she asks, "Forgive me, but have I interrupted something? If so, I can take a stroll in the garden."

"No, we've just finished." Emma adds a parting word for us both. "I'll take your advice, Carl. I will – I must – concentrate my life round the children. They have a special need of me now. As for you, Toni, Carl tells me you'll be directing his analysis. He has great faith in your skill. I hope, for all our sakes, it's justified. Which reminds me, you must have him

129

show you the notes he wrote last night. They're very revealing!"

The door closes, a shade too loudly, on her exit. Toni asks with somewhat edgy humour:

"And what, pray, was all that about?"

This time I cannot lie; the best I can do is defuse the drama. I tell her with a shrug:

"We had a few sharp words. She thinks I should go into analysis with Freud. I told her I want to work with you."

"And she of course said, 'Oh how splendid! The best treatment for any psychosis is a tumble in the hay with Toni.' "

That sets us both laughing; but our mirth has an uneasy ring to it, like the giggling of children listening to ghost stories around a dying fire. We kiss, we embrace. I am full of desire for her but she disengages herself quickly and retreats behind her desk. Clearly, she is still punishing me for the Spielrein letter. She mentions Emma's comment about my notes. It is easier to show them to her than to explain. Her reaction is identical with Emma's.

"Good God! This is a farrago of nonsense!"

"Toxic fatigue." Again I try to shrug the matter off. "I've been up five nights in a row."

"You'd have been better off spending them at my place."

"I agree, my love; but I can't very well go creeping around the countryside at two in the morning."

"You'd have found me awake. I need you, too, you know."

Once again we are on the edge of a quarrel. Always it is over the same thing – the precedence of wife and mistress and other women in my very complicated

130

life. I sometimes think it would be wonderful to have the power of bi-location as certain Christian mystics and primitive witch doctors are supposed to have. On the other hand, it might not be such a good idea after all. Quarrelling with two women at once could be a very exhausting experience.

I decide it is time to be businesslike. I return to my desk. Toni brings her notebook. We begin the analysis of the new elements in the chaos dream. I must say this for Toni: no matter how irritable she gets about our love affair, in clinical matters she is one hundred per cent professional. The first point she makes is the presence of the black stallion in the dream. She recalls to me that the horse is always myself. Always, too, the animal is handicapped. In the earlier dream he was dragging a great log. In this one he is trying in vain to find a foothold in the floodwaters. Finally he is drowned – as I am afraid of drowning in a sea of personal troubles.

Next, we talk of Elijah. He is a conductor in the dream. He controls the train and the destiny of everyone on board. We can sleep safely under his tutelage. He is for me the archetype of the perfect father figure.

Salome, however, has changed her role. She is no longer the daughter, lover, protector of Elijah. She is the hostile woman playing the role of naked seductress to me, a man who has no desire for her. There is a clear connection here with Sabina Spielrein, who I had thought was out of my life for good. Now she has written herself back into it. I do not want her. I have Toni. For the first time Toni steps out of her professional role and asks me a very pointed question:

"Have you ever thought that the day may come

131

when you will be talking about me exactly as you are talking about Sabina Spielrein?"

I protest stoutly that my feelings for the Spielrein were pure infatuation. I was betrayed into them by pity and by her dependence upon me during her illness.

"Which is exactly how you and I came together," Toni reminds me sweetly. "I, too, have progressed from patient to pupil to colleague and mistress."

"Then as a colleague, please remember that we are in a clinical situation where you have no right to intrude your private sentiments."

She blushes. Her eyes fill up with tears. She protests bitterly.

"My God! You can be brutal sometimes!"

"And you are tactless, stupid and unprofessional! At this moment I am not your lover, I am your patient. The fact that I am in control of myself makes no matter. In other circumstances with another person, you could do great damage."

"Forgive me, doctor!" she blazes at me. "I have so little experience in these matters. This is my first affair with a married man."

"And may I remind you that you walked into it with your eyes open."

"So I did. But I also walked into it with all of me, body and soul. I am not like you. I can't divide my life into neat little slices and hand them round like sponge cake. This one's for you; this one's for Emma. This one's for Aunt Mary! I'm me – Toni Wolff! – all of one piece; and if you don't like that, I'm sorry."

"On the contrary, I like it very much. As your former physician, I am proud of your mature and stable personality!"

132

She bursts into tears, slams her notebook on my desk and runs towards the door. I shout at her like a drill sergeant:

"Stop right there!"

She stops. I berate her brutally.

"You are not a child. You are an intelligent woman, free to make your own choices about your own life. At this moment, however, you have the responsibility of a healer. I am in desperate need of your help with this analysis. Now compose yourself and let's get back to work!"

I see what it costs her to control her emotions. It is a physical effort, painful to watch. Finally her head comes up proudly, and she turns to face me again.

"I am at your service, doctor. If you agree, I think we should now consider the death wish element in both the versions of the dream."

I tell her that I would rather not get too involved in the smaller details. I would rather discuss for a while the larger context: the vast flood obliterating the land. She reminds me with cool formality:

"I know what you would rather do; but have you not told me over and over again that the subject which the patient least wishes to discuss is that which is nearest to the heart of his problem? So, if you don't mind, let's talk about your death wish – for Emma, for Freud, for your own children. Let's ask what you will do instead of killing them . . . because the ritual has to be accomplished in fact or in symbol."

MAGDA
En voyage

I am travelling by wagon-lit to Zurich in a compartment reserved exclusively for myself. I shall dine in the restaurant car, then retire early and read myself to sleep. On my arrival I shall establish myself at the Baur au Lac in a suite with a view over the lake. Once there, I shall consider how best to make contact with this famous Dr. Jung.

Now that I have begun my journey, I feel almost light hearted. Life has at last simplified itself to what Lily used to call Hobson's choice. If Jung can help me – if he can show me how to come to terms with the past, and devise a tolerable future away from demon country – then I shall accept with thanks. If he cannot, then amen! It is a very short stride into nothingness. I carry the key in my reticule: a small blue bottle sealed with red wax.

In the old days, before I was married – and after! – I was passionately fond of train travel. It gave me always a heightened sexual excitement. There was no telling whom one might meet in the corridors or in the dining car, what midnight assignations might be made between the soup and the cheese. This time, however, I feel no such excitement. I have no urge for casual encounters. I cannot cope with the threadbare rituals of love with a stranger. Even my bedtime reading is chosen to distract me from sexual preoccupation: a novel about the English detective Sherlock Holmes and his chronicler, Dr. Watson.

Nevertheless, I dress carefully for dinner and I am not unconscious of the admiring glances and the whispered comments of the male diners when I enter the restaurant. The head waiter places me, as I have asked, at a table for two. He has promised also that he will find me, if possible, a woman guest to share the table. When I arrive, however, the other place is still empty. I am already beginning my second course when my dinner companion arrives. The head waiter introduces her as Mademoiselle de Launay. For an instant I gape at her, dumbstruck. She is the living image of Ilse Hellman. Reason tells me there can be no possible connection. This girl is only in her early twenties. She is French. Ilse was Austrian and had never borne children. I try to bridge the awkward moment with a smile and an explanation.

"Forgive me. You are the image of a girl I once knew. Please sit down. I hope you will allow me to tell you that you look very, very pretty."

The meal goes pleasantly enough. She is well mannered and charming. She tells me she is going to stay with relatives in Locarno. I am not really interested. Her looks continue to distract me. Whenever she turns her head in a certain fashion, I see Ilse Hellman, companion of my school days, who married the man I wanted for myself.

The adventures of Mr. Sherlock Holmes are pale stuff beside this piece of personal history. The book remains unread while I lie wakeful in the darkness, rehearsing the drama which began in those distant days and the last act of which is yet to be played out in Zurich.

When I was fourteen years old, Papa decided that I must be removed from what he called "the company of peasants and country bumpkins". I must be trained for my destiny as a young lady of quality. In short, it was time I went to boarding school. After much correspondence and consultation with friends, Papa

135

and Lily decided that the best place for me was the International Academy for Young Gentlewomen. This high-sounding establishment was situated near Geneva and was run by a very formidable lady called the Countess Adrienne de Volnay.

The regimen promised by the countess included: "a broad education in the arts, constant training in the social proprieties, regular exercise in conformity with the needs of the feminine physique, carefully supervised leisure, including visits to museums, concerts, operas and folk festivals, regular but well chaperoned contacts with young gentlemen of good family and impeccable morals."

Looking back now, I recognise her for an educator, far in advance of her time. She turned out literate and polished women. She gave us a comfortable living, a tolerable but efficient discipline and considerably more freedom than other similar establishments of the time.

I enjoyed the place – probably because I was better prepared for it than most of my peers. Lily had taught me well, and I was easily able to hold my own in the academic subjects. More than that – thanks to Papa! – my sentimental education was much more advanced than that of my companions. I had started menstruating at twelve. I understood my own anatomy and its functions. I had been taught to regard myself as a woman, albeit a young one. The sexual functions and precautions had been explained to me. The rising tides of desire in my own body were not unfamiliar nor for that matter were the means of satisfying them.

So, it was all too easy to set myself up as a leader, a kind of Keeper of Mysteries at our International

Academy. My friendship was courted. I was not ashamed to profit from it. Everyone wanted me for a "special friend"; but the one I chose was Ilse Hellman, who came from the eastern part of Land Salzburg and was therefore almost a neighbour. It was I who gave her her first experience of sex between girls. She was a prize to wear in my bonnet, too, because she was tall and slim and rich and easily the prettiest of us all.

Looking back now, I can see that there was one fundamental difference between us. I was the only child of a very exotic alliance. Ilse was the fourth of six children, with three older brothers and two younger sisters. Whatever I had – comfort, opportunity, love, deference – was mine by right. If it wasn't offered, I didn't argue about it. I simply entered into possession. I annexed things, people too, for that matter. Mademoiselle Félice who admired my talent for languages, was *my* French mistress. Rudi, who taught us equitation was *my* riding master. Laurent, who was the handsomest of the young gentlemen who came to our dancing classes was *my* partner – until I chose to hand him down to Ilse or one of our junior admirers.

Ilse, on the other hand, was well trained in social strategy. She had to be, to survive with three sturdy males, two junior sisters, an anaemic mother and a father who was a big entrepreneur in the mining and metal business. She wanted to be protected. She liked sexual comfort. She needed a girl friend to bolster her confidence with boys. She was happy to pay tribute for these services; but once she fixed her notions on a prize she would use every pirate's trick to get it. Strange as it may seem, it was she who first taught me to be jealous.

It was Papa's custom to visit me once in mid-term, usually when he was on his way to Paris with some new lover. Lily came twice a year, and I was instructed always to introduce her as "Tante Liliane", my dead mother's sister from England. The first time Papa came, he took Ilse and myself out to lunch at a lakeside restaurant in Geneva – very chic, very expensive. Two minutes after we were seated, Ilse was playing up to Papa like a young Sarah Bernhardt. She fluttered at him. She touched his hand; she admired his clothes; she giggled at his jokes. Papa played back like the veteran Casanova he was. I was so angry I wanted to be sick in my soup; but there was never any point in being angry with Papa. You had to play his game, toujours gai, always the happy cavalier. However, I knew very well that, if I ever invited Ilse to Silbersee, there would be love under the stars the first night and hell to pay ever after for Lily and me!

I said nothing to Ilse. Not for anything would I let her know she had upset me; but after that I began quietly and slowly to replace her as my court favourite. I told Lily about the incident on her next visit. She gave an unsteady little laugh and a wry comment.

"You were absolutely right, lassie. While your Papa's getting older, his follies are getting younger *and* more expensive. We'll have to watch him, you and I, otherwise some little tart from nowhere will end up sporting the Kardoss arms and wearing your grandmother's diamonds!"

It was probably this exchange of confidences which prepared us both for what happened at Silbersee on my seventeenth birthday. I was home for the summer holidays. Papa had arranged a daylong party for me:

138

lunch in the garden with friends and neighbours, a gypsy orchestra brought down from Salzburg, dancing on the terrace as night fell, a champagne supper, carriages calling at ten-thirty so that those with young families could be home by a decent hour. Ilse Hellman was there with her parents. I had invited her because she was my nearest schoolfriend, and she couldn't get into too much harm with her parents on the premises. Even so, she flirted outrageously with Papa; and I have often wondered how much her presence had to do with what followed.

It was nearly midnight, I remember; we were all together in the upstairs suite, Lily, Papa and I, drinking a last glass of champagne and reminiscing over the events of the day. There was a moment of drowsy silence, then, apropos of nothing at all, Papa said:

"Lily my dear, don't you think our Magda is beautiful?"

"Very beautiful."

She bent and kissed me on the lips. I remember telling them, a little fuzzily, that they were beautiful, too – the most beautiful couple in the world. Then Papa kissed me, too – a lover's kiss – and drew me to my feet, lifted me and carried me into his bedroom. He told me with a smile:

"You have one more birthday surprise, my love. You're going to be changed from a girl into a woman."

Somehow I had always known it would happen just like this. They had both led me, step by pleasant step, to the moment of initiation. They had taught me enough ways to satisfy myself so that this moment would be theirs and theirs alone. Together they undressed me, together they excited me slowly and with an infinity of small pleasures. Then, when it seemed I could bear the waiting no longer, Papa, with Lily as witness and mistress of ceremonies, made me a woman – and made sure that no man, ever again, would blot his memory out of my mind or my body.

Even now, as the train clatters, clickety-clack, through the night, the ecstasy repeats itself, all too briefly. When it is over, I weep quietly in the dark. Papa is long dead, and Lily is a little old lady who lives with her cat in a small stone cottage in the Cotswolds. She has a pension from me, paid every month by the Ysambard brothers. We have never seen each other since she left Europe after my marriage. The local parson keeps an eye on her for me. I have sometimes thought I would like to visit her and salvage a little of our lost love before she dies. However, the parson tells me she is almost stone-deaf – and I cannot imagine shouting all our secrets up and down the street in an English village.

Does this sound strange? The thing I cannot forgive Papa is that, after that extraordinary rite of passage, he made me go back to school for another year. I had to matriculate, he said. I had to qualify for entry into a university medical school. I pleaded with him, begged him on my knees to find me tutors and let me work at home in Silbersee. No, he would have none of it. The International Academy for Young Gentlewomen had done a splendid job. I must finish the matriculation course with them. To this day I cannot understand his reasoning. How could he do it? What did he expect of a healthy young animal he himself had awakened so fully? Didn't he understand that all the company I had at school was pubescent girls and "young gentlemen of good family and impeccable morals"? And even if their morals were not impeccable, what possible charm could they have for me now?

So, for the last year at the academy, I went wild – jungle-wild! – with a calculated ferocity which surprised even myself. Papa wanted me to matriculate? Good! I would do it with high distinction. I wanted freedom? Good! I would buy it with bright coinage. My conduct at school was beyond reproach. As a result, I was given liberties and privileges that were denied to others. I went twice a week to Geneva to do research in the university library. I took an advanced course in dressage at the riding school. I had weekend voice lessons at the Opéra from Madame Corsini, a pupil of Jenny Lind.

I also managed, on the same timetable, a regular session in the hayloft with Rudi the riding master, a couple of interesting interludes with one or other of the students at the university, and a sporadic but highly dramatic affair with a bel canto tenor who practised down the corridor from Madame Corsini.

At the end of the academic year I came home completely exhausted, with high marks in all subjects and a bad attack of pneumonia. Papa treated me. Lily cosseted me. The clean mountain air completed the cure. Papa told me he had procured a place for me at the University of Padua, which has one of the oldest and most distinguished faculties of medicine in Europe. I was delighted. Life went on its placid summer way in Silbersee.

It wasn't the same. It would never be the same again. We three still shared the apartment. We still wandered about in all stages of undress. Sometimes we all climbed into bed together and played the old games; but that was different, too. Now there was no real fun in the play. It was uneasy, unsatisfying, contrived.

Papa, I noticed, was putting on weight. Lily still kept her trim, girlish figure. She exercised every day and insisted I do the same. Her hair was greying a little and the first telltale lines showed in her face. Although her smile was still wonderful and there were always flashes of the old salty humour, she was clearly insecure, and sometimes unhappy. She was jealous of Papa and possessive of me. I didn't blame her. While I was at school, Papa left her alone for weeks at a time, and she rattled around the empty Schloss like a pea in a dry pod. She confessed to me that she had had one or two brief affairs: one with Hans Hemeling and another – God forgive her! – with a junior priest at the Pfarrhaus, whose superiors had smartly moved him back to Vienna. But neither of them had proved satisfactory, "because your Papa's the best, lassie! He knows how to deliver everything a woman wants. The trouble is he gets bored before we do! It's the first buds he's after, not the full blooms."

I knew what she meant. I wasn't a fresh bud any more, and Papa was bored with me too. Like Lily I was pleasant to have close, to fondle and to enjoy as a playmate. But as soon as he was fresh again, it was heels up and over the fence to the fillies in the next meadow. I asked Lily what she thought we could do about it. As always she had a plan – a secret which only she and I must know.

"Your Papa's slowing down, as you see. He can't stand all this trotting backwards and forwards to Vienna. He's got a girl in Salzburg whom he's quite serious about – at least as serious as he'll ever get! It's been going on for a year now. He'd like to bring her down here; but I'm in his way and so are you – and besides we might spill secrets, eh? So here's what I've suggested. You'll be going to university in Padua. He doesn't want you living alone and unprotected. He doesn't want you getting a bad name at the university. So I talked him into letting me set up house for you in a decent place. There'll be a room for him when he wants to visit – which he will, believe me, because he's set his heart on this career for you. You and I will go our own ways; and if our men don't work out we'll always have each other. What do you say, lassie?"

"I say I love you, Lily! I love you so much I could eat you alive!"

The record of the next five years is almost irrelevant to my present case. Papa set us up in an elegant apartment with functional plumbing and a ceiling by Tiepolo. He also paid for a daily maid and a cook. It was a good time, a happy time. Lily and I lived like two sisters, caring for each other, sharing confidences, laughing over misadventures. At the university I was first an oddity, then, when the year's results were posted, a minor phenomenon. I had more attention than I needed as a woman; but I managed to conduct my love affairs out of sight of my student friends. It was not too hard. I needed mature men. Life was too precious to waste on mothering puppies.

Papa came to visit from time to time, always alone, but always on the way to or from some complicated occasion of the heart. In the long summer terms, depending upon the state of our love lives, we travelled together to new places, to Scandinavia, to Africa, to England and once to Petrograd to visit the Hermitage. It was then that Papa made his famous "mot" which in the end turned out to be prophetic.

Lily and I had spent the whole day playing a complicated flirtation game with two handsome Swedes in our tour party. They were married. Their wives were with them. We had set ourselves to attract their attention and if possible get them into conversation. Finally Papa exploded in exasperation.

"My God! Now I know what Catherine the Great must have been like! God save us from predatory women!"

When I reminded him that he had spent his whole life being chased by them, he objected.

"Not at all! I chase my own game! The minute a woman looks like Diana the huntress I'm off! But you two! I wouldn't let you loose in a mortuary!"

As a medical student I spent more than enough time in mortuaries; but the effect they had on me was only to reinforce the sense of futility which haunted me in the dark hours. As I reflect on it now, listening to the mourning wail of the train whistle, I see that I am completely different from Papa. I am – or I was – a very efficient doctor. My diagnoses were good; my surgery precise. But I had none of Papa's gentleness, his care for tissue, his hatred of unnecessary trauma. I suppose I saw medicine always as a post-house, a place of easement on the road to extinction. Death had no terror for me, and by corollary, life – even my own – commanded little respect. What was involved for me was not compassion – but combat: a question of power; how quickly I could ease the unbearable pain; how long I could defer the inevitable end. Strange that I should remember this now, while I myself am making this journey just to choose between living and dying.

But love has been like that for me, too – an exercise of power: to attract, to hold, to command satisfaction, to dismiss when I choose. The only ones I have never loved like that are Papa, my husband and Lily. What they gave I have never been able to find with anyone else. I couldn't command them. I never wanted to dismiss them. It was they who finally absented themselves. I wonder what is missing in me, and how I came to lose it. Was it perhaps taken away when Mamma disappeared, or when Papa invaded my first womanhood and left me no dreams at all, but only memories and desires?

Another thought comes to me in this noisy but solitary progress towards Zurich. I was brought up in Austria, in a Catholic province. I spent five years in Padua, the city of Saint Anthony the Wonderworker, whose massive tomb is encircled every day by pilgrims seeking favours. I have visited monasteries and churches, and been medical adviser to nuns and priests, but none of their beliefs or attitudes have rubbed off on me, let alone penetrated the armour of my scepticism. I wonder why? Is it, as Gianni di Malvasia suggests, that the gift of credence has been withheld at the whim of some divine comedian? Or is it a lack in me, an absence of some faculty like taste or smell or colour perception? To this point it has never bothered me; but now it does. I have never felt so lonely in my life as I do at this moment. If I decide to end things quietly, it would be nice to have someone to talk to before I go. Even if God is an illusion it would be comforting to have someone breathe His name in my ear. I would settle even for less – to sit in a warm bath like Petronius Arbiter, with a friend holding my hand and making pleasant talk, while life bleeds quietly away without pain.

There is a whole litany of objections to my enjoying so peaceful an end. I recite it to the rhythm of the wheels on the iron tracks: "I cut the roses, I beat the dog, I bloodied the horse, I married the man, who lived in the house of Johann, Ritter von Gamsfeld."

JUNG
Zurich

Toni and I are still grappling with the analysis of my death wish. We have gone over together all the records of my dreams; and it is astonishing how often and in how many different contexts the motif recurs. What we are trying to do now is relate the dream wish to its object in real life and examine my own connection with that object.

Today we are happier together. Last night I responded to her challenge. While Emma was sleeping, in the small hours of the morning, I slipped out of the house and cycled over to Toni's place. We had four wonderful hours together, and I left just as the false dawn was breaking over the lake. When Emma woke and came looking for me, I was shaved and tidy and working assiduously at my desk. No smoking this time! No brandy stains on what has turned out to be a very useful set of notes!

Toni, too, is much calmer in mind. It is not simply the sexual release, although that, she assures me, was enormous; it is the fact that I dared something for her. My midnight visit was an escapade that might have cost me dear, if Emma had found out. Her outburst the other day still troubles me. I have always assumed that, like good respectable Swiss, we shall stay wedded, no matter what happens in the enclave of our

146

marriage. Now I am not so sure. If Emma finds my delinquencies intolerable, she may well decide to take the children and go back to her family, who would without doubt receive her and comfort her. On the other hand, if my reputation gets too much mauled, I may just decide to say to hell with them all, toss my own cap over the windmill and go away with Toni. She would be quite happy for us to live together with or without benefit of clergy. I discourage talk of this; but I know it is in her mind and it lurks always at the back of mine. After all, Freud seems to survive this kind of situation better than I. I suspect that "amortising his marriage" means that he has some kind of accommodation with his wife's sister. Which would explain why he is so devilishly sensitive to my published views on the incest taboo. Well, he's going to hear more of the same in Munich, come September. Freud is, of course, the clear object of one death wish, and Toni continues to hammer at this single subject.

"Freud is the new father figure in your life. You adopted him to replace your natural father who failed you when he was alive, about whom you feel guilty now that he is dead. You have a deep emotional attachment to Freud. Yet, you are going to kill him."

"No, that's not accurate. My subconscious entertains the death wish. It expresses itself in dreams. My conscious – and my conscience – reject the thought."

"Not true!" Toni is very resolute. She will tolerate no hedging on this argument. "You are going to kill Freud. You are going to do it at the Munich conference. You will disavow publicly one of his key doctrines. You will fight him for the presidency of the

Psycho-Analytical Society and you will probably win. What is all that but a duel to the death?"

It is true, of course. I admit it and pay her a compliment on her precision and sagacity. She waves it aside impatiently.

"Please, Carl! Don't do that with me. Not now! This is much too important. We're just beginning to make progress. There's something else behind this Freud situation; we have to find it together. In the last chaos dream you saw the black stallion. Right?"

"Yes."

She riffles through her notes until she comes to the reference and reads it back to me.

" 'I saw his forequarters and the great muscles in his neck.' But you didn't see his hindquarters?"

"No."

"How did you know it was a stallion?"

"Well, I suppose the build of the beast, the strength, the . . ."

"The hindquarters were hidden, but you knew there was a penis there and testicles. What are you trying to hide that has to do with your maleness? Please, Carl! You have to be honest, otherwise I can't help you."

Suddenly I want to tell her. The words come pouring out: the guilty joy, the bitter shame, the transference to Freud of this unresolved homo-erotic episode, my fear of how she herself might regard it. At the end I am blubbering like a schoolboy, my pride in tatters. Toni strokes my bowed head and repeats over and over, "There . . . there . . . there," as if she is soothing a stricken child. When all my tears are spent, she sponges my cheeks and cups my face in her hands and smiles at me with grave tenderness.

"Now at last I know you love me, Carl. You've given me the greatest proof possible: your trust."

"I've given you the rottenest part of myself."

"Don't say that! Don't ever say that to me! What did you expect of yourself – a boy, a parson's son, with a man he loved and trusted? I only wish you could have enjoyed the whole thing, instead of carrying the guilt of it all these years. Don't you see, Carl, this is a big part of your problem. Everything with you is half done, half finished, half enjoyed. Me, Emma, all the others who pop in and out of your life, your children, too! You want them and you don't want them. Everything is a transaction. You always try to calculate whether what you get is worth what you're paying. There's no joy in that!"

"Then perhaps today will be the beginning of joy."

It is a wish more than a hope. She is very pleased with herself because she has flushed out one small demon from the thickets of my soul. She does not realise that there are legions more lurking in the undergrowth. Still, she has cause to be proud, and I to be grateful, that this sordid little history is out in the open.

I am calm now. She asks whether I am ready to continue the session. I tell her yes. So long as the water flows, don't close the sluice gate. Her next question shocks me, as she intends it to do.

"How will you kill Emma and the children?"

"That's monstrous!"

"No. It's the logic of the psyche. What you dream is what you wish. What you wish, you will try to accomplish, in fact or symbol. So please, my dear, my love, try to answer. Don't retreat now!"

I do retreat. I will not tell her my thoughts about

divorce, remarriage, all that social chaos. Instead I toss a bait to distract her from the subject.

"I told Emma yesterday that she must let me go my own way. She must concentrate her life on herself and the children."

Toni reflects for a long moment. Finally she nods assent.

"If you meant it, yes, that's a death sentence for a woman. If ever you tell me that, I'll be sure it's over between us. But are you certain you did mean it?"

Now I am really sliced by Occam's razor. If I say yes, I am a horror of a man, who marries a woman, breeds five children out of her and then leaves her to her own devices. Toni sees my hesitation. She continues the inquisition.

"Do you love Emma?"

"Yes."

"Do you love your children?"

"Yes, yes!"

"Then why do you dream their death?"

"Because they stand between me and you."

"But why can't you love us all?"

"There isn't enough of me for that."

"Ah! So you kill them to save yourself, not to possess me!"

"This is dialectic, not analysis! Let's drop it."

She has made her point. She is prepared to drop the argument without protest. Now she begins, more placidly, to develop another line of enquiry. This time I am prepared to cooperate, because it interests me, too. She asks:

"The train. You say it was coming from somewhere in the North."

"It seemed so, yes."

"Where was it going?"

"Home, here to Switzerland."

"And the flood didn't stop it?"

"No. It just kept going. The waters never seemed to threaten the train."

"That's why you wanted to stay inside?"

"Until I saw the stallion, yes."

"Do you see any pattern there, any analogy with your own life?"

Once again I am self-conscious, reluctant. Toni forces me to fit the jigsaw pieces together and admit the connection between dream and reality.

"I am, for the present at least, in a kind of retirement. I need that. I cling to my privacy here. I need the security of a family routine. If this marriage were to break up, I don't think I would be able – at least in this moment – to cope with it. If I lost you, I too would be lost. When you didn't meet me on the train, I was terribly troubled."

"So let me ask you something important, Carl. Your present is here. You need the security of your home place; but where do you see your future?"

"There will be another home place, not far from here. My future, my real future, is inside my head. I know that. I am absolutely certain of it. Wait, I have something to show you."

I bring out the sketches I have made of my tower, of the ground plan which is at once a mandala and the Tetragrammaton. I explain them with loving care. I tell her I have not yet found the land, but I will one day. I tell her how even as I made the sketches I saw it as a place where we could be together. Her face lights up with pleasure. She is like a young bride looking at the plans of her first home. When I put away the

151

sketches, the light is quenched and her questions take on a more sombre tone.

"Why is Salome blind?"

"I'm not sure. I've been fishing around for connections with that one. You know that, in the Orient, blind girls are often trained as prostitutes. They are much in demand by older men because they are skilful and sensitive – and they cannot see the ravages of age in their clients. Also, here in Europe, the blind are trained in massage and physiotherapy. They are excellent manipulators. The two ideas are related in the dream. Salome is a person of low origins. She is also the wife, lover and protector of an old man."

"So, let me ask you another question, Carl. In your very first important dream, the one in the underground cave, you saw the phallus as a giant one-eyed god. Was it blind, too? And how blind are you, Carl?"

"I don't understand."

"I'll put it another way then. You made love to me last night. I know you make love to Emma when you can. What's the difference? Or are we both just two grey cats in the dark? No, don't get angry! This is important, and you know it!"

The humour of it hits me and I burst out laughing. Toni is disconcerted. She demands to know what is so funny. I tell her that perhaps I should call Emma and have her join us so that I don't have to go over the same explanation twice. Where would she like me to start? The physics of intercourse? The oestrous cycle of women? The varieties of stimuli for each sex? Does absence excite desire? Does propinquity kill it? Finally she laughs, too, and agrees to drop the question.

Then she tosses another in my lap. This one really takes the prize!

"Carl, how do you see yourself? What are you?"

I know what she is asking. I know why. We have had many discussions, made many tentative definitions about the nature of mental health. We have arrived together at a notion of one-ness, a settled state in which the individual recognises himself as an entity, not necessarily complete or perfect, but acceptable and endurable. I have coined the word "individuation" to express both the process of growth and the state of arrival.

The cat does not question that she is a cat. The zebra does not seek to change his stripes. So, when Toni asks me who I am, I have to tell her honestly that I don't know yet. This is the nature of my sickness. I have lost the certainty, not only about my goals, but about who is the real man behind the "persona", the public face of Carl Gustav Jung. As I try to explain, she listens in silence, holding my hands between her own.

"My love, I am like the man who lost his shadow. Because I have no shadow I have no proof that I exist at all. This is why I need you. You prove that I'm solid, substantial and not just a fantasy of my own fantasies. This is why I am unsatisfactory to Emma and she to me. She is bringing up a family, bearing a new child. She needs a sure man to sustain her and her offspring. She cannot carry me too, like a suckling at the breast. So, we resent each other and hurt each other. I know that she has more grounds for complaint than I; but that doesn't help. Her grip on reality is stronger than mine, as is yours. Just now, I am in the cloud of unknowing! So, you see, the real question is not what I am, but what I'll turn out to be. Have I ever told you that, when I began my university studies, I wanted to be an archaeologist?"

"Then why didn't you?"

"Simple economics. Basel was near home. My parents couldn't afford to send me anywhere else. But Basel had no chair in archaeology. So, I took a medical degree instead. Now look at me – a compromise! And compromises never work too well."

"Don't underrate yourself. You're a very good doctor."

"I used to be, at the clinic. Now I'm the patient – and like all patients I'm centred on myself. Yet something tells me that although I've travelled much and will travel more in the physical world, my real exploration will be in the undiscovered country of the mind. Remember the old tag, 'Non foras ire: in interiore homine habitat veritas. Truth dwells inside a man. He doesn't have to go outside to find it.' Sometimes it's a frightening journey. I feel often as if I'm toppling off the edge of the world. But I must go on. Perhaps my final destiny is not to be a healer, but one who risks his own sanity to bring back the healing herbs and the magical formulae for other men to use."

Perhaps! It is all a great perhaps until she puts her arms around me and makes my manhood rise again and turns herself into my shadow so that I can stand, for a brief while at least, solid in the sun. To which, as always, there is an ironic afterthought. The shadow, once reunited with the substance, never, never leaves!

MAGDA
En voyage

At four in the morning we are halted at the Swiss frontier for entry and customs formalities. I put on a dressing gown and walk out into the corridor to watch the small bustle of passengers, porters and vendors on the platform. The conductor offers me a cup of coffee in his little cabin, where a young Swiss is inspecting passports. He smiles and gives me a "Grueszi" and asks politely if I am taking a vacation in Switzerland.

I tell him I am going to visit a very distinguished Swiss medical man, Doctor Carl Jung. The name means nothing to him. He is a country boy from Appenzell. He makes a little joke of his ignorance. He tells me in Schweizerdeutsch that he doesn't know any Jungdoktor but there is a beautiful Jungmädchen he is going to marry when he gets his promotion.

He looks at my rings and asks if I am married. I make my little joke and tell him I'm no longer a Jungmädchen but I am a Junggesellin, a bachelor girl. That same moment he flips open my passport. He will make high rank one day. He does not bat an eyelid as he reads my age in the document.

There is still a three hour journey ahead of us, so I go back to bed and try to interest myself in the life and death drama of Sherlock Holmes and the infamous Moriarty. Vain effort! My own tale of love and violence is much more vivid, and I have to set it in some kind of order before my meeting with Jung.

The first question any doctor asks of any new patient is: "What's the trouble? What brings you to me?" How shall I answer? "I've always liked violent sex games; now I'm going crazy and I'm afraid I'll kill my next partner." Or again, "It starts with incest and builds up to murder. I have a taste for both. So you see, doctor, there's an area of difficulty." Perhaps it would be simpler to say, "Let's spare each other's blushes, dear colleague. Hand me your copy of *Psychopathia Sexualis* and I'll mark the relevant passages."

Set down in linear script, it reads like bad farce. But today or tomorrow Jung will ask the routine question and I shall have to answer it in words that will not brand me immediately as a criminal, a lunatic or a pathological liar. My best tactic may be to act like the majority of patients: present a long list of non-specific symptoms and let the physician ferret out the real illness for himself. At least that way I'll have time to size up this psychic wonderworker before I commit myself to an outright confession. Besides, if he is, as Gianni suggests, a notable womaniser, we may have an interesting session: two physicians, each making a diagnosis of the other's sexual maladies!

By nine in the morning, I am installed in the hotel, bathed, dressed and ready for judgment day – which I would like to have over as soon as possible. I summon the manager. I tell him I wish to remain incognito during my stay: I am to be known under a nom de guerre, "Madame Hirschfeld". I also desire him, if he will have the kindness, to call Doctor Carl Gustav Jung at his home in Küsnacht and make an appointment for me under the same name. He will identify me only as a guest, recently arrived from Paris and recommended by a distinguished medico in that city, Doctor di Malvasia.

The manager is only too happy to oblige. He understands the idiosyncrasies of the rich – and I have to be rich to afford my present accommodation: a large suite with a view down the lake, which today is slate-grey and oily under a thundery sky. The manager is also discreetly informative on the subject of Herr Doktor Jung. He was, until recently, Clinical Director at the Burghölzli – the huge cantonal clinic for the mentally afflicted, which I will see on my way to Küsnacht. He was also a lecturer at the university, but retired quite recently. He has become a well known, if somewhat controversial, figure in the new psycho-analytic movement.

"But of course (this in deference to my sensibilities), he is a man of high reputation and undoubted talent. Our medical standards in Switzerland are among the highest in the world. If Madame will excuse me, I shall be back shortly."

It is twenty minutes before he returns. Contact with Doctor Jung has proved rather difficult. He has spoken first with the wife, then with a Fräulein Wolff, who appears to be some kind of special assistant. Finally, after much delay, he has been able to speak with the great man himself. He was quite brusque at first, obviously reluctant to concern himself with a new patient dropping out of the sky. In the end however – the manager gives a little self-righteous shrug – the matter was settled by a discreet hint that Madame was well able to pay for his trouble.

The Herr Doktor will see me at eleven. The manager has taken the liberty of arranging for a chauffeured automobile to take me to Küsnacht, wait and bring me back to the hotel. The place is not far, a fifteen minute drive, no more. I thank him profusely. He is equally profuse in his deprecations. "Anything you need, Madame, anything!" Then he leaves me, with an hour to kill before the moment of final judgment.

I spend the time in a dressing-up game, looking for the costume in which to present myself. The image must be soft, summery, feminine: lace or sprigged muslin, a picture hat, a flowered parasol. Let Doctor Jung discover for himself what a variety of characters is hidden under the finery.

The maquillage must be soft and subtle, no hard lines, no heavy rouge. There! I have to confess that I am pleasantly surprised by what I see in the mirror. There is a touch of youth, a faint souvenir of innocence, which I have not noticed for a long time.

I check the contents of my reticule: a lace handkerchief, perfume, lipstick, a compact, a comb, visiting cards, an envelope stuffed with Swiss francs, so that, whatever happens, Doctor Jung will feel adequately recompensed – and, of course, my passport to oblivion, the small blue phial sealed with red wax. Time to go. Time to say a prayer – if I knew even a small one.

My suite is on the first floor. I walk ceremoniously downstairs. In the lobby, heads turn. Even the stolid Swiss take notice as La Dame Inconnue makes her entrance. A page rushes to open the door for me. The porter salutes and hands me to the chauffeur, who settles me in regal splendour in the back seat of a vast Hispano Suiza. As we move off, I am conscious of a certain irony. Here I am, a murderess, riding in state like a queen, while Marie Antoinette rode to the guillotine in a tumbril. The only problem is that I've lost the nerve to enjoy it wholeheartedly.

The house of Doctor Jung is a pleasant but undistinguished dwelling, right on the shore of the lake. It is a tall, square house of two storeys, whose outlines are broken by a circular tower, the base of which forms the entrance and whose topmost floor looks out over the lake on one side and the foothill countryside on the other. The grounds are not overly large. One approaches the house from the road by a long straight path flanked by orchard trees: pears and cherries and apples. There are flower gardens along the borders of the lawn and a kitchen garden by the far fence. As I approach the front door, my eye is caught by an inscription over the archway. It is in Latin. "Vocatus atque non vocatus, deus aderit. Whether he is called or not, the god will be present." I seem to remember that a similar phrase in Greek was inscribed over the shrine of the oracle at Delphi.

I ring the bell. After a longish pause the door is opened by a tall, good-looking woman in her late twenties or early thirties. She is pleasant but a trifle flustered. She apologises for having kept me waiting.

"I've just sent the children out for a picnic with Nurse; it's the housekeeper's day off, so I'm the maid-of-all-work." She smiles and her whole face lights up. "I'm not very good at it either. Please, do come in. I'm Emma Jung. You must be the new patient. Frau . . . There! It's gone right out of my head!"

"Frau Hirschfeld. And please! I'm very grateful that the doctor would see me at such short notice."

She ushers me into a small waiting room off the hall and leaves me, promising that the doctor will be ready in a few minutes. I have the idea she is probably pregnant. Her face has that curious masklike appearance and there are deep, dark circles under her eyes.

She looks like a woman breeding too quickly, while her firstlings are still clinging to her skirts.

I pick up a magazine from the pile on the table. It is the 1912 edition of the *Yearbook of Psychoanalytic and Psychopathological Research*. It contains a long essay by Doctor Jung entitled "Mutations and Symbols of the Libido". I have hardly read two pages of the dense prose when Emma Jung returns to summon me into her husband's presence. When I stand up, I find I am a little dizzy. I take a deep breath, smooth my skirt, straighten myself up like a soldier for inspection and follow Emma Jung upstairs. When we reach the landing outside the doctor's study, I know that I have reached the point of no return.

JUNG
Zurich

This morning is Föhn weather, hot, still and humid, the air pressing down on the valley like a thick grey blanket. Everyone is ill humoured. The children are fretful. Emma has a worse than usual bout of morning sickness. Toni is in a bad humour with menstrual cramps. I am fed up to the back teeth with everybody – myself included.

I insist that Nurse take the children out for a picnic. Emma protests that there may be rain and she does not want the children caught in a thunderstorm. I tell her that I will have old Ludwig Simmel take them out in his pony trap; if the rain comes they can shelter under the canvas cover. But at all costs, they must be out of the house; otherwise we shall all drive each other crazy.

Emma submits with reluctance. I walk half a

kilometre down the road to make arrangements with Simmel. He, like everyone else, is suffering from the Föhn and does not want to go out. I offer double the amount he normally charges. He agrees with ill grace. I stride back to the house in worse humour than before.

I am halfway to the front door when I stop dead in my tracks. I feel as if I have run into a steel wall. I see nothing; but I can feel the obstruction at my finger-tips. It is like the testudo of the ancient Romans, a barrier of interlocked shields behind which the legions advanced. I feel that the legions are here, too. I know that in this moment they are hostile to me. They belong in the deepest level of my unconscious; but now they are released as a maleficent influence to plague me. Their power is enormous.

I try to step forward to penetrate the invisible wall. I cannot. I turn on my heel and walk back towards the front gate. Before I have taken three paces, I am stopped again. I am surrounded by a solid ring of hostility. I stand absolutely still. I raise my voice in a great shout for help: "Elijah! Elijah!" A moment later I can sense that the wall is melting away and that the creatures behind it are retreating into the darkness from whence they came.

I walk back to the house sweating and trembling like one in fever. I tell Emma to prepare a picnic lunch and Nurse to have the children ready to leave in half an hour. Emma follows me to my study where Toni is opening the morning mail. She tells me that during my brief absence there has been a phone call from the manager of the Baur au Lac. One of his guests, a Frau Hirschfeld, wants to see me this morning. Some fashionable physician in Paris has recommended her

161

to me. I tell Emma that the last thing I need in the world today is a new patient. Emma is unexpectedly stubborn. She tells me flatly:

"I think you're making a mistake, Carl. God knows, we're not so well off that you can afford to turn away patients. You've said yourself many times that you would like to have a connection with the big tourist hotels. Well, here's your opportunity."

This is the moment Toni chooses to assert her authority as my analyst. She says snappishly:

"I don't think you should see any patients for a few days. We are making such excellent progress with the dream analysis that I'd rather not see you distracted."

This is entirely too much. I turn on her in fury.

"Shut up, Toni! I'll make my own decisions!"

"As you wish, of course, doctor."

She turns back to the mail, using the letter opener as if it is a dagger and the envelopes are my living flesh. I am not prepared to have this exhibition of bad temper in front of Emma. I tell Toni curtly:

"Please call the Baur au Lac and tell the manager I would like to speak with him." Then I make my oblique apology to Emma. "You're quite right, of course. I'll see this woman, whoever she is. As you say, the Baur au Lac is a good connection."

"Thank you, Carl."

She gives me a small, grateful smile and goes out. Immediately Toni storms at me.

"My God! You're an absolute beast! I was only trying to protect your privacy and you cut me down like some little clerk."

"You deserved it. Never, never interfere in a situation between my wife and myself."

"Never interfere." She is almost choking with anger. "Dear Christ! I'm your whore, I'm your nursemaid, your lover . . . and you tell me not to interfere. I'll never, never understand how your mind works."

I reach out to take the phone. She snatches the instrument away and puts the call through. When the manager comes on I agree to see Frau Hirschfeld at eleven. The name of the man in Paris who recommended her, Malvasy, Malvoisier, something like that, means nothing to me. Still, as Emma says, it is all money – and God, do we need it! I tell Toni:

"I'd like you to sit in on this consultation."

"As you wish, doctor."

"Are we going to carry on this silly quarrel all day?"

"There is no quarrel, my dear doctor. You've taught me my place. Be sure that from now on, I'll stay in it."

"Good! Then bring your notebook over to my desk. I want to get something down immediately."

I begin dictating the experience I have just had in the garden: I see her anger abating as her professional curiosity is awakened. She seizes instantly on my description of the "testudo", the wall of shields. She points out, quite rightly, that the shield is not a weapon but a defence. Could it be that the invisible legions were trying to protect themselves from me? She labours to explain this odd thought:

"You've often described yourself as haunted or inhabited by a daimon. At other times you've called yourself a 'numinous' person: one in whom power resides without his being aware of it, or even being able to control it . . ." She breaks off as if searching for words, then with an odd unexpected warmth she

163

continues: "Has it never occurred to you that you might be the hostile influence and that these spirits, emanations, personifications – whatever you like to call them – are afraid of you?" She gives me a side-long, tentative smile. "I'm not trying to be nasty, believe me. I know I'm bitchy today. I've got my period, and I feel like hell. But you're the one who's been setting everyone's teeth on edge. The children must go for a picnic! Old Simmel charges too much! Mind your manners, Toni! Yes I want, no I don't want! No wonder you scare off even the spooks in the garden!"

We laugh in spite of ourselves. We kiss and make up. We drink a surreptitious glass of brandy just to toast our reunion. I light my pipe and we talk again about the phenomenon. Suddenly out of the blue I remember a quotation from Goethe's *Faust* which exactly describes the constellation of personages or influences which I experienced. "It walks abroad, it's in the air."

There is a key here to a puzzle which I have not yet been able to solve. It is the puzzle of time: past, present, future, now, then. I am dredging up mem-ories, symbols, myths, archetypes, whose roots are buried in the mists of prehistory. Nevertheless, they are mine, too. I give them another shape. I endow them with another numen and pass them on. Or do I? Have they perhaps taken possession of me, as the wind takes possession of the hollow reed, making its own music from a passive instrument? I know this is not science. There is no method to it, no logic, no sequence of cause and effect. Rather it is an act of spontaneous creation. Fra Angelico dreams heaven and lo! there it is, limned on the vaulted ceiling.

Dante dreams hell and the words ring plangent down the centuries. "Nessun maggior dolore che ricordarsi del tempo felice, nella miseria."

I, too, am searching for words to express the nature of the Godlike act when Emma announces that Frau Hirschfeld has arrived. Instantly I am beset by an irrational terror. I do not want to see this woman. No good will come of the encounter. It is too late and I have no valid reason to refuse her entry now. Two minutes later she steps into my study – and takes immediate possession, like a queen entering the domain of a vassal.

She has all the beauty of maturity. She is elegantly gowned. She has a splendid assurance of gesture and movement. She dominates my scholar's retreat as a great actress dominates a provincial theatre. I feel the impact of a strong will and a passionate spirit.

My irrational fear subsides into awe and then into a very lively lust. I hope neither Toni nor Emma will read it in my face. I realise that all my desires have been for younger women and for those emotionally dependent on me. I wonder what it would be like to fall in love with someone who knows how to spell all the words. Then I ask myself: if she knows how to spell the words, why the devil has she come to me? God help you, Carl Jung, for a mealy mouthed Swiss hypocrite! You're head over heels and gone for this one, and you can't wait to lay siege to her!

MAGDA
Zurich

This Carl Jung is a good-looking man. He is tall, flat bellied, strongly built, and he carries himself like a soldier. His hair is cropped short and his eyes are bright with intelligence. His handshake is firm and dry. He reminds me vaguely of Papa as a young man – something in the look perhaps, the hint of mischief, the sidelong way he scans you, like a good horse-trader inspecting a promising filly.

The girl is interesting; not pretty, but with a kind of elfin, gypsy charm. She is full of brisk business, very possessive, very much the assistant to the great man:

"May I take your hat and parasol, Madame? Please be seated there, by the doctor's desk. We need to get a few personal details before we begin the session."

We? I'm very sorry, my pretty one, but one or other of us will be gone in five minutes, I promise you! Jung is at pains to make me feel at ease. I hand him Gianni's letter of introduction. He reads it and hands it back. He grins and makes a pedantic joke.

"Etymologically it's not quite accurate. You're pseudonymous, not anonymous. Well, Hirschfeld will be as good a label as any – for the moment! The name is less important than the person; but we do need some facts about her. Miss Wolff will take the notes. I'll ask the questions."

He perches himself on the edge of his desk, swinging his long legs. Miss Wolff, notebook in hand, sits in his chair facing me. I have the notion that this is some kind of ritual to establish her as a personage on the

166

stage. I am still determined she won't be there too long. Jung begins the interrogation:

"How old are you, Frau Hirschfeld?"

"Forty-five."

"Married or single?"

"I am a widow."

"For how long?"

"Fifteen years."

"Any children?"

"One daughter."

"And how old is she?"

"Nineteen."

"What is your nationality?"

"Is that important?"

"It may be; it may not."

"Then let's say I'm European."

"What is your mother tongue?"

"I am equally fluent in English, French, Italian, German and Hungarian."

"How do you occupy your time?"

"I used to practise medicine. I gave it up after my husband's death. Since then I have been running a country estate, where I breed horses and dogs."

"Where did you do your medical training?"

"Italy and Austria, with some post-graduate work in London."

"Can you give me a summary of your health in medical terms?"

"As a child I had mumps, measles, chicken pox and the common cold. In adult life I have had no major illness and no surgery. I have no respiratory, cardio-vascular or urinary problems. Although I am forty-five, my periods are still regular and I have not yet experienced any symptoms of menopause. I take regular exercise. My muscle tone is excellent."

"What about sexual activity?"

"I have no permanent lover, but I am adequately entertained."

"How often?"

"Very adequately, doctor, thank you."

"Well." He gives me a wide, happy smile. "You're in excellent health, you have a very adequate sex life. What is troubling you?"

And there it is, flat and pat as a pancake, the question I have been dreading. I am still not prepared to answer it. I tell him with studious formality:

"With the greatest respect, doctor, and with all deference to Miss Wolff, I desire to consult with you alone."

He does not refuse outright. Clearly, he has to save the blushes of his young colleague, who is not, I think, as demure as she looks. He tells me first:

"Miss Wolff is my assistant and my trusted colleague. Her insights are extremely valuable in diagnosis."

"I am sure they are. Nevertheless . . ."

"Please!" He holds up an admonitory hand. "Please let me finish. I respect your desire for privacy; but as a consulting physician yourself, you will understand the precautions one must take with a new patient. Some of mine can be quite violent. One threatened me with a loaded revolver. Among my women patients there are those who entertain delusions – and spread false gossip – that they are the objects of lustful desire or attempted rape."

I assure him, with my most modest smile, that I am neither violent nor deluded. He yields the point with good humour. He tells Miss Wolff to leave us alone.

He should be ready for her in about two hours – which, he explains to me, is the upper limit of endurance for patient and analyst in a single session. As Miss Wolff makes her exit, I remark that she seems a very competent young lady – and a beautiful one. He is obviously flattered by proxy.

"She's quite brilliant, a fine poet, an outstanding analyst."

"And, clearly, she is devoted to you."

"As we are to her. In this business one needs loyal and discreet colleagues."

I give him full marks for that: no concessions, a salute to the absent, a terse little homily on professional trust. I brace myself for a new round of questioning. Instead he gives me an encouraging grin and some gentle advice.

"I know how you feel. It's like being asked to undress in the middle of the Bahnhofstrasse. Let me try to explain how we work. It's quite different from physical diagnosis, where the parameters of the body and its internal structures and functions determine the logic of our investigations. So unless there is a malfunction in the brain itself, we analysts are dealing always with intangibles, giant jigsaw puzzles with pieces scattered all over the board, in the past and in the present. We're concerned as much with dreams as with realities . . . with crimes that are never committed and those that are perpetrated in a strange kind of innocence. You must understand that the analyst is not a judge. He is, rather, a detective like that famous Englishman, Mr. Sherlock Holmes. He hopes that he may be a healer as well; because much of our mental health depends upon our understanding of ourselves and on coming to terms with what we understand. So,

169

two things to remember. You have nothing to fear from me – and nothing you can tell me will surprise me. I've heard it all. I've dreamed it all – because what we miss, good and bad, in our daily lives, we make up in dreams."

It is as if he has thrown me a lifeline in the midst of a raging sea. I grasp at it desperately. I tell him eagerly:

"That's one of the things that brought me to you. I am having a recurrent nightmare which disturbs me very much and leaves me always exhausted and depressed."

"Then tell me about it. I'll make some notes as you talk."

Now that I have begun, it is a relief to talk. I find myself reliving all the details of the dream, the wild hunt, the vast burned solitude of the desert, the small bloody carcass of the fox, myself naked and shorn, sealed in the glass ball, rolling over and over under the mocking eye of the sun.

Jung listens in silence. He is studiously neutral. His eyes watch every expression on my face, every gesture. He seems to take notes in a kind of shorthand. When I am finished he asks:

"Have you ever told that dream to anyone else?"

"No. Why do you ask?"

"You recount it so vividly. You are a natural story-teller. Now I'd like to ask you some questions about it. Try to answer spontaneously – not construct anything just to please me. If you can't answer, say so. If you don't want to answer, say that, too. Understood?"

Understood. He is telling me the rules of this new game, and that he understands them better than I. The first question is a surprise.

"What sex was the fox?"

"Female." I am surprised to hear myself answer so positively.

"Can you tell me the names of any of the people on the hunt with you?"

"No."

"Who killed the fox?"

"I don't know. I suppose the hounds did."

"Why did your horse throw you?"

"I don't know that either."

"What kind of women have their heads shorn?"

"Nuns, criminals, women who need cranial operations."

"Which one are you in the dream?"

"Well, I've never wanted to be a nun and I've never had a cranial operation. I suppose that leaves criminal. The ball is certainly a prison."

"What makes you say that?"

"That's what it feels like – and after the dream I always feel guilty."

"Do you feel guilty during it?"

"Not really. I feel ridiculous, as if a voyeur is staring at me in the bath."

"And the sun is the voyeur?"

"Yes."

"Tell me how you wake up."

"How? Oh, I'm curled up, in a foetal attitude. I have to make an effort to straighten up and face the new day."

He makes a few more notes and then gives me a grin of approval.

"You're doing very well. Stay relaxed. Just let the stuff flow out. It's a pleasure to deal with an intelligent woman – and a beautiful one."

I thank him for the compliment. I know I am being flattered; but I am glad of it. I wonder how long this little pavane can go on. Then the questions begin again.

"Do you have any religious convictions? Do you belong to any sect or communion?"

It is Gianni's question all over again. This time I answer it differently.

"No. Papa was an old fashioned rationalist who taught me that life begins and ends here and that we have to reach out and grab the best of it while we can."

"And you still believe that?"

"Absolutely."

"What was your father's profession?"

"He was a surgeon, a very good one. He used to say, 'I've cut 'em living and I've carved 'em dead, and I never caught any glimpse of God or a soul.' I loved Papa very much. I suppose I simply adopted his convictions and habits of mind."

"Was your mother a believer?"

"I don't know. She left me when I was a babe in arms."

"Left you?"

"Left us both. I was suckled by a wet nurse. Lily and Papa brought me up."

"And your mother?"

"We never saw her again. Papa never spoke of her. Quite recently I discovered by accident that she died a duchess in England." I realise that I have made a blunder and told more than I intended. I try, awkwardly, to repair the damage. "You see there are good reasons for my wanting to remain anonymous – or is it pseudonymous?"

Jung smiles and nods assent; but now I sense that he

is wary. Perhaps he thinks that a duchess in the family is one snobbery too many! He asks:

"You mention a Lily. Who is she?"

"She was my mother's companion when she came to Europe to give birth to me. She fell in love with Papa and stayed to look after me. She was all the woman I needed – mother, sister, friend!"

"But your father and she never married?"

"No. He wanted desperately to marry my mother – but after that – no! He lost all interest in matrimony."

"Since we're on the subject of family, tell me about your husband, your daughter . . . anything you can remember."

"Well, I married when I was twenty-five, a year after I had finished medical training. My husband was Austrian, the heir to a large estate and a minor title. He was in his early thirties. I was his second wife. His first had died very suddenly, without bearing him any children. He was a wonderful man and I was desperately in love with him. We lived on his estate and I practised medicine in the surrounding villages. I got pregnant the first year and we had a daughter. We had hoped for a son, to carry on the title, but still it didn't matter. We were both young. There would be other children. It didn't turn out like that. When my daughter was coming up to her fourth birthday, my husband contracted cancer. The invasion was rapid. Soon there were metastases everywhere. We both knew there was no hope. *His* only wish was to die at home, with me, in our own house. *My* only wish was to make his passing as easy as possible. I hired a nurse, but undertook the medical supervision myself. As a doctor, you will understand my treatment."

173

"You have yet to tell me what it was."

"Increasing doses of sedatives to keep the pain under control."

"Also to depress the cardiovascular and respiratory systems, and so cause early demise?"

"Yes."

"And your husband died peacefully?"

"As peacefully and quickly as possible without rousing suspicion and enquiry. But there were long, bad weeks. And when the wasting and the symptoms became too terrible, I had to keep my daughter away from the sickroom. That was when the trouble started."

"What trouble?"

"After a while, I noticed that she seemed to be afraid of me. I tried and tried to find out why. It was the nurse who finally explained the reason. She would hear her father groaning and crying. She would see me coming out of the sickroom with instruments to be sterilised and bloody cloths to be burned. The idea became fixed in her mind that I was some kind of witch trying to kill her father."

"Which, in a fashion, you were."

"Right. But the child had no way of knowing that."

"Children don't have to *know* things. They absorb them like sponges. Did you ever try to explain things to your daughter? Not the treatment, but the problems of her father's illness?"

"Often, but I never seemed able to reach her. She retreated further into herself. The terrible thing was I found myself resenting the child. She was like a constant accuser; and at the end of a long and bitter day with a dying man, I found her presence unbearable. There were moments – frightening moments –

when I almost wanted to kill her. I knew I could do it, too. So, finally, I talked with a sister of my husband who had a large family. She volunteered to take the child until it was over."

"And how did that work out?"

"She was very happy – except when I went to visit her. Then there would be terrible hysterical scenes. Even after my husband's death, there was no way she could be persuaded to come home. So, it seemed kinder to leave her as a member of a large, happy family."

"Have you ever regretted that decision?"

For the first time, I am faced with a question to which I have to ponder the answer. I am not tempted to lie about it. It is simply that always in the past I have declined to face it. Finally, I can put it into words.

"Regret it? No. I think it was the best solution for us both. I am a very passionate woman; but I don't believe I have any real talent for maternity."

J UNG
$\overline{\textit{Zurich}}$
We are hardly twenty minutes into the session and already I am deeply disturbed by what I have heard. The most impressive – no, the most frightening – thing about this woman is her total lucidity, her wholly rational grasp of what she is and the story she is unfolding to me. I am not deceived by her answers about the dream, which is the clearest possible projection of an enormous guilt about some matter still to be revealed.

She is as clear about the sex of the dead fox as I was about the sex of the stallion in my chaos dream. The

175

glass ball is clearly a womb as well as a prison. She wakes in a foetal position, unprepared to face a hostile dawn. It has not occurred to her, or she is concealing her knowledge, that infants are born with very little hair. She has also dealt very summarily with the mother who abandoned her, and her own child whom she has abandoned in her turn.

She describes herself as very passionate. I am aware of her as a quite explosive personality, capable at one moment of a singular self-control and at another of a devastating outburst of energy. She is like a stick of dynamite, inert and apparently harmless in the hand, but capable of demolishing a whole building. In my own unstable state, I feel threatened by her; but the threat is ambivalent. On the one hand, there is a powerful sexual attraction. On the other, I sense a latent hostility as strong as that of the invisible archetypes in the garden. Her death wishes correspond in sinister fashion with my own. She admits to having hastened her husband's demise – albeit for compassionate reasons. She admits to moments of murderous resentment against her own child. Most certainly there are other love-hate relationships hidden behind the symbols of the dream.

Therefore, I do not want to extend this analysis a moment longer than is necessary. Having begun it, I cannot ethically terminate it in a brutal and dangerous fashion. I must at least be able to recommend her for treatment to someone else. For this, I need to see how far her lucidity extends, how swiftly her reason will take us to the root of her problem. To ease the tension that has already built up, I suggest we take a stroll by the lakeshore while we continue our talk.

On the way out we have to pass by the kitchen. My

patient goes ahead of me into the garden, while I pause to ask Emma if she will send some coffee up to the study. My hand is already on the door handle when I hear Emma's voice and Toni's raised in anger. I stand very still and shamelessly eavesdrop on the altercation. It is Emma who seems to be in control of the argument.

"Don't you understand that we have a very sick man on our hands?"

"Of course I do. I spend more time with him than you do – eight hours a day in that study, sometimes more."

"If he gets worse, do you think you can cope with him?"

"Why ask me? You're his wife."

"And you're his mistress!"

"I love him."

"I love him too. So, we should at least try to be honest with each other. You're not the first rival I've had. You probably won't be the last."

"Don't patronise me!"

"I'm asking you to help me."

"My God! You're an extraordinary woman!"

"Look, I've got four children. I'm carrying our fifth. Carl's rages terrify us all. The little ones don't understand their father's problem. He's blind to theirs. I have to protect them and hold the family together as long as I can. I can't fight you. I'm not sure I want to. I see Carl manipulating you as he does everyone else. All I ask is that the pair of you play outside – not in *my* house! Well?"

"Why do you put up with him?"

"Why do you?"

"I love him."

"So do I. And that's the only reason I put up with you, my dear."

"It can't go on like this."

"So long as he wants it, it will go on!"

I have heard enough. I am shamed and saddened – and fool enough to find a scrap of comfort in the fact that two women love me enough to fight over me. This is, in any case, hardly the moment to ask for coffee. I creep away and join my patient down by the boat-house, where she is inspecting the toytown I am building with stones from the lakeshore. I use it as a text for what I have to tell her.

"I began it as a therapy. I, like most people in their middle years, am passing through a psychic crisis. I have put myself into analysis with Miss Wolff, whom you met. All analysis involves a journey backwards to pick up the signposts we have passed. This is a model of the village where I was born. The man you see before you was shaped here, not merely by his parents, by everything and everybody around him, but by everybody who had gone before: the men who built the church, the masons who hewed the stones, the women who baked the bread and passed down the folk remedies for people's ills. We are all reflectors of a past which we have forgotten, but which is buried deep in our subconscious. Our dreams recall that long and ancient inheritance. Do you see that street there, the one leading down from the church?"

"Yes. What about it?"

"One day I saw the devil walking down it."

She laughs. The laughter has an open innocent sound.

"You're joking."

"No, I mean it. What I saw was a Roman Catholic

priest in a black cassock and a black shovel hat, which looked like a pair of horns. But to my little Swiss Lutheran mind, he was the devil. It was years before I could enter a Catholic church without a shiver of terror."

"How strange!"

"And yet not so strange. The same thing happened to your little daughter, when she began to identify you as a witch. I still struggle with the memory of my own mother, who most of the time was a warm, simple, talkative countrywoman, but who had a strange gypsy side to her nature that used to terrify me."

She bends and picks up an elongated stone and lays it like a lintel over the doorway of an unfinished cottage. In a small, quiet voice she says:

"I know what you are trying to do. It does help to know that other people have problems not unlike one's own. But you have to understand that I've lived a very strange life – and met some very odd characters. I find it extremely difficult to trust people – even in our medical profession. Last week in Paris, my own bankers, the men who manage my estate, tried to push me into a compromising situation with a very wealthy man whom they wanted as a client."

"And you think I'm capable of something like that?"

"We all are, Doctor Jung. We all are."

"What would you accept as proof that you can trust me?"

"What can you offer?"

She says it quite baldly, like a countrywoman haggling in a market; but I sense that she means it. I reflect for a moment. I ask myself why the hell I have to trade at all. She's a grown woman; clearly sane.

179

Why should I put myself in jeopardy for her cure? For once I am prepared to be honest: because I desire her, because I want to have her in my debt. So I propose the bargain.

"If you are prepared to trust me with your secrets, I am prepared to reveal to you two pieces of information about myself: the one very personal; the other professional. Either one could damage me greatly if it were bruited abroad. That way each of us holds the other's surety. Equal threat, equal fidelity. It seems like a reasonable bargain."

"It is. But why should you care so much? I wouldn't cut off my finger to persuade one of my patients to have an appendectomy."

I am angry now at her manipulation and I snap at her:

"Perhaps because I have a different view of my patients."

"How do you view me, doctor?"

"That's just the point, Frau Hirschfeld. It's not you! It's all of us: we do not live alone. We live together. We depend on each other. The moment we forget that, we are lost – like fiery particles flung off from the solar system to be quenched and lost for ever in the outer darkness of space. When you came into my house, did you notice an inscription over the door?"

Much to my surprise she quotes it back to me, verbatim:

"'Vocatus atque non vocatus deus aderit.'" She also translates it in its original sense. "'Whether he is called or not, the god will be present.' I wonder what that signifies to you, doctor?"

"It signifies the reverse of what you say you believe:

180

that human life is a pointless trip to nowhere. I'm not an orthodox Christian any more. I can't even set a meaning to the word God; but I know that I am groping towards a truth about who He is and what we are. I know that however many mistakes I make in my life – and God knows I've made plenty – I cannot abdicate the search for a meaning. You're someone I've met on the pilgrim road. If only for that reason, you're important to me. I can't pass you by and let you die in a ditch!"

I am surprised at my own vehemence. I am even more surprised when she reaches out and takes my hand like a child and says meekly:

"I'm sorry. I believe what you're telling me. I want to trust you, truly! I accept your bargain."

I point once more to the village, to the very cottage on which she has just laid the lintel stone. I tell her:

"Here's the first fact, which I've told only to one other person in my life. That cottage was the house of a man, a friend of the family, whom in my boyhood I loved and trusted. One day he raped me. It was an experience which festered in my mind for a long time and coloured many relationships in my adult life." She opens her mouth to speak. I silence her instantly. "Please! I don't want to discuss it. The second fact is that somewhere in this country there is a woman walking around free, whom I know positively to be a murderess. She was in confinement at the Burgholzli for an acute depressive illness. The prognosis was negative. I managed after much labour to identify the cause of the malady. In deep distress over an unsuitable marriage, she had murdered one of her children. The fact that she could share the knowledge brought her a long way towards a full cure. I altered the

181

record, suppressed the incriminating evidence and discharged her. My signature is on the document; so I am technically guilty of a criminal act. Again I don't want to discuss the details. Now I've given you my surety; are you prepared to trust me?"

"First, you have to explain what you want of me."

I am appalled. I am committed; but she is still trying to avoid any contract. I take her roughly by the arms and force her to face me.

"Very well. I'll tell you! You must take me by the hand and lead me into the desert country of your dreams; into that glass ball where you are curled up, shaven, not like a nun, but like a criminal, with all your private parts showing. You have to show me what the red eye of the sun sees, what your little daughter saw and fled from. I want to know the secret that drove you to my door and is now driving you again to destroy yourself."

She thrusts herself free and retreats from me. It is an act of bitter rejection. She shakes her head vigorously from side to side. She spits the words at me.

"No! No! No! It's still a bad bargain."

I am furious now and I mince no words with her.

"What are you afraid of, woman? Dirty stories? I know all the words in the book. I know men and women who eat shit to get their orgasms. Murder? I know about that, too. I've been attacked by a patient with a kitchen knife. What else can't you bring yourself to talk about? Rape? Mutilation? Incest? Your life is on the block, Madame! Don't let a few rough words stand in the way of saving it!"

Her reaction is strange. Instead of being shocked, as I have hoped, into submission or hysteria, she becomes suddenly icy calm. Her tone is almost one of compassion for my stupidity.

"You still don't see it, do you, doctor?"

"See what, Madame?"

"It's not the questions I'm afraid of; it's the answer *you* may give me at the end. If that answer is the wrong one, I'm finished."

She fumbles in her reticule and brings out a small blue bottle sealed with red wax. She holds it out towards me. I have to make a step forward to take it from her hand. The label is that of a pharmacy in Paris. It is inscribed in a careful open script: "Prussic Acid, Poison, Not To Be Taken". The woman watches me as I read it. She is expecting some violent reaction from me. She does not know I have played this scene before. Neither does she know that I am not opposed to suicide when life becomes intolerable. I shrug and hand the bottle back to her.

"It's not what I would choose to make an end of myself. Still, it's your life, Madame. Don't try to blackmail me with it."

"You still miss the point. I'm not blackmailing you. I'm stating a fact. You're the one loading the pistol. I'm the one playing Russian roulette. If you fail me, I'm out of the game. I make a swift and final painful exit. All you lose, my dear doctor, is a patient you didn't want in the first place."

"Not true, Madame! I have offered you the only surety I have: the last of my rather tattered reputation. As for a cure, you know damned well there are no guarantees! Your father was a surgeon. He never knew what he was going to find when he opened up some poor devil on the operating table. It's kill or cure for all of us. A bad bargain? Yes, but it's the only one we're offered – any of us! If you don't like it, too bad! Pull down the shutters and put yourself to sleep for ever!"

I turn on my heel and leave her. I do not look back. She can follow me or not as she chooses. I approach the kitchen on tiptoe and pause to eavesdrop again. The argument is over. My two women appear to be engaged in a quite peaceable discussion about how to bake an apple cake. I put my head round the door and enquire meekly whether we may have coffee served in the study.

MAGDA
Zurich

I am fascinated by this man. I sense his weaknesses. He is obviously a skirt chaser and his lust is as transparent as a farmboy's. He has a coarse tongue and a quick temper. I think if anyone, man or woman, pushed him too hard, he would hit back. I was goading him, deliberately, because the manager at the Baur au Lac had suggested that it was only the prospect of a fat fee that had induced him to see me.

He probably is venal. Medicine is a profession that deals in costly magic; this medicine of the mind is an expensive novelty, but I have no doubt about this man's sincerity. When he talked about the search and the pilgrim road, that wasn't just rhetoric. He meant it. He cares – and he's furious because he thinks I'm trying to cheat on our agreement.

So what now? Do I play out the game, or pick up my hat and parasol and go home? Jung will not bend to me. Either I tell my story or he will show me the door.

184

Conclusion? I swallow my pride, put another stone on the toy village, follow the master back to his study and hold out both hands for the thumbscrews!

"So . . ." he announces, as he dips a biscuit into his coffee, "we go back to the things which trouble you, the things that drive you to seek help. First, there is the recurrent nightmare. We'll return to that. What are the other problems?"

I take the plunge – not the big one from the high board, but the small one into the shallow end of the pool.

"I have trouble on my estate, a kind of peasants' revolt. My people think I'm a witch. My studmaster tells me that unless I stay away for a long time, the whole staff will quit. If I try to run the place with foreigners, they'll burn me out."

"Is your studmaster telling the truth?"

"Yes."

"Why do your people think you're a witch?"

I tell him about the horse and the hound and the roses. He stabs the tip of his pencil at me and snaps:

"Tell me the rest of it."

"What do you mean, the rest of it?"

"Please, don't play games! Why did you ride the stallion past the mares?"

"For curiosity, I suppose."

"The hell, you suppose! You breed animals. What is there to be curious about? You know what happens when stallion smells mare. Were you in heat yourself?"

"Don't be vulgar, doctor!"

"Don't lie to me then! What time of the month was it for you?"

"All right, I was in heat, too!"

"And you knew that riding the stallion would bring you to climax. Yes or no?"

"God, you've got a dirty mind!"

"It gets dirtier. It had happened before, hadn't it?"

"Yes."

"And always there was cruelty. You had to hurt somebody, break something."

"Not . . . not always. In the past, it happened only rarely. Now it's happening frequently, and I'm afraid. Once upon a time, it never happened at all. You have to believe that."

"I do believe it; but that doesn't close the matter. We'll come back to it again." He is gentle now. He is like me. When people submit, he is calm and pleasant. He makes a note or two and then says: "Tell me about the once-upon-a-time, when these nasty things never happened."

He dips another biscuit in his coffee. I laugh and tell him that Lily used to do that. She called it "dunking". He asks was Lily part of the "good times"?

"Oh, yes. She was the biggest part and the best – after Papa, of course. Funny! One of my earliest memories is of Lily bouncing me on her knee and saying the English nursery rhyme:

> Ride a cock horse to Banbury Cross
> To see a fine lady upon a white horse

I used to feel all shimmery and shivery with pleasure at the motion and the smell of her perfume and the rustle of her clothes against her skin. Strange how things like that stay with you and excite you."

I wonder if he knows that I am excited now – and if

he does, why doesn't he respond a little? He looks a sturdy enough stallion. I ask him:

"Do you have sexual memories?"

"Everyone does; but at this moment I'm interested in yours. Tell me more about you and Lily."

"Well, when she went to live in Silbersee . . ." The word is out before I realise that I have given him another clue to my identity. Hoping he has missed it, I hurry on. "We had a small horse breeding operation – hacks and draught animals for the local hunters and farmers. Papa insisted that both Lily and I learn to ride. After we were confident enough, we would ride out with Papa to visit the local gentlefolk. If Papa wasn't home, Lily and I would go visiting together."

His next question catches me unaware.

"Did your father ever speak about your mother?"

"Never. I asked him about her only once. He looked at me in the strangest way and said, 'Be glad she's gone. She never loved me. She never loved you. She was the Snow Queen, who had a lump of ice instead of a heart. But we don't need her, do we? I'm your prince; you're my princess; and Lily will look after us both for ever and ever, amen. Now promise me you'll never talk about the Snow Queen again! Never, never, never!' So, of course, I promised."

"And you never thought about her?"

"Sometimes I did. Once I remember I saw a picture of the Snow Queen in a book of fairy tales. I was surprised that she looked so beautiful. I was tempted to take it to Papa and show him – but Lily said I shouldn't. It would only make him angry. I was afraid that if he got too angry he would stay away and never come home. He was away so much; that was a very real fear for me."

Suddenly, I am self-conscious. I am giving a solo performance. I say as much to Jung. He laughs and waves me on.

"That's the best thing that can happen. Tell me more about your life at . . . where was it? . . . Silbersee."

I begin, haltingly at first, then with lively enthusiasm, to tell him about my childhood in the Schloss, with Lily and me living our enchanted existence, while Papa came and went like some gallant from the golden days. I tell him about Papa's homecomings and the happy sensual intimacies we shared. I find, to my surprise, I am happy to share the memory with my new friend, Doctor Jung.

"One morning, while I was still quite small, I came into Papa's bedroom and found him making love with Lily. She was straddling him and riding him like a jockey. When Papa caught sight of me, he laughed and beckoned me over and had me join the game. I sat on his chest. Lily put her arms around me and sang 'Ride a cock horse', while the three of us bounced and laughed as if it were just another nursery game. Does that shock you, doctor?"

"No. Should it?"

"Well, some people might think it strange."

"Did you find it strange?"

"No. It was pure pleasure. And it got better the older I grew. I had the best of two worlds – life on a big estate, the sowing and the reaping, the cutting of timber, the mating and birthing of animals, and lovely, cosy hours in our private heaven in the Schloss. Lily and Papa prepared me for puberty. Lily taught me girl things. Papa showed me his medical books, taught me how babies are conceived and born, and

188

how women should conduct their sexual lives. I adored him. I would do anything to please him. I wanted to be as like him as possible. That's why I made up my mind to be a doctor.''

"What was your father's name?"

"Oh no, you don't, doctor! That's not fair!"

He grins at me, mischievously.

"A little test. Why is your name so important? You're telling me much more intimate things."

"Because this way I can tell them like fairy tales. If I don't have a name, they don't belong to me, do they?"

"I understand. Please, tell me more fairy tales."

"It was a terrible wrench when I had to go to boarding school and learn to be a young lady of quality. The hardest thing was to keep quiet about the things I'd learned from Lily and my father. I felt so much older and wiser than all the silly little girls giggling in the dormitory after lights-out. I felt lonely, too, sometimes."

"But obviously you settled down in the end?"

"Of course. I learned how to make capital out of my secret knowledge. I became a leader, not a follower. I began to build up contacts outside the school. The way I did this was by enrolling in what were called 'optional courses'. These were given by private teachers in their own homes or studios. For example, as soon as I became a senior, I persuaded Papa to let me enrol at an advanced riding academy near the school. The academy was run by a former captain of cavalry and his two sons. One was a bit of an oaf; but the other, Rudi, was very handsome, and in the saddle he looked like a prince. He knew it too, and I teased him all the time about his arrogance. I knew he

189

wanted me, because every time we talked I could see his erection straining at his tight breeches. One day, he challenged me to ride a big black stallion which the academy had just bought for stud. He was a beautiful beast, but bad tempered – a real rogue. I was hardly in the saddle when he reared and bucked and tried every trick to get rid of me. I hung on, determined to best him if I died in the attempt. I flogged and spurred him and drove him round and round at a bolting gallop until the moment when I knew I had him mastered. My excitement was so great that I came to orgasm – a wild burst of pleasure that excites me every time I remember it. Even now, my dear doctor."

He does not take the bait. His eyes are fixed on his notebook. Still writing, he asks:

"And what happened then?"

"I rode the stallion to a standstill, then dismounted and tossed the reins to Rudi. I was wet and smelling of sex. Rudi stared at me and said, 'Christ! I wish you'd ride me like that!' I laughed and said, 'Why not?' We climbed up into the hayloft and made love. But after the stallion, Rudi was a great disappointment. He had no staying power."

I mean it as a joke. He does not react. He scribbles another note and asks another question.

"How old were you when this happened?"

"Oh, seventeen – a little more, perhaps."

"But clearly it wasn't your first sexual experience."

"Oh, dear no! I'd made all the usual experiments – no, that's the wrong word, they weren't experiments. I'd learned how to stimulate myself to climax. I had a quite happy lesbian relationship with a girl at school – and various episodes with male students in and around Geneva. None of them was important. I knew more than they did. Most of them were too eager or too inexperienced. Papa used to say a good lover needs as much training as an athlete."

"Was your Papa a good lover?"

"The best! The very best! He was everything a woman . . ."

I break off, horrorstruck at what I have told him. I feel a blush like a tidal wave flooding over my breast and my cheeks. I cannot meet Jung's eyes. I bury my face in my hands. A moment later, I hear him, as if from a great distance, saying:

"There now. Cry if you want. I'm going to pour some brandy."

As he passes, he lays a hand on my head, as if he is imparting a blessing. I am absurdly grateful for the gesture. At least it proves that I am not a leper.

J UNG
$\overline{Zurich}$
I confess to a singular satisfaction. The woman's narrative – so vivid and at times so joyful – about her childhood and her relations with her father convince me that I am right and Freud is totally wrong on the incest taboo. I can say, without vanity, that I have much more experience than he in this matter.

Freud is a city man, born and bred. I am a country fellow. In Switzerland there are many small mountain communities where incestuous relations in various degrees of consanguinity are quite common. The commonest are those between father and daughter in a large family, between brother and sister, and between close cousins. Unless violence is involved, or a

191

total destruction of the bond between husband and wife, incestuous relationships are often durable and happy. They excite little hostility in the small closed community, which accepts them as the slightly abnormal fringe of local mores.

There are, however, deeper questions involved – and it is on these that I have taken issue with Freud and his minions. Incest has always had a mythical, a sacred aspect. The kings of Ancient Egypt married their sisters. Many of the regeneration myths are incestuous in character.

This woman's narrative has all these characteristics. She lives in a closed world – a heaven of childish pleasures. Her father is a prince; she is a princess. As a lover, he was the best, always! Even the lost mother is a beautiful Snow Queen. Lily, the surrogate mother, is at once handmaiden, duenna and confidante at court. It is only later, when reality invades this Eden, that their three-cornered relationship will inevitably deteriorate. If I can trust the story I am being told, the same mythic attitude prevails with the father. He never brings women home. No outsider invades the upper rooms. The enchanted garden remains inviolate. The spell will be broken if the gate is opened and strangers from the outside world gain entrance.

This is when the trouble starts – and we are still a long way from definition of what that trouble may be. The childhood and girlhood narratives are clear, vivid and coherent. The others – with the exception of the dream – are still only sketches. She wants to be done with them as soon as possible. "Yes, I was cruel to the stallion and the dog. Yes, I was sexually excited by the experience. I loved my husband. I missed him when he died. My daughter thought I was a witch. I lost her. Sad, sad, sad! And if you don't save me, reward me with peace and justification after all the trouble I'm going through, I'll kill myself with prussic acid." She's a doctor. She knows there are easier, if not quicker, ways of dying than by cyanide poisoning; but the little blue bottle with the poison label is a dramatic threat directed at me.

I know that little piece of theatre, too. I remember the girl at the Burgholzli – also an incest case, but one who had been violated – who had retreated into a world of total myth and fantasy. She lived on the moon. She met a winged demon who turned into a beautiful man. All the magical transformations of ugliness into beauty! She was finally cured and restored to a normal life. On the day I signed her certificate of discharge from outpatient treatment, she presented me with a loaded pistol. If I had failed her, she said, she was going to shoot me . . . Well, this one can't shoot me with a phial of hydrocyanic acid. She can, however, decide to stage a suicide scene on my doorstep. I hope she is too rational for that; but one can never be sure.

As we sip our brandy – I am interested to see how she handles a moderately large dose of alcohol – I take pains to impress on her that the incest experience is relatively common and that she must not feel humiliated by it. Her reaction is one of genuine surprise.

"Humiliated? By that? Never! I was prepared for it, don't you see? My father was the one man who could make sense of a bizarre universe. Nothing shocked him. Nothing was unforgivable, except hypocrisy."

"But he never forgave your mother's desertion."

"That's true."

"And you had to be sure you never incurred his displeasure – otherwise you, too, might have been cast out of Eden for ever."

"I've never thought of it that way." She does not reject this thought. She examines it, with an odd air of sadness. "Still, it could be so. I told you Papa's comings and goings were always rather capricious. But yes, if he was away for longer than I expected, I would become restless and tearful. I used to wonder if something had happened to him – or if some other witch woman had carried him off."

"Did he ever punish you, threaten you?"

"Never!" She is very emphatic. "It was Lily's job to discipline me. Papa just enjoyed me. I enjoyed him. So long as he was there, my world was a Garden of Eden. Everything was possible. Nothing was forbidden. I was the lucky Eve who had the run of the place."

"Let us be specific now. When did your father first have full intercourse with you?"

"On my seventeenth birthday. He told me it was his special gift."

"Tell me about it – everything you can remember."

Once again her narrative flows freely and simply. Her pleasure in the recollection is obvious. She is disappointed because I seem not to share it. Equally vivid – and this it seems to me is a very significant point – is her description of her anger and disappointment at being sent back to school after this rite of passage. I put it to her in the terms of our original metaphor.

194

"So, when you went back to school this time, it was like being cast out of Eden?"

"Yes, that's what it felt like. I was a hothouse plant suddenly transplanted to a cold climate. For the first time, I saw myself as an oddity. What I resented was that I had no preparation for the experience."

"So, how did you cope?"

She gives a small rueful laugh and takes a mouthful of brandy.

"I told you – I took control of the situation." She sets down the brandy glass and takes off one of her rings. It is a signet ring. The stone is jade – imperial jade – carved with a device in intaglio. She tells me: "That's Papa's coat of arms. The device is a mailed fist holding a mace. The motto, which is very hard to read, is 'Nemo me impune lacessit. No one provokes me with impunity.' As I got older, Papa used to remind me of it from time to time. He would say: 'You don't have to use the club. Most of the time, you just have to wave it around and look fierce, and you'll get what you want.'"

"But you've done more than wave it around, yes?"

"Sometimes."

"You've broken stallions. You've brutalised a dog. You've cut down roses with a hatchet. What have you done to people?" I hand back the ring and wait while she slips it back on to her finger. "You're out of paradise now. It's winter in your world. Clearly, you feel threatened. What do you do, for example, with lovers who have crossed you?"

This is indeed a sensitive spot. Her face clouds over. She reaches for the brandy glass. I stretch out my hand and take it from her. I smile and say:

"You don't need that to answer a simple question."

195

She snaps back instantly:

"It isn't a simple question. It's a lot of different questions all mixed up together."

"You're right. I apologise. So, let's be very simple. You have brutalised animals. Have you ever brutalised people?"

"Yes." It is a curt, reluctant monosyllable. Then she adds, "And if you want me to tell you about it, I am going to need that drink."

I refill her glass and hand it back to her. I ask, as casually as I can:

"Do you have any dependence on alcohol? Please! It's a clinical question, which I'm sure you'll understand."

She gives me a sidelong smile and raises her glass in salute before she drinks.

"Clinical question, clinical answer. I enjoy alcohol. I am not dependent on it. Neither am I addicted to nicotine, opium, morphine or any other drugs. I've experimented with them all. I've learned not to trust any of them. I owe that to Papa, too. He used to say: 'Try everything. Depend on nothing but yourself. Alcohol destroys the brain cells, syphilis plays hell with the constitution – and depressant drugs do no good for your sex life.' Are you answered, doctor?"

"On this subject, yes. Now answer my first question."

"Have I ever brutalised people? Yes, I have. I still do. In the circles I frequent, I have a reputation for it. I've also developed a taste for the game. I am frightened, really frightened, that one day I'll go too far and end up with a dead body in my bed. Most of the time, I am absolutely under control, as I am here with you, but sometimes I go berserk and I really want to hurt

196

people. You ask why I came to see you. I had to leave a certain European city because of a sado-masochist incident. The man – a willing partner, mind you – was badly injured and had a heart attack as well. I had to get out in a hurry. Now that frightened me. It was like . . . like . . ."

"Like breaking the stallion, beating the dog almost to death?"

"Just like that."

"And you experienced orgasm in each case?"

"Yes."

"How do you feel about these incidents?"

"I feel a freak, because they're excessive. I feel threatened because I could have the police on my neck."

"Do you do this sort of thing for money?"

"No. I do it for fun. If anybody pays afterwards, I do."

"These are very dangerous games."

"I know."

"Do you feel guilty about them?"

"No. I'd like to be different – normal if you like. But guilty? I suppose the truth is I don't know what the word means. I'm not sure I've ever experienced guilt. Look! I know what I want to say; but I have to find the right words. This is terribly important to me. May I walk in the garden for a few minutes? No, you mustn't come! I need to be alone."

I agree. She walks out alone. Thank God, she is still lucid, still rational. This again is an experience I should like to communicate to Freud and some of his very dogmatic colleagues. In a clinic like the Burgholzli, one deals always with real casualties. In private practice a large number of one's patients are people in middle age, whose psychic supports – religion, family life, career achievement or, quite simply, the myth pattern by which they have lived so long – have collapsed beneath them. They are like climbers caught in a blizzard on the Jungfrau. They have lost all sense of direction. They grope desperately for handhold and foothold. They cling like limpets to the cliff from which a sudden gust may snatch them and whirl them into emptiness. They pray for the guide to come and pick them off the icy rockface before they die.

This woman is one of those. She is as sane as I am – probably a lot saner, according to Emma and Toni! The session we are having now is not analysis. I am simply eliciting a confession. Whether it will be a full confession remains to be seen. What will happen when she asks for absolution, God only knows! While she is walking in the garden, composing herself, I rummage quickly through her reticule. It is a precaution I have practised for years with women patients. Some carry guns; some carry knives; and I have come across some very lethal nail files.

The only significant items are the small blue bottle of prussic acid and half a dozen visiting cards tucked into the inside pocket. In the upper left-hand corner of each card, there is engraved a coat of arms – a knight's helmet, surmounting a shield, on which is the emblem of a mailed fist holding a spiked mace. The motto reads, "Nemo me impune lacessit." The name engraved on the card is: "Magda Liliane Kardoss von Gamsfeld".

Now I know, though I can never reveal, who my patient is. In Hungarian, of which I know a little from my contacts with Ferenczi, Kardoss means a fist. In Austrian dialect, the word "Gams" means a chamois.

In German, a "Hirsch" means a stag. Her pseudonym is based on a simple switch of names, easy to decipher. Subconsciously, too, she is scattering small identity clues for me to follow: her father's coat of arms, the name of his estate, Silbersee, the fact – or is it a fiction? – that her mother was an English duchess. This is encouraging. She wants me to follow the paperchase. She wants to lead me to the truth. But then, as Hamlet says, then what dreams may come! Ah, there's the rub!

I put everything back in the reticule, take down from my shelves a copy of Friedrich Creuzer's *Symbols and Mythology of Ancient Peoples*, and settle down to read until she has finished her meditation and – please God – is ready to tell me why she likes hurting people and why she has no concept of guilt.

M AGDA
Zurich
This time I take my promenade under the orchard trees in the front garden. The apples and pears are ripening. There is a scent of roses and honeysuckle and a bourdon of bees, drowsy in the still air. My head is buzzing like a hive, with a multitude of thoughts for which I cannot find words. I have never been under this kind of inquisition before, and I understand now what a large step it is to surrender your privacy to another person.

Somehow, at least for me, physical privacy hardly matters any more; but since childhood ended with my virtual banishment to the International Academy for Young Gentlewomen, I have guarded my inner life like the secrets of the Signoria. It became something of an obsession with me that only I should know the whole logic of my affairs. Indeed, the success of my adventures depended on secrecy. Now this Carl Jung is dissecting me like a corpse on the slab and I am powerless to complain.

I have hardly made my first circuit of the lawn when Emma Jung comes out, with basket and gloves and shears, to cut roses for the house. She greets me agreeably and asks:

"How is it going?"

"I don't know. Suddenly I began to feel confused. I came out here to compose myself."

"That's good. The first session is always an ordeal. You mustn't let Carl push you too hard."

"So far he's been very considerate – though I think I've made him angry a couple of times."

She makes a little shrugging gesture of resignation.

"That's his way. You just have to get used to it. I tell him it doesn't work with all patients. I'm an analyst myself. Carl trained me and I correspond a lot with Freud. I work mostly with women. Since the children came, of course, I've been very much the Hausfrau."

I am drawn to her immediately. She is open and warm and unassuming. I offer to hold the basket while she cuts the blooms. She seems glad of my company. I explain that I have practised as a physician and I am interested to know how the analytic procedure works. I am struck by the simplicity of her answer.

"For my patients, I liken the formation of a character to knitting a garment. You know what happens when you make a mistake? The whole pattern is spoilt. Then you have a choice: you can finish the garment; but it will always be botched and ugly; or you can unravel the knitting right back to the first mistake and start again. That's basically what analysis is about. It's a tedious job. The patient is scared and sometimes hostile. The analyst has to lend patience, honesty and courage. Now, remember, I've dealt only with fairly simple cases. Carl handles much more difficult ones than I would dare to attempt. Sometimes he adopts a very stern approach. I tell him that's like chopping parsley with a meat cleaver. He snorts and tells me to mind my own business. He's a brilliant man." She smiles, a small, tolerant, woman-to-woman smile, and adds an afterthought: "Difficult to live with at times, but full of concern for his patients. May I ask who recommended you to him?"

It turns out she knows Giancarlo di Malvasia, had sat next to him at lunch during the Weimar Conference, was charmed by his elegance and wit, and could make no headway at all against his Florentine snobberies. I tell her I had exactly the same experience. We laugh together. She snips a yellow rosebud and hands it to me.

"It goes with your dress – which, I must say, is beautiful. You have very good taste."

"Thank you."

"Would you let me offer you a word of advice?"

"Please! I should welcome it."

"I have found that there are two danger points in every analysis, especially for a woman. The first is when transference occurs."

This is a new word to me. I ask what it means. She explains:

"It is a process, unconscious at first, by which the patient identifies so intimately with the analyst as to become completely and sometimes morbidly dependent on him. Sometimes the analyst, too, is caught in the same trap. He – or she – becomes deeply attached to the patient, who is as dependent as a child. It's really very much like falling in love. Indeed, Freud is quite definite about it. He told me once, 'The cure is effected by love.' Be that as it may, the next danger point is when the patient is brought to see clearly the defect or the incident that has caused the neurosis. That's always a terrible shock; because it's never quite what you expect. It's rather like losing someone you love. You know it happens to other people. You never expect it to happen to you. And you have to face it alone. You cannot turn back to the guide who brought you to the moment of revelation. Forgive me! I know you're a strong and intelligent woman. You'll come through all right. I'm just trying to prepare you a little."

She is also warning me: "Keep off the grass." Normally I bristle when a woman does this to me. It's like a challenge to a duel, and I am instantly on guard. But not this time, not with this one. I find her wise and gentle and well meaning. I try to tell her so. She refuses the compliment:

"No! It's just that I've seen so many casualties in this profession. It's full of clever and dedicated people; but they're dealing with highly flammable material: the human psyche. Not all of them know how to handle it. In our group we've had two suicides and a lot of near breakdowns. Carl himself is under great stress just now. We all are in this household."

She is clearly inviting a response. I ask, gently:

"What are you trying to tell me, Frau Jung?"

"The moment I met you, I felt that you were a quite unusual woman. I was instantly attracted to you.

Under other circumstances, I should ask you to be my friend. Now, I simply tell you: be careful! Be careful of yourself; be careful of my Carl. I fear you may be dangerous for each other." She takes the basket from my arm and gives me a gentle push in the direction of the house. "Now you should go in. You are paying for every minute of time!"

I still have the rosebud. I wonder if I should make an entrance wearing it between my teeth and clicking castanets like a gypsy. Jung is reading. He closes the book and gestures at me to sit down.

"Rested and ready again? Let's move along! You were telling me you didn't understand guilt. Do you ever disappoint yourself?"

"Often."

"What do you do about it?"

"Put it to the back of my mind and get on with the business of living. Sometimes when I remember it, I curse myself for a fool."

"That's guilt; whether it is you, or the woman next door, or God himself who passes judgment on the act. Why did you have to make such a mouthful of it?"

"Because I still think there's more to it than that – and I wonder why I haven't felt it. You're patronising me, doctor! Please don't do it. I'm paying you to help me." I take out the envelope full of francs and wave it at him. "You see! There's the fee. Do you want it now or afterwards?"

I know it is an insult, but I think it is time to trade blow for blow. He is surly and combative. He slams his hand flat on the desk.

"Money doesn't buy my services, Frau Hirschfeld."

"And bullying doesn't command my confidence, doctor."

He stares at me in silence for a long moment; then he laughs, gets up, takes my hands and raises them to his lips. There is no hint of gallantry in the gesture. I find it simple and touching.

"I'm sorry. These are tricks of the trade. With a new patient one goes through the repertoire, looking for the right approach. May we start again?"

"Yes. I know I need help; but I'm not the village idiot."

"You might be safer if you were. They don't execute idiots for murder. And that's what could happen to you if you continue these bizarre exercises. Tell me what happened that scared you so much."

I gave him a terse description of the affair of my colonel at Gräfin Bette's house of appointment. He is not satisfied. He wants more.

"I need to know what goes on in your head before, during and after such an episode. Take your time. Try to step back and take a clinical view."

It isn't easy; but I manage to set it out for him.

"First, it always happens when I'm bored, lonely, depressed – when I feel ugly about myself and the world. I begin to make fantasies about sexual acts. All of them – except those with women – involve violence, and I am the aggressor! The fantasies become obsessive until I must absolutely do what I am dreaming. That's why I use the houses of appointment. There are lots of wealthy amateurs like me who pay for the accommodation but not for their partners. Of course, if there are no amateurs available, then I hire a professional. By the time the game begins, I am in a high state of excitement, rising rapidly to frenzy, and turning abruptly to black rage. In that instant, I could tear my partner to pieces. I don't love him. I hate him. If he is strong and battles with me, we fight each other to climax. If he's weak and submissive, I beat him without mercy until I come to orgasm. Until that moment, I am quite out of control. Afterwards, I am exhausted, affectionate, grateful, the best of company. I bathe and dress in my finest clothes and go out to dine."

"With your partner?"

"Never! That's a closed world. If we meet outside it, we meet as strangers."

"Or as enemies?"

"Sometimes, perhaps. Blackmail is not unknown."

He is silent for a while, studying me over the tops of his interlaced fingers. Then he takes a new tack.

"Something puzzles me about your story."

"What in particular?"

"First, you have this enchanted childhood, this magical and beautiful awakening to womanhood. Then comes a gap – which you'll have to fill in for me – your unmarried years as a student at university. Next we have a wonderful, tumultuously happy marriage which ends, sadly, with the premature death of your husband and the alienation of your only daughter. It's a shame, but at the time of your husband's death you were thirty years old, rich and beautiful. I should have laid odds on an early remarriage for you. Statistically and psychologically that's the pattern. Instead, you launch yourself on a sordid and promiscuous sex life, sado-masochist in character and so disreputable that it has brought you to the attention of the police. Can you tell me why? What set you off on this long walk on the bad side of town?"

That, I tell him, is a long and tangled story. He will need to be very patient with me. He asks if he may smoke. When the pipe is drawing well, he uses it like a pointer to gesture to me. He orders me, curtly:

"Go ahead! Go ahead! You're wasting my time and your money!"

I snap back at him instantly:

"Don't talk to me like that! You hack at me like a butcher. Leave me a little dignity."

He shakes his head in weary resignation. It is clear that he does think I am the village idiot.

"Dignity, Madame, is a thin cloak in a black winter. Please do go on!"

JUNG
Zurich
Finally, I think I have her launched on the crucial part of the story, the one which should take us to the graveyard where the bodies are buried. I use the words in a metaphorical sense; but I have the uneasy sense that the metaphor is very close to fact.

I am not well acquainted with the demi-monde. When I was young in Paris, my poverty, my Puritan upbringing and my fear of infection kept me tolerably chaste. In my better years I have managed to find some diversions from monogamy; but I have never had enough money to indulge in the diversions or perversions of the rich – which in any case are not widely available in Zurich! However, I know enough of the gilded world to understand that it protects its privacy very well, and that Magda Liliane Kardoss von Gamsfeld may be exaggerating her risky follies to conceal a far graver matter.

There is another possibility which I must not dismiss: that she is suffering as I am from a progressive fragmentation of the personality, so that it seems that all the beasts of the subconscious are set free to threaten her. In this case, it is quite possible that all I am hearing is an elaborate fairy tale.

We have not even begun to analyse her dream. I am hoping that what she is about to tell me will illuminate some of its meanings. As she begins her narrative, I notice a distinct change of style. She is no longer reliving the sensuous joys of childhood and trying to make me a vicarious partner. Now she is a young adult – sharing her delight in travel and intellectual discovery.

"Papa gave me Padua as ancient princes gave territories and domains to their sons. He made me aware that the gift was a precious one, a share of his own youth. He had studied medicine at 'Il Bo' when Padua was still a Habsburg city, where Austrian police patrolled the alleys and Metternich's spies mingled with the plotters of the Risorgimento at the Caffè Pedrocchi. Because Papa was young and Hungarian he had no time at all for Austrians, Czechs, Slovaks or Croats, and gave all his sympathies to the Italian cause. Because he fell constantly in love with Italian women, married and unmarried, he became an assiduous and practised plotter. He had a fund of tall stories about hairbreadth escapes from jealous husbands and zealous agents of the Emperor. We arrived, the three of us, just after Ferragosto, to find an apartment and complete the formalities for sojourn permits and my admission to the university. Papa lodged us in the best hotel, hired a coachman to attend us every day and set out to display my new inheritance: Venice, Vicenza, the Euganean hills, all the summer splendours of the Lombard plain – and Padua itself, the city of St. Anthony the Wonder-worker, of Livy and Petrarch, Boccaccio and Tasso and the greatest names in medical history.

"Papa boasted that he could walk the city blindfold and recite all its glories like a litany: 'Giotto and Mantegna painted here. Erasmus lectured in philosophy, Vesalius taught anatomy, Fracastorius proposed the first valid theory of contagion, Morgagni described renal tuberculosis and hemiplegic lesions, Leonardo da Vinci made anatomical drawings for texts by Marcantonio della Torre!' "

She breaks off, embarrassed by her own eloquent recitation. I encourage her eagerly.

"Please go on! You are wakening to a wider world. The experience is important and exciting. So, you fell in love with Padua?"

"With the city – and all over again with Papa. The room in my heart which had been closed since the day he forced me to go back to school was opened once more."

"And once more you were lovers?"

"No. I had a new role now. I was the son with whom he could share the experiences of his own youth."

"And you enjoyed that?"

"Of course. It seemed to complete things between us."

"Did your father prescribe the role, or did you just adopt it instinctively?"

She thinks about that for a while and then admits reluctantly:

"I would say Papa prescribed it – not in so many

words, he never did that – but by indirection, yes."

"How, exactly?"

"Well, first there was the question how I, a woman, would fit into the rough-and-tumble of medical school. Not that women students were unknown in Padua. There's the statue of a woman at the top of the main staircase: Lucrezia Cornaro, daughter of a noble family, who defended her thesis as Doctor of Letters in the great hall. But medical school was something else! So, Papa grinned at me in that funny way of his and said: 'Personally, I'd suggest a mannish look, à la George Sand! This is the age of the dandies. You'll look damned attractive in trousers. They'll think you're odd of course; but after a month you'll be part of the scenery – and you won't have their hands up your skirts at inconvenient moments. As a matter of fact, I know just the woman who can fit you out. She's the wardrobe mistress at the Fenice in Venice. She designs clothes for Duse!' So that was how I came to wear my first trouser suit, to understand how much Papa had wanted a son – and how complicated was the love he bore for me."

"Did you feel comfortable in male clothes?"

"They weren't male clothes. They were mannish in cut. That's all. But yes, I felt comfortable; I still do – but now of course I'm in fashion."

"Did you enjoy the masquerade?"

"It wasn't a masquerade. It was – how shall I say it? – an expression of attitude. I wanted to work on equal terms with male students. I wanted to be as much of a son as I could to Papa. Does that sound so strange?"

I wish I could tell her that to me, Carl Gustav Jung, it is not strange at all but disturbingly familiar. She who faces me at this moment is my Salome to the life: daughter, lover, protector – son too, perhaps. Is that what the snake means in my dream? I press my patient for more details.

"How else did your father prescribe your role as a son?"

This time she gives a small laugh of embarrassment.

"Again it was by indirection. He was worried, he said, about my physical safety. Paduan students were traditionally a rough and roistering lot. In the old days they had a pleasant custom called 'Chi va li'. Literally it meant 'Who goes there?' It was a challenge to any stranger who passed by the wine shops or brothels near 'Il Bo'. The passer-by had either to pay a tax or be beaten up by drunken scholars. So, Papa decided I had to learn to protect myself. He took me to a salle d'armes run by a Piedmontese called Maestro Arnaldo who taught me the elements of fencing and how to fire a pistol.

"Then Papa bought me a swordstick and a small pocket pistol which he called a derringer. I never used the swordstick; Lily kept that by her for protection in the apartment. The pistol came in useful on a few occasions – once with a very drunken Englishman on a boat ride down the Brenta!

"Apart from that, Papa provided me with certain male privileges: a member's card for the Club della Caccia where Lily and I could always hire a mount, an entrée to a gambling salon in Venice, which was also a place of rendezvous for lovers or lonely hearts, and a comfortable credit arrangement with the local office of the Banco Padovano. As for other entertainment, Papa told me: 'You'll have to find your own. If you're ever stupid enough to get pregnant, come straight home to me. At least you'll get a clean job and no reproaches!' "

"A clean job and no reproaches." I seize on the phrase and try to force her to examine it with me. "Doesn't that strike you as terribly cold blooded from a father to a daughter – or even to a son! Didn't he teach you any morality at all?"

She ponders the question for a few seconds, then answers with a shrug:

"Some, I suppose; but it was all very simple and pragmatic. Don't lie, because you'll trip yourself up in the end. Why steal? You have more than you can use – and besides you lose friends and end up in gaol. As for sex, it's a game until you want to marry and have children; but if you play in the mud, you'll get dirty. That was about the size of it."

"Does that still satisfy you?"

"No; but it's all I have. I have no religious sense at all. Apparently you have. That's why Gianni recommended you."

"Gianni?" The name eludes me for an instant. Then I remember: "Oh yes! Our Italian colleague. What's his name?"

"Di Malvasia. Your wife remembers him quite well. They were dinner companions at Weimar. He's a Roman Catholic. He's also homosexual and he let his family talk him into marriage. He's very unhappy; but he claims that his religion has helped him to come to terms with the situation. Do you believe that's possible?"

"Most certainly it's possible."

"I wish you'd explain how. Gianni tried, but I felt he was a rather biased witness. With him the important thing was that you could confess your sins to a priest

211

and be sure you were forgiven by God. It's very comforting; but how can anyone believe a thing like that?"

We have touched on this matter before, but briefly and tentatively. Now she has brought me back to it. I am not sure whether she wants to create a diversion, or whether she is genuinely seeking enlightenment. In either case, I must offer her a reasonable answer. I begin on a light note.

"Let's see how well they trained you in Padua. Let's define the terms. What is religion? Give it to me simply and plainly, as you understand it."

She ponders a moment and then with more than a hint of mischief in her smile accepts the challenge.

"Very well, doctor. Incominciamo . . . let's begin! Religio: a Latin noun. Generic meaning: a bond, a duty, an obligation to reverence. Religion: a system of belief and worship. Examples: Christianity, animism, Islam. Enough?"

"You're doing very well, dear colleague."

"Then will you give me a definition in return?"

"If I can."

"What is insanity?"

"Again a word of Latin derivation. Sanus, healthy. Insanus, unhealthy. Generic meaning: not of sound mind, mentally deranged. However, in common speech, the word is loosely used to cover a whole variety of symptoms, from simple hysteria to fixed delusional states or violent dementia. May I now ask the point of the question?"

"Let's put the two definitions together: religion and insanity. Let's take a concrete example to test our logic. Gianni di Malvasia believes in God, the Roman Catholic Church, auricular confession – the whole book! You believe in a god. You don't know who or

212

what he is; but you carve your belief over the lintel of your door. 'Called or uncalled, the god will be present.' Me? I believe none of that: no god, no Church, nothing but what I see, smell, hear and touch. Now we can't all be right. One of us, at least, has to be insane by definition: victim of a fixed delusional state. Which one is it? Gianni, me or you?"

"The answer, dear colleague, is simple. None of us is insane. The definitions are inadequate and the logic is defective."

The words are hardly out of my mouth when I realise that I have made a ghastly mistake. I have let her trap me into an academic argument for which I am in no wise prepared. If I allow it to continue in these scholastic terms, we shall both end with our heads against a brick wall – and she will be the one still laughing. For once, it seems, I am forced into an act of humility. I have to admit my own ignorance. I am, however, still vain enough to dress it up as wisdom. I get out my sketch pad and a heavy black pencil. I have her stand behind my chair. As she leans over my shoulder, her perfume envelops me, the nearness of her body excites me. I draw a semicircle. Then, I draw three little stick figures – man, woman and child – standing on the straight line of the diameter. I explain the illustration.

"This is man's simplest and most primitive concept of himself and his habitat. He lives on a flat earth under a domed sky. The earth is full of creatures, great and small. The sky has the sun by day, the moon and stars by night and an ever-changing pattern of clouds out of which come thunder and lightning and rain. Between the earth and the sky, the winds blow, balmy or blustery, according to the season. Man and his partner, woman, are animals who dream, animals who ask questions. Who lives up there beyond the clouds? If we walk far enough, will we fall off the edge of the land? Who made us? What happens when we die? What makes the thunder and lightning? Man and woman have no answers; so they invent them. They make fairy tales, myths which they pass on to their children. On the myths, their children build religions, systems of belief; they construct rituals, constitute authorities. They make images of their gods, build temples to enshrine them and symbolise their presence in human affairs. And everything fits nicely, everything works, until the system is overworked or overburdened by events. If the king becomes a tyrant, his people revolt and kill him. If pestilence strikes the land and the god is blind to all the offerings laid at his feet, then he is tumbled from his pedestal, his shrine is laid waste and the puzzled tribe looks for a new protector."

Suddenly she draws very close to me. Her hands touch my cheeks, then cover my eyes. Her lips brush my ear as she whispers:

"You're a very clever man, Doctor Jung. I wonder if you believe the half of it?"

A moment later she is back in her chair, demure as a schoolgirl waiting for praise or reproof. I decline to offer either. I finish my little homily, though a little less rhetorically than I began it.

"And that's the state you find yourself in now. The ethics of Eden don't work in the big world. The song birds have disappeared; now there are only vultures and carrion crows. Papa isn't there any more, and the other men you meet don't want to take his place. For that matter, neither do I!"

Instantly she is in a fury. I half expect her to leap from the chair and strike me. I note with clinical concern how swiftly the change occurs, how hard she has to battle to control herself. I smile and try to placate her.

"Don't be angry, please! I'm not mocking you. I like to be caressed – especially by a beautiful woman. But it wasn't me you were playing peekaboo with; you were re-enacting a scene: happy days in Padua with Papa."

She jerks up her head, in that now familiar gesture of defiance.

"Not all of them were happy! Don't believe that! In the end Lily and I were glad to see the back of him."

"Why?"

"For the first time in my life I saw him drunk and violent. It shocked me. What shocked me more was that Lily could handle him and I couldn't. He wouldn't let me near him; he threatened to kill me if I touched him."

"Don't you think we should talk about that?"

She gives me a pale, unsteady smile and points to my sketch.

"It isn't a pretty story like yours."

I dare not tell her now that my story is a fairy tale, a myth. It never happened. Man is a fierce and dangerous animal, ugly in rage, brutal in rut, desperate in death. The only hopeful thing about him is the angel-spirit that peeps sometimes from his savage eyes, that teaches, all too rarely, a gentleness to his lethal hand.

MAGDA
Zurich

I have to admire this man. For all his weaknesses – and there was no doubt at all about his response when I stood close to him and fondled him! – he is both sympathetic and skilful. He accepted my request for anonymity – yet already I have told him more than I intended. Still, no matter! I admire his subtlety. He has run me like a balky horse, now coaxing, now cutting at me with the whip, to make me face the first big hurdle: my strange mixed-up relationship with Papa. I am ready to take the jump now. I can feel him nursing me between his knees, giving me my head, waiting for the moment when I need him for the last lift over the bars. Well, if we get this one behind us, the others won't look quite so formidable. So, here we go, doctor dear! Here we go!

"We were installed in the apartment – the one with the Tiepolo on the ceiling and bathrooms as big as the Terme di Caracalla. Lily was breaking in the servants. I was disputing with the decorator over the matching of draperies and bedcovers. Papa had been restless for days. 'Like a prowling hound!' Lily said. 'I wouldn't be surprised to come out one night and find him baying the moon!' Then, at breakfast, he announced that he had done his duty to us and was now about to divert himself. If we needed him – God forbid that we should! – we might find him at the Danieli. Failing that, his old friend Morosini would know where to find him. Lily snorted disdainfully: 'Morosini, fiddlesticks! He's found a new woman. Oh well, at least we'll have some peace for a while!' I too was glad to have him out of the house. I was stuffed full of Paduan history: Harvey and Linacre and Dante

216

Alighieri and the 'nations' and 'tongues' who made up the foreign population of the university. I had bought all my texts. Now I wanted to nestle into the apartment that was to be home for Lily and me for the next five years. It was my first experience of housekeeping and I was enjoying it; but Papa treated the place like a post house, where the serving maids were either virtuous or boring."

I break off, because Jung does not seem to be listening to what I am saying. He is writing assiduously in his notebook. I am irritated because I am trying hard to make the story interesting. He looks up, frowning, and demands to know why I have stopped.

"Because I seem to be boring you."

"Nonsense!" He is brusque and irritable. "You're not an actress. I'm not an audience. This is a clinical interview. Just go on, for God's sake!"

I have to compose myself again. This time I give him the story, flat and plain.

"Three days later Papa came home. It was nearly midnight. Lily and I were in our night clothes, reading in the salone. We heard a battering on the front door and Papa's voice shouting obscenities. We rushed to let him in. He was drunk and filthy. He pushed his way past us and staggered upstairs to his room. Lily and I followed. When he saw us standing in the doorway he flung his valise at us and ordered us out. I went to him. He seemed not to know who I was. When I reached out to touch him he slapped me, very hard across the face, so that I staggered and almost fell. Then he began to abuse me with every foul word he could lay his tongue to. The next instant I saw Lily running at him across the room. She had the skirt of her nightdress hoisted above her knees and she was wearing

217

embroidered Turkish slippers with pointed metal toes. I remember thinking she looked like an angry hen defending her chicks. She said one word, 'Bastard!' then kicked Papa very hard in the crotch. He retched, doubled up with pain and fell writhing on the floor. Lily hustled me out of the room, locked the door on him and left him. She took me to her room, made me get into bed, fed me a large brandy and a dose of chloral hydrate and stayed with me until I fell asleep. That's a potent mixture, as you know. I didn't wake until noon the next day."

"And that's the end of the story?"

"That's my part of it. The next is Lily's; so it's secondhand. While I was sleeping she went back to Papa. He was sprawled on the floor, snoring in his own mess. She stripped him, washed him, dragged him into bed, then cleaned the room and got rid of all the soiled clothes. She let him sleep until nine, then woke him, fed him breakfast, told him what he had done to me, heard what had happened to him and sent him out to visit the barber and the Turkish baths. After that, apparently, he hired a horse and went on a wild ride through the campagna towards the Euganean hills. When he came home, just before sunset, he took me in his arms and cried like a baby. He begged me to forgive him. I did, of course. I could never refuse him anything. But after that nothing was ever quite the same. Two days later he left for Silbersee. We were both glad to have him gone."

Jung cocks his head on one side like a quizzical parrot and asks:

"Now may I know the reason for all these drunken dramatics?"

"It seems Papa had taken his new lady love to the

Fenice theatre for a performance of *Don Giovanni*. There, facing him from the opposite box, was my mother, her English husband and a youth who was clearly their son. Papa left his companion in the box, went back to the Danieli, packed his valise and, in company with the boatman, who took him across to Mestre, embarked on a forty-eight hour drinking bout that landed him, by some miracle, home on our doorstep. When he saw me, he thought I was my mother – apparently I am very like her – and he heaped on me every scrap of abuse he had stored up for twenty years. So, you see it was really very simple – and terribly sad!"

"My dear woman," Jung chides me gently, "I think it is not half so simple as you would like to make it. You've never completely forgiven your father for that night, have you?"

"No."

"What exactly was it that you couldn't forget or forgive?"

The words stick like a fish bone in my throat. They will choke me before I can utter them. Jung snaps at me:

"Say it, girl! Say it, for Christ's sake!"

"He was talking to my mother, not to me."

"I know that! Go on!"

"But he was talking *about* me. There was a – a horrible kind of triumph in his voice. He said, 'You got away; but I've got Magda! She's your daughter, but she's better at the game than you'll ever be! She'll be the best whore in the business when I'm finished with her. Your daughter! Your goddamned beautiful daughter! Maybe we'll mate her with that little colt who was with you in the box, eh?' "

219

I am crying now. I can't stop. I hate to be like this. Why has he forced me to humiliate myself so? Why doesn't he say something? I feel as if I am back in my glass ball, rolling over and over in the empty desert. Now, thank God, he has come to me. He squats in front of me, unclenches my fists and puts a handkerchief between them. Then he tilts up my chin so that I am forced to meet his eyes. They are kind and full of compassion. He gives me a funny little grin, kisses the tips of his fingers and transfers the kiss to my lips.

"Good girl! It's rough, I know; but now we can begin to make sense together. Dry your eyes. Stand up and walk around for a few minutes."

He helps me to my feet, holds me until I am steady and then leads me to his bookshelves to show me his collection of works on alchemy. It is a simple stratagem; but it works. I begin to calm down. He sits at his desk, makes notes, and, while I am still moving about, begins to chat quite casually about Papa and me.

"For you, of course, it is a terrible shock. The fairy tale has reversed itself. Your prince has turned into a toad. The words of love have changed to obscenities; the gestures of love have become acts of violence. You are no longer the object of your Papa's affection. You are the instrument of his vengeance on the woman who left him. It's all very ugly, the more so because commonsense tells you that the ugliness has been festering in his mind for years. You feel dirtied, humiliated, corrupted. Eve is cast out of Eden. She tries to cover her shame with fig leaves . . . and she begins to hate the man who shamed her. She has never been wholly sure of him. Prince though he was, she has known a long time that he was spoiled, selfish and perverted. Now she is totally disillusioned. Where does she turn? To Lily? She, poor woman, is herself caught between the millstones, at once a conspirator and a victim. No, our disillusioned princess turns to her mother, the Snow Queen, with the heart of ice. Mother was right to abandon this monster. Mother's cruelty was totally justified because it had made her invincible and invulnerable. Am I making sense to you?"

Yes, he is making sense; but I wish it were as simple as it sounds. He tells me I should reflect on what he has said. I should ask myself whether the pattern he has described fits all my behaviour. I, too, must begin to take an active part in the analysis. He looks at his watch. He tells me my two hours are up. We have made good progress. We will pick up the story at the same point in our next interview. Tomorrow perhaps, at the same time? Fräulein Wolff will make the appointment. Tomorrow? The word puts me in a blind panic. I hurry across the room. I plead with him desperately.

"If I leave now, I know I won't have the courage to come back. Don't you understand? It's like the big jump at the puissance trials. Once you're set for it, you have to go. If you check, ever so little, the horse will balk and you're kaput. Please, let's keep going!"

He does not like the idea at all. Already I am showing signs of strain. It is difficult for him as well. This is not like physical diagnosis. The indicators are often concealed in some simple phrase or gesture. If the analyst is not alert, he may miss them. I argue with him strenuously. Finally we compromise. I will go back to the hotel, have lunch and return at three. We will work until five-thirty at the latest. There is, however, a condition. By that time, I must complete what he calls my biography: the outline sketch of my works and days. The analysis will come later; but I must be prepared to put all the facts at his disposal today.

Our pact once made, he seems in no hurry to dismiss me. He watches me with a smile as I repair my make-up at the mirror. He puts his hands on my shoulders and turns me round to face him. He tells me:

"I'm very pleased with you. I gave you a rough passage this morning; but you came through it very well. Enjoy your lunch. Oh, by the way, now that we know each other, you don't have to dress quite so formally. Wear something casual. It will help you to relax."

I have a sudden impulse to kiss him, but I hold back. I do not want to be one of those foolish ones Frau Jung told me about who lean like children on their analyst. At the door I offer my hand and thank him for his help. He laughs and quotes me the old proverb: "The wounded physician makes the best healer."

As he walks me to the gate, through the apple trees and the roses in full blush, I am aware of his authority, sensible of his physical vigour. He is a big man, burly and thrusting. I wonder how he would be in bed – and which of us would conduct the symphony.

JUNG
Zurich

I watch as she drives off in that vast car and I wish that I could afford one half as large. Her opulence irritates me. It is an affront to my own modest estate. Until now, this one has never had to count the cost of anything. I was deeply offended by the way she waved an envelope full of cash under my nose; then immediately I understood it as a gesture of desperation. Her arrogance, the brutality she claims to practise, contrast strangely with the picture of the young girl systematically debauched by a profligate father and a conniving nurse.

The image of the dominant female, the "mater terribilis", is endemic in male mythology. It is repugnant to most males, but enormously seductive to others. I personally find no pleasure in it. I am more moved by the spectacle of innocence, ravaged and exploited, which perhaps is what makes me so easy a prey to dependent women, and makes this Magda Kardoss von Gamsfeld so fascinating a study in typology.

I stroll for a while, alone in the garden, trying to fit together a clinical summation. First and foremost, she is quite rational. In any court of law she would be held sane and accountable for her actions. Given her background and education, any plea for mitigation in a criminal case would most certainly fail. Why have I begun there, with an assumption of criminality? I know it is a potential in her case. I have no evidence that it is actual. The colonel in Berlin was a consenting partner, as presumably are all her other associates. The cruelty to her animals was never made a subject of charges. Nonetheless, the content of her dream, and her questions about forgiveness, her fear that she may lose courage and flee, all suggest an enormous, subconscious guilt.

Yet she has very little moral sense. In sexual matters, she is promiscuous with both sexes. In her episodes of nymphomania, she seeks catharsis by cruelty, but is more concerned with police intervention than the damage to her own psychic life. The roots of her malady are clear enough: excessive sexual stimulation during the prepubertal and pubertal life, the long standing incestuous relationship with her father, who was himself an obvious psychotic, the ambivalent situation with Lily, the surrogate mother.

Once again I am impressed most strongly by the similarity of our natures and our symptoms. The *animus*, the male principle, is strong in her, as the *anima*, the female principle, is strong in me. There is violence in both of us. There are moments when I am tempted to administer a good old country thrashing to some of Freud's toadies. I, too, am obsessive and becoming more so. I am subject to sudden rages and sharp swings into depression. I am haunted by guilt which I cannot always define, and by ambivalent sexual urges and experiences.

Even our dreams concord strangely. We are both imprisoned in a transparent world, she in the globe of glass, I behind the window of the railway carriage. We both see the stallion in a context of death and disaster. It did not escape me that, even when she was pleading to continue our session, she used a horse metaphor: the "puissance", the trial of strength for jumpers.

So, there is between us the possibility of wordless communication, of instinctive interaction, which may be either fruitful or dangerous. The good thing is that we have both been educated in the same discipline of medicine – she more richly than I, who had to settle for Basel, while she was plunged immediately into the mainstream of tradition in Padua, where arts, letters and medicine all flourished together. Perhaps, one day, if I have any success with her, we may be able to share some field of study. At least she is more mature than the Spielrein girl, who really turned into a near disaster for me!

Which reminds me, I must ask two questions. Why did she give up medicine? What will she do now that she can no longer return to her estates in Austria?

Normally Toni and I take a midday snack in my study, so that the rhythm of my work and the privacy of our communion are not interrupted. Today, because the children are absent, Emma suggests that the three of us lunch together. There is no way I can decently refuse; but these three-cornered occasions are always fraught with tension as each woman tries to assert her claims on my person and my attention.

Now I am caught in a new dilemma. I do not, as a rule, discuss my private patients with Emma. It is not fair to her; it is not fair to them. Zurich is a small city, and the doctor's wife must be above all suspicion of gossip. With Toni it is different. She is my pupil, my colleague, my archivist. She must be privy to everything that goes on. At lunch, however, both women are curious about my new case; so, to keep the peace, I have to be a little more forthcoming. Both are surprised – suspicious would be a more accurate word! – when I tell them that Magda Hirschfeld is returning after lunch. Emma remarks tartly:

"I've never known you to do that before, Carl. You've always said that two hours is the limit for an effective session."

"I know; but this is an unusual subject. She has opened up very quickly. She could as quickly lose courage and fall silent again. I gave her extra time on condition that we completed the biographical survey this afternoon."

"Has she told you her real name yet?"

It is Toni's question. I could kill her for asking it. I answer that she has not told me, but it is a matter of no consequence.

"Isn't that a bit risky? If anything unforeseen happens, you'll look a little foolish if you don't even know your patient's name."

"Not really." I am irritated by this sidelong reference to my past indiscretions, but I try not to show it. "I have a note from her medical advisor in Paris who urges me to grant her anonymity. In extreme need, the management at the Baur au Lac will have a record of her identity documents. Besides, the fact that I acceded to her first request has helped to elicit other and more relevant information."

"She's very beautiful." Emma's admiration is not altogether guileless. "And those clothes must have cost a fortune!"

"She's a rich widow – and a merry one." Toni is an excellent mimic and she does my patient's accent perfectly. " 'I have no permanent lover, but I am adequately entertained.' I'll bet she is! I'd say she was a real man eater!"

The moment she says the words, an extraordinary thing happens. It is as if I have been struck by catalepsy. I am dumb and rigid; I am no longer at my own table; I am back in the underground cave, looking up at the great, blind phallus god, while my mother's voice admonishes me: "Look well! That's the man eater!"

It seems an age before the vision dissolves and I am back to normality. Yet, neither of the women has noticed anything strange, because Emma is saying in her calm, judicial fashion:

"A man eater? She didn't give me that impression. I talked with her in the garden. She's very intelligent and altogether charming. But that doesn't signify, I suppose. I'm sure there are intelligent and charming man-eaters. What's your opinion, Carl?"

I am not going to be drawn into that little snare – not for all the tea in China! I tell her:

"I don't have too many opinions yet. I've established that there is an acute father fixation, with related sexual obsessions. I'm hoping to make some sense of those this afternoon."

Both women understand the warning; but Toni is prepared to risk more than Emma. She asks solicitously:

"Would you like me to write up your notes before she comes back. It would only take an hour."

And that would put her exactly where I don't want to have her, right in the middle of a relationship which I have only begun to nurture. Thank you, my dear, but no! You have privileges enough already. I need some private ground to stroll in! I tell her I'd rather leave the collation until the session is finished. She can take the afternoon off and I'll drop the notes round to her apartment this evening. She accepts that with good grace. It means we can have an hour or two in bed. Emma affects to ignore this transparent little stratagem and turns the conversation back to my patient.

"I'll be very interested to see how this case works out."

"Works out? I'm not sure what you mean."

"Well, she is of a certain age – in full bloom, you might say. Most of your problems in transference situations have arisen with much younger women."

There is no reproach in her tone. Her eyes are innocent of malice. I try to look wise and professional as if I have not seen the blade under the velvet sheath.

"I don't expect too much trouble. She's quite rational about her problems. She's a trained physician. If I have any fear at this time it is that, rather than face a progressive breakdown, she would commit suicide. The impulse to destruction, which is evident in her sexual relations, could vent itself finally in self-destruction."

I have said more than I wanted about the patient, but it helps us over the bad moment. Toni seizes on the thought and asks:

"How does this destructive impulse demonstrate itself?"

"Periodic obsessional nymphomania, culminating in sado-masochist episodes."

"I told you." Toni cannot resist the small triumph. "A man-eater, a real one!"

"It doesn't follow." Emma's cool retort surprises me. She is normally reticent in discussion and would rather be silent than precipitate an argument. "Perhaps she doesn't really like men; so every episode must end destructively. There are men like that, too. They would die if you called them homo-erotic, but their relations with women are always tainted by cruelty. Don't you agree, Carl?"

I can do nothing else but agree – and make my escape as quickly as possible. I understand now, with a curious lurch of fear in my gut, that Emma has taken me at my word. She will let me go my own uncertain way; she will ignore my vagaries and concentrate her life around the children; but she will do it without illusions and she will reserve the right to be what she pleases and say what she pleases in her own house . . .

Before Toni goes home for the afternoon, we have a brief, unhappy interlude in my study. She is boiling with anger and she does not mind if I get scalded, too.

"I ask you, Carl, how long can this go on? I had one session with her in the kitchen this morning. She told me she thought you could well be going out of your mind – and what was I going to do about it. She's prepared to abdicate everything except being the Frau Doktor Jung. What kind of marriage is that? Why do you and I have to skulk around like criminals because we love each other? And that scene at lunch! My God, she was slicing us up like apples for a strudel and you just sat there, nodding and consenting, as if . . . as if you were discussing the morning headlines! Well, I've had enough, I promise you, Carl! I'll jump over the moon for you. I'll pack my bags and run away with you any time you like. But I will not stay here and take this kind of torture. I won't let you take it either!"

She is deaf to argument. She will not be coaxed. In the end I let her go. By the time evening comes she will be penitent and hungry for loving. I don't blame her for being angry. I don't blame Emma either. I myself am the culprit. I am like the greedy monkey with his fist caught in the jar of lollipops. I want all I can grab. I won't have any unless I settle for one at a time!

Truth to tell, there are days, like today, when I am bored with all these well bred women and their shopping list of demands. I yearn to be out of this stuffy town and in some savage place where I don't have to argue and discuss and define, but only dance to the wild drums, and couple in the dust under the bushes, and give not a hoot in hell afterwards.

A thought, by way of postscript. I wonder what would happen if I dangled the same idea in front of Magda Liliane Kardoss von Gamsfeld. My guess is that she would say, "Fine! Let's saddle and go!" The sad thing is I've never learned to ride a horse. Still, with a good teacher, I could learn very quickly.

MAGDA
Zurich

When I left Jung's house, I felt like a child let out from school. I wanted to shout, sing, dance, roll in the green meadows. Before I was halfway to the hotel, reaction had set in. I was plunged into black melancholy. The air was heavy with menace. The hills seemed about to lurch over and bury me. When I walked through the foyer of the Baur au Lac, it was as if I had been stripped of my skin. Every glance, every whisper, was an intolerable pain.

Alone in my room I was beset by panic and confusion. My head was full of tiny mice, squealing and scurrying this way and that. I wanted to scream aloud. Instead I stood in the middle of the floor, dumb and rigid, trying to regain control of myself. When, finally, I succeeded I was trembling in every limb, bathed in sweat like a fever patient.

I stripped off my clothes, took a hot bath, put on a Japanese kimono, ordered coffee and English sandwiches sent to my room, then lay down on the bed and considered my situation. There was no doubt now: I was much more fragile than I had believed. I remembered how Professor Lello in Padua used to describe the progress of certain pneumonic infections: "The change from sub-acute to acute and critical condition is often sudden and dramatic. The patient is not prepared for it. Even an experienced physician may be taken unaware."

I myself had noted often that patients who had resisted or deferred medical treatment for a long time deteriorated very quickly once they put themselves in the hands of a doctor. Their will to resist seemed suddenly to drain away once they surrendered themselves to a professional healer. Now the same thing was happening to me. My brief separation from Jung – no more than a lunch hour – had put me in a gibbering terror, as if, in a raging sea, I had been snatched from the hand of the rescuer. When the waiter brought my lunch, I held him as long as I could with idle talk. He was a garrulous old man and I was glad of it. Anything was better than the squeak and scurry of mice inside my head.

When he had gone, I ate and drank with deliberate care, cutting the sandwiches into geometric designs, making each mouthful last a long time, trying to compare the taste of this coffee with all the other coffees I had drunk during all my years of travel. Finally, when it seemed I was stable again, planted with reasonable firmness on the plane of simple reality, I began to think of Carl Gustav Jung.

I still do not know how far I can trust him, how much I can lean on his strength and his judgment. I was touched by his offhand remark that the wounded physician makes the best healer. That reminded me again of Professor Lello, who used to deliver as his opening address to undergraduates a discourse on the Hippocratic oath. He was a man of singular simplicity and when he reached the phrase "primum non nocere . . . first do no harm" he would say: "When you get sick, when you cut your finger or drop a hammer on your toe – remember the experience. It will teach you never to inflict unnecessary pain on those who already suffer."

To this profession of faith and ethics I am, of course, renegade and traitor. I inflict pain to pleasure myself. This is why I need more from Jung than compassion and understanding. This is why I got angry with him when he dismissed the question of guilt in so offhand a fashion. This is why his talk about religious fictions, myths and fairy tales left me with a nagging question: whether he is afraid of certainty, makes a profession of doubt, because at bottom he is as confused as any of his patients.

I remembered Emma Jung's quiet but poignant words: "In our group we've had two suicides and a lot of near breakdowns, Carl himself is under great stress just now. We all are." If my guess is right, he is trying to cope with the stress exactly as I am – by sexual release. I wonder if he understands, as I do, that as time goes on you need more and get less – and pay more dearly. A Frenchman, as usual, described it best, with a pen dipped in acid: "L'amour coûte cher aux vieillards. Love gets expensive for old men." And for old women? I am not yet old, but I pay more – much more than most – for very special dissatisfactions.

But I am still hedging the question of Jung and myself. When I have laid out all my history in front of him like a pack of tarot cards, what then? I know already what I am and I hate myself. I know – at least in part – why I am so; and Jung, no doubt, can help me to understand the rest. The real question is what he can teach me, promise me, to change myself and make tomorrow endurable.

It is not an unusual question. It presents itself every day to every physician. What do you say to the patient, man or woman, in whom you have just diagnosed a terminal disease? Professor Lello used to say cryptically: "The patients will tell you that; provided you are wise enough to understand what they are saying." But I am saying so many contradictory things to Jung; how can he possibly be sure what I mean? How can I be sure myself? My fear is that, as in the past, I shall find myself in a single suspended moment, a winter time, with only a yea or a nay between living and dying.

This was Jung's first brutal admonition: "Your life is your own, Madame; don't try to blackmail me with it." Emma Jung's warning was more humane but no less definite: that the moment of revelation will be a terrible shock and that I shall have to face it alone. Suddenly the meaning of that new word, "transference", is very plain to me – plain as my sexual appetite for Carl Jung. I will do anything – anything at all – to bind him to me so that at the final moment he will not abandon me.

He would like a change of clothes? Good! Something casual? The tenue de matelot which Poiret designed for me: trousers of blue shantung, blouse of striped cotton, open sandals, a head scarf. It is more Côte d'Azur than Zurich, more yachting than Kaffeeklatsch at the Baur au Lac; but – to the devil with it! – what the man asked he shall have.

As for the biography, that will be as near to the truth as memory can bring me. I have discovered something. Sexual confession is easy with this man. Under his professional formality there lurks a lusty peasant who enjoys a dirty story and who knows that women enjoy them, too. But when we walk further and begin to explore the dark side of the moon, what then? He is full of middle-class mannerisms and, I suspect, middle-class prejudices. The bluff and bawdy peasant dresses and lives and talks like a petit-maître. If my guess is right, he runs a three-cornered marriage; but he runs it like a bourgeois and not a bohemian.

It may be, of course, that he cannot afford better. Gianni di Malvasia was quite definite that analysis is a profession in which one does not prosper quickly. I wonder what would happen if I tossed a purse of gold coins on this one's desk and said, "Come on, my friend! Let's do some really interesting research together." My first guess is that he would grab the gold, kick up his heels and be out of the house without waiting to pack a shirt. My second is that I would wake up one night and find him squatting naked at some wayside shrine, waiting for the dumb god to speak.

My third guess is that I would probably be fool enough to strip off my clothes and join him.

Time to go. Heads turn again as I cross the foyer in my Poiret sailor suit. I hear an English voice, very high coloratura, say: "My God! What an extraordinary woman!" I am tempted to turn and tell her that she doesn't know the half of it – and if her husband ever wants to get rid of her, I can offer just the right prescription!

J UNG *Zurich* By our sober Swiss standards she is dressed like a French tart. For my taste she is beautifully turned out. The trousers show off her long dancer's legs and her slim waist. The blouse emphasises the thrust of her breasts, which are neither too large nor too small. The head scarf confines her hair and shows the fine bone structure of her face, cleancut as an old cameo. I pay her a compliment. She accepts it with a smile. Then, immediately, we are down to business. I ask her to sketch for me her student life in Padua, to describe in detail any incident or encounter which was significant in her later life. Without hesitation she plunges into the narrative.

"What Papa had done to me was a terrible shock. It had, however, the same effect as his sending me back to school for matriculation. I was determined to succeed, to establish my own credentials in this new world of university life. You must understand that Padua was a proud place, where students of all tongues and nations congregated. The English and the Scots had long ago established themselves as a

235

'Nazione' with special rights and an honourable tradition. Thomas Linacre, physician to Henry the Seventh of England, Edward Wootton, physician to Henry the Eighth, both studied there. The medical schools of Leiden and Edinburgh, Philadelphia, Columbia and Harvard, all had their roots in Padua. We were taught this from the beginning. We were taught to be proud of it – arrogant if need be – with outsiders. Ours was the most reputable degree in Europe – if you'll forgive me, Doctor Jung."

I forgive her. I am happy to see her so excited by so pure a memory of youth. I ask myself cynically how long it is likely to last.

"Even now I'm a good student. If I take up something, I have to do it well or not at all. The Paduan style of teaching threw great responsibility on the student, and the examinations, both oral and written, were rigorous. So, during the week I lived a very regular life: lectures in the daytime, an hour or two in the coffee house, then home to Lily to bathe, change, dine and write up my notes for the day. I was not eager for intimacies among the students. I felt too vulnerable. I had too many secrets. I was content, at least for the beginning, to play the exotic bluestocking, unfamiliar with the student scene, dependent – oh so dependent! – on the chivalry of her escorts. I did, however, learn very quickly that Italian males are incurably spoiled by the time they are ten years old and that any woman who marries one needs the tolerance of Patient Griselda. The senior professors were the best in the world. The juniors were badly paid and of variable quality. Some of them were not above accepting an envelope of cash at examination time in return for a good report and a good raccomandazione. It was suggested to me that I might like to pay in kind. My standard reply was that if I needed to peddle my body for a pass mark, I would rather deal with the chancellor or a senior professor."

"But all in all, your academic life was uneventful?"

"Yes. I had one or two small romances; but they came to nothing. I had no taste for teaching young men the facts of life. Besides, I had made another discovery. Love affairs in Italy are highly public. Names, dates, places and sexual manners were bandied about freely. I wanted no part of that scene!

"Weekends were another matter. From Friday to Monday I lived in another world: the Club della Caccia, the gaming salon in Venice, the theatre, the whole social round. You see, there was something about Papa which I had never realised until this time. His name was good; his credit was good; and none of his women ever had a bad word to say about him. So, of course, Lily and I profited from that. Nobody quite knew where I fitted into the chronology of Papa's life. It was clear that I had been born on the wrong side of someone's blanket; so, my presence at a party was always good for an hour's gossip. Lily had schooled me well in social diplomacy. If I wanted to keep our entrée open, I should defer to the dowagers in public, permit myself to be courted respectfully by their sons, and flirt with their husbands in private."

"Did you have any thoughts of marriage at this time?"

"Not only thoughts; I had a serious proposal."

"From whom?"

"The son of a very old, very wealthy Venetian family. I believe one of his ancestors had been a Doge."

237

"But you didn't accept him?"

"I did. Why not? He was handsome, romantic, rich and just stupid enough so that I was sure I could manage him."

"What happened?"

"I had forgotten about the small print on the contract. He was Roman Catholic. I was nothing – atheist in fact. He would have to get permission from the Church to marry me. It would be a hole and corner affair. The ceremony would be performed behind the high altar or in the sacristy. I should have to take instruction from a priest to understand my husband's moral and religious convictions. I should have to promise that all my children would be brought up in the Roman faith. It was all too much. I declined with thanks. His mother was so happy she embraced me and told me I was a noble girl with a beautiful nature. She would write to her brother the bishop and have him say a mass for my intentions. My intentions being all bad ones at that moment, I didn't see the point of the exercise. However, I kissed hands and cheeks and went back to Padua."

"Broken hearted?"

"Anything but. I was wild and ready for mischief. The next week at the Caffè Pedrocchi I was telling the story – with dramatic embellishments of course! – to a group of friends from my anatomy class. This lot were all 'spiriti liberati', free thinkers and anti-clericals. One of them offered me a bet: that I wouldn't dare go to confession in the duomo. I asked what he would put up as his side of the wager. He offered a dinner for us all with a chitarrista thrown in to make music. I agreed. Then the boys – all convent trained, of course! – set about teaching me the ritual and the Act of Repentance I must recite at the end. It was short enough for me to get it word perfect in a few minutes. The next thing was to choose a good list of sins. We settled on fornication, adultery and what we agreed to call abnormal acts. This, according to my friends, was bound to lead to some interesting dialogue with the confessor, all of which I must report to my friends as part of the wager."

"And you went through with it?"

"Without a tremor. No, that's not true. When the time came I was scared. I felt as though I were meddling with something magic. I felt the same thing when . . . but that's another story. Let me finish this one."

I do not see where all this is leading; the story of the marriage proposal and her rejection of it was told in a flippant, offhand fashion like a piece of drawing-room gossip. Perhaps it was no more than that; but she seems more interested in this new anecdote, more eager in tone, more expressive in gesture. So, I make no comment and let her run on.

"On Saturday afternoon – that's confession day for the Romans; they scrub their souls in preparation for Sunday – the boys walked me down to the cathedral, and knelt with me in the prie-dieus near the confessional. There was quite a line ahead of me, so I had to wait, getting more and more nervous with every moment. What made it worse was that, up ahead in a side chapel, I could see a long line of pilgrims passing by the tomb of Saint Anthony, touching it, kissing it, leaning against the stones, as if the magic of the Wonderworker communicated itself to lips and fingertips. It was quite eerie. These devotees really believed they were in communication with the long dead saint, and that they could count on him to answer their whispered prayers. So, you see, by the time my turn came to enter the confessional, I was ready to cry off and pay the wager myself. The boys would have none of it. They pushed me forward, and the next moment I was inside the box.''

Now a curious thing happens. She gets out of her chair and begins to act out the scene, using me as the priest figure, kneeling on the floor beside me, resting her hands on the arms of my chair.

"The priest was sitting where you are now; only he was behind a little grille. His head was bowed, his chin resting on his hand. I couldn't see his eyes; but I could smell what he'd had for lunch – garlic and rough wine. I knelt down as I'm kneeling now. I crossed myself and said, as the boys had taught me, 'Bless me, Father, for I have sinned. It's been a year since my last confession. I've done a lot of bad things since then.' He asks what sort of things. 'Oh, I've slept with a lot of men. The man I'm sleeping with now is married. Sometimes I do it for money and then, often, the clients want – well – strange kinds of acts.' Then I had my big surprise. He asked quite gently, 'Have you no other way of earning a living? Do you have to prostitute yourself?' I wasn't prepared for this. I mumbled something about how difficult it was to find work. He said, 'If you're sincere about it, go to the Mater Misericordiae hospital. I know they're looking for kitchen maids and cleaners for the wards. It's rough work, but at least you'll be independent.' Then he read me a little lecture about reforming my life and trusting in God's mercy. He told me to repeat the Act of Repentance, made the sign of the cross over me and told me to go in peace and mend my life. When I walked out of the church the boys crowded round me wanting to know what had happened. I tried to make a big joke of it; but the joke fell flat. I really wanted to believe it could happen: that someone just wiped out your past with a few magic words. Silly, isn't it?"

She says it with a laugh; but she is very close to tears. I am tempted to take her face in my hands and kiss her on the lips to comfort her; but I dare not. I've been caught this way before. First, she wanted me to be Papa; now she wants me to play Father Confessor. It is very tempting to join the game; but I am her only anchor to reality; I cannot surrender my own hold on it. I help her to rise and tell her to be seated again. She pouts like a disappointed child and complains:

"You don't like my story. Did I tell it badly? It really did happen."

This little girl act is so alien to her normal persona that I fear for a moment that she may be unconsciously regressing to avoid an unpleasant reality that lies ahead in her narrative. I apply the old remedy, a sound scolding.

"For God's sake, don't try these tricks with me! You're a mature woman. Your story is fascinating – but you don't have to dress it up like a nursery tale for your dollies!"

As I hope, she is furious and storms at me:

"God damn you! Don't talk to me like that. You don't know how hard I'm working to give you what you want!"

"That's the point! You're working too hard. And I don't *want* anything. What we both need is the truth – and the more simply it is told, the better. Don't try to guess how I will react to it, or why. That's my business. How would you feel if a patient of yours wasn't

241

content with telling you his symptoms but insisted on making the diagnosis as well? Do you understand?"

Yes! Yes! She understands; but I have to understand too. Never before has she revealed so much of herself to anyone. When she falls into acting, it is out of panic, not because she wants to make an exhibition of herself. So again we have a truce. I remind her that she has mentioned another story. Something with an element of magic in it.

"Magic? Oh yes, I remember now." She begins to take on another character, the bluestocking scholar, possessor of curious learning. I wait, respectfully. "Have you ever drunk Caffè alla Borgia?"

"To the best of my knowledge, never. What is it?"

"It's coffee, apricot brandy, cream and cinnamon. It was the ritual drink at the monthly meeting of the Scotus Society."

So we are in for another game. I tell her I have never heard of the Scotus Society. She is delighted with her small victory.

"But you do know the man it was named for."

"I do?"

"You have his works on your shelves."

"Have I?"

"Indeed! It's Michael the Scot, thirteenth century. He translated Aristotle from the Arabic version of Averröes and taught the text in Toledo, Salamanca and Padua. He was supposed to be a wizard. He wrote three works that have survived: *On Physiognomy*, *On Generation* . . ."

"*On Alchemy*!" I leap to supply the answer, and so am sucked into the game. "Of course! And Padua was always known as a centre for the alchemical arts and for necromancy."

242

"Bravo!" She applauds me and hurries to embellish the story. "Did you know that there is even a version of the Faust legend in which a scholar of Cambridge named Ashbourner sold his soul to the devil in return for a doctorate of divinity at Padua. When he tried to welsh on the bargain, he was found drowned in the Cam!"

"And how did you stumble on all this?"

"I didn't stumble on it. I read up on it. The whole point about studying in Padua was that one was grounded in the liberal arts as well as physical medicine and surgery. The Scotus Society was founded in my father's time. It purported to be an association of scholars interested in occult phenomena. In fact, it was a cover for anti-Habsburg and anti-clerical activities. In my time it was still anti-clerical but rather more frivolous. Its members played at black magic, diabolism, the revival of ancient rites and cults. You've probably forgotten how fashionable all that was in its time. Remember what a big stir Huysmans made with *Là bas*?"

I am suddenly aware that she is not simply acting the bluestocking. She has read widely. She knows what she has read in its social frame. I am still not clear, however, where this story is leading. She continues:

"But I always felt uneasy with it. I wasn't an unwilling participant. As an unbeliever I had to agree that it was all mummery anyway; and most of the time it was an opportunity for some fairly theatrical sex. We used to meet at a country house near Abano, and hold our ceremonies in an abandoned chapel in the grounds. The only role I boggled at was being the naked woman lying on the altar slab during the Black

243

Mass. First, I didn't like the man who was playing Satan, and second, I felt vaguely that we were dealing with something dangerous. I didn't realise that the danger was in me, not outside."

She hesitates. I wait. If she can break through this block without prompting, it means we have made great progress. Finally, in a roundabout fashion, she does it.

"You said this morning that my story contradicted itself . . . a happy childhood, a happy marriage and then what you called 'a promiscuous sex life, sado-masochist in character'. Remember?"

I do remember. I was not aware that she had taken the question so much to heart.

"So I kept asking myself, where did it begin? How did it begin? It sounds exaggerated, but I think it began with the Scotus Society."

"With the Black Mass?"

"No, with something else. Do you have any reference here on the excavations at Pompeii – pictorial reference, I mean?"

I am sure I have. My interest in archaeology has never waned. I find the volume. We leaf through it. Finally she stops me at the pages dealing with the Villa dei Misteri, where it is believed the frescoes depict the celebration of the Isis cult. One of the most notable of the paintings is that of a young woman stripped and bowed over the knee of a priestess, being flagellated by an attendant. I glance at my patient. She is pale and upset. Her voice is unsteady.

"That's it! We acted out that whole ceremony at one of our sessions in Abano. I was the one who did the scourging. I – I was surprised how much the victim and I enjoyed it. She was studying sculpture at the School of Fine Arts. It was the beginning of an affair between us that lasted nearly a year. I didn't try to extend the experience at the time. We found other games to play. But later, when the big crisis came in my life, I suppose I was already prepared. Strange though, that it should be associated with a religious act!"

"Not so strange." I feel very gentle towards her at this moment. She is working with me and not against me as so many patients do in the early stages of analysis. So, I try to share with her some observations and insights. "Religion, sex and suffering make, perhaps, the most constant trinity of human experiences. Think about it for a moment. Religion, which we have already defined together, treats of mystery, the mystery of our origins, our ends, our relationship with the cosmos, with the mystery of pain itself. What is the symbol that confronts you in every Christian church? The crucifix: the body of a tortured man nailed to a wooden cross. Sex is an act both godlike and animal. It is the beginning of life. It is also the little death. The fury of lovers is not far from the fury of rape and slaughter. The first impulse of the disappointed lover is to inflict pain upon the once beloved. Look at the pictures of Hieronymus Bosch and you will see the pleasure-pain principle contorted into a sexual vision of hell."

"That's exactly how I have felt lately: as if hell is a madhouse and I'm locked up in it."

It is the simplest and most poignant admission she has made since we began our session. I decide to continue this way for a little while, setting conversational lures and watching how she responds to them.

"Let me ask you a question. It may sound insulting.

It is not meant to be so. You've spoken several times, quite calmly and openly, of your sexual attachments to women. They are non-violent. You find great satisfaction in them. Your relations with men on the other hand are aggressive and violent. Do you feel split between the two sexes? Do you feel yourself part woman, part man?"

"No I don't." She is emphatic but quite calm. "I perceive myself as a whole person, a woman. My tastes are not everybody's; but they are mine and I am me."

"Are you satisfied with yourself?"

"You know I'm not. I'm deathly afraid."

"Of what?"

"That this me is an incurable accident. You've seen monster births. We all have in medicine. There is no hope for them at all. They are beyond reason, beyond love, even beyond care. I feel like that about myself."

"And this is why you are grasping at various religious ideas, because admission into any religious society is associated with rebirth. Put off the old Adam, put on the new Christ. Eve, who brought about man's downfall, is now Mary, the mother of God, who carried the Saviour in her womb."

There is a long moment of silence, then she gets up from her chair, comes to me and kisses me on the forehead. I touch her cheek in acknowledgment and ask:

"What was that for?"

"To thank you for being so understanding. I'm sorry I've been rude to you."

A little cautionary bell begins to chime in my head. I tell her that I understand some of it but not all. We

246

have still a long way to go. Neither of us can afford to be complacent.

"For instance, this sculptress with whom you shared the flagellation scene and then embarked on a love affair, could you tell me more about her?"

"Her name was Alma de Angelis. She was twenty-five. She came from the South – Capua if I remember rightly. She was small and dark with long, lustrous black hair and wonderful eyes that seemed too big for her face. Sculpture, you know, is the most laborious of the arts. You're working either in stone or wood or bronze, and the sheer physical labour is enormous. One vivid memory I have is of her hands. They were hard and chapped like a labourer's. I remember asking Alma why she wanted to do such work. She told me her father was a stone carver who worked in marble for funerary monuments. She was the only child. He desperately wanted a son to whom he could pass on his skill and see him do something better than carve crying angels on gravestones. So he scraped together enough money to send Alma to Padua for study. In that respect she was very much like me; except that, a true Southerner, she was desperately afraid of having to go home and confess that she had lost her virginity. So she was ripe for the kind of affair we had; and I promised that, before she went home, I would do the traditional surgical restoration of her maidenhead! However, we broke up long before that and lost touch with each other."

"Were you happy, while the affair lasted?"

"I think so. It was one of those things that went by fits and starts: high drama one day, boredom the next. Great scenes of jealousy. Much pouting and sulking. Very Italian! There were elements of calculation for both of us. She took me into the bohemia of painters, sculptors and craftsmen of all kinds. I gave her a taste of luxury she had never known and could never have afforded. Lily coddled her and – I found later – used to send her money long after our affair was over."

"I notice, if you'll forgive my saying so, that you seem to be telling all this with considerable detachment. It's not at all like your narratives about your childhood. Why is that?"

"Because I do feel differently – very differently – about this period. After that terrible scene with Papa, I was resolved that nobody, ever again, would be able to manipulate me through my emotions. So, in a sense I became an actress. I could laugh, cry, make love, enjoy myself in every conceivable way; but the only time I took off the make-up and became the real me was at home with Lily. I knew everything about her; she knew everything about me; and we still loved each other. If ever I had any doubts, they were always stilled by that vision of Lily with her nightdress hauled up, rushing across the floor to kick Papa in the balls!"

The word comes out with such singular relish that we both laugh. I take advantage of this relaxed moment to feed in another suggestion.

"Has it ever occurred to you that in Padua you were trying to live exactly the same life as you had enjoyed at Schloss Silbersee? Your apartment was still a private Eden where very few outsiders were allowed to penetrate. True or not?"

"True, of course." She makes no demur; she goes even further. "You see, children who grow up in a big family and go to school with their peers are very lucky. By the time they're adults they're accepted as part of the group. Even their follies are open and shared; their adventures are part of tribal folklore. For me it was totally different. I was the odd girl out. I knew very early, because Lily and Papa so taught me, that all my privileges depended on secrecy. I began with one guilty secret; a Mamma who ran away and never came back. Later, of course, I had many: my sexual relations at home, my adventures at school and the whole hothouse life that I felt more and more guilty about because I couldn't share it with anyone."

It is on the tip of my tongue to remind her that in our morning session, she was most emphatic that she had never experienced guilt, could not define the sentiment. Fortunately I remain silent. She reverts to our earlier discussion of faith and forgiveness. She asks flatly:

"Do you think there is any possibility of a religious solution for me?"

"If you want one, there probably is."

"I don't understand that."

"Let me try to explain. You can go to any one of the religious groups in the world – Muslim, Buddhist, Calvinist, Roman Catholic, Lutheran, Quaker; the list is endless. You present yourself to a minister, as people came to my father, for instance. You say, 'Please, I am lost and in darkness. I am told you have the light. Will you share it with me? I am unclean, I wish to be cleansed.' The answer will be the same from everyone: "Yes, we have the light. We are willing to share it. There is always forgiveness and a new life for the penitent. Come in! Let us instruct you. Then, when you are ready and disposed to grace, we will receive you into the community of the elect.' "

"But which community do I choose? Which way is the right one? Whose god is the true one?"

"If any."

"Exactly! If any. But I have seen people calm and happy and totally at peace in religious convictions."

"I'd like to hear about the ones who impressed you most."

"Are you laughing at me?"

"God forbid! But in this kind of analysis the small facts are very important."

"Very well! Here's an example. All the time we were in Padua we used to get calls from mendicant monks and nuns collecting for various charities: hospitals, orphanages, refuges for fallen women. The monks came alone. The nuns always came in pairs, one young, one older. My favourites were a pair of Poor Clares from a foundling home near the centre of the city. The elder one was a big woman with a round smiling face who looked and talked like a village washerwoman. The younger was singularly beautiful. Her skin was white as milk. She looked as though she had just stepped out from a della Robbia ceramic.

"Lily and I would always have these two in for coffee and apple cake. They were glad to rest their feet after a long tramp round the city; so we got to know them quite well. The elder one was exactly what she looked like, the daughter of a peasant farmer near Ferrara. The other was the daughter of a judge from Siena. Her name in religion was Sister Damiana. She was highly educated, spoke English, French and German, and played the piano beautifully.

"When I asked what had made her enter the convent, she gave me a very strange answer. 'I was called. I answered.' When I asked her how she was called – by voice or trumpet or heavenly post horn – she laughed and said: 'It's like falling in love. There are no words to describe it.' When I asked her if she'd ever fallen in love, she said yes, she had even become engaged, but her fiancé had died a month before the wedding.

"She used to call me Dottoressa, and when the big typhoid epidemic hit Padua, she asked Lily and me to help with nursing the children in the institute. All of us senior medical students were recruited for public health duty; so by the time I got to the orphanage, I had often been on my feet for eight or ten hours. But the devotion of those women, especially my young friend, shamed me and kept me going. Come to think of it, she was the only one who ever could shame me, without saying a word!"

"Did you ever share any confidences with her?"

"About my own life? Never. Damiana never asked; and what I had to tell was hardly convent talk. However, there was one strange day, just before the epidemic began to subside. I was sitting on a bed in one of the dormitories, trying to spoon liquid into a frail little mite who I knew was terminal. I was raging inside about the stupidity and ignorance that caused this kind of outbreak to happen. Damiana came and laid her hand on my forehead and said softly: 'Such stormy thoughts! So much anger! Such a hungry heart! Be calm! Love will come to you in his own time.' I burst into tears. She held me against her until I was quiet again. I remember thinking that I couldn't feel her breasts through the coarse cloth of her habit."

"Did you keep in touch with her afterwards?"

"She died the year before I left Padua. She had T.B. but she could have been saved. I've hated those primitive conventual orders ever since. They may be better now; but in Italy in those days they'd set out to

251

save the poor and ignorant for Christ – and kill off their own people with malnutrition, overwork and sheer inhuman neglect."

It is the first time I have seen her angry about anyone but herself. I content myself with a quiet comment.

"It's plain you were very fond of her."

"I loved her. I loved her in a way I've never known before or since. Thank God she never knew the kind of woman I was!"

"Perhaps she did."

"She couldn't have. She died too soon. I should be glad of that, I suppose."

She is very near to tears. I note how hard she tries to hold them back. Finally she manages an unsteady smile and demands to change the subject.

"Very well. What else can you tell me that was significant about your life in Padua?"

"Significant? That's a loaded word if ever I heard one. Significant. Let me think. Well, for one thing I became a good physician. I understood what the trade was about. I was deft in surgery and accurate in diagnosis. Professor Lello used to say I had everything a great doctor needs – except heart. He was right. I was always plagued by the idea that medicine is a profession dedicated to futility. All our patients die in the end. We bury our successes and our failures in the same grave."

There is something odd about the last phrase, but I cannot for the life of me think what it is. It is like hearing a distant bell with a tiny crack in it. I ask one of the questions I have on my list.

"Why did you finally give up medicine?"

She looks at me in mild surprise.

"Oh! I thought I'd explained that. I nursed my husband during his final illness. That was one failure too many. I quit the game for good."

I am still interested in how she buried successes and failures in the same grave; but no matter, I make a note and hope that it will clarify itself later. I ask whether there is any more useful material to be mined out of the Padua period.

"What else? Oh yes! Lily had a big, big love affair. It lasted only a year – less than that even! – but it was the most extraordinary thing that had ever happened to her. One weekend Lily and I were riding in the hills when we came to a tiny village called Arqua. Lily, who carried a Baedeker even to bed, announced that this was the place where Petrarch had lived during the last years of his life and that the signatures of Lord Byron and Teresa Guiccioli were to be found in the visitors' book.

"We found Petrarch's house, perched high on a hilltop with the poet's cat, mummified, in a glass case over the lintel. We found Byron's signature – and Teresa's, too. We strolled in the tiny garden overlooking the hills and the vineyards. Then, just as we were mounting up for the ride home, Lily's great love came ambling up the road on a big bay hunter."

She is obviously enjoying this part of the story, so I let her savour the drama of it.

"A beautiful horse and a most extraordinary rider! He was not young. We discovered later that he was in his late sixties; but he carried himself like a prince in the saddle, ramrod straight, with his great arrogant head held high, like Donatello's Gattamelata outside the duomo in Padua. His face was lean, with a long beard and heavy drooping moustache. He had a great hooked nose like an eagle's beak, a pair of dark piercing eyes and a thin slash of a mouth which rarely smiled and always carried a hint of cruelty. He reined in and saluted us in Italian. Lily gaped at him for a moment, then in purest Lancashire announced:

" 'My God! I know you!'

"The stranger grinned – and the dark eyes softened into a boyish twinkle.

" 'You do Madame? Then for the love of God tell me who I am. I should hate to perish in ignorance.'

" 'You're – you're that explorer fellow. Richard . . . I'm sorry, Sir Richard Burton. I've seen your picture in *The Times*.'

"He swept off his hat and made extravagant thanks.

" 'Madame, you have saved my day from utter disaster! I am indeed the explorer fellow, presently Her Britannic Majesty's consul in Trieste. You find me on vacation from my post, unchained from my desk and mercifully on leave from a wife I love dearly but cannot tolerate for more than a month at a stretch. That's not her fault. I am myself a quite intolerable spouse.'

"After that Lily made a breathless introduction of herself and of me. We did a second tour of Petrarch's house and garden, stood respectfully under the fig trees while our new acquaintance declaimed two of the *Sonnets to Laura* and then rode back with him to the club to return our horses and pick up our coachman. The obvious move was to invite Burton to dinner. He accepted. Over the meal, he was charming and outrageous and full of splendid stories about his early days in the Sind, his ill fated exploration with Speke and so much more that by the time he left, Lily and I were floating all over the map.

"On the next visit – only forty-eight hours later – he was taken ill with a violent attack of malaria. We put him to bed in Papa's room. I examined him. It was clearly a chronic case. His liver and spleen were grossly enlarged. I prescribed for him; Lily nursed him. By the time he was well enough to travel again they were lovers. When I remonstrated with Lily, she retorted: 'What did you expect? He's an urgent man. I'm a ready woman. As for his lady wife, she must have had a lot worse competition than me. He's done everything and seen everything – and thank God I was practised enough to be ready for him!'

"Then – this was tender and rather sad – she took my hands and held them against her breast and begged me, 'Please, Magda, love! You won't try to steal him from me, will you?' I swore I wouldn't and I meant it. He was too old for me and – I know this will sound strange – he frightened me. He knew too much about everything. He had made the pilgrimage to Mecca, disguised as an Arab doctor. He had entered the forbidden city of Harar in Ethiopia. He had spied for Napier in the Sind, and written a scandalous account of male and female prostitution in Karachi which dogged him for the rest of his career. He had no morals to speak of. He had killed men. He was engaged in translating the two erotic classics of the Arab world, *The Thousand and One Nights* and *The Scented Garden*. I always had the feeling that he was looking into my head and laughing at what he saw.

"His attitude to Lily was quite different. He loved her earthiness and her spit-in-the-eye vulgarities. When he got too boisterous or too angry drunk, she could scold him into submission. He came at all hours and went away without warning; but his pockets were always full of odd gifts: a bracelet of elephant hair, an amulet of carved amber, a bezel ring from some Balkan goldsmith.

"One day he arrived just before noon. Lily was out with the maid buying fruit and vegetables. I sat down with him to have coffee. He took me by the shoulders and turned me to face him. His grip was like iron. His dark eyes were hypnotic. He spoke very quietly, almost in a whisper, 'You're a wild one, Magda. I used to tame falcons in India, so I know what you need. The only reason I haven't touched you is because I'm too tired to care. Lily's just right for me. She knows what I want and when I want it and when I just need to curl up and sleep. Problem is I'm not going to be around much longer. You know it. You were punching around at my liver during that last malaria attack. I've got all sorts of other bugs that I've picked up from Salt Lake in Utah to Jeddah in Arabia. I'd like to leave something for Lily; but I'm a poor man and whatever I have goes to my wife Elizabeth. She's a good woman, with the heart of a lion; but I've always needed a string of fillies and sometimes a colt or two for a change. So I've brought something I want you to hold for Lily and give to her when I'm gone. She'll get a laugh out of it. And if I leave it to Elizabeth, I know she'll burn it.'

"He handed me a small, flat bundle sewn in canvas with a sailmaker's stitch. He begged, 'You won't open it, will you? That's Lily's privilege.' Then he gave me a long appraising look. I knew he was deciding whether to kiss me or not. Finally he shook his head and grinned at me. 'No, no, no! It's too early for you and too late for me. I'd like to be young enough to enjoy you. I'd hate to be the man who failed you.' He died three months later. Lily was broken hearted. It took her a long time to recover. She kept the package for weeks before she could bring herself to open it. Inside, written in Burton's own hand, was a translation of *The Scented Garden*. We used to sit up in bed reading it to each other. Later, I heard that Elizabeth Arundell Burton was accused of burning this and a number of other Burton's erotica. Perhaps she did and this was a copy which he made specially for Lily. I don't know. I presume Lily still has it. I wonder what the parson will say when he finds it after her death among her belongings. I understand she's become such a prim old lady!"

She ends the story on this odd elegiac note; so I am almost sure we have done with Padua. She herself is weary of the tale. I suggest a few moments' break and offer her a brandy or a cordial. We both settle for the brandy. By way of a diversion we rummage together through my books and come up with more snippets of useless information on Michael the Scot. We find that Dante has him in the fourth circle of hell, that Boccaccio rates him among the great masters of necromancy and that he crops up in a fresco in Florence – a small, slight fellow with a pointed beard, dressed like an Arab. I also learn a little more about my client. She knows very well how to use research material. She does read Latin and Greek – but then so did Messalina, who was a very bawdy and a very dangerous lady!

I must have poured an over-large dose of brandy. I can feel it going to my head. Normally I like the first wave of relaxation that comes with a noggin of liquor; but not now. We are coming up to the moment which the old Greek healers called the "experience of the god". It is an instant of great danger in which the patient will either submit to the Presence or run berserk in a destructive fury. So, dear Madame, if you're ready, let's recollect ourselves and begin our consideration of the last things, your private Eschaton, the day of judgment and dissolution, when the scales fall from your eyes and you will see everything plain!

MAGDA
Zurich

I see now why Jung was reluctant to prolong our session. It is only four in the afternoon and I am already conscious of fatigue. The drink helps at first. It makes me feel relaxed, open and agreeable; but it also loosens my controls and makes me vulnerable to any sudden pressure from outside or stress from within. I know I have been talking very freely, and I am surprised how much forgotten material has been revealed by Jung's curious inquisition. I have not thought of Sister Damiana or Alma de Angelis in years. As for Lily's affair with Sir Richard Burton, I thought that was consigned to the attic decades ago!

Jung tells me that he still wants me to follow the chronology of my life, but not to linger too long on tenuous or unimportant recollections. He says, quite rightly, that the landmarks are usually visible from a long way off. I tell him that the two years after university were very important in my personal development, and it is essential to spend some time on them.

I say this not entirely without guile. I know my

history. He doesn't. I need time and a new infusion of courage to get me to the moment of truth and past it. Jung understands, I think. For all his burly frame and his very obvious reactions to my female presence, there is a lot of the female in him. There are moments when he stops reasoning and guesses – and the guess is generally right. I can sense, too, when he is indulging me and when he is moving to block me. This happens always at moments when I am trying to play a confidence trick on myself.

However, I think I have convinced him that I do have a mind, that I read more than fashion magazines, and that I can spell all the words in the medical dictionary. So, he asks, are we ready? I assure him we are. He opens with a simple affirmation.

"You left Padua with a medical degree."

"A very good one, in fact."

"What plans did you have for a future career?"

"They were still vague, because I hadn't yet finished my training. Papa had procured me an internship at the Allgemeines Krankenhaus in Vienna. Your colleague Freud worked there too, if I remember rightly. After that I wanted to do post-graduate study in Edinburgh or London; but Papa, for obvious reasons, wasn't too happy about that. Afterwards? Well, I had a vague idea that I would like to design my life as Papa had done: keep Silbersee and practise in Salzburg or Innsbruck. But first there was the grand ocean voyage which Papa had promised me as a reward for my graduation.

"I was ready for change. We all were. Papa was in his fifties now, still chasing the girls, but beginning to wonder whether he shouldn't find some comfortable, titled widow with a competence of her own and settle down! Lily, beginning to be middle-aged, was more possessive and occasionally rasping. Me? I was tired. The final year had been brutally hard: long hours at the hospital, late nights with my texts, very little diversion – and, to cap it all, a bout of bronchitis in the winter that I simply couldn't shake off. I had no regular lover and little inclination to go chasing one. All I wanted was to get through the year and earn a freedom I had never enjoyed."

Jung looks at me with a mischievous grin and says:

"That's an odd thing to say. I should have thought you were the freest of mortal women, with your own establishment, plenty of money, a complaisant chaperone, and even more complaisant parent."

"You don't understand. What I wanted most to be free of was my past – all the things that seemed to set me apart from other people. The voyage that Papa had planned would, I hoped, be a punctuation point from which I could begin a new chapter."

"Did it turn out so?"

"Yes, it did. Though not quite as I expected. The voyage itself was a wonderful experience. We embarked at Rotterdam in first class accommodations on the flagship of the Royal Dutch Line: separate cabins for each of us because, as Papa put it, 'We're all old enough to need privacy!' My God! I thought, so late in the day! Our outward route lay through the Suez Canal to Aden, Colombo, Singapore, Surabaja, Saigon, Shanghai and Hong Kong. Our fellow passengers were a mixed bunch of merchants, officials of the Dutch colonial service, British traders, and an assortment of wives and children. Don't worry! I'm not going to give you the whole Baedeker tour; but I loved every day and every night of it. I did feel free. I did feel a woman in my own right.

"I made friends with the ship's doctor, who, once he got over his astonishment at finding a colleague in skirts, became a comfortable if somewhat persistent escort. I was, however, much more interested in a man who joined us at Aden. The moment she saw him Lily clutched my arm and said, 'That's what Dick Burton must have looked like when he was a young man!' He had the same arrogant bearing, the same hawk face and piercing eyes and cynical mouth. But his manners were ten times better than Ruffian Dick's. He spoke softly, drank little and was full of small, unobtrusive courtesies. His name was Avram Kostykian, which caused Papa to dismiss him with a shrug: 'Armenian Jew! You find 'em everywhere there's trade. I wouldn't spend much time on him if I were you.' I didn't like Papa's tone and I told him so. I also told him I would keep what company I chose. He shrugged and walked away. It was the first time I had realised how deep his prejudice was. When I told Lily, she laughed and said I didn't know the half of it. No Jew in Austria could ever hope for promotion in the army or in the civil service. Even an army surgeon rarely got above the rank of captain."

I am surprised to see Jung blushing and fidgeting with his pen. I ask him pointblank:

"Don't you like Jews either?"

"Not very much." At least he has the grace to be frank. He also feels the need to explain himself further. "My colleague Freud is of course a Jew; but even with him I run up against certain limitations which are peculiarly Semitic. The Aryan heritage, the Aryan unconscious, is much richer in potential than the

Jewish." He grins and shrugs in deprecation. "I'm probably just as prejudiced as your father. None of my affairs with Jewish women has ever turned out very well!"

I try not to show it, but he has disappointed me. I ask myself: if he is prejudiced against a whole race, how will he be when he knows my very special category? Also, his confession of other affairs sounds more like a boast in bad taste than a slip of the tongue. He knows I have met his wife. I would rather he kept his affairs to himself. And if they haven't turned out well, must it be the woman who is to blame? I find a perverse satisfaction in extending the story of my encounter with Kostykian.

"He was, as Papa had surmised, a trader, but a very special one. He dealt in precious stones: rubies, emeralds, sapphires, but especially in pearls. He travelled all over the East, wherever the pearl divers worked, to bid for their stocks. When he found I was interested, he would sit for hours showing me his treasures, telling me tales of the divers and the captains who drove them until they collapsed with the bends, and the Chinese and Indian and Malay merchants, who sat around for hours betting on the value of a pearl, as the 'peeler' worked on it. Do you know what a peeler is?"

"I confess I do not, Madame. But I'm sure you will tell me."

For some reason Jung is huffy and a little impatient. I tell him he should be interested because the peeler does exactly what he, the analyst, is trying to do with me.

"A pearl is made up of many layers of nacre deposited by the oyster over the original irritant in the shell. Sometimes even a fine pearl has defects in the outer skin: pinhole pittings, tiny indented marks. These greatly reduce the value of the jewel. However, if they are not too deep, they may be removed by peeling off layers of nacre until you reach a perfect, unblemished skin. It's delicate, finical work and a mistake can be very costly. So you can imagine the scene in a Malay kampong or a Chinese godown: all those impassive faces watching as flake after flake of skin is removed, no one knowing whether the whole pearl will be pared away or whether a priceless beauty will be revealed. It takes a lot of nerve to bid blind on the ultimate value.

"Kostykian told the story wonderfully. He had a poet's feel for places and people. And, best of all, he taught me how to do the peeling! He challenged me, saying, 'You're a surgeon. You've got a scalpel and a pair of tongs. Here! I'll show you.' He handed me a pink pearl, nearly a centimetre across. It was badly pitted and probably worthless. He showed me how to start the operation and continue it with tiny, patient strokes. At the end of two hours I had a perfect pink pearl about a third of a centimetre in diameter. Kostykian gave it to me as a present. I had it mounted in a pendant; but I mislaid it somewhere, after I was married."

"A very charming story." Jung makes a dry comment. "But can you tell me what it has to do with our concerns?"

His manner irritates me as much as his slighting attitude to Jews. I give him a testy answer.

"Yes I can. Kostykian was one man who gave me a lot and never asked anything of me. He took me ashore with him. He walked me round the jewel marts

263

in Colombo and Bangkok. He showed me how to read a stone; the silk in an emerald, the distribution of colour in a sapphire, the difference between a Siam ruby and the rich pigeon blood of Burma. He was so attentive and yet so apparently passionless that I wondered whether he was like Gianni di Malvasia and preferred the love of men. The night before we parted in Singapore, he told me the reason: 'I'm married. I have a wife and four little boys in Alexandria. They are the centre of my life. Although I am home only four months of the year, they are with me, every day and every night. I live a strange existence, as you see. I meet strange people in wild places. Life is cheap, women are cheaper. I am often offered a girl, just for the first option on a big pearl. I am a man of strong passions. I have to keep them very much under control, even in trade. Jewels are eerie things. One can lust after them just as one lusts after a woman. I know that once I slip, once I let down my defences, I am lost. I shall become like a spinning top whirling from port to port, arriving nowhere. You, my Magda, are the biggest and the sweetest temptation I have ever had! Now, let's kiss good night and goodbye. I'll be off the ship before you're awake in the morning.'

"When I went back to my cabin I found a package on the pillow. Inside it was a small but very pure sapphire, rich blue and quite brilliant. There was a note too. I remember it word for word. 'The weight is two carats. There is a small inclusion at the apex, but it will take an expert to spot it. Nothing is perfect in this world. For the first time in my life, I'm regretting something I haven't done. Thank you for the great, great pleasure of your company. Avram.' "

"I wonder." Jung laces his hands together, makes a church steeple of his fingertips and peers at me over the top of it. "I wonder why you tell that story with so much satisfaction."

"Because after all my other affairs, from Papa and Lily onwards, I have always felt used, deprived of some special freedom that should have been mine by right. I was never quite sure what it was – even a whore's wage on the mantelpiece might have helped! But with Avram Kostykian, the Armenian Jew, everything was a free act between friends. When I said as much to Papa he just grunted and said grudgingly, 'Well, it's always a mistake to generalise.' Lily gave me a surreptitious kick under the table and a terse reminder. 'Never say I told you so. It's the height of bad manners!' "

"Perhaps that's the answer to your problem." Jung leans back in his chair and chuckles mischievously. "Find yourself a virtuous married Jew who brings you sapphires and doesn't want to sleep with you!"

"Don't think I haven't considered it!"

I laugh in spite of myself. Jung presses on impatiently.

"Is there anything else you want to tell me about the voyage?"

I mention the Malay who ran amok in Surabaja and was shot in front of our eyes. I speak of the similarity between my own violent fugues and his demented, murderous dash through the streets. Jung writes copious notes at this point and then poses an unexpected question.

"The end for the man amok is a bullet in the head. Are you saying death is the only solution for you too?"

"It may be. I have to face it, don't I? If you can't do anything for me . . ."

He slams his hand on the table and launches into a tirade.

"I told you at the beginning! Don't blackmail me with your life! I didn't give it to you. I can't take it away. I'm not a miracle worker either. I don't cast out devils – though I know some Gadarene swine I'd like to send them into! Analysis isn't surgery. You don't chop out the diseased organ, sew up the patient and send her home to tea and sandwiches. This is a mutual effort to define the cause of a psychosis and, if possible, eliminate it, or at least make it possible for you to live with it. Live, you understand! Live! Of course, if you want, you can think yourself into dying, like the native under the witch doctor's curse. If that's what you want, I can't help you!"

This time his anger is not an act. I realise that he, like me, is getting tired. I must not tease him any more. I must not let him tease me either. I apologise. I tell him that I understand we are both under stress, that I really am trying to cooperate. He is quickly mollified and smiles at me again.

"At least you know now that analysis is not a game for children. When you start rummaging about in the unconscious, you never know what strange animals will pop out. Try to sum it up for me. Was the voyage a success or not?"

"For me a total success. I saw a world I had never expected – a beautiful, cruel, indifferent world in which an individual existence meant nothing. In China girl babies were exposed on rubbish heaps. In Japan fathers sold their girls into prostitution. Through all of Asia, millions died in floods, famines and epidemics. In India the British despised the off-whites they fathered. In Java the Dutch married them. In Siam the king dispensed death at every meeting of his ministers. In Borneo the Dyaks hunted human heads for trophies. These experiences put me in my place – my small obscure place – and I was grateful.

"Even so, it was good to be back at Silbersee, with three months still in hand before I had to take up my appointment at the Allgemeines Krankenhaus in Vienna. The estate had aged like all of us. Coming home for vacations I hadn't noticed the change so much; but now it was clear that everything was running down. The Schloss and the tenant houses needed paint and plaster, our furniture needed recovering, the gardens were scraggy, the accounts untidy, the staff indolent and offhand. Papa was away so much that when he came home he wanted simply to relax and play the country gentleman.

"For the first time I understood how much a son would have meant to him at this period of his life. For the first time too, I understood how spoiled and self-centred a creature I was. I knew that I could run Silbersee. With Lily as my lieutenant, I could run it and still do my internship in Vienna. The problem would be to get Papa to agree. I had no idea of the disposition of his will. I knew very well the disposition of his mind: that women were made for bed but not for business. A frontal attack on his prejudices would get me nowhere.

"My opportunity came when, a couple of weeks after our return, he fell ill with pneumonia. It was a bad siege and it left him very weak and more dependent than I had ever seen him. He was quite childish at times, querulous and demanding. Finally, after a long talk with Lily, I decided to face matters out with him. I was amazed at my own vehemence. I told him nobody could play as he played, run a busy consulting practice, keep a steady hand in the operating theatre and manage a country estate the size of Silbersee. I couldn't run his practice and I certainly wasn't going to orchestrate his love life; but I could and would take on Silbersee, on two conditions: that I knew it was deeded to me and everyone else knew I was the Chief, the Boss, the Arbeitgeberin!

"Papa tried to waltz me round the linden tree to the tune of 'Tomorrow, someday, very soon'. I told him plainly that if he didn't like the deal, I was leaving and setting myself up in Vienna. I mightn't make a fortune; but at least I would eat and stay out of the rain. Finally, male pride being satisfied, he consented. Papers were drawn deeding Silbersee to me with an entail that would stop my husband from taking possession if I married. During Papa's lifetime we would share the income equally. After his death, I would undertake to pension Lily. Whatever other commitments Papa had – to women or children I didn't know about – he could provide out of his personal funds, which I knew were substantial. So, finally, I was a landowner, with my feet firmly planted on my own soil."

"From which," Jung reminds me coolly, "you are now in exile. Have you thought where you are going to go, what you are going to do?"

"Silbersee is up for sale. I'll probably do very well out of it. War in Europe seems inevitable. The armies are paying high prices for brood stock and stud farms."

268

"And where will you go then?"

"At this moment I don't even know where I shall go when I leave Zurich."

"Perhaps we may induce you to stay in Switzerland."

"If you can help me, my dear doctor, I'll be happy to take up residence next door!"

"My wife might object to that; but I'm sure we could find you something quite beautiful round the lakeshore."

It is one of these light-headed exchanges which carry a whole gamut of sexual overtones. I am still happy to respond; but after his comments on Kostykian and on his own affairs with Jewish women, I am wary. He adds an unexpected afterthought:

"Joking aside, if you are to continue in analysis with me, we will need to be reasonably close to each other and to establish a routine of conference and communication. Occasionally I find it helps to visit a patient, though I do not make a practice of it. However, we can discuss that later. To get back to your life story. You were the mistress of Silbersee, you were a trained physician with a bright career ahead of you. You had learned that in the cosmic scheme, your unconventional past was of little consequence. In short, all the odds were in your favour. What happened next?"

"I took control of Silbersee, with Lily as my faithful adjutant. I scoured every corner of the estate, went over every detail of the accounts. I promoted Hans Hemeling from head groom to studmaster and began selling off the scrubby breeders that had been our stock-in-trade for too long. I made Lily chatelaine of the Schloss. She could storm like a fury over dusty furniture and wasted food and the next minute have the whole staff in fits of laughter with her bawdy jokes in dialect. We were being cheated in the Stüberl and the guest house and grossly underpaid on the timber contracts. Our cattle were sold through a local auctioneer, who played games with a bidding ring of butchers from Salzburg and Innsbruck.

"I went around swinging right and left, not caring whom I hit. At the end of the first month we almost had a new peasants' revolt. I was nicknamed *Zickzackblitz*, forked lightning, because nobody knew where I was going to strike next. But when painters and carpenters began to work on the Schloss and afterwards on the houses of the estate, when the gardens began to look tidy and we got better prices in the market, and Hans and I came home with our first good Arab stallion and a dam to breed with him, then the atmosphere changed. Fräulein Zickzackblitz became the *Meisterin*, and word of our reformation began to spread around the countryside.

"Then Lily suggested that we set up a local hunt club on the English model, with some fashionable trimmings that we had learned in Lombardy. It would give us a market for our horses. We would make the Stüberl the assembly point for the meet. We would import English and German hounds and breed them for the pack. Papa loved this idea. It gave a whole new dimension to his rather faded social life. After the first meet, he remarked happily, 'Marvellous. I never knew there were so many good-looking women still hiding in the woodwork!'

"By the time I left for Vienna, the place was a going concern again. I could trust Lily and Hemeling. I myself would be back every two or three weeks to check the operation and enjoy my own domain. The night before I left, Papa asked me to join him for brandy in his study. This was a rare event. He was never one for face-to-face confidences. He liked to float through our domestic life like a philosopher in residence, bestowing words of wisdom, an offhand caress to me or Lily, an enthusiastic pat on the bottoms of the servant girls – and only the illusion of intimacy. This time, however, he had obviously taken a great deal of trouble to prepare a special speech for me.

" 'We've had a funny life, Liebchen, all three of us; but we seem to have survived it pretty well. You've done better than I ever dreamed. I'm very proud of you, even if I'm not very proud of myself. I wish there were some way I could pass my title on to you, but there isn't. Even if you have a son, there's nothing I can do except petition the Emperor to grant him a patent of nobility. One of my girl friends at court might just manage to slip it under his nose. There'd be a bar sinister in the coat of arms, but that wouldn't matter. The point is that I can't make a petition until there is a grandson. So, that's the question: what are your thoughts about getting married? I know you've got a year to do in Vienna. There's a year in England, which I'm not happy about; but you can do it if you want. After that, you're about as ripe as any girl can risk being for a decent marriage. You've got a handsome estate in your own right. You're damned good looking and although I know you don't live like a nun, you've got to settle down some time. Question is, with whom? I don't want to see you picked up by some shabby merchant with lots of money and no breeding. On the other hand, if we're talking of breeding it

271

means someone who's coming into the marriage market second-time around – a widower in his forties perhaps, with a young family or, better still, without. The problem is that all the young bloods are already pre-empted for girls just coming out at court. I'm sorry, but that's the way it is. You're ten times the woman they are; but your birth certificate betrays you. At least you haven't had to become a dancer or a chorus singer! You do have a profession and money in your own right. So, what are we going to do about it, eh? I can have Louisa von Grabitz scout the market if you like. She charges a fee, of course; but she's the least gossipy of all these matchmaking dowagers.'

"The longer he talked, the angrier I became. I kept thinking: the gall of the man! I didn't ask to be born. I didn't ask to be Papa's child bride! And if I was damaged goods in the marriage market, pray tell, whose fault was that? Finally I burst out: 'The fact is, Papa dear, I don't want to get married yet; and when I do, I'll choose my own husband, even if I have to make another trip to Hong Kong to find him!' "

"And how did your father take that announcement?"

"With relief I think. He didn't really want to be bothered. He'd done his duty. If I wanted to skip to the moon on a wooden leg, that was my affair. Whatever his shortcomings, he had kept me out of the music halls and off the streets. In his curious, élitist ethos that was more than most bastards had any right to expect from their progenitors."

"So, when you went off to Vienna, you parted friends?"

"Only just. That night when Papa and Lily were getting ready for bed, Papa asked me to join them –

'Just a cuddle, Liebchen, for old times' sake!' I was about to tell him the old times were long gone and I never wanted to hear of them again, when Lily – God love her! – saved us from another nasty scene. She laughed and said: 'Listen, you old goat! Don't waste yourself on the overture. Save yourself for the big aria!' Then she dragged him off to the bedroom singing 'La ci darem la mano'.

"That night I dreamed of my mother. It was midwinter. I was waiting in the snow outside the gates of Schloss Silbersee. Mother came driving by, in a sleigh drawn by white horses with silver bells. She was wrapped in white ermine. I knew it was she from a long way off. I stood out in the middle of the road and waved to the driver to stop. Instead he whipped up his horses and drove right past me, while Mamma sat there, with the cold, cruel smile of the Snow Queen."

Jung ponders this piece of information for a while then turns back through his notes. He marks several passages and remarks:

"Here's something else I find curious. Why, in all these years, did you never press for information about your mother – if not from your father, then from Lily? Why didn't you just go to London or to your birthplace and find out what you wanted to know? It would have been a very simple piece of detective work. Another thing I can't understand is Lily's reticence about the matter, especially when you were older and capable of understanding."

"The answers, my dear doctor, are so simple that they're pathetic. Why didn't I press for information? Because I'd been conditioned all my life not to do it. Why didn't I go to England and ferret out the truth? Because I was afraid of exactly what happened in the dream: that my mother would cut me dead in the street. Why didn't Lily tell me the truth? Because, as I've only recently discovered, Lily was the reason for the break-up. Lily was sleeping with Papa during my mother's pregnancy. Lily was conspiring in my seduction to hold on to Papa. Lily was the perfect opportunist. She loved me, yes! No question, no doubt! But Papa paid her wages and what Papa demanded, Papa got. What he needed most of all was silence. Until the day she left to go home to England, what Lily told me about my mother tallied exactly with what my father told. My life, my happiness depended on them both. Why should I risk them for the cold, disdainful smile of the Snow Queen? That's why I've never tried to intrude on my daughter's life. She probably feels the same way about me."

"Have you never written to your daughter?"

"Several times, in the early days. I never got an answer."

"For God's sake! She was only a child!"

"I know. But after a while, you yourself can't find the words. What do you say? 'I'm not a witch, I'm your mother and I love you. I want to hold you and kiss you and make up to you for all the lost years?' It's beautiful! But if you shout it or write it or sing it long enough in an empty room, it will drive you mad. You've talked of your own love affairs, doctor. Have you ever wanted to unsay something and found no one's there to listen? Have you never wanted to say tender things only to hear them echo back from a wall of stone!"

JUNG
Zurich

Her declaration is too poignant, too simple to be anything but truth. Her dagger thrust at my jugular – "your own love affairs, doctor!" – was aimed with a steady hand and an unblinking eye. The rest of it – the Scotus Society, the flagellation scene, profane passion with Alma de Angelis, sacred love with Sister Damiana, platonic attachment to Kostykian the Wandering Jew who puts jewels on ladies' pillows and leaves their virtue unsullied – is all too much. It is a hodgepodge of truth, dream stuff and archetypal wish fulfilment.

I do not propose to challenge her on it. The material is valuable anyway. However, I am not prepared to swallow it like the bolus of pitch and hemp that Daniel fed to the great dragon. What is important is that the nearer we come to the moment of revelation, the more my patient divides herself, like an amoeba. So far we have three separate personae: the damned soul, grasping at images of lost innocence, Fräulein Zickzackblitz, mistress of Silbersee, sane and practical, laying about her with a riding crop; the desolate mother mourning her lost child, bereft even of the skill to communicate her love and her grief. Well, we shall see in due time which of these personages is the most durable!

She is sitting bolt upright in her chair waiting for me to continue the interrogation. I say nothing. I go to her, stand behind the chair and begin to massage her shoulders and her neck. Her muscles are hard as boards, knotted in spasm. After a few moments she gives a sigh of pleasure and relaxes under my touch. Then she undoes the top two buttons of her blouse and throws back the collar so that I can work on her

275

bare skin. I begin to coax her in rhythm with the movement: "Let go now. This is easier than talking. It tells us both more too. Close your eyes. Here you are free from nightmares!"

For a while she abandons herself quite happily to my touch; then she reaches up, imprisons my right hand and draws it down to touch it with her lips. Quite calmly she declares:

"That's enough. Thank you, my dear. I enjoyed it very much. Any more and we are both in hot water."

I note the endearment with pleasure and her pleasure with delight that I have been able to arouse her. I draw her head back and kiss her on the forehead, then retreat to my chair. She buttons her blouse and sits facing me, half sombre, half amused, sensual as a cat by a fire. I am elated. Physical contact has been made. The first bastion is breached. Time and patience will bring us into the castle keep itself. Then she startles me with a frank declaration:

"I fear you haven't been listening to me, my dear doctor. I keep telling you I seduce easily and then behave very badly. I think you seduce easily too, and then wonder why things get messy afterwards. You and I should not start any games that we're not prepared to play right to the end. But thank you for wanting me. That helps more than you know."

I smile and shrug and thank her in my turn. I, too, like to be wanted at a moment in my life where I feel often like the ugly duckling. Then, the interlude over, we are back to reality. I ask her to tell me about her life as an intern at the general hospital in Vienna. She is not ready for that yet.

"I'd like to tell you first about Ilse."

"Ilse? I don't remember that name."

276

"We haven't discussed her."

"Is she important to your story?"

"Later she is most important."

"Tell me about her."

"She was my friend at school in Geneva. She also lived in Land Salzburg. Her father was a mine owner and a big financier. I had a schoolgirl affair with her. Papa would have liked to seduce her, too; but he didn't, because I wouldn't invite her to stay with us. However, she was pretty, personable, rich and almost endearingly stupid. She and her two brothers were among the first members of our new hunt club. Ilse was prime meat in the marriage market. Her mother was a doleful, anaemic creature. Her father was rich, rich – and very anxious to find a titled husband for little Ilse. Our monthly hunt meets at Silbersee were an ideal occasion to parade the promising young colts on whom she wanted my expert opinion. She was one of those girls who live in a rose-pink glow of illusion. She recalled incidents from our schooldays in Geneva that never happened, never could have happened. Our schoolgirl affair, which ended the day I saw her setting her cap at Papa, was for her a lifelong bond. I must be bridesmaid at her wedding, godmother to her children, friend of the heart to her and the husband she hadn't even found yet. A session with Ilse was like gorging yourself on Sachertorte. You ended up sticky and creamy and utterly surfeited with sweetness."

"A very clear portrait. I now have Ilse graven on my heart. May we pass on, please?"

"You wanted to know about Vienna. From the beginning that was an odd experience. I told you Papa had procured me an appointment as an intern at the Allgemeines Krankenhaus. He gave me letters of introduction to the registrar and to three or four of the senior men with whom he had worked over the years. He set me up in a pleasant apartment between the Alsengrund and the Josefstadt, an easy walk from the hospital. He gave me a note to his bankers. And that was it! No social contacts, no women friends, nothing! He had lived a private life for all these years; there was no reason to have it complicated by a bluestocking daughter with a defective birth certificate!

"I was hurt, of course, and angry; but by now I had developed an automatic reaction. If these were the rules of the game, I would play them to the limit – no favours asked, no quarter given! I made my bows to the senior staff, thanked them profusely for their good offices on my behalf, and retreated resolutely to the ranks of the juniors. I made contact with Gianni di Malvasia, who was lodging with a young male friend in a rather seedy apartment off the Herrengasse. The friend was a student of piano and composition, and neither their apartment nor their neighbours', could accommodate a grand piano. I offered the use of my apartment for practice, and an occasional home cooked meal in return for their escorting me to concerts and introducing me to the young life of the city.

"It worked well. Gianni, in his stuffy fashion, was very protective. I understood his needs and his occasional agonies. Soon we had a small circle of friends who made the rounds together: cheap seats at the opera, wine and dancing in Grinzing, booths in the cheaper and seamier night spots in the old city. I met all sorts of interesting people. At Silbersee there's a portrait of me by Klimt. It's semi-nude. I'm wrapped in a multi-coloured drape that he painted afterwards. I met Schnitzler and didn't like him. I found him an insufferable snob. Lina Loos took me up for a while; but she got bored with me because I couldn't paint or write. It was a strange frantic time. They called it the Gay Apocalypse, but it matched our mood.

"You've worked in a public hospital. You know what it's like. You're all terribly young. You spend your days and a lot of your nights with the sick, the dying, all the bloody casualties of a big city. You think you're tough, but you're not. After a while the sheer futile mess of the human condition begins to appal you."

I turn back through my notes and remind her that she has made a similar remark before. I quote it back to her: "We bury our successes and our failures in the same grave." I ask, can she explain it to me?

"I'll try; but please, be patient with me. I have to take it one step at a time. You must know what I mean about the futility. Didn't you ever get depressed when you looked down at all those rows of beds and realised how much the patients expected of you and how little you could really give them. It did me a little good. It taught me to be kinder. On the other hand, it did me a lot of harm."

"What sort of harm?"

For the first time she seems embarrassed. Then she makes a big effort and blurts out:

"For quite a long while it played hell with my sex life. I'd wake up beside some beautiful young body and wonder what terrible things were going on inside it. Gianni said the same thing happened to all medical students. You just had to get over it. He made a joke. 'They say justice is a blind goddess. I think love has to be blind, too.' My trouble was that, in the end, the blindfold fell off, just at the wrong time."

I note that phrase, too. I underline it several times; but, mindful that she is prepared only for one step at a time, I let her go on.

"One result was, of course, that in our free time we played hard, just to forget the tragedy; but it still shoved itself under our noses. My introduction to the underside of Vienna came very early. One winter's night, just about eleven, I was curled up in front of the fire reading when Gianni knocked on my door. He had a carriage waiting. He wanted me to dress immediately, get my instruments and go with him. Why me? I wanted to know. I thought it might be a botched abortion. There were a lot of those and young interns were often called in to do the repair job. They had no licence to practise privately, so there was always an element of risk. Gianni told me the mistress of a friend of his was having a baby. It was a bad delivery and he needed help. He took me to a grimy block of apartments near the Burggasse. They're still there. They call them *Bassena-Wohnungen*, basin apartments, because there's one watertap on each floor and a single communal toilet. The place was as grim as a gaol; and the Hausmeister who peered at us from his little glass cabin looked like a snarling old mastiff. Gianni handed him a bank-note and he let us pass.

"The patient was a girl, no more than eighteen, thin and undernourished, far gone in a difficult labour. The lad with her was a student from the conservatory, who scraped up food and tuition money by playing the accordion in a wine cellar. The apartment was little better than a hovel; Gianni himself had brought the towels and the linen, a basket and blankets for the baby. It was a breech birth, difficult and messy. We had to use high forceps and finally cut to get the child out alive. It was a close call, and we sat until dawn coaxing the mother back from the edge of dying. As soon as the stores opened we sent the young father out to buy provisions. He was hardly out of the door when the Hausmeister came storming in, shouting scandal, threatening eviction, the usual performance of that very special breed.

"I was starting to shout back, but Gianni restrained me. He put on the most beautiful performance I have ever seen. We were, he explained, doctors on an errand of mercy. Surely a few hours' disturbance was better than a death in the house. As for scandal, well, as an officer charged with public health, he had noticed a number of quite scandalous and dangerous infractions in this building – unsanitary toilet facilities, filthy wash-basins, accumulations of rubbish, rats which were known plague carriers. Then he broke off and with an air of great surprise and concern asked the Hausmeister to put out his tongue, cough, bend and touch his toes, a whole comedy of medical nonsense. Then he said, 'My friend, you need help almost as much as this mother and child. Come and see me at the hospital. Ask for me in casualty between three and four. I can't promise anything – one never can in cases like yours. But I'll do the best I can for you – provided, of course, I can count on you to take care of my friends here!'

"The fellow was almost grovelling with panic. He begged to know what was the matter with him. Gianni suggested I should take a look at him too, and give a second opinion. I put him through the same routine. My opinion was that he was in a very bad way. He had an acute case of serpiginous scatology which, if left untreated, would develop into incurable proctalgia.

281

By this time the wretch didn't know whether he was shot or poisoned. Gianni assured him gravely that he would do his best, provided there was no more annoyance for the new mother and child. At the hospital Gianni treated him quite successfully, with a heavy purge and a week's dose of placebos. I visited the mother and child every day until they were both out of danger."

I tell her it's a charming story. If she did it on the stage at the Burgtheater, there wouldn't be a dry eye in the house; but please, I would like to know the point of it!

"The point, my dear doctor, is that the child died a month later. The couple split up shortly after. The girl went back on the streets and used to send her friends to me to make sure they were fit for inspection by the city health people. The father of the child is now a well known conductor. You asked me about burying successes and failures. There's your answer."

I am sure it's not the whole answer; but for the present, it will suffice. I ask a simpler question.

"Affairs of the heart – anything important during this period?"

"No! It just wasn't possible. I worked like a dog at the Krankenhaus. In spite of all the prejudices that festered in that place – against women, against Jews, against psychiatry, reforms in administration, socialism and Hungarians! – I was determined to prove myself first rate. So, playtime was only playtime. And I still had to have a place and a time that belonged only to me."

"And when you were alone, what did you do?"

"I read; I played the piano; I cooked; I mended my clothes; I day dreamed."

"About what?"

"About Silbersee mostly. What I would do when I next went home, the improvements I could make. I even planned a big hunt ball and worked out every detail in my head – except one."

"What was that?"

"Who would be my escort. There was no man that special in my life."

"Had there ever been?"

"No. Only Papa. The rest were friends, bed companions. I never really needed them enough to want to keep them."

"So, really, in spite of your education, your travels, your training as a physician, a part of you had remained anchored in childhood, and the sexual experiences of adolescence. You tried to shut the door on the incest experience; but no man ever matched your Papa as a lover. Your attachment to Lily had all sorts of elements in it; she was mother, sister, confidante, lesbian companion. Yes?"

"I've never arranged it that way in my mind; but yes, it's true."

"And for each of these people, about whom you feel guilt and shame – or at least embarrassment – you have provided yourself with an idealised Doppelgänger. For Lily, you have the beautiful and devoted virgin, Sister Damiana, called untimely to God. She understands you as Lily does. She reads your mind; but the relationship is untainted by sex. Therefore, you cannot feel her breasts under the habit. In place of your Papa you have the noble voyager, Avram Kostykian. He is straight out of the Grail legend: the gentle knight, pure and beyond reproach, who shows you the mystery of the pearl, leaves you an almost perfect sapphire, but never wants sex with you."

I expect her to be angry. I would be happier if she were. It would mean that we were coming close to the heart of the argument. But no! She is quiet, quizzical, even a mite patronising.

"Are you telling me, doctor, that I have invented these people?"

"Not at all. I am saying that, unconsciously, you have – how shall I put it – re-arranged them in your mind, the way a portraitist re-arranges his sitter as he sets her down on canvas. It's a matter of editing, of emphasis, of light and shade. It's an act of artistic creation."

"Or to put it bluntly, a lie."

"On the contrary! It is an act of truth. You are telling not only what these people were in themselves, but what they were to you, what they have become to you with the passage of time. I could tell you the Kostykian story three different ways. The facts would be the same in each case, but the meaning would be quite different. Would you like me to try?"

"No thank you." She laughs. "I take the point. What I should like to know is . . ."

We are interrupted by a domestic commotion. The children and their nurse have arrived home. There is much high pitched shouting and bidding for Mamma's attention. A moment later, Emma knocks on the door and ushers in the nurse. Her hand is bound with a bloody scarf. She has torn it on a piece of barbed wire. The cut is deep. It runs from the base of the little finger down the fleshy heel of the hand. It will need stitches. I ask Emma to boil water, bring me gauze, cotton wool, disinfectant, and a needle and thread.

My patient offers to help. I accept. She has told me she used to be very deft in surgery. So we can test that story at least. She wraps a towel round her middle, scrubs up at my wash basin, then with little fuss and a minimum of discomfort to the victim, she cleanses, disinfects, stitches and bandages the wound. The nursemaid is grateful. Emma is delighted; she knows I should have taken twice the time, grumbled all the way through it and left the nursemaid in tears. For my part, I am discreetly pleased. It is one more small intimacy. I save my compliment until we are alone:

"That was a very stylish demonstration, my dear colleague."

"What else did you expect? A first year student could hardly have botched it. But I'm glad you approve. I have the feeling you think that half of what I'm telling you is fiction."

I decide to be blunt with her. We are too far along now to be dealing in half-truths. Once again I invite her professional understanding of what we are about.

". . . Let's be frank with each other. In all diagnosis one has to be sceptical. You know that every alcoholic with cirrhosis of the liver will tell you he's a moderate drinker. The ulcer sufferer confesses only to occasional indigestion. In our interview I asked you how your episodes of sadism began. You said – where is it now? ah here! – you said 'whenever I feel ugly about myself'. In other words, your view of yourself changes. Therefore, what you tell about yourself changes too. I cannot accept simply the persona, the mask, in which you present yourself to me at one moment. I have to discover all the other constituents of the self behind the mask. Our dreams and even our daydreams represent the dynamic elements in our lives. The simple facts – the colour of a house, the direction of a street, whether we drank tea or coffee at a given meal – these are the static elements. So please, please! It's too late in the day to become self-conscious. Just tell me the tale as you remember it."

"And you, my friend, please remember I need much help from here on."

"I will. I promise. You finished your internship in Vienna. Presumably you were granted a licence to practise medicine and surgery."

"I was offered more. A teaching post if I wanted it. There was an opening for an assistant in abdominal surgery. It was the first step on a high ladder. I wasn't sure I wanted to make the climb. I used the excuse that I wanted to do a post-graduate year in Edinburgh or London. After that I would feel more confident of my capacity. I kissed hands again, bowed out, threw a wild, wild party for my friends in a Hungarian restaurant and then came back to Silbersee.

"Papa, I found, was in Munich. 'In rut,' Lily sniffed, 'for the diva in Fledermaus.' I wished him luck and settled down to check the accounts and the stud-book and ride the rounds of our domain and listen to Lily's rehash of the local gossip. I had hardly been home a week when I got a letter from Ilse Hellman. Surprise! Miracle! Star-bursts all over the sky! She had fallen in love with a most wonderful, wonderful man, Prince Charming himself. His name was Johann Dietrich. He was titled, too, Ritter von Gamsfeld. He had proposed. She had accepted. Papa had consented. The betrothal would be announced at a grand supper dance, which was now being arranged. I would get a formal invitation very soon. All three of us must come, Papa and Tante Liliane and me. And, of course, everything we had planned could now happen: I would be bridesmaid, godmother, ever-loving companion in their wedded bliss. It sounded like purgatory in pink ribbons; but there it was!

"We looked up von Gamsfeld in the *Almanach de Gotha*. The title was minor but quite old. It was first given to one of the brothers of Wolf Dietrich, the warrior archbishop of Salzburg. The manor estate was located not far from Bad Ischl and was rated by our local informants as 'considerable'. So, it seemed my little Ilse would have her dream come true, and Papa Hellman would achieve the financier's dream, a wedding of agriculture, mining and good, gold Austrian crowns. It made Lily's testy question not at all unreasonable: 'If that little cottonhead can grab herself a catch like that, why not you? Think about it, luv. You've been working too hard, too long – and the night games don't help your complexion either!' To which, of course, I had no ready answer, except to tell her I was going to take a ride up to see the timber-cutters. If she wanted to come, she was welcome, but please, no more lectures on the holy estate of matrimony!"

"But obviously you thought about it."

"Of course! Every girl does; and Lily had touched a tender spot. I was the bright one. I was beautiful, rich and capable – but little Miss Cottonhead was the one who got Prince Charming!"

"So what did you do about it?"

"The same as Lily. I started thinking about clothes. The engagement party was to be a lavish affair – a grand ball at the Hellman mansion near Bad Ischl. Guests would be accommodated overnight at the Hôtel Drei Mohren which was rented from cellar to attic for the occasion. It was to be all opulence and old regime but in a country mode, to compliment the local dignitaries. Lily and I decided that we would go in *Landestracht*, and we made three trips to Salzburg to have the full-dress dirndls designed and fitted. By the time Papa showed up again, pale and frayed from his long waits in the diva's dressing room and late, late suppers afterwards, the dresses were ready. He was so impressed with them that he decided that he too would go in local dress, and that – for the first time, mark you! – he would let me wear his mother's jewels, beautiful, heavily worked pieces made in Hungarian style by goldsmiths in Vienna and Budapest. Grandmother must have been a big woman, because some of the pieces were far too heavy for me; but there were others that matched beautifully with my costume, a pendant necklace and a pair of bracelets. For a ring I wore the sapphire which Avram Kostykian had given me, and which I had had set in Vienna.''

Once again I am struck by the extraordinarily complex nature of this woman. What I am hearing now is all woman talk, guileless and natural: dress and jewellery and social chit-chat. I wait for the shadow figure to emerge, the dark spirit that prompts the anger in her eyes and her orgiac furies in the house of appointment. I try to coax the shadow out with an unkind question.

"Why didn't your Papa just give you his mother's jewellery? I don't imagine he wore it himself. Why did he keep it locked away when he had a grown daughter to wear it?"

"I don't know." Her answer seems frank and open. "It wasn't anything that bothered me. It was his property. He could do what he liked with it. Lily had the theory that he was keeping it in case he ever got married; so that he could pass it on to his wife. I know he bought jewels for his girl friends, but he never gave away grandmother's." She looks up at me and gives a little embarrassed laugh. "You're a nice sober Swiss. You don't know how crazy the Hungarians can be. They're like quicksilver. You can never hold them steady enough to make sense of anything."

"What happened to the jewels in the end?"

"He gave them to Lily."

"What an extraordinary thing!"

"Perhaps not so extraordinary; but I'll tell you about that, later. Where were we?"

"At the preparations for Ilse Hellman's engagement ball."

"Oh yes! The invitations arrived – wouldn't you guess? – perfect autumn weather, clear and calm, the leaves, not fallen yet, still gold and russet and amber. There were special arrangements for me. Papa and Lily were lodged at the Drei Mohren. I was taken to the Hellman mansion, lodged in a room next to Ilse so we could gossip together, dress together. I wondered if she would want us to spend the night in bed together after Prince Charming went chastely to his couch! Forgive me! This is all retrospect. I didn't feel quite as bitchy at the time; but – oh dear! – it was a little hard to swallow all that sweetness!"

"And what about Prince Charming? Was he as hard to take?"

The change in her is startling. It is as if a light has been switched off. There is a terrible winter sadness in her voice that chills the heart. She does not look at me, she stares down at the backs of her hands which lie, slack and motionless, in her lap. She says simply:

"Oh no! He wasn't hard to take at all. He was the most beautiful man I had ever seen. I wanted him more than anything or anybody else in my whole life."

I wait in silence for the rest of it. Slowly she lifts her head to face me. Her eyes are bleak. Her cheeks are bloodless, like white marble. I am reminded of her descriptions of her mother, the Snow Queen with a lump of ice where her heart should be. She needs no prompting, the words come pouring out in a steady, remorseless flow.

"It was the real coup de foudre. If you've never felt it, nobody can tell you what it's like. Here was this beautiful creature, tall, blond, bright eyed, oozing maleness, decked out in the dress uniform of the Imperial Cavalry, bending over my hand and telling me how pleased he was to know me, how much Ilse had talked about our friendship, *et patati et patata, und so weiter*, for ever and ever. I could feel myself blushing from navel to forehead – me of all people! I kept praying I wouldn't make a fool of myself and faint clean away at his feet. I see you smile. I don't blame you. I'm forty-five years old and I still remember that moment as vividly as if it were happening now. We've talked about being reborn. Well, somebody was born in me that night, somebody so wild and passionate I've never been able to subdue her. I wanted Johann Dietrich with all my body and soul, and here he was betrothing himself to this melting little caramel cake! When I danced with him it was worse. I found he was intelligent, too. He had heard of what I was doing at Silbersee. He asked if he might visit one day and look over the brood stock. Perhaps I could advise him about something similar at Gamsfeld. We might even found a hunt there. We needn't be in competition, we could perhaps set up a joint enterprise. As a cavalryman he was interested in . . .

"Then Ilse came and whisked him away; but I treasured every word as if it were a diamond. He wasn't lost to me yet; not until they were married. Please God, not even then!

"When at last the ball was over, and the pre-dawn breakfast was served and the two lovers had exchanged their last chaste kisses, Ilse came to my room. She was too excited to sleep. She crept into bed with me and talked and talked, while I listened with most loving interest, filing everything away for future reference. I wanted to know as much as she did about this paragon from Gamsfeld. When she tired at last and snuggled into the crook of my arm, I began to make love to her as we had done in the old days in Geneva. After a night of waltzes and frustrated love, she was too excited to resist. She protested weakly that though she still loved me she wanted to save herself for Johann. I didn't know what there was worth saving; but I told her the same sweet lies Lily and Papa had told me: that she was robbing Johann of nothing, only enriching him with a ready and experienced body. She fell asleep with her lips against my breast and her leg thrown over mine and her hair brushing my cheek. I was still awake when the sun came up and farmboys began bringing in the herds for milking. I could hear the sound of the cowbells, clear across the valley. I looked down at Ilse and thought how wonderful it would be if she just disappeared – blew away like an autumn leaf."

As I look at that pale, beautiful face and those lustrous eyes, peering backwards into a landscape that only they can perceive, I feel a sudden terror, as if an icy finger is probing at my heart. I understand perfectly what she tells me. This is the death wish that we all make, some time in our lives. I have made it lying beside Emma, while my mind and my body are engorged with another woman. I have made it against my father. I have made it against Freud – and Toni, relentless inquisitor of my secret heart, claims that I am determined to fulfil it in Munich.

Then, in the deep recesses of my unconscious, an iron door opens and a thousand strange creatures rush out to besiege me: a hideous dwarf with Freud's face, a hopping bird with the face of a little girl, the clanking skeleton of some prehistoric monster, a Siegfried, surpassingly beautiful, with a gory wound in his breast, who cries, "You have killed me, you, you, you!" The siege seems to last an eternity; but when I look at my patient she has noticed nothing. She is still caught in the enchanted moment of the love wish and the death wish, the moment of corruption which must precede the moment of possession.

Once again I am aware of the strange concordance of our psychic experiences. The dissociation which I have just experienced, the sensation of being out of my own control and under the influence of alien forces, is exactly the same as that which she experiences in her orgiac moments. No, wait! It is not exactly the same. I am constantly besieged. She is always the aggressor. Suddenly I am aware that she is no longer seated but standing before me, with hands outstretched. I ask defensively:

"Yes. What is it?"

She begs me, humbly, like a little girl:

"Please! I'm very frightened; will you hold my hands for a moment?"

I look into her eyes. I see no guile, no malice. I am not sure that she perceives me at all. She is staring into the kaleidoscope of her own self and not into my confused brain-box. I take her hands. I stand up. I draw her to me and hold her close against my body. I feel a prickle of lust for her. She does not respond. She does not resist. She accepts my warmth with a kind of despairing gratitude. My lust subsides quickly. After a few moments she withdraws from my embrace and thanks me with the quaint formality of childhood.

"Thank you. I needed that. You're not displeased with me, are you?"

"Why should I be displeased? I'm happy that you trust me – and I have much respect for your courage. Are you ready to go on?"

MAGDA
Zurich

I go on, because I must. It is late afternoon. My time is running out. I have promised to complete my biography by the end of this session. Immediately after that, a decision must be made. Can this Carl Jung help me or not? More important still, will he help me once he knows the whole story?

If he cannot or will not, then I leave Zurich immediately. There is an overnight wagon-lit to Milan and Rome. I shall be on it. Whether I shall ever get off it is another matter. There is a certain irony in the notion of beginning a journey among the puritans in Zurich and ending it, a pilgrim of eternity, somewhere on the road to Rome, the eternal city. I hear Jung's voice asking me:

"Something funny? Do you want to share the joke?"

It is easier to lie than to explain the humour of death on the wagon-lit. I tell him:

"I was just remembering our journey back to Silbersee after the ball. Papa was nodding in the corner seat, making little grunting noises as his head tapped against the carriage window on each curve. Lily was wide-awake, but slightly dishevelled after a long night and a hasty toilette. I was red-eyed and weary; but my head was full of little dancing devils. Lily pointed to Papa and grumbled: 'I don't know where he got to last night. He disappeared after the last waltz and the next I saw of him was when he walked into breakfast saying he'd just paid a visit to the barber. I don't know whom he picked up at bedtime; but, give the old devil his due, he's as quick as greased lightning. And what about you, Miss? I saw you dancing with Dietrich. You'd better get those stars out of your eyes; because nobody is going to break up that engagement. I got the whole story last night from Frau Hellman's widowed sister. Now there's a pantomime character for you! She looks like one of the ugly sisters from Cinderella! Anyway, Dietrich's mother died five years ago. His father died last year. Johann gets the title, of course; but the estate does not revert to him absolutely until he's married. Until then he gets only the revenues. Apparently the old man didn't want the property pledged for gambling debts or dissipated on fancy ladies. However, there are other legacies to be paid – to relatives and retainers and one quite hefty amount to the woman Daddy was keeping when he died. So, young Johann needs ready cash. What quicker way to get it than a money marriage? I'd say he's got it both ways, love and money. Ilse dotes on him; and he seems to be very fond of her. But you see what I mean: if you'd been around, you could have been in the market, too!' I was very tempted to tell her that I was already in it and I intended to stay in it until the last bids were called. But I was too tired for argument. I simply told her that Johann Dietrich wanted to talk with us about a joint breeding operation and perhaps another hunt club at Gamsfeld.

"Lily thought about that for a few minutes and then decided it made sense. With larger capital we could bid for the best bloodstock. Gamsfeld had certain advantages over Silbersee for training. There was more flat land. It was nearer to the railhead junction for Vienna, Munich, Carinthia and Italy. We could mate and breed and raise the young stock at Silbersee, then ship them to Gamsfeld for training. Hans Hemeling was excellent at his job. I could doctor animals as well as I could humans. All in all, a splendid idea – provided I kept my hands in the pockets of my hacking jacket, at least when Ilse Hellman was around the place. That's what I was smiling at; you had to get up very early in the morning to trick Lily Mostyn!

"Papa had a comment to make, too, when he was jolted awake on a particularly sharp curve. Apropos of nothing at all, he announced: 'I'm very impressed with young Dietrich, very impressed. Much more brains than you'd expect from a cavalry officer. He's got a widowed aunt who keeps house for him at Gamsfeld. Her name is Sibilla. Good-looking woman, soft tongued and light on her feet. I've invited her to visit us at Silbersee.' I didn't comment. I thought, why not before? Why the devil couldn't you have spent a few thoughts on your daughter's marriage prospects?"

Suddenly I am aware of Jung's scrutiny. His eyes never leave my face. He is not writing notes, just tapping the end of his pencil against his lips. I know what he is thinking. He is as bored as I with this gossipy nonsense. I throw out my arms in a gesture of surrender.

"All right! I'll say it plain! I wanted Johann Dietrich. From that very first moment I was hell bent to get him. I had no plan. I had a big place in Ilse's heart, a small handhold on Johann's life. I had to start from there – and I did as soon as we got back to Silbersee."

"Tell me what you did." Jung grins at me with mischievous amusement. "I have a lot to learn about women in love."

"I wrote letters. To Papa Hellman and his wife, many and fulsome thank-yous for their hospitality, which I hoped they would permit me to return at Silbersee. To Ilse, a veritable book of loving compliments: how beautiful she looked; what a splendid man she had found; how happy I was to know she was happy; how Johann had mentioned he would like to see our farms at Silbersee and perhaps set up a joint venture with us; how delighted we'd be to have him visit, with Ilse of course – with his aunt and her Papa and Mamma and the cat and the dog if they felt like it! And how soon would they like to suggest? In Johann's letter I was very formal and well bred. Ilse was my dear, dear friend. I was happy for her and for him. As for his visit to Silbersee, please, any time! We were making some interesting changes from cold bloods to

296

warm bloods. I talked about Hanoverians and Holsteins and English Thoroughbreds and experiments I had heard of with cross-breeding Connemara ponies. I told him of my forthcoming visit to England, and planted the thought that we might invest together in a good English sire."

"As a matter of interest," Jung quizzes me amiably, "how much time did you have before the marriage was to be sealed?"

"From autumn to Easter. True to form, little Ilse had to be an Easter bride and Johann had to complete two more months of duty with his regiment before he resigned his commission."

"Not much time to break up a betrothal as solid as that one."

"I know. It would have been easier to rob the Landesbank! However, I was ready for any gamble at all."

"But you had no idea, surely, how Johann Dietrich felt about you."

"That didn't matter. I knew that whatever Ilse had I had more; whatever she did for a man, I could do twenty times better."

"Such confidence!"

He laughs in my face. I burst out laughing too.

"It's a form of madness. You're absolutely convinced that the world outside works by the same rules as the world inside your head. In my case it seemed to do just that. A few weeks after the betrothal, Johann and Ilse came to visit us at Silbersee. They were chaperoned by Johann's aunt, the one who had made such an impression on Papa and who seemed to be equally taken with him. As part of the changes at Silbersee and to provide for our hunt club guests, I had converted two of the nearer cottages into guest lodges. This was where we put Ilse, Johann and Aunt Sibilla. We rode around the estate together with Hans Hemeling as guide. Hemeling made an excellent impression on Johann, who was by no means the idle heir. He talked frankly about his problems.

"His father had run the estate very efficiently; but he had never allowed Johann to take part in the management. In the latter years of his life there was a certain estrangement, because the old man had moved his mistress into the manor. So, Johann stayed away with his regiment on full-time service. Now, there was a lot of ground to make up. He was eager to hear how we had reorganised ourselves at Silbersee, and how we had succeeded in restoring morale among our tenants. Then, he said something that rekindled my hopes like a wind blowing through hot coals: 'I hope you can pass some of this on to Ilse. She's a dear girl and I love her very much, but she's never had to fend for herself; and once we're married I'm going to need a lot of help at Gamsfeld. You're different. You've had a professional education. You're tremendously self-reliant. I admire that so much. Then of course you've got Lily. I love that woman, she's got salt on her tongue and the devil in her heart! I like your Papa too. He's got a lot of style.'"

"So much for compliments; but was there no holding of hands, no kisses, no little moments of revelation?"

"None. I was as prudent as a nun."

"And Ilse?"

"Was overwhelmed. Now I must play little mother as well as all the other roles and teach her the elements of running an establishment. Johann's Aunt

Sibilla was a very managing woman, and Ilse didn't want her taking over as mistress of the house. I promised that Lily and I would do all we could to have her ready for installation as chatelaine.

"At the end of the day, we fed them a country style supper at the Schloss, and packed them off to the guest cottage. Papa intervened at this stage and offered to drive them into the village for zither music and Schuhplattler. I knew he wanted to cultivate Aunt Sibilla; the lovers wanted to be alone. Lily and I opted for an early bedtime.

"When they left next morning, Johann Dietrich handed me a promissory note for three thousand gold crowns as a half share in an English Thoroughbred stallion, if I could find the right one. So, a few weeks later I was off to England with Hans Hemeling to attend the yearling sales at Newmarket. Hans would bring the animals back home. I would stay on for two months' post-graduate study at Saint Mark's Hospital in the East End, where good work was being done on the study of fistulas and malignant growths.

"It seemed a proper move. Papa had promised to stay at home and look after Lily and the estate. I saw no sense at all in waiting for Johann Dietrich to work up a grand passion for me. The sooner we settled down to trade together, the more we'd see of each other. Absence might not make his heart grow fonder – but at least we would be in partnership for three thousand gold crowns apiece. Many a great romance had flowered out of smaller seeds than that. I had another idea."

"Stop a moment!" Jung holds up a peremptory hand. "You were going to London. You were going to be there alone, for two months. Was there no mention of your mother? No discussion with your Papa or with Lily?"

"There was discussion, yes."

"And?"

"As always, it led to a dead end."

"Please explain how."

"Papa took the line he always did: no information, no discussion. So far as he was concerned, my mother was dead, buried and forgotten. My need of information was like a summer colic; I would get over it."

"And Lily?"

"Lily took a different tack this time. She understood my feelings, always had. She herself was an adopted child. It was the first time she had ever admitted that; and I'm still not sure it was true. However, she claimed to have felt the same pangs of curiosity about her parents as I had about Mamma. But, she said, it was like the locked room in Bluebeard's castle; once you opened the door, you might find things you didn't like and couldn't forget ever after. She said something else, too, which has stuck in my mind. 'There's a cold streak in the English, luv, especially in their aristocracy. They can be very cruel and very clannish when their interest is threatened. I'd rather not have you risk that. I was a nanny, remember, a cut above the housemaid and the cook; but I never got to sit down to dinner with the gentry. You're gentry yourself now. Why have some hoity-toity madam look at you through her lorgnette as if you were a slug on a lettuce leaf.' Does that explain it?"

"It will suffice. How did you get into Saint Mark's Hospital?"

"The way I did everything else, those days. I wrote

and sent copies of my qualifications and letters from my professors in Padua and Vienna."

"And so, leaving romance simmering on the stove in Gamsfeld, you arrived in London . . ."

"With a letter of credit to Coutts bank and an introduction to His Imperial Majesty's ambassador at the Court of Saint James. Since I had no patent of nobility there was no danger of my being taken up by society; but my professional credentials made me a respectable, if exotic, name in the embassy guest book. I went to Newmarket with Hans and bought our first important sire. We named him Macedon, because we hoped he would father a world winner like Alexander the Great. When Hans came back to Austria, I signed in at Saint Mark's, took lodgings in Baker Street ·and rode back and forth from work every day in a hansom cab. It was the most miserable period of my life. The only thing that kept me going was pride. I couldn't let Papa or Johann see me coming home like a whipped puppy."

"What was the problem?"

"Everything! The weather was vile: pea-soup fog or drizzling rain for weeks on end. My lodgings were a frozen wasteland. The Englishmen I met seemed anchored in a sexual Sea of Sargasso, between masturbation, masochism and Greek love in the Turkish baths. And Ilse Hellman married Johann Dietrich, by special dispensation, a week before Christmas."

"Good God!" Even Jung was startled by that piece of history. "What happened? Don't tell me she got pregnant at Silbersee. That would be too much!"

"No. Her mother fell very ill. It was thought she might die before Christmas. She wanted to see her little Ilse married before she departed this life. Johann didn't raise any objections. It meant he was confirmed earlier in his estate. Papa Hellman was happy to have everything neatly buttoned up. Ilse's Mamma died on New Year's Eve – while I was peering through a microscope at a sarcoma section in Saint Mark's Hospital!''

The next instant Jung and I are both spluttering with laughter. It really is too much for credibility. And yet, that was exactly how it happened. Except I wasn't laughing in London when Lily's telegram arrived. I was crying my eyes out in rage and disappointment.

''There was snow ankle deep in the streets, but I walked all the way to Piccadilly and talked my way into the Café Royal, where I watched a fat lipped fellow making epigrams for a table full of young men who hung on his every secondhand word. No, that isn't true! I thought he was giving a rather good performance. I remember walking over to the table with a glass of champagne in my hand to tell him so. When I introduced myself by name and profession – and with reasonable sobriety! – he took me by the hand and announced with a flourish: 'Madame, you are magnificent! A physician indeed and a surgeon! Gentlemen, there is hope for us yet, if – Heaven forbid – we are stricken with the pox! Do you dance, Madame? Splendid! I have just written a play about a dancer with an interest in surgery. Her name is Salome. She dances for King Herod who presents her with John the Baptist's head on a dish. Do you think you could play the part?' ''

Jung is beginning to be impatient. He is certainly not interested in my sketchy reminiscences of literary

London. He urges me back to the main line of my history.

"You finished your term at Saint Mark's. You went back to Austria. What then?"

"I went to Gamsfeld to visit Johann and Ilse. Johann, the young Lord of the Manor, happy to be out of the army, had a head full of plans for the estate. Ilse, the young bride, still blooming, was trying desperately to fall pregnant. I was welcome on both counts: as business partner for Johann and physician-in-ordinary to Ilse. Even Aunt Sibilla was glad to have me as a house guest. I was a link, even if a tenuous one, to Papa, whose attentions had become rather sporadic. Johann and I decided that, as soon as spring came, we would open the hunt club at Gamsfeld and thereafter run the two studs in tandem, each concentrating on the development of different blood lines."

"And with all this intimacy, there was still no affair? No sexual interest on Johann's part? No advances from you? No jealousy from Ilse?"

"No affair. No jealousy. Sexual advances? Don't forget, my dear doctor; I had great experience of this kind of manipulation. People get used to situations that other folk would consider scandalous. It was the most natural thing in the world for me to be in Ilse's bedroom, to ride the rounds with Johann at Silbersee or Gamsfeld. It was quite usual for the four of us – because Aunt Sibilla was an ally in Gamsfeld as Lily was at Silbersee – to sit around in our night clothes, drink a night-cap together, embrace before we parted for bed. The embraces could mean whatever you chose to think. The last thing in the world I wanted was a scandal. I wanted to be exactly what I was: Mistress of Silbersee, the Frau Doktor Kardoss, beloved of my patients, friend of the heart to Johann, Ritter von Gamsfeld, and his rich and adorable wife."

"That must have been quite a complex relationship."

"On the surface it was very simple."

"And you worked hard to sustain it."

"Very, very hard."

"What did you expect to get out of it?"

"Exactly what I did get: to marry Johann Dietrich, to bear his child and become the Lady of Gamsfeld."

"Presumably you will explain how all that came about."

"I think you already know, my dear doctor. I killed Ilse Hellman."

JUNG Did I already know? Do I know
Zurich now? Do I want to know any
more? My conscious self struggles to set her bald statement within a frame of reason. In evidentiary terms, I did not know she had committed murder. I still do not know. I am a doctor of sick minds which distort reality. I have listened to a narrative, every word of which may be a fiction. I have had no time to test its truth or analyse its hidden meanings.

On the other hand, the unrest in my own subconscious – the sudden release of archetypes of terror and violence – affirms that what I am hearing is truth. It is as if a chord struck on a pianoforte has set up a whole series of sympathetic vibrations. Whether the truth is what the words say – that is another matter. When Toni tells me that I intend to kill Freud at

Munich, she is talking of a moral act with moral consequences, not an offence under the criminal code.

Do I want to know more? I must. I have seen what this confession has cost my patient. I know what it has cost me. Each of us must draw some benefit from the experience. There is another reason, too. I am so joined to her, even by this brief day's experience, that everything that touches her, touches me in a special mystery of conjunction. We are not joined in body yet; but our subconscious selves are very close. Nevertheless, I have to deal – and deal very carefully – with the conscious. I get up from my chair and pace the room slowly, taking care not to pass too close to her until I have finished what must be said.

"This morning we made a bargain, to guarantee that what passed between us in this room would remain secret. That bargain stands. Having come this far we have consummated a kind of sacrament." Before the last words are out I am aware of myself as a pompous idiot, mouthing banalities like my father in the pulpit. I am standing by the bookshelves. She comes to me. She has her own word to say.

"I'm not worried. That part was settled in my mind hours ago. You see, once you've joined the *Vogelfreier*, the outlaws, the next stop is the sky. I can make that flight whenever I choose."

"I know that; but I have to be sure of something. There's so much metaphor and symbol in this business. Did you actually and physically kill Ilse Hellman?"

"Actually, physically and by premeditated act. But no court in the world could ever convict me."

"Did you have accomplices?"

"No."

"Did Johann know?"

"Never."

"Who then?"

"No one. Lily guessed. Papa guessed. But no one ever knew, until this moment."

"How did you do it?"

"Is that important?"

"From this moment, everything is important. You are my patient. It is you who are in jeopardy now."

"Do you care so much?"

"I care."

"Why?"

"I don't know! But I care. Now for Christ's sake, let's have the rest of the story!"

I turn away from her to go back to my desk. She catches at my sleeve, turns me in mid-stride and kisses me full on the lips. The mystery of conjunction is complete; for a long moment we are glued together like those little copulating dolls one finds in curiosity shops. The moment passes. She pushes me away and seats herself again in the patient's chair. She gives me an odd, half-sad smile and an ironic comment: "Now I understand why the Romans use a wire grille in the confessional." I remind her with a grin that I am an analyst and not a confessor, so the rules of the game are different. Then she begins again; and as she talks, the realisation grows that I have just embraced a murderess and found it a most stimulating experience.

"Everything was planned around that first hunt at Gamsfeld. We had organised it as a full day's festival: the fox hunt in the morning, a parade of our bloodstock after lunch, a hunt ball in the evening, with fireworks and a Bierfest in the village for the locals. We were bringing in some of our own people from Silbersee as handlers and grooms, so that the two enterprises would be seen to be working together. Can you let me have a pencil and a sheet of paper. There's a certain amount of geography involved. It's easier if you see it on paper."

She pulls her chair up to the desk and draws a figure eight with the top loop much larger than the lower one. In the lower loop she marks a cross.

"That's Gamsfeld itself: the castle, which is small but very old. It's perched on a hill, surrounded by a wall, with dwellings inside the enclosure for the household staff. Below, in this first round valley, are the home meadows, three hundred acres of them. The perimeter is all hills, with meadows on the lower slopes, then pinewoods, then the snowline, crags and stunted growth. That's where the *Gams*, the chamois, could still be found. Here, where the two parts of the figure touch, is a defile, about a quarter of a mile wide between two hills. Beyond that, as you see, the country opens out again into pastures, meadowlands and orchards, each divided by low walls of stone. At the top of the figure eight is the village. Very old, quite beautiful in spring and summer, but grim and depressing in winter.

"We knew we would have a big cavalcade for the event and Johann wanted to ingratiate himself with the village folk. So, we arranged to assemble the huntsmen and the hounds in the village square itself, with breakfast and a stirrup cup and favours for the children. That way the butcher, the baker, the innkeeper, the farmers and the working folk all got a share of the proceeds. After breakfast we would move out to the open meadowland, where there was the best chance of flushing a fox. The hounds would be slipped and the hunt would be on. We would try to drive the fox back through the defile and on to the home estate where the going was rougher but the risks of damage to farm property were less.

"At my suggestion, Johann had arranged some insurance against accidents. We had the farm boys trap a fox and keep it penned. If we didn't flush our own fox before we hit the defile, the boys would release the trapped animal about a quarter of a mile ahead so that hounds and horsemen would have themselves a runnable quarry. The second insurance was to invite the local doctor to join the hunt – and bring his bag of tricks with him. That meant there would be three of us to deal with any casualties, which would be picked up by a farm brake following the cavalcade.

"Finally, the four of us, Johann Dietrich, Hans Hemeling, Ilse and myself rode the whole course, across and around, to note any hazards for novice riders or those unfamiliar with the country. There were several: a bank on the mill stream where the timbers of the chute had rotted, a rabbit warren, honeycombed with burrows, where both horse and rider could come to grief, and a stone wall, higher than the rest, part of an old building complex, with a rubble-filled ditch on the other side. A good rider on a good mount could take it in one stride, a poor one would risk his neck. We agreed to mark the hazards and warn the huntsmen before we set off.

"I asked Ilse how well she rode over the jumps. Johann answered for her. 'She's quite good. We've been out a lot together; but I don't want her taking any risks. I suggest she ride with you, Magda. She doesn't have to prove anything against these big country fellows on their heavy hunters, or my friends from the cavalry who are trained to take risks. I've warned her however, if she has any doubts, to pass up the jump. When the pack is in full cry, it's catch as catch can!'

"For the first time I heard a jangle of jealousy among the silver bells. Ilse didn't want to be lectured in front of me. Ilse was perfectly able to take care of herself. The Mistress of Gamsfeld had a name to keep up. She wanted her Johann to be proud of her. Amen! So be it! I was absolved from responsibility. Which was exactly as I had planned it."

"But surely, Madame . . ." Even to me, the sober Swiss from Küsnacht, an obvious question presents itself. "Surely it is the fox who makes the running, not the huntsmen? How could you calculate on hitting this or that obstacle where your accident was to be staged? After all, your neck was at risk, too – from the hangman if things went wrong."

She gives me a brief patronising smile and shakes her head.

"You miss the point, dear colleague. The danger spots were a diversion, a distraction. There was no guarantee that we would ever come near them at all; but in a steeplechase, a point-to-point, a hunt across country, there is danger at every instant. Accidents can happen very easily. Ilse Hellman was a mediocre horsewoman. She rode sidesaddle like a perfect lady. I am a good rider – a very good one – and I've always ridden astride. So you see, the odds were all in my favour. Johann and his friends were out for a fox. I was after the vixen. I would be riding neck and neck with Ilse Hellman until the kill."

There is no doubt that the voice which issues from her mouth, the fire which lights her eyes, are expressions of the shadow, the dark and primitive element of her self. I begin to understand how deep is the split within her psyche, and what she really means when she claims, on the one hand, to have no religious or moral instincts and, on the other, gropes so desperately for a handhold on faith. I am reminded vividly of accounts which I have read of so-called diabolic possession. I am sure that many of these are phenomena belonging to states of dementia praecox. I am convinced that this woman, while acting with complete rationality is, at certain moments, cut completely in two like a tomato. I urge her to continue. I have to confess that I am irresistibly intrigued by this account of an assassination by the assassin herself.

"At Gamsfeld we all rose early, in order to welcome the guests as they arrived in the village. It was a beautiful spring morning, sunny, crisp, with rime still crackling underfoot and the first faint buds breaking on the winter-bare branches. Johann, Ilse and I set off together. Johann, bred to the cavalry, was riding his favourite mount, a big Furioso from Hungary. I had brought Celsius, a Hanoverian that I had schooled myself, a handy jumper, seventeen hands and steady as a Swiss clock. Ilse's mount was a gift from Johann, a pretty little half-Arab mare from the stud at Radautz. She was young and mettlesome and Ilse, splendid in a new riding habit, matched her for beauty and line, if not for intelligence.

"I know it sounds strange, a compliment to the woman I wanted to kill; but what would you have instead? A lie? She did look beautiful. Her mount was a beauty too; though I didn't know how much heart she'd have under pressure. But of course there would be no pressure today. We were out for good, honest country fun, with the village band playing oom-pah-pah in the square, the girls in starched aprons and Sunday dirndls dashing about with beer and bread and sausage, and all the gentry for miles around ready to join a fox hunt *à l'Anglaise* at Gamsfeld!

"As we trotted off, Ilse was next to Aunt Sibilla. I drew alongside them and reminded Ilse of Johann's warnings. Let the men take the lead. Once the view halloo sounded, all those big seventeen-handers would go charging forward like a regiment of hussars. She was nervous now and glad to have me by her. The little mare was restive, too, and hard to hold. Ilse complained, 'I don't know her well enough. I'm not sure how she's going to respond.' I told her to ride with a firm hand. We were in no hurry. If she wanted her head at the fences, give it to her. If she faltered, pass up the jump rather than risk a tumble. I would ride with her all the way but take each jump ahead of her. My Celsius had a big, steady stride, and he would lend confidence to the little mare. Aunt Sibilla added her own counsel. 'You can trust Magda. Just stay with her, she'll get you home safe.' Which was exactly what I needed: clear evidence that I had a great care for my dear friend Ilse. Then the master sounded his horn, the hounds moved off, we trotted after them, out of the square, down the cobbled street, over the little arched bridge – nine centuries old they said! – and into the open meadows, where the hounds were slipped and the horsemen fanned out across the pastures.

"Our luck held. Half a mile from the bridge we

flushed our fox, a big, sleek male who appeared from the lee of an ashlar fence and loped away towards the defile, with the hounds two paddocks away from him. At the first cry, Ilse was off at a hand gallop, as I knew she would be. She was jostled in the first rush, was almost thrown, and then fell back to join me and Aunt Sibilla at the tail of the chase.

"Sibilla scolded her. I, the dear and faithful friend, encouraged her. 'We'll catch them up. Let's take it easy over the next two fences, then we'll move up into the pack.' She settled down then, we took three stone fences, in beautiful rhythm. By the time the little mare was gathered and ready, I was over and cantering until Ilse caught up. It was child's play, a training exercise that I used to do with Rudi in the old days in Geneva. The next two fences we took more smartly. Ilse was flushed with excitement. She called out: 'Now let's go! Now!' We were three fields away from the main group. We had to take two stone fences, a brush fence with a ditch beyond, and then, looming up from a different angle altogether, the stone wall with the rubble ditch.

"This was the moment. I knew I had to decide – now or never. The rubble ditch might kill us both. If I judged it right, the brush fence could be the last frontier for Ilse. I answered her cry, 'Go! Let's go!' and took the first two fences, flying, with Ilse ten feet behind me. She stumbled a little after the second, but recovered and was hard on my heels as I made for the brush fence. Johann and I had noted this one as we made our rounds. The ditch on the other side was wide and steep; but any clean jumper could take it with ease. Even Ilse. She was only a length behind me when I jumped, not straight, but slewed slightly across her path. I cleared the ditch easily; but the little mare, thrown off stride, propped at the last moment and Ilse went sailing over the brush fence, to land head first in the ditch.

"There are no good falls – only lucky ones. This was a bad one. She was alive but unconscious, her body grotesquely twisted. There was bleeding from the nose and ears, and one side of the skull was impacted against a small sharp rock embedded in the wall of the ditch. The first riders to come on the scene were Aunt Sibilla and Papa. Aunt Sibilla – old regime to the tops of her riding gloves – looked down, stricken but tearless, and announced: 'I saw it happen. Poor child! Her timing was all wrong. Dear God, what a mess! I'll get some help.'

"Papa knelt with me, made a quick examination and muttered to me: 'We'll be lucky if she's alive when we get her back home. If she is, then we'll work on her together. The local man can do the anaesthetic; you assist me.' Then the men arrived with the brake. We lifted Ilse into it and made her as comfortable as we could. Papa and I rode back with her to the castle.

"Johann was horror-struck, but he carried himself like a soldier. He sent his major-domo and my Hans Hemeling to deal with the guests; then came upstairs to the bedroom where Sibilla and Lily were undressing Ilse while Papa and I and the local doctor were scrubbing up for whatever surgery seemed possible – which was little enough. There was a large depressed fracture of the skull, fractures in the central vertebral structure and, by the look of things, a profuse cranial haemorrhage. Johann asked, 'Is there any hope?' The village physician left the answer to Papa. He was gentle but firm in his opinion. 'Not much, I fear. We might do a little better in a hospital, but she'll die before we get her there. We need your agreement for emergency work now – but don't count on any miracles.'

"Johann was grim and pale. He said simply: 'Do what you can, please, gentlemen.' Then he bent and kissed Ilse on the forehead, shepherded Sibilla and Lily out of the room and left us to our work. The physician from the village proved both competent and judicious. In his opinion the cranial damage was major and irreparable. The spinal fracture would probably mean permanent paralysis. All in all, it would be a mercy if she did not survive. Papa nodded agreement. I, being in the presence of my seniors, had no opinion to offer. Papa suggested that we deal first with the cranial depression and see what sort of mess we had inside. It was a mess, too. After an hour of useless work we simply sewed back the flaps, bandaged the skull, composed her in the bed and called in Johann.

"It was Papa who delivered the verdict. She was not going to survive. The most merciful thing was to let her die quietly with no more butcher's work. Johann broke down completely. He knelt by the bed, his face buried in his hands, sobbing like a stricken child. The physician asked tactfully whether we should not have the priest in to give her the last sacraments. Aunt Sibilla had already sent for him. I, who had never seen this service before, stood with the rest and listened to the words of dismissal, and felt – would you believe? – joyful that it would soon be over.

"But the end was not yet. The vigil was longer than any of us expected. About eight in the evening, I was sitting in the bedroom with Johann and Aunt Sibilla. I was longing to take him in my arms; but dared not give so much as a hint of what I felt for him. I was keeping watch with Ilse, my dearest friend, companion of my woman's heart.

"Suddenly she began to roll her head on the pillow and utter strange animal cries. Sibilla and Johann looked at me and asked what was happening. I explained as best I could that the synapses in the brain were all askew and that these were reflex actions only. Then Johann cried out: 'But she's hurting can't you see? She's hurting! Please help her! Please!' I told him I would do what I could. I asked them both to leave the room. I poured a little chloroform on a pad and waved it under Ilse's nose. The smell would make it appear – to all but Papa – that I had administered more anaesthetic. Then I killed her with an injection of air into the femoral artery, where the pinprick would not be noticed.

"Ten minutes later I called in Papa and the local man. They pronounced her dead. There was the usual bedside grief. The local man signed a death certificate. My father witnessed it. The priest gave the last blessing, offered his condolences to the family and took his leave. Johann, frozen in a terrible grief, refused to leave the room until the women came in to wash the body and prepare it for the undertaker.

"The rest of it is a sequence of rituals, unreal as the scenes painted on an ancient vase. Aunt Sibilla begged us to stay at Gamsfeld until after the funeral. For the first time, I began to be wary. It was no part of my plan to be talked of as a possible consort for the widowed Ritter von Gamsfeld. So I made the excuse that I had things to do at Silbersee and would take the same train as Hans, who was taking the horses back home. I promised faithfully that I would be back in time for the funeral.

"Lily was less than happy. She was jealous of Aunt Sibilla's attentions to Papa, and had some sour words to say about the gentry being always gentry and settling their own affairs without care for anyone else. I suggested she come home with me and Hans and let Papa work out his own destiny. On the train journey she sprang a surprise. She had decided to take a vacation in England, very soon, while the spring flowers were out and the gardens at their best. She hadn't been home for so long. She was getting a kind of hunger to see the old place again.

"I told her it was a marvellous idea, just what she needed. I knew Papa was getting to be a trial; and I was always busy. 'So busy, luv!' Lily told me sadly. 'So very busy! And so clever that I wonder where you learned it all!' There was a barb in that bait too, but I ignored it. I was sure a holiday in England was just what Lily needed. I promised a gift of fifty crowns to help her on her way.

"The funeral at Gamsfeld was a big affair, very feudal, full of strange local protocols that made no sense at all to us Ausländers. On one side of the grave, Johann stood with Aunt Sibilla and other members of his family. Facing them were Papa Hellman and his sons. I stood with the Hellmans – a mute and mourning witness to my own sad loss. Papa Hellman held my hand and put his arm around my shoulder, and told me he would always look on me as his second daughter.

"As we moved out of the churchyard, Johann caught up with me. With a humility that moved me to tears, he begged: 'Please, would you be willing to go on working as we planned? I need desperately to keep busy, and Ilse was so wrapped up in the project, I'm sure she'd want it to go on. Aunt Sibilla wants it, too. She thinks you're one of the bravest and most complete women she's met – and she loves having you around. I want to come to Silbersee sometimes; if you'll have me. Gamsfeld is going to be a very lonely place now.' If I could have moved in then and there, I would have done it; but that little colony at Gamsfeld was full of sharp peasant eyes and clacking tongues. If I had learned nothing else in life I had learned to sit patiently behind my defences and wait for the time to strike."

"Tell me! Through all this, did you feel no guilt, no doubt, no fear?"

"I felt nothing but triumph."

It is an extraordinary statement; yet I believe it absolutely. All my own death dreams have prepared me to understand it. She is telling of a moment when the shadow, the dark element of the self, is in complete control, when all guilt is suppressed, and one feels like a conqueror marching into a vanquished city over a carpet of corpses, without even a twinge of remorse. Only later, a long time later perhaps, does the conqueror discover that he has taken possession of a plague town, where the bodies of the dead pollute the wells and the scavenging rats are carriers of the Black Death.

Her dream makes sense now. All its elements are contained in the macabre story I have just heard: the hunt, the fall, the dead vixen, she herself locked in the globe of glass, naked under the accusing eye of the sun – the primal God symbol. It is the glass ball itself

317

which interests me now. It is at once a prison, a place of exhibition, a womb, a capsule in which she can maintain herself alive and safe, beyond the touch of hostile hands. I mention all these matters briefly. She does not contend with them. The dream has served its purpose. It has brought her safely to me, exposed but still untouchable. I remind her that we have a time limit and we must press on. I ask:

"After the funeral did you go back to Silbersee?"

"We went back, yes; but it wasn't the same. It would never be the same again."

"Why not?"

"Because my heart was with Johann in Gamsfeld and a strange, dark alchemy had begun to work between Papa and Lily and me. It began with the complicated chemistry of age. Papa – handsome, charming, agreeable, utterly selfish Papa! – was now a rather portly gentleman in his late fifties, with a well trained eye for young girls and an increasing dependence on the company and the ministrations of women long past their first youth. He needed to be coddled. He needed to be reassured that all his male parts were in working order and that his musk could raise all the females in the vicinity. What he didn't need, what he fled like the plague, was marriage. So when someone like Aunt Sibilla, practised, persuasive and persistently urbane began stalking him, he tended to indulge himself first, then flee in panic – only to find himself hunted by other predatory ladies with money on their minds.

"What he could never see was that the only person with whom he could possibly be happy in marriage was Lily. She would have indulged him to the limit, forgiven him all his infidelities and still had love and body warmth to share when he came home. I tried a hundred times to persuade him; but no! He could not, would not see it. All his education was-against the notion. A gentleman never married beneath him. He could tumble the common folk to his heart's content, but he never raised them to his own high estate. Charge him with these ancient snobberies, and he would huff and puff and tell you 'Nonsense! Nonsense!' but he clung to them just the same.

"So, Lily, ten years younger but trapped in the shoals of the spinster forties, became more and more bitter. She was still a good-looking woman; she still exercised every day; but there was grey in her hair and a certain matronly look and fewer smiles in her eyes – and, after we came back from Gamsfeld, a strange, furtive withdrawal from me. For a while I pretended not to notice. I was busy all the time, with Silbersee, with the Gamsfeld project, and with a clinic which I had opened in the village to take some of the weight off our ageing medico. However, one day she irritated me so much that I attacked. I told her I was sick of her childish sulks and if she had something on her mind, now was the time to say it.

"She said it. She said it loud and long in purest Lancashire. She had given the best years of her life to Papa, to me, to Silbersee. She had finished in a dead end street. She was nothing but a glorified housekeeper. She had no respect, no love. Papa preened himself like an old turkey whenever that Sibilla woman was around – and then expected Lily to rub his back and warm his front and wind him up for his next big affair. It was all too much! 'And as for you, young Miss, I've loved you as if you were my own flesh and blood; but I don't know you any more. You frighten me now. Oh,

I know you say you love me! You probably do, in your own weird way. But if you wanted something badly enough, you'd walk all over me to get it. There's a devil in you, lass! I've seen him looking out of those beautiful eyes. I know what you've done. I know what you're doing now. I don't want to be around to see what comes of it!' Then she burst into tears and ran to lock herself in her room.

"My first reaction was a cold rage – too cold for words, thank God! I said nothing to defend myself, nothing to answer the veiled accusation. As I calmed down, I realised that silence was the only armour I needed. With Johann's family and Papa Hellman on my side, any accusations that Lily might make would only be interpreted as the vagaries of a spinster lady in menopause.

"Later in the day she came to me, pale and penitent, and begged me to forgive her. She hadn't meant half the things she'd said. She wasn't well. The affair at Gamsfeld had upset her terribly. Much as she loved him, Papa was sometimes a monster. I took her in my arms and kissed her and told her it was just a bad moment, best forgotten. The sooner she could get away on her holiday, the better.

"Then she sprang another surprise. While she was in England she might – just might – look around for a little cottage in the country, a place where she could retire and live quietly when the time seemed right. She had some capital saved and Papa had always said she had a pension coming. I assured her she had; but was it necessary to think so far ahead? I had always hoped she would stay with me and help me to bring up my own children.

"She gave me a long searching look. Her eyes filled

up with tears. She shook her head. 'I've thought of that too, luv; but it wouldn't work. The kind of life we've lived – you don't want to pass that on to your children. My guess is that Johann Dietrich will ask you to marry him, and you'll do it and he'll want a son, and you'll probably give him one. If you can keep everything clean after that, you're home and happy; but it's not easy, as I have good reason to know!'

"A few days later, she left for London. Papa was operating in Vienna. Hans Hemeling drove her to the station. I was glad to be rid of her for a while. Johann Dietrich was coming to Silbersee."

MAGDA
Zurich

It is very strange. I have confessed, without restraint, to a whole catalogue of crimes and, finally, to premeditated murder; yet I have not been too much at a loss for words. I have even, at times, been carried away by the vividness of my own recollection and the unbidden eloquence of an actress. Now, when I am come to talk of love and marriage, I find myself stammering with embarrassment.

Jung, who is beginning to look as tired as I am feeling, fidgets in his chair and asks testily what the hell is blocking me. I try to make a joke. I tell him this is a love story and I haven't been loved in a long time. Jung snaps at me:

"Nonsense! What have you got to hide? The seventh veil fell off long ago! Get on with the story. Johann was coming to visit you. What was he coming for? Business, pleasure, to propose marriage? Well?"

"I told myself it was business. I wasn't building any dream castles yet. Presumably he wanted the pleasure of my company as well. That he could have; but he would have to jump a lot of hurdles before he got anything more. I was a girl with a defective birth certificate. I had learned from Lily that the mistress rarely arrived at the marriage bed. So, much as I loved him, much as I wanted him, Johann would have to play by the rules.

"Lily had departed for London; Papa was in Vienna. Therefore, discretion was demanded. Johann would be lodged in the guest house. Hans Hemeling would appoint one of the young grooms as his valet. If Johann pined for me in the night, so much the better. He had only to confess his love, offer me a marriage contract, and I would melt into his arms – after the ceremony!

"There was another reason for my caution. I was head over heels and gone for him; but I didn't really know him intimately. Ilse had waxed ecstatic over her honeymoon experience; but then Ilse had been ecstatic with me long, long before the honeymoon. I had worked with him, yes. I liked the presence of the man, the impression he gave of strength and solidity, even of rectitude. I had also seen him shattered and weeping at Ilse's bedside. I had to know how much room she still occupied in his heart and how hard it might be to have her vacate the premises. There was a lot to learn, you see; and he had to learn something too: that here in Silbersee I was the Meisterin, the Frau Doktor, and it was I who sat at the head of the table and rang the bell for service."

"Bravo!" Jung claps his hands in mocking applause. "This is a real love story! I know I'm going to

322

cry into my handkerchief! Strength, solidity, rectitude! Woo me with love, not diamonds! I will be wife not mistress! Christ! What's got into you? You committed murder because you had a fire in your belly and you thought this was the only man in the world who could put it out. But he had to prove it. True or false?"

"True!"

"Then get on with it, for God's sake! What happened when Johann Dietrich arrived?"

"Why, Doctor Jung, do you have to be such a bastard?"

"Because I'm tired and you're still playing stupid games."

"I'm sorry but I'm tired, too! The instant I saw Johann, my heart bled. He had lost weight. He was so tight, so controlled, that you felt one touch would set him twanging like a fiddle string. Yet he was very calm, very considerate, grateful for the least service. He came on the morning train; so lunch was our first meal together. That was a kind of fencing match: tentative questions, polite answers, some careful skating around painful areas. After lunch I suggested we ride up, through the timber lands, to the top of the Silberberg, where there was a magnificent vista of the countryside – three lakes and a view across the cols to the peaks of the Tauern Alps.

"It was a slow, ambling ride. We picked our way along the loggers' paths until we broke out at the snowline, on to rocky ledges and patches of sodden tussocks. Up here the air was like wine – Greek wine with the taste of pine sap – and the space was like a silent explosion that blew open every door in the mind.

"At the top of the Silberberg there are twin peaks: high needles of rock that the locals call the Cuckold's Horns. Between them lies a small, deep tarn, black water, reflecting the horns and the clouds and the stars at night. We tethered the horses at the pool's edge and sat, side by side, on a rock ledge looking southward towards the sun.

"Johann, who had been very quiet on the ride, said with sudden vehemence: 'Christ! I'd forgotten what it was like to be free! These last weeks I've been living like a troll in an underground cave.' I wanted to reach out and take him in my arms. Instead I sat, pitching pebbles into the water and saying all the usual sympathetic nothings: it was still early days; time was the great healer; thus and thus. He gave me an odd lopsided smile and laid a fingertip against my lips. I had it all wrong, he told me. The last thing he needed was time. The less of it he had to brood in, the better. And please! No sympathy. That was the worst possible prescription. If you were a Dietrich you bit the bullet, soldiered on like the old man, like Aunt Sibilla.

"What was plaguing him more than Ilse's death was his own responsibility for it. His responsibility? I could hardly believe what I was hearing! No, he assured me, he felt guilty – sometimes suicidally guilty – about the whole terrible business. It was difficult to explain, but he had to talk it out. He had loved Ilse very much. Their marriage, brief though it was, had been very happy. However, deep down, he knew that it was a mistake. Ilse was a child, a loving beautiful child with a rich dowry – a perfect match in the old style. She adored her husband, would go on adoring him, growing up like a young tree in the shadow of the

324

great oak. The trouble was he didn't want a child bride. He wanted a companion, a lover, a friend. If Ilse had lived – he would probably, in the end, have gone out and found a mistress as his father had. Ilse had been spared that unhappiness; but if he hadn't married her, she would still be alive. The last scenes in that bedchamber at Gamsfeld haunted his dreams and his waking moments. There! At last it was out. He was sorry to burden me with his problems; but he felt better for telling me."

"And you?" Jung is still testy and teasing. "You must have felt a whole lot better, too. No suspicion, no rival in the memory room! What happened then?"

"The way you are now, doctor, I'm not going to play you the balcony scene from *Romeo and Juliet*. We dined and sat up late, as we used to do at Gamsfeld. I was wild for him. By bedtime, I could hardly contain myself; but I managed it. I sent him off to the guest cottage and spent a miserable, solitary night in my own suite. The next day, we worked in the morning and rode in the afternoon. As we were having a drink before dinner, he proposed, very formally."

"What did he propose?" Jung is chuckling like a mischievous schoolboy. "Companionship? Love? Friendship?"

"And marriage! As soon as the banns could decently be posted, dispensations obtained – oh yes! there was no escaping Mother Church this time! – and settlements arranged."

"And you, of course, accepted?"

"Wrong, my dear colleague! I put him off. I told him I loved him very much, had loved him from the moment of our first meeting. I was deeply moved, deeply honoured by his proposal; but the memory of Ilse was still too fresh for me and for him, too. I could not bear to share his heart with a ghost. I was an all or nothing woman. There were other things he had to understand, too. I was no child bride. I was a liberated spirit, with my own career and my own properties. I would not relinquish either in any marriage settlement. I was not a virgin either. I had loved and been loved; but if I married him, I would be faithful to death. As for the Church, well, in Austria and the Empire we were stuck with that. I would not convert. I would consent to the children being brought up as Roman Catholics. It wasn't all said as bluntly as I'm putting it to you, but that was the gist of it. I asked him to think about it very carefully and write to me when he got back to Gamsfeld."

Jung throws back his head and bellows with laughter.

"You really were playing a rough game. 'You want me; put it in writing!' My God, that's cheek for you! And how did he react?"

"He was much more of a gentleman than you, my dear doctor. He didn't laugh. He told me that he knew what his answer would be. He loved me. He wanted me for his wife. He wanted me to be the mother of his sons. Nothing could change that. But he would respect my wishes and write to me from Gamsfeld. The next day he went home. Ten days later his letter arrived. It was as tender and passionate as I had ever dared to hope. There was other good news too. The archbishop had consented to our marriage; and in consideration of my total willingness to have the children baptised and educated as Catholics, he had granted a dispensation for a public wedding in the church at Gamsfeld. Under the marriage settlement, I would hold Silbersee in my own right, and in default of a male heir, Gamsfeld would pass to me in the event of Johann's death."

"So, finally you had it all. How did Lily put it?"

"I was home and happy."

"And were you truly happy?"

"At that time? Absolutely."

"In spite of Lily's suspicions?"

"As I said, who would listen? What could she prove? Beside, she was going home. She depended on me for a pension – and in spite of it all she still loved me."

"You're very sure of that, aren't you?"

"Yes."

"How did your father take the news?"

"Well. That's worth a footnote at least! We were sitting at dinner on his first night back from Vienna. Old fashioned fellow that he was, he had taught me to talk business only between the pear and the cheese. So that's when I told him. He didn't seem surprised; but he seemed at a loss for words. Finally he said, with a kind of reluctant admiration: 'Well, I have to salute you, my girl! Even your mother wasn't as tough as you are!' Then he filled his wine glass and raised it in a toast. 'To your marriage! I wish you well. I hope you don't talk in your sleep!' "

There is silence in the room, now. Jung is scribbling rapidly in his notebook. He is no longer smiling. Something has changed quite abruptly between us. I realise – perhaps too late – that he is a very skilful interrogator, at one moment terse, at another tender, at another a bawdy buffoon. He has manoeuvred me into disclosures which a few hours ago would have

327

seemed impossible. He looks up at me and points the tip of his pencil at me like a divining rod. He tells me gravely:

"We are finished with history now. You have already told me the basic facts of your marriage, your husband's illness, your alienation from your child, your husband's death. But something's missing. I have a sketch, not a picture. I want to know more about your marriage – not chronology, not events – the taste of it, the feel of it, and when it changed and how it changed. I know this part is hard; but for your own sake, please try."

"The taste of it, the feel of it? There wasn't one taste or feeling. There were hundreds. They changed every day. You'll probably smile when I tell you that when I stood at the altar with Johann I really did wish I was a virgin bride. In bed that night, I was glad I wasn't. It was an ecstasy that seemed to blot out the past for both of us, a rebirth into a pristine world. We made a pact that all our yesterdays would be blotted out at sunrise. For both of us there would be only today and tomorrow. Johann told me how much he had felt the alienation from his father and how much he wanted a son. I told him how much I, who had never had a mother, wanted to be one. It was a summer idyll and we were happy.

"We worked well together, too. Johann had a natural flair for command and organisation. The village men and the estate folk had much respect for him. He liked physical labour and it pleased him that he could hew wood and pitch hay and school a horse with the best of the country folk. As for me, I was my husband's consort, not some homebody scolding the maids and knitting and serving tea. It took the Gamsfelders a little time to get used to the Lady of the Manor sitting on the fence of the schooling yard or, when we got our annual epidemic of gastro-enteritis among the babies, making the rounds with the village doctor. My proudest day was when Johann came in, late from paying the fruit pickers, and told me: 'You must have arrived, my love. The baker's wife has named her first daughter after you.'

"At the beginning, I left Lily and Hans Hemeling to run Silbersee. Lily, after her vacation, seemed more relaxed, less fretful about herself and her future. She had bought her cottage; it was being made ready for her. As soon as I was properly settled into matrimony, she would take her leave. When I fell pregnant, four months after the wedding, I asked whether she would change her mind and stay on as Nanny for the baby. She refused, quite firmly. I told her it was sad that with so much happiness to share, I couldn't share it with her. She gave me a strange look, half hostile, half pitying and said, 'I wonder, lassie, what it will take to teach you the truth. We're both whores. We're both lucky. I'm ending respectable. You've married rich, and by God's sweet grace you're having a baby. But don't push your luck any further; you can't afford the gamble.' I couldn't afford to be angry either. I shrugged and dropped the matter.

"I told her to feel free about leaving. Hans Hemeling could run Silbersee when I wasn't there. I would write to Coutts bank immediately about her pension arrangements. She had, as always, the last word: 'You're mistress of Silbersee, luv; but I've been your Papa's mistress for a long time now. He's the one that must tell me when the time is right.'

"How and when he told her, I never knew. I know

he gave her his mother's jewels, because he told me, in his offhand style, after it was all done. I know he travelled with her to London. He told me that, too. I was at Gamsfeld when it all happened. Lily didn't say goodbye to me. She left a note for me with Papa. I read it and burned it."

"What did the note say?"

"It was just a quotation from the Bible. Something about the Lord setting a mark on Cain."

Jung nods in recognition and gives me the quotation word for word:

" 'And the Lord set a mark upon Cain that whosoever found him should not kill him. And Cain went out from the face of the Lord and dwelt as a fugitive on the earth, at the East side of Eden.' "

He is obviously more impressed by it than I was. He forgets that I am not bred in the same context of thought as he is. I explain that while I was wounded by the dissolution of my relationship with Lily, I was quite happy that she was gone. It was only later, much too late, that I felt the sadness and understood how much we still meant to each other.

"Aunt Sibilla stayed on at Gamsfeld. I was happy about that. She could run the castle. I was left free to work with Johann. Besides, Aunt Sibilla's presence was constant testimony to my innocence. Every week we would go together to lay fresh flowers on Ilse's grave. She would accompany Johann to church so that I did not have to apostatise from my respectable unbelief! For my part I encouraged her in the project of snaring Papa, who, with Lily gone, was becoming rather desperate and footloose. In short, it was family life; but now it was my family and Johann's and I felt I had earned all the happiness we had."

330

"Earned it?" Jung was shocked out of his silence. "By murder?"

"Why are you angry with me? You asked me to tell you how I felt then, not how I feel now."

"I'm sorry." He apologises instantly. "I was distracted for a moment. Please do go on."

I am irritated by his lapse. After all, if he is having an affair now, if he has had them in the past, he must know that the enjoyment depends on an illusion of innocence, a justification by some code or other. One fornicates for lovers' fun. Adultery has to be blamed on the partner: the wife who doesn't understand, the husband who can't give satisfaction. Cat burglars are acrobats manqués. Even murderers don't need a very complicated charter to justify their trade; arms peddlers like Basil Zaharoff don't need a charter at all! Jung wants to know what's bothering me. I tell him in so many words. He is annoyed.

"Let's leave the polemic, shall we? I've apologised. I meant it. Go on, please."

"Well, the baby comes next, I suppose. We were both disappointed it wasn't a boy; but there was still lots of time and lots of loving and this was a beautiful, healthy child. Johann wanted her to have my name, Magda. I told him I'd settle for Anna Sibilla. This gave her part of my name and all of Aunt Sibilla's. Then, for good measure, we tacked on Gunhild, which was the name of Johann's married sister. Again, what do I say? With a baby in the house and a proud father and a healthy mother with plenty of milk, it had to be a happy time. There was much stitching and sewing and embroidery so that Anna Sibilla's christening day was like Saint Nicholas' Day, with gifts piled high in the hallway.

"It was also the first time I had ever seen Papa unable to cope with an occasion. When I put the baby in his arms, so that he could be photographed with his first grandchild, he became acutely embarrassed and fled, immediately afterwards, to the privacy of Johann's study. I found him there an hour later contemplating a very large glass of brandy. He was not drunk enough to be angry; but only a few paces away from being maudlin. When he saw me he raised his glass and said: 'To life – eh? It goes on regardless!' Then he took me by the hand and drew me towards him. I stiffened immediately; afraid he might be just far gone enough to try to maul me. He dropped my hand as if it were a live coal.

"Then without warning he told me: 'Your mother's dead. It happened while I was in London with Lily. I didn't want to upset you while you were still carrying the child. Anyway, that closes the account for both of us!' All I could say was, 'Thank you, Papa. Thank you for being so considerate.' Then I walked out and left him, picked up the baby and took her upstairs to give her the breast. I remember thinking, 'You're coming on quite nicely, my darling. At least you've got your own mother to feed you!' Then for no reason at all I began to cry, and I couldn't stop and Johann had to come and comfort me, while Aunt Sibilla explained with lofty tolerance: 'Post-partum depression. Lots of women get it. It'll pass in a few days. Then you'll be merry as a cricket again!' "

"And were you?" asks Jung drily.

"Yes. When I got tired of feeding the baby, Johann got a wet nurse from the village; so very soon I was able to be out and about with him again. Silbersee needed a visit. Hans Hemeling was doing well; he just wanted me to stiffen his authority from time to time. Then we began to travel, visiting the great stud farms, Einseideln, Lipizza, Bois-Roussel, Landshut, Janow Podlaski. It was too early for us to join that distinguished company, but we began to be known as judicious buyers whose breeding records would bear watching. Yes, it was a merry time; and homecomings were always wonderful. Anna Sibilla was a happy child, and why not? Her parents adored her. Her aunt doted on her. A whole army of admiring servants existed only to serve her. I was still trying to start another baby – a son this time for sure! – but somehow it wasn't happening.

"There was no discernible reason. We were both healthy and potent. Then Johann began to complain of feeling listless and tired. He lost appetite and weight. One night while we were making love, he cried out and complained that I had hurt him. I put on the lights and made him lie quiet while I examined him. There was a hard swelling in the scrotal sac. The lymph nodes in the groin were enlarged. Early in the morning I sent a telegram to Papa at the hospital in Salzburg. He came immediately, examined Johann and confirmed my diagnosis; testicular carcinoma, which already had disseminated itself through the lymph nodes. You know what that meant twenty years ago, doctor – even today in 1913! It meant an orchidectomy and a long and painful decline to death.

"Together Papa and I delivered the death sentence to Johann. Don't ever believe breeding doesn't count. In horses or men, it shows! I was never so proud of my man as I was at that moment. He held me tightly in his arms for a long time. Then he told me to get the hell

333

out of the room. He needed to be alone for a while. He would join us downstairs when he was ready.

"While we were waiting for him, Papa and I walked out into the sunshine and held a council of war. The operation would be done in Salzburg. Then we would bring Johann home to Gamsfeld with a pair of nurses. I asked Papa how long he might last. At a guess, Papa said, six months, certainly less than a year. Then he asked me, 'How is your nerve?' I asked him why. He said flatly: 'Because you're going to have to decide how much you and he can take. If I were in his place now I'd be loading my pistol and finding a nice quiet place to blow my brains out. That's why I suggest you treat him – I'll work with you as the specialist surgeon – and keep the local man out of it as far as you can. He's very religious. Any whiff of scandal and he'll back away instantly. Remember the Catholics still bury suicides in unconsecrated ground. You and I will sign the death certificate.' "

"Was your father suggesting a death pact with Johann?" asks Jung.

"On the contrary. He was asking me if my nerves were strong enough to terminate Johann's life alone, when the time came. I told him yes. He nodded approval and said, 'Good! Hold to that. You don't know how bad it will be.'

"Just after that Johann came out to join us. He was pale but composed. He said he was going to walk down to the village and talk to Father Lukas, the parish priest. I offered to go with him. He kissed me and told me he would rather go alone. I felt hurt and shut out. Papa said calmly: 'Let him be. Each of us has to make his own terms with the Reaper. Religion helps, if you're a real believer.' I burst into tears. Papa held me close and kissed my hair and then walked me slowly round to the rose garden, where we came on little Anna picking blooms with Aunt Sibilla. Papa said, 'You take the child. I'll break the news to Sibilla.' I picked up the little one and carried her off to see the new foals in the far meadow.

"Dinner that night was a sombre meal. Papa and I were leaving the next morning to take Johann to the hospital in Salzburg. I would stay at a hotel until he was ready to come home. Aunt Sibilla would stay at Gamsfeld and look after little Anna. Over the coffee, Johann said: 'I'm sorry to put you through all this; but there's something I'd like you all to know. I've never been especially religious; but I had a long talk with Father Lukas today. He heard my confession, helped me make a kind of peace with what's going to happen. I'm telling you this because I don't want you to grieve for me. Just hold my hand and help me to get through it like a man!'

"I know this is going to sound quite irrational – but it was as if he had slammed a door in my face. I had killed to get him. I was ready to die for him. I was ready to lie down beside him and go out with him if he wanted. Instead, at one stride, he had removed himself, stepped into a secret room that was barred to me. For that single, crazy moment, I hated him. I hated his God. I hated Father Lukas, everything, everything. Then Aunt Sibilla's calm voice cut across my black musing: 'When Johann comes home and the nurses move in, we'll need more space. There are two spare rooms along from mine. I suggest we make those over as an infirmary. If you agree, I'll have it done while you're in Salzburg.' In an instant I was sane again; but – I hope this makes sense – I'd seen the black

335

devils and I knew they were always lying in wait for me."

"It makes sense." Jung is gentle now and solicitous. "When something like that happens in a family, it's a rough ride for everyone."

"I can't tell you how rough it was. For Johann there was the trauma of mutilation, the constant pain, the long days and nights of coming to terms with dissolution. For me there was the daily horror of seeing what had been done to that beautiful body that I had killed to possess, of knowing what was going on inside it, and of seeing the spirit that inhabited it withdraw further and further from me into its own twilight world.

"I would come in to soothe him and find him with a rosary in his hands, telling the beads, staring at the crucifix as if he drew strength from that other mutilated figure. Father Lukas came every day to give him the communion and pray with him. One day he came out of Johann's room and said, 'Your husband is a man very close to God. He has accepted his suffering and offered it as a sacrifice for your well being and that of your little girl.' He meant it kindly, I know; but I found the notion grotesque. What kind of a god made a trade in human suffering?"

"Tell me about your days," says Jung mildly. "How did you accommodate? What did you do?"

"Well, we had day and night nursing, so I was able to build up a tolerable routine outside the sickroom. I would work with the nurses while Johann was bathed and his dressings changed. Then I would be about the business of the farm until lunchtime. Usually I took Anna with me, driving around in the pony trap, which she loved. At midday I fed Johann his lunch, then

336

went to my office to catch up on correspondence and accounts. Aunt Sibilla took over Anna at this time. She taught her to read and sew and draw. She also kept insisting, 'The child needs company of her own age. I'm going to bring up some of the village children to play with her.' She did several times; but it never seemed to work. The gap between the gentry and the village folk was too wide – even the dialect was a barrier.

"As her father got worse and worse, Anna began to have problems. She couldn't stand the smell of the sickroom. She could not associate the pale, shrunken figure on the bed with her once handsome and vigorous father. She suffered from nightmares: mixed-up versions of local folklore that she had heard from the servants, trolls and giants and krampus figures and vampires and werewolves. I began to have my own nightmares as well: Ilse, in her grave clothes, sitting on Johann's bed telling him how I had killed her; Johann holding up the crucifix and cursing me with it; most horrible of all, making love to Johann and finding myself embracing a rotting corpse. After a night of bad dreams I used to hate going into the sickroom. The figure on the bed, with the patient suffering eyes and the wan smile, was too close to my fantasies. The touch of his emaciated hand on my cheek burned me like fire. It was about this time that I began to notice Anna's fear of me and how she cringed away from my embraces. Also Johann's condition began to deteriorate rapidly. The pain was constant now and we had to keep him heavily sedated with morphia. As each dose wore off he would begin to scream, a high choked cry of agony that tailed off into a litany of broken prayers: 'Jesus, Mary, Joseph, help me . . . help me . . .' It was after one of these screaming sessions that Anna saw me coming out of the bedroom with the syringe and the dish in my hand, and fled from me like a terrified animal.

"That night I spoke to Aunt Sibilla, who recommended sending her away to stay with Johann's sister, Gunhild, and her young family. Aunt Sibilla offered to accompany her and stay until she was settled. I agreed instantly. The child's obvious revulsion for me was one nightmare too many. The day after they left, Papa arrived for his weekly visit from Salzburg. When he saw the state Johann was in, he swore softly and told me enough was enough. He wouldn't let a dog suffer like that.

"This time we were partners in the deed. We filled him up with morphia so that the heart was barely pumping. We called up the parish priest and asked him to administer the last rites – and incidentally provide a clerical witness to Johann's terminal condition. That night, as we were settling him down, I sent the nurse out of the room on some pretext or other, and Papa gave Johann enough morphia to kill him. When the nurse came back, Papa said brusquely, 'We could lose him tonight.' The nurse crossed herself and said, 'It will be a mercy. The poor man has had enough.' An hour later, while I was dozing in my room, it was all over. The nurse folded his hands on his breast, twined the rosary round his fingers, closed his eyes; then called me in to see him.

"I couldn't cry. I didn't know how to pray. I bent and kissed his cold forehead, drew the sheet over his face and walked out. I went to Papa's room. He was lying on the bed, in trousers and shirt sleeves, reading. He didn't say a word. He handed me a white pill with a glass of water and made me swallow it. He drew me down on the bed beside him, cradled my head on his arm and crooned over me as he used to do when I was a very little girl:

> Sleep then, my little one, sleep,
> Angels will watch over thee.

"My last thought as I tumbled down a deep dark hole in the ground was: 'Angels? Now Papa's got religion too. Soon I'll have no one to talk to . . .' And that, my dear doctor, is my life story. Now you know it all!"

"Except for one thing."

"What's that?"

"The transition. The change from mourning wife to black widow – the spider that devours its mate."

"You really are a bastard!"

"The transition! How did it happen?"

"What does it matter?"

"Because I need to know and you need to tell. It's five o'clock. You've got half an hour. There's no time for waltzing round the mulberry bush. The transition: how, when, where?"

"Let me get to it in my own way."

"Just so we get there!"

"We buried Johann beside Ilse in the churchyard at Gamsfeld. Everyone was touched by the gesture. Love conquers all! My God, if they'd only known! Then I travelled to Gunhild's place near Semmering to pick up little Anna. It was the same story all over again. She fled from me, screaming. Gunhild, a warm motherly woman, was as distressed for me as for the child. She offered to keep her, bring her up in the happy hugger-mugger of her own family, until she was old enough to rationalise her terrors. I was only too happy to accept. My emotions were rubbed raw. I was in no state to deal with a disturbed child.

"I went back to Gamsfeld and talked over the situation with Aunt Sibilla. If she were content to stay on as chatelaine of Gamsfeld, I would do a tour of all the major stud farms in Europe, introduce them to our breeding books, and make the contacts we would need for the future development of both Silbersee and Gamsfeld. Sibilla was happy with the arrangement. She had substantial monies of her own. With free residence and an annuity for her services at Gamsfeld, she could maintain herself in style and still keep up the never ending courtship of Papa. She would rather not marry him now, she told me wryly; it would take some of the spice out of living.

"I went to Vienna to buy clothes for the trip. Papa met me there. He bought me dinner and offered me some simple, vulgar advice. I was a new widow, rich and ripe; a natural mark for fortune hunters. He suggested – no, strongly urged! – I put all thoughts of re-marriage out of my head for a while and enjoy myself. Since I was now also a woman in business, I didn't want to get a bad reputation. I'd be moving with a sporting crowd; but if I wanted to make money out of them, I would need a cool head and a certain basic discretion. So, it would be useful to have an entrée to certain establishments where ladies like myself, widowed or simply wandering, could find the amusement and the company they needed without personal risk or social stigma. He presented me with a handwritten list: Paris, London, Vienna, Berlin, all the European capitals. He also gave me a handful of his personal cards, each inscribed: 'Introducing my dear friend Magda. Please take care of her.' I hadn't the heart to suggest that it looked perilously like pimping for his daughter. He wouldn't have understood. I had learned long ago, on that drunken night in Padua, that he really did see me, not as the fruit of his loins, but as the work of his hands – the best whore in the game!

"You asked how I started as the black widow. That's exactly how – through Papa! When I left him after dinner I was just drunk enough and reckless enough to telephone the number of the Vienna lokal. A woman's voice answered. I introduced myself as Magda, a friend of Doctor Kardoss. I was asked to wait in the foyer of my hotel. A carriage would be sent for me. It would, if I so desired, also bring me home. A fee was named, payable in gold crowns. The fee covered all services. It was quite substantial. I was asked to wear an evening dress.

"The carriage arrived. I was handed inside. The windows were painted black; so I had no idea where I was going. Half an hour later I was ushered into a luxurious villa surrounded by parklands. No questions were asked about my identity. The money and Papa's card were enough. My hostess, a well dressed, well spoken woman in her forties, asked what my pleasure was. I asked what she offered. Anything and everything. I told her that, as this was my first night in this lovely place, I should like to work through the menu. And that, my dear doctor, was exactly what I did. I found several dishes I liked and I order them wherever I go. The rest you have already in your notes. You see I didn't hold you up, did I? We still have twenty-five minutes!"

My flippant tone annoys him. He snaps at me:

"I don't see anything funny in what you've told me."

"Neither do I!" It is my turn to be angry. "But what do you want? Blood? You can have that. I'm bleeding inside. The husband I loved died horribly. To my only child I'm a nightmare. My own father sent me out on the brothel route, because he thought that was the safest way for me to travel. The fact that he was right doesn't make it any easier. What else do you want? A room by room description of orgies in an expensive casino? You can look it all up in Krafft-Ebing – unless you want me to undress and demonstrate! But put this down in your notebook, dear colleague. At least when I'm there, I know I'm alive. I may be half out of my mind with lust; but I'm celebrating life, not death!"

"You're a liar, Madame!" He dismisses me with cold brutality. "For you, every love story ends in a chamber of horrors. Your own dreams tell you the truth. You're wedded, not to life, but to death!"

Suddenly it is all too much. I cannot bear to look at his stony, accusing eyes. I am sick of this day-long, shabby, useless inquisition. I burst into tears.

It is a long time before I recover. When I look up Jung has disappeared. His wife is standing in front of me with a glass of cordial. She smiles and hands it to me.

"Carl asked me to bring you this. He'll be back soon. He's walking in the garden, getting his thoughts together. This has been a long session, exhausting for you both. Drink it, please."

I sip the drink and dab my eyes, and wonder why I feel as though a steamroller has flattened me out on the pavement. Emma Jung perches herself on the edge of the desk and talks to me in her calm, persuasive fashion:

"I did warn you, didn't I? I don't know what your problems are; but clearly you've hit the first crisis point. It's always distressing. You feel naked and ashamed, as if you are the only one out of step with the world. But you're not. The hardest thing to learn is to accept yourself for what you are, to be glad of the good and forgive yourself for the bad. Oh dear! I didn't mean to run on. You're Carl's patient, not mine; but I know he's very concerned for you."

"He has a funny way of showing it."

I try to make a joke, but it doesn't turn out right. I am on the verge of tears again. Emma reaches out, takes my hand, imprisons it between her palms and holds it in her lap. I feel strangely comforted, as if there were a lifeline holding me to sanity. Her calm voice soothes me like a lullaby.

"I have to explain something about Carl; because at this moment in his life, he's not very good at explaining himself. Although he was brought up in a very narrow world, as the son of a country parson, his forbears on both sides were strange and brilliant people. His grandfather, for whom he is named, spent a year in prison in Berlin, as a suspected accomplice in the assassination of a Russian official. Then he went on to become a brilliant doctor, Rector of the University and Grand Master of the Swiss Freemasons. He was a playwright and essayist. He also found time to father thirteen children! Oh, and there's a kind of family legend that he was the illegitimate son of Goethe. However, nobody's too sure about that. Carl's maternal grandmother was supposed to have second sight; and apparently his mother had quite uncanny insights into people." She laughs and pats my hand. "It's an odd inheritance to cope with; when you add to it Carl's own restless curiosity and his stubborn refusal to come to terms with the ordinary things, well . . . there are problems for us and advantages for his patients. It's strange. You two are very much alike. I felt it from the moment we met. I don't know whether that's a good thing or a bad thing; but there it is. Oh, I almost forgot! Carl wants a little more time with you before you leave. Then he would like to ride back to town with you in the car. He has papers to take to Miss Wolff."

"I could have the chauffeur deliver them. It would save your husband a trip."

Her grip tightens a little on my hand.

"I think he wants to do some work with her. He's told me not to make dinner for him."

"In that case, may I invite you to dine with me at the Baur au Lac? If you don't mind leaving the children with Nurse for a couple of hours, I'd love you to come. Tonight of all nights, I don't want to eat alone. I'll have you picked up here and brought back."

She hesitates a few moments then accepts, on condition that I arrange it with her husband.

"I don't want him to think I'm poaching on his territory; but I know he'll be out late and – oh dear! – I don't want to dine alone either!"

We settle on eight o'clock. I will arrange to have dinner served in the suite. We can make girl talk – kick off our shoes and be comfortable. Suddenly I find myself calm again. The floor is solid under my feet. This little female conspiracy, and the certainty that Jung is having an affair with his assistant, restore

my shaky hold on reality. These are matters I understand. The rest belong in the chamber of horrors. I
wish I could forget the horrors; but I cannot. The door
to the chamber is open now and the black bats are
flying across the face of the moon. Emma Jung gives
my hand a final affectionate squeeze and admonishes
me:

"Tidy yourself up before he comes back. Your nose
is shiny and your lipstick is smeared. There's a mirror
by the wash basin."

I am grateful for her sturdy commonsense. In some
ways she reminds me of Lily. I wish my own grip on
reality was as strong and as stubborn as theirs.

JUNG
Zurich

I am shamed by what I have
done. I stand here, fumbling with
the stones of my unfinished vil-
lage, and ponder my cruel folly. I have taken the
words of a patient, spoken to me in trust and confidence, and I have used them as a lash to beat her into
submission. I have turned the truth she has told me
into a lie, and thrust it back at her in mockery. Then,
when I saw its shattering effect, I fled. I called Emma
from the kitchen, made a hasty excuse about a long
day and a hysterical outburst from my patient and left
her to cope with the crisis.

I do not know what damage I have done, how far I
have thrust her back into her psychotic situation. I do
not know what I can salvage out of the mess. All I
know is I cannot let her leave like this. I have to go
back and talk with her again. The small blue phial in
her reticule is not a stage prop. It is an instrument of

death, and I am convinced that she has the nerve to use it, once her last hope is extinguished. I must go back to her – but not yet. I have asked Emma to hold her on any pretext at all, until she is composed again and I have my head set on straight.

Why did I do this incredible thing? Why? Why? There is no point in raging at myself. That's another lie. I know damned well why I did it – for twenty reasons, all bad! This Magda Hirschfeld is probing and tapping at my weaknesses, testing the locks on all the secret doors of my unconscious. She is like Salome's black snake, coiled inside me, tightening its coils as it settles deeper, hissing quietly to tell me: "I am here. I am waiting!"

I know what she is waiting for; she has told me clearly from the beginning. She read the sign over my door. She read it, rightly, as a promise, that the dumb oracle would speak, that the hidden god would present himself. When he does not, she will blame me, because I am the man who carved the sign and who solicits the belief and the offerings of the pilgrims. I do not want to be unmasked as a charlatan. I hate her for the threat she poses to my unstable persona.

I hate her, but I envy her, too. What I dream in secret, she has dared and done. She has played all the roles in all the sexual mysteries. I have only dreamed priapic pomps and enjoyed my little lusts furtively, in secret. She has dared murder, too, and escaped scot free. I have dreamed murder; but the closest I shall ever come to it is a pamphlet, a speech, a cavil at some conference, some petty spiteful act before bed or after. God help me for a coward and a sham!

You see, that's what I mean! Which god do I invoke? The old whitebeard, up in the empyrean who obliterated my cathedral with his great turd? Or the blind, dark phallus god in the cave? Or is there another to whom I am wilfully blind, of whom I am mortally afraid, about whom I weave webs of fantasy, to shut out the pure white light of his reality?

Which one will I show to Magda Hirschfeld when she asks: "Can you open my eyes and make me see what my husband saw, mumbling his litanies in the long, dark nights of his agony?" I know she will ask that – and I have tried to pre-empt the question by accusing her of a passion for the dead!

Elijah! Where are you? I need you now. I have to walk back to the house and up the stairs and into the room where Salome waits for me. It's a long way. I can't endure it without your company. You see, I love Salome, but I'm afraid of her, too. Her black snake is inside me; but how can I penetrate her? That's what I was trying to do, you understand, break down the door, get inside, out of the storm.

I am in panic. I feel myself slipping out of this ambient world into that far, other land of the unconscious. I grasp, like a drowning man, for the nearest tangible object. It is the trunk of the apple tree which overhangs the boathouse and shelters my toy village. I lay my cheek against its rough bark. I reach up and shake the branches. Small unripe apples fall to the ground. One of them thumps me on the head. Like Isaac Newton I discover that the law of gravity still prevails. I am back on earth. I walk reluctantly towards the house. My patient is calm again. She has repaired her make-up. She is chatting amiably with Emma. She offers a brief deprecation.

"I'm quite recovered now. Your wife has been most kind. She tells me you are dining out tonight. I've asked her if she would consent to take dinner with me at the Baur au Lac. I'll have her picked up and brought home safely. I hope you don't mind. I dread spending this evening alone."

Mind? Of course not! Why should I? I shall have a whole evening free with Toni – and no possible reproaches afterwards. I shall also have a useful complaint to hold in reserve: I do not approve of my wife becoming intimate with my patients! Then – because nothing in life is as perfect as one would wish – I have a private disappointment. I cannot now call on my patient at the hotel, as I had proposed to do after my visit to Toni. I shepherd Emma out of the room and try to make my peace with Magda Hirschfeld.

"You've had a rough day; but you've come through it very well. I know my last remark sounded harsh and brutal. In analysis, one uses this technique sometimes, to force an abrupt change of direction. You were being flippant about a quite serious question. That indicated an opposite attitude. You were under great stress. You might attempt to avoid or conceal something important. I had to remind you, sharply, that we were not playing games."

She gives me a long searching look and a doubter's smile.

"You called me a liar. You said I was wedded to death, not to life. Both are ugly accusations. If I'm a liar, I'm wasting time and money here. If I'm wedded to death, I have a first class ticket to the honeymoon. In short, you were being gratuitously cruel. That's *my* vice. I recognise it quickly. You owe me an apology and an explanation."

Her attack takes me by surprise. I have no choice but to apologise.

"I'm sorry. This has been a long day for both of us. Let me write in another appointment for you tomorrow."

"Before you do that . . ."

"Yes?"

"I'd like to have the explanation."

"Of what?"

"Your accusations. Do you really think I'm a liar?"

"No; but as a prudent professional I have to consider the possibility. I have to test your story before I can accept it as a basis for diagnosis. So far I haven't had time to do that. Don't be offended. I deal all the time with the most elaborate fabrications. People wander into police stations and confess to murders they couldn't possibly have committed. Women in menopause report rape attempts. Elderly spinsters are visited by angels in their beds."

She laughs lightly and throws out her arms in surrender.

"No rape. No angels. More's the pity! Now another question: am I insane?"

"No."

"What's the matter with me?"

"Exactly what you've told me. Whatever name I give it won't change the fact: you indulge obsessively and with increasing frequency in sado-masochistic encounters alternating with lesbian adventures. That's fact. The whys and wherefores will emerge during analysis. If we work well together, they will emerge quickly and a psychic adjustment will be that much easier to make. All we've done so far is set down a case history in outline and established a sketch of symptomatology."

"And the prognosis?"

"It's too early to make one. There's a lot more work to be done."

"Is the work worth doing?"

"You have to answer that. How much do you value your life, your self?"

"Not very highly."

"Then what do you expect of me?"

"I'm not sure." She frowns over the question for a little while and then in piecemeal fashion sets down her answer. "Papa and Lily reared me in a private paradise; but they turned me into an exotic animal unfit to live anywhere else – not only unfit but dangerous, because all I think about is myself and my own survival. So, now I suppose I'm looking for someone like Papa – no, like Johann really! – to show me how to find a place in the everyday world. I can't go back to the womb and be born again, so I need a guide, a mentor. You're not the only candidate, of course."

She says it with a little secret smile that irritates me again. I am too tired for teasing. I demand to know.

"Who is the other fortunate fellow?"

"Basil Zaharoff. He's reputed to be the biggest arms dealer in the world. He sells everything you need to run a war. He does a lot of his selling by bribery and through women. He's offered me a job – as madam of all his houses of appointment and controller of his women agents. His opinion of me is the same as Papa's – and again I quote verbatim – 'If you turned professional, my dear Magda, you'd be the greatest in the game!' "

"And you're seriously interested in that?"

"I have to be. The pay is large and protection is guaranteed."

350

"But you haven't accepted yet?"

"No. Gianni di Malvasia suggested I see you first."

"Why me?"

"He said – and again I quote – 'Jung embraces religious experience; even though he does not always define it in orthodox terms.' "

"He's right. I embrace it in this sense: I accept that it exists, and that for many people – millions all over the world – it modifies life most profoundly. But let me be very clear, Madame. I cannot *give* you religious experience. I cannot endow you with any faith. I will not argue any system of belief with you. You come to me Christian; you go out Christian. You come atheist; you go home atheist. I don't peddle absolutions either, like the Roman Catholics!"

"But you have a promise, carved over your door: 'Whether he is called or not, the god will be present.' Where is he? We haven't heard from him yet."

"You don't believe in him. I haven't discovered him. So we have to get on without him."

Our brief debate seems to have exhausted her. She gives a dry little laugh and a shrug of resignation.

"If Lily were here now, she'd say it was Humpty Dumpty time."

"Please? I've never heard the expression."

She explains that Humpty Dumpty is a character in an English nursery rhyme. She recites it to me, slowly, so that I will not miss any of the words:

Humpty Dumpty sat on a wall,
Humpty Dumpty had a great fall.
All the King's horses, and all the King's men,
Couldn't put Humpty together again.

It is an amusing jingle; but, to a bullet-headed Swiss from Basel, it doesn't mean very much. I ask:

"Who was Humpty Dumpty?"

"He was an egg!"

"Oh, I see! And then he fell from the wall. Oh, of course! You cannot put a squashed egg back together again. Very amusing!"

It is obviously not amusing for her. In a tone of mortal sadness she puts the question I have been dreading.

"I've killed a dog and a horse and a woman. I've ruined the life of a child. Can you put me back together again? Can you make me whole?"

I am touched almost to tears. I, too, wish the god were present to teach me the healing words. I reach out and draw her to her feet and hold her at arm's length and tell her, as gently as I can, the only truth I know:

"I can't change what's done. There's no cure for murder. It isn't a disease. It's an act that carries condign penalties. They can never be enforced against you. You're like the soldier, home safe from the killing ground. You're lucky; because with help – the kind of help an analyst can offer – you can still change yourself."

"Into what?"

"Whatever you want to be. Habits can be altered. Obsessional syndromes can be modified. You're a doctor; you know that much! For the rest, you can always find a tolerant corner of the world to indulge your sexual preferences."

"But don't you see? It's the reason I need, the motive, the urge."

"You don't like what you are. Isn't that reason enough?"

"Strangely, it isn't. I can stop being what I am, at any moment. One dose, one pistol shot and everything's over. But if there were something else, if I could believe I had a soul that would be saved by repentance, admitted to some eternal paradise, that would be a very good reason to change. I watched Johann during his illness. He had something that made all the rest of us, all our love, all our care, totally dispensable. He believed absolutely in an afterlife. But for me, sadly, an afterlife is a myth."

"Even so, why waste the good years? You've got a lot of living still ahead of you."

"What sort of living?" She tries to wrench herself away from me. I hold her until she relaxes again. "Don't you listen? I've had it all! Love, passion, childbirth, money. Even the ultimate thrill of snuffing out a human life like a candle flame and knowing that I was safe, free! What else are you offering, doctor?"

I release her. She turns away and walks to the window that overlooks the lake where the thunder clouds are banking and the water is slate-grey and ominous. Nothing will serve now but total honesty and what I can command of wisdom and what I can share of love that has been too widely and too cheaply dispensed. I go closer, but do not touch her. I choose the words as carefully as if they were jewels on a golden tray:

"Dear colleague, dear woman! I don't know any way to answer you, other than by trying to share with you the experience I'm going through now. I beg you to be patient with me. It isn't easy to put into words. I am – I have been for a long time – in a state very

353

much like yours. I have monstrous dreams. I am obsessed by fantasies of lust and criminal violence. I am, I think, in a worse condition than you, because often I lose grip on reality and find myself in dialogue with emanations from my own unconscious. But I do know, from my own experience and from long contact with the mentally ill at the Burghölzli, that the barrier between fantasy and act is a paper wall, easily breached. So I understand your crime. I understand all your excesses. I understand your fears. I could be very happy playing the same games on the same circuit as you. I would fit very easily into the freak show, believe me! I have suicide impulses as you have – and murder dreams. Often I lock myself in this very room to wrestle with my dark Doppelgänger.

"But something else is happening to me also – something strange and good and beautiful. I'm learning more and more about how the human psyche works, how the past weaves itself into the tapestry of our dreams, how the future grows to reality out of our wildest imaginings. I have to battle to make sense of it. Often I am scared to death; but sometimes – just sometimes – the vision is almost blinding, like seeing the sunshine after a week of storms. You ask what's next for you. I tell you, an infinity of new experiences, new visions, new hopes, new loves too perhaps – but you'll never see them from a brothel bedroom or the inside of a coffin!"

I can say no more. She stands head bowed, face averted from me. I wait, empty and immobile like Omar Khayyám's goblet, downturned upon the grass. When finally she turns to face me, I am shocked to the marrow. Her face is a mask of hate, her tongue a lash of contempt.

"Words, my dear doctor! Rhetoric, all of it! Convert me if you can! Turn the cannibal into a Christian like the missionaries; but don't sell me smoke!"

I am with her in a stride. I grasp her wrists and swing her round to face me. I pull her close so that she can take my words – anger instead of kisses – mouth to mouth!

"How dare you patronise me, you stupid bitch! How dare you bring your brothel tricks into this place! You come begging for help. When it's offered, you reject it! There are tears in what I've told you – tears and blood and hurts to me and my family. I've tried to turn them into coinage that might buy you and other patients a respite from the nightmares that plague you. But no! You don't want that! You want the freak show and the dance of death. Enjoy it then! But don't stage it in my house!"

I release her and turn away in disgust. She stands rubbing her bruised wrists. I am still in rage; so I round on her again.

"You've got debts to pay, Madame! You can't resurrect the dead. You can't give your daughter the childhood she missed. But you can still make some amends. You're trained in the healing arts. There are places and people crying for good doctors. How much do you pay for the privileges of debasing a human being in a house of appointment? There are charities that could put those monies to good use and . . ."

She rejects the whole idea with a gesture of disgust and a new burst of venom.

"Oh Christ! Here it comes again – the same old cliché! Purify yourself with good works. Pay dole money to join the good folk. My husband did that. My own father castrated him, and he offered up his balls and his life and his suffering to buy himself and me and my daughter a place in heaven. And who'll be there when I open the door? Nobody! Nobody!"

It is a cry of pure desperation and I make the mistake of answering it. Gently now, I try to reason with her.

"Please! You've got it all wrong. I'm not offering tickets to heaven. I don't know where heaven is; but I do know where hell is – right inside our skulls! And we create it for ourselves!"

For one brief moment it seems that she will bend to me. The next, she launches herself at me in a fierce physical attack, pummelling my chest, trying to rake my face with her nails, snarling like a tigress over and over.

"God damn you! God damn you for a bloody Swiss hypocrite! God . . . damn . . . you!"

I am an old hand at this from the clinic, where, with two thousand patients, you had to have strong arms and eyes in the back of your head. I grasp her wrists and lock them in a cross so that she cries out in pain. She is terribly strong; but I force her slowly down, while a fierce sexual urge sweeps over me and I give her insult for insult.

"Two can play at that game, my girl! This is what you wanted all along, wasn't it? Salvation in the hayloft with Papa or Rudi or maybe even the stallion in the stall!"

She struggles still, but now she joins the game of abuse.

"You see! You're more mixed up than I am. You like hurting people too. You're a fraud! Your God's a confidence trick. At least I can admit what I am."

I force her down on her knees. She cries out that she

has had enough. I release her. She clasps one hand round my thighs and with the other tries to unbutton my trousers. Before I can thrust her away, before she can take hold of my erection, I come to climax and I stand there trapped like a fool, pumping out seed that stains my trousers while she still kneels like some disappointed worshipper, groping at the shrine of the blind god who is turning into a worm before her eyes.

When the sorry little moment is over, I lift her to her feet and tell her curtly to tidy herself up. I inspect the damage to my trousers. Not too bad. The smock will cover the worst of it. While Emma is seeing my patient to the door, I can slip upstairs and change. It is an embarrassing event; but nothing new in the history of many a hurried congress. While Magda Hirschfeld is tidying herself, I sit down at the desk and put down the last notes. She seats herself in the patient's chair and says, demurely:

"Well, at least you've seen how it happens – rage, violence, surrender. I climaxed at the same time as you did. I'm sorry it wasn't fun. It seems to work better with professionals. Where do we go from here?"

"Nowhere, I'm afraid."

"Why? Because I've embarrassed you? Because I've damaged your self-esteem, your authority?"

"All that, yes; but that's my fault and not yours. I knew the game. I didn't have to play it. No, there's another reason. You and I are dangerous to each other."

"Because we'd end up in bed?"

"No, we'd end in a double madness, folie à deux, and you'd be the one to survive, not I."

"You don't have a very high opinion of yourself either, doctor!"

"No, I don't; and that's another point of resemblance between us. We are both possessed by daimons – of rage, of destruction. You're the caged bird let loose among the predators; so you become the strongest and the cruellest of all. Love makes you vulnerable, so you have to kill it. Do you remember the end of the Snow Queen story? The only thing that melted her icy heart was a tear drop."

"And who, pray, will weep tears for me? Will you, Carl Jung?"

"I did – and you tried to kill me as you killed the horse and the dog and the woman."

"Can I ever be changed?"

"Only if you want it enough."

She ponders that for a moment, then shakes her head.

"As a physician in Italy, I re-made a few virgins in time for the wedding night; but there's no surgery that will turn a Messalina into a Sister of Charity or a murderer into a Mother Abbess. Even the great Carl Jung can't pull God out of a conjuror's hat. Don't bother with the notes. I'll save you the trouble and write the summation for you. 'The patient's condition is irreversible. Prognosis negative.' But I'd still like to have dinner with your wife. I hope you'll allow her to come?"

"She's a free agent. How could I prevent her?"

"Very easily. So, thank you."

"May I ask for your discretion about what happened here?"

"What did happen? Words were said. A man and a woman wrestled a little. Seed was spilt that might

358

have been spent more happily. What does it signify? How much talk can one spend on it? I must go."

She stands and offers her hand. I take it and raise it to my lips. I should like to kiss her on the mouth – but that moment is lost long since. She takes my hands and turns them palms-up, palms-down, as my mother used to do to see whether my nails were clean and whether I had scrubbed my knuckles. She tells me:

"You'd make a good horseman. You have the hands for it, very strong."

"I need them. People are harder to handle than horses."

She picks up her reticule, takes out the envelope full of Swiss francs and hands it to me.

"The fee, doctor – with my thanks."

"There is no fee."

Her manner changes instantly. She is brusque and imperious.

"Nonsense! Of course there's a fee. I've taken up your whole day. I'm a doctor, too, remember. I expect to be paid whether the patient lives or dies. Take it!"

"It's too much!"

"I have no use for it. Spend it on your wife."

She tosses the envelope on the desk. I leave it there. I have earned it. We do need it. She reminds me:

"Your wife mentioned you'd like to be driven to Miss Wolff's house. I'll talk to her while you change your trousers. Mistresses are much less tolerant than wives."

"For a woman with little to be proud of, you're most impertinent, Madame!"

"Not impertinent, just scared. I'm hurrying down a dark street, listening to my own footsteps and my own heartbeat. I don't know where I'm going or what I'll do when I get there. So I make bad jokes; I'm sorry."

"I wish . . ."

"No! Don't! Lily used to have a proverb about wishes. How did it go? Oh yes. 'If wishes were horses, then beggars would ride. Put beggars on horseback and then – woe betide!' Hurry now. I'll go and chat with your wife."

As we drive towards the city, the storm which has been brewing all day bursts over the lake. The rain, mixed with hailstones, beats against the windscreen. Thunder rolls up and down the valley. Forked lightning slashes across the tumbled sky. Magda Liliane Kardoss von Gamsfeld takes her leave with an irony:

"Fräulein Zickzackblitz makes her exit and the powers of heaven are moved. Beautifully staged, doctor! I have new respect for the Swiss. Enjoy your evening!"

By the time I reach Toni's door I am looking like a drowned rat. At least it's a good excuse to get my clothes off quickly. It is, I find, easier to strip off a wet shirt than the memory of folly, failure and professional ineptitude.

M AGDA
Zurich

The moment I am back at the hotel I regret having invited Emma Jung to dinner. I am suddenly weary – so weary that I can hardly drag myself upstairs. I am sick of talking, sick of being talked at. My dearest wish is to be deaf, dumb and blind, tranquil in the amniotic fluid of some primal womb.

I draw myself a bath and soak in it for an hour; then put on a housecoat and stretch out on the chaise-longue with the latest edition of *Die Dame*, a new illustrated magazine for women published in Berlin, which is becoming very popular. After two minutes I have lost the thread of what I am reading. I am too languid, too empty even to be melancholy. As for my plan to take the midnight train to Rome, wild horses will not drag me out of this room tonight.

Tomorrow I will make decisions. Tomorrow or the next day, it makes no matter. I have survived the rack and thumbscrews of a psychiatric inquisition; I can certainly survive a night at the Baur au Lac. I ring for the floor waiter and place my order for dinner to be served at eight-thirty. I also have him ice a bottle of champagne to welcome my guest. I want her to be impressed. I want her to remember a joyful evening. I desire very much that she may like me.

My self-esteem has never been lower. That shabby little scene in Jung's office – which I staged, not he! – makes my flesh crawl every time I think of it. Fräu lein Zickzackblitz indeed! And as for going out in a thunder of Wagnerian music, I was more like Miss Dirty-Face, offering rough trade with her sisters, up and down the Limmatquai. I wonder how Emma Jung would react if she ever found out what happened. It is not impossible. I have the nagging suspicion that Jung is a man who stores up small malices which vitiate his compassion and his very real understanding. It is one more reason to make this meal a memorable occasion for Emma.

When she arrives, I have a completely new impress-ion of her. At home, with her brood clustered about her, she looked the grave young matron, the Frau

361

Doktor, the well bred mistress of a well ordered house. I had guessed her age at thirty-three or there-abouts. Here, at the Baur au Lac, she looks very much younger, very pregnant and very, very vulnerable. When I offer her champagne she hesitates. Carl has a good head for drink; she tends to get tipsy and talkative. She doesn't want to upset the baby. I remind her that she has a very good physician in attendance and a chauffeur to drive her home; so she accepts the drink. I make her take the chaise-longue while I settle myself in an armchair near the bell pull and make the toast: "To a new friendship and, of course, to a healthy new baby!" We drink. Then she asks the first and most awkward question:

"When is your next appointment with Carl?"

"I haven't made one. He feels I should look elsewhere for counsel."

"Oh dear!" She frowns unhappily.

"Please, don't be distressed! Your intuition was right in the first place. I have no complaints. Your husband tried very hard to help me. I tried to cooperate. It didn't work. No blame to either of us."

"Then tomorrow Carl must write to your physician in Paris. That's very important. It's not only courtesy. It's essential for you too. I'll have Toni remind him in the morning." She gives me a small embarrassed smile. "That's the protocol in our house. All professional business goes through Toni. I suppose it's natural enough. I married when I was twenty-one. Carl was seven years older. It was he who set the rules. I followed them without question. Very Swiss! After a while it becomes a habit. So much of my time is taken up with the children, I just have to let Carl go his own way. I know that isn't good for him – especially at this stage of his life – but I can't fight him any more."

She is anxious to talk. I am happy to listen. I pour more chanpagne and prompt her gently.

"You mentioned your husband was under great stress. What's the problem?"

"I wish I knew! No, that's not true. I do know part of it, a large part. I just don't like to admit it; and Carl, of course, hates to discuss it with me. He's always chosen to believe that a wife has fewer brains than other women." She laughs a little unsteadily. "As a matter of fact, he's right. Otherwise why would we let ourselves in for marriage and childbirth? Was your marriage happy?"

"All but the last year. That was horrible. My husband died of cancer."

"Oh dear. I'm sorry."

"Please! It's long in the past."

"Do you have any children?"

"One daughter. She's married now. We're not close."

"That's sad. And you've never wanted to get married again?"

"Well, let's say I haven't met anyone who'd want to spend a lifetime with me – or with whom I'd want to spend more than a month. I lead a busy life. I run two stud farms. We sell horses all over Europe. I travel a lot."

"I envy you that – the travel, I mean. Carl is the traveller in our family. He's been to Paris, England, the United States, Italy, Germany. I've gone with him to a couple of conferences; but there's not much fun in that. Carl needs to be the centre of attention. I'm not very good at being the modest wife deferring to the great man and his colleagues. I have a few ideas of my own I'd like to air sometimes!"

"You told me your husband trained you as an analyst."

"He did, but I wasn't thinking of that. I was thinking of the other side of the story. These people, my husband included, are handling high explosives and they're as careless and jealous and stubborn as children! You have no idea the backbiting that goes on at these conferences, the cabals and cliques that form around each old leader, each new theorist. I'm dreading the meeting that's coming up in Munich. My husband is preparing for a big fight with Freud. They've been friends for so long. Now they're sworn enemies. I like Freud. He's always been kind and understanding to me. He even admits I have a brain. So I'm caught in the middle. Oh dear! I told you I shouldn't drink. Here I am running on like the village gossip. You talk to me for a change. May I call you Magda? I hate feeling distant from someone. That's another problem. I'm getting more and more distant from Carl."

I have a fine ear for malice. I hear none in what she is telling me. Rather I hear regret and the insidious sadness of a woman lonely too soon, imprisoned in a nursery, while her husband, the sportive gaoler, goes off about his business, safe in the knowledge that the children will hold her more securely than locks and bars.

I want to hear more of this clever fellow and how he runs the rest of his life, and what, if anything, I have missed by not submitting myself humbly to his guidance. Because I do not want to offend my Emma – open and vulnerable but relaxed at last – I walk the long way round to get the eggs. I tell her how I did my final training in Vienna, while Freud was teaching there, and how Gianni di Malvasia and I spent our student nights in the glow of the Gay Apocalypse. The tale carries us up to the moment when dinner is served and the consommé is disposed of. Then she is ready to pick up the thread of her own story.

"That's what Carl missed most, I think – the carefree days. He was always on the move. The family had little money. He had to thrust his own way upwards and he did it by sheer hard work and brains. He lived then, as he would like to live now, largely and lustily. That's what made me fall in love with him. Everything he did and said – drinking, yodelling, debating – was dramatic, almost greedy. With me it was different. I took everything for granted. My family was rich. I'd always had whatever I wanted. We were big people in Basel. Folk bowed and doffed hats to my parents. I took that for granted, too. Carl resented it. He still does. I have to be very careful in company never, never to push myself forward in his presence. Perhaps I should have fought it from the beginning, but it's too late now. Carl's not the king of the profession. Freud still wears the crown. But Carl is certainly the crown prince. He has his own court – and oh dear, oh dear! – his own ladies-in-waiting, who adore him and hang on his every word. He has his mistresses too, as a proper prince should have. Toni, as you've probably guessed, is the latest – and I think she'll last longer than any of the others."

"And you approve that?"

"I'm not asked to approve or disapprove. It's a fact of life. I accept it because of the children. One can only fight so long; after that it's not home any more but hell on earth. Carl makes it difficult, of course, because he insists on having Toni round the place morning, noon and night. I wish he'd set up another establishment away from the house, and do his business and run his love life from there; but he won't. He says we can't afford it. I try to point out that we're both spending too much life on this mess. He won't listen. I'm sure the stress of all this is contributing to his breakdown."

Breakdown? I have heard "problems", "stress", "strain". But breakdown is a new word – and for me a bad one. Is it possible I have made this painful and dangerous confession to a man who is off the rails? There has been talk of scandals, involving other women. Is it possible that Jung, not I, is the clown in this absurd circus? My blood turns to ice. The hairs rise on the nape of my neck. God almighty! Who here is the crazy one? With great calm, with singular sweetness, I ask Emma:

"What form does the breakdown take? How does it show itself? It must be very difficult for you and the children."

JUNG
_____
Zurich

"Hullo Paris! Hullo Paris! I wish to speak to Doctor Gianni di Malvasia. No! Mal-va-sia! I will spell it out for you."

I am lying naked in bed, while Toni is trying to raise Magda Hirschfeld's doctor in Paris. The reason is simple – so simple that, in my excited state, I missed it by a Roman mile. This woman is suicidal. She carries poison in her reticule. I have rejected her as a

366

patient and a sexual partner. My wife is dining with her at the hotel. I have consented to the arrangement. What better prelude to a really spectacular suicide!

Toni saw the possibility as soon as she heard my carefully expurgated edition of the day's events. She insisted that I call Malvasia in Paris and shift the responsibility back to him, as the physician of record. Whether he intervenes or not, it will be some protection against the scandal which will inevitably break if the woman decides to do away with herself, tonight, in the Baur au Lac.

"Hullo Paris! Hullo Paris! Yes! I am still waiting for Doctor Malvasia. Understand please, it is a medical emergency. Yes, an emergency!"

It is more than a medical emergency. It is make or break for me. I am out of a job and subsisting on private practice. I have acquired a reputation as an eccentric. Some of my colleagues suspect that I am unstable. There has already been too much gossip about too many silly affairs with women. I know there are some indiscreet letters lying around. So, all I need is a suicide at the Baur au Lac and a headline: "Rejected by Local Analyst, Woman Kills Herself". Finally it seems Toni has been able to get through. I hear her saying:

"This is Fräulein Wolff, assistant to Doctor Carl Jung. Yes, the doctor speaks both French and Italian. A moment only! I will pass you to him."

She hands me the receiver. I introduce myself in my best Tuscan. The line crackles continually; but we are able to understand each other.

"This is Carl Jung. Can you hear me?"

"This is Malvasia. I hear you. What's the problem . . ?"

"This patient you sent me."

"What about her?"

"There is no way I can help her. She is not a suitable subject for my type of analysis."

"I'm sorry to hear that."

"I have spent six hours with her today. As therapist and patient we are totally incompatible. She is, however, in bad condition – very bad."

"Is she certifiable?"

"No! No! No! She is more rational than you or I. There are certain things one should not say on a telephone; but I will try. Obsession."

"Understood."

"Sado-masochist – increasing frequency, increasing violence."

"Understood."

"Great guilt about past episodes which are not – definitely not – for discussion at this moment. A strong suicidal urge. That's why I am calling you. Does she have relatives who could assume some responsibility?"

"Close ones, no. The husband is dead. His family would help, but she would not apply to them. Her father died shortly after the husband. There is a daughter; but she seems to be totally alienated. How grave is the risk?"

"Very grave. She carries a phial of prussic acid. I've seen it."

"Hell! Where is she now?"

"At the Baur au Lac. My wife is dining with her. They met only today and immediately established a rapport; which of course I approve. But you have to understand, doctor, that, once that dinner is over and my wife returns home, I can no longer be responsible for your patient. She has paid me for today's session. I have told her I cannot help her further."

"Can you recommend her to anyone else?"

"No. Because I am not the physician. You are!"

"Dio mio! What time is it in Zurich?"

"Nine in the evening."

"There's a train that leaves Paris at ten or ten-thirty. It gets to Zurich in the morning. I'll try to be on it. Is she likely to do anything silly tonight?"

"I doubt it. My guess is that she will not want to shame my wife – and so, she will stage the suicide somewhere else. I emphasise, however, that one can never be sure."

"I understand. I'll want to see you as soon as I arrive."

"Come straight to my house. You have the address. I'll hand you all my notes and pass on certain matters verbally. We should most definitely confer before you meet your patient."

"Thank you for the call and for your efforts, Doctor Jung."

"A pleasure, I assure you. A sadness one was unable to do more. Until tomorrow then!"

Toni throws herself on the bed beside me, chanting triumphantly:

"Tomorrow, tomorrow, tomorrow! I don't care about tomorrow any more. It's all out in the open now. Emma knows. She's told me in so many words it's my job to look after you. And, starting now, that's just what I'm going to do! First, we make love; then we get up and have supper; then we make love again. And if you get home before morning, it won't be my fault. In fact, if you never go home at all, I don't care!" She straddles me and pins me to the bed and stares into my eyes. "One question though! Our Magda. You didn't play games with her, did you? When I left, you had that lecherous look in your eye."

Und so weiter. And so it goes, the sweet and silly night, when we pay long homage to the blind god who is not a worm any more but a great strong pillar, when I don't have to think about Emma, because she has finally acknowledged my right to live free. As for Magda Liliane Kardoss von Gamsfeld, well, her physician is on the way from Paris. I'm sure she will be in good hands. Nonetheless, I regret her. She was an experience lost, a moment that found me unready.

Never mind! I am here, celebrating the mystery of conjunction with her who is sister, lover, protector, all in one. I love you, Toni my love! You are my Salome. The snake is our friend. He coils himself about us, binding us together. No. I don't want to sleep! I want to lie close to you until the snake stirs again. Tonight of all nights, let no dreams come!

MAGDA
Zurich

"The breakdown!" Emma wipes a morsel of salmon from the corner of her mouth, takes a sip of wine and explains. "It's hard for us all, yes! He gets into these great shouting rages, which are really quite childish, but terrify the children. They're still very young, as you saw. However, from my point of view and from his too, I think, the withdrawals are worse than the rages. He locks himself in his study or goes wandering off along the lakeshore muttering to himself and sometimes shouting about people whom only he can see. He dreams a lot – bad nightmares! – and flails about in bed. To tell you the truth, I'm quite glad when he doesn't sleep with me now. I'm frightened he's going to hurt the baby."

I watch her as she takes another mouthful of food. She is not beautiful, and yet there is a grave and tender charm about her that tugs at my heartstrings. It makes me wonder, for one poignant instant, what my own daughter looks like. I ask her:

"Is he a good father?"

"Yes. When he can be. I know that's a silly way to put it; but he really is two people, more perhaps! One of them is a kind and loving man; the other is a dark dreamer, a kind of troubled poet, swinging all the time between hope and black despair. That's the one I don't like. I'm very ordinary, you see. When Carl was working at the Burgholzli and lecturing at the university, he was much better, at least for us, than he is now. There was how shall I call it? – an architecture, a structure that held him together. He had routines; he had colleagues; he had a standing place. Now he doesn't have those things. Just when he needs them most, he doesn't have them. I can't supply them. I'm at the wrong stage of life. I have children tugging at my skirts all day. I'm wiping noses and treating coughs and settling nursery quarrels. I don't have time – even if I had the talent – to sit down and help Carl work things out. Besides, I'm not sure that's what he wants. He gets bored with people very quickly. Watch him eating an orange! He sucks the juice out and tosses the pulp and the rind away. That's why women are so attracted to him at first and so angry afterwards." She laughs and splutters over the wine. I

371

reach out and wipe her lips. She pats my hand in thanks. "He gives them his whole attention, makes them feel like great, complicated romantic heroines. Then he walks away and leaves them screaming or crying into their handkerchiefs. He hates to be committed, you see. He has to spread himself to feel safe."

I can restrain myself no longer. I have to ask:

"What about Toni? Will that happen to her, too?"

Emma takes a long swallow of wine and waits until I refill her glass. This time she has to labour a little over the answer.

"I don't know about Toni. She's young and attractive; so she'll probably hold Carl longer than the others. But there's more to her than that. She's got a first-class mind, very subtle, very well organised, but highly imaginative, too. She writes good poetry. Carl claims, seriously, that she's a female Goethe. That's an exaggeration, of course. He's just besotted with her! But she *is* very good. I know this sounds strange coming from a wife, but she's very good for Carl, too. Oh yes, she's passionate and she enjoys sex, but that's not what I mean. Carl is wandering in very strange country just now. Toni seems to understand the geography, to be able to hold his hand and share the experience, without getting herself lost, as Carl often does. I don't know if that makes sense, but . . ."

It does make sense. It also disturbs me. I have to take a risk now and ask her a question she may not care to answer.

"You told me that I was very like your husband and that you weren't sure whether that was good or bad."

"I remember."

"Your husband went further. He said he couldn't

continue the analysis, because he and I were dangerous to each other."

"I think he was right. I'm glad he had sense enough to recognise it."

"Can you explain what he meant?"

"I think I can; but please . . ." She gives me a dubious little smile and reaches out to clasp my hand in that familiar protective gesture. "Please don't be hurt or angry. We're friends now. I want us to stay friends. Promise?"

"I promise."

"Well. Let's go back to Carl. One of the things that is happening to him – and he is making it happen, too! – is that his unconscious life, all the memories, fears, hopes, fairy tales, myths and legends, everything, everything in his past, is coming to the surface. He can't cope with the experience. It's as if a great fountain were welling up from the deepest part of the ocean and creatures he has never seen, never dreamed of, are now swimming about on the surface. There are people, and you're one of them, who seem to have power to unlock those mysterious fountains and set them gushing out of control. It's not something you do deliberately. It just happens. In Carl's case, however, it's bad and dangerous. He can no longer shut down the fountain; he can no longer cope with the strange creatures. He's trying to, but I think he's making a great mistake. He's going about it the wrong way. He's trying to open more and more caverns in the deep. That toy village he showed you in the garden. I find that sinister. He's trying to rebuild his childhood and his primaeval past too, stone by stone. I say it's a terribly dangerous experiment. He claims his only hope is to make the backward journey.

So you see, I'm glad you're not going on with Carl, but I'm sorry you're not staying with me."

"I set no fountains gushing for you, is that it?"

"On the contrary. How often do you think I talk to anyone as I've talked to you tonight? I feel good with you: good and tender and loving. Oh yes! You've turned on a fountain; but it's a small, happy, bubbling spring of clear sweet water."

Suddenly, without warning, I find myself weeping quietly. The next instant she is standing by my chair holding my face against her breast, my breast against her swollen body, so that I feel, or dream I feel, the stirring of the new life she carries. She rocks me gently to and fro and croons over me:

"Have your cry. It's good for you. Emma's here."

Afterwards, I ring for the waiter to remove the food and bring us coffee and brandy, because tonight, says Emma, she has the right to be a little crazy. Over the brandy she tells me:

"I'd like to do something for you, my dear."

"What's that?"

"I'd like to write to your daughter and ask her whether she'd consider either meeting you or at least opening a correspondence with you. I'd find the words to say, believe me. After all, you want to contact her, but you just can't find the right way to do it. She probably feels the same; but even if nothing comes of it, you'll feel better because you've tried. Will you let me do it, please?"

I cannot tell her that I shall probably not be here to see the end of the correspondence; so I agree. It is a tender thought. I am touched and grateful. I give her Gunhild's address in Semmering. She will forward the letter to Anna Sibilla. I give her the address of Ysambard Frères in Paris. They will know where I am, dead or alive! Then I have a question for Emma: how does she propose to order her life now that she has virtually accepted a ménage à trois with Toni Wolff?

"I've thought about it a lot. I think I've got it straight in my mind – which doesn't make it easier by any means! I'm going to go on living at Küsnacht, just as we are now. I'm not going to quarrel. I'm going to try to enjoy what is still left between Carl and me. It's quite a lot, one way and another. I'm going to hold the family together, make sure they respect their father and that he still gives them what love and affection he can. I'll be nice to Toni. However, a line will be drawn. The study is Carl's territory and hers. The rest is mine. I want no invasions, no advice, no nothing! And that's as far as I've gone. The rest will have to sort itself out, day by day."

"There's one thing you haven't mentioned."

"What's that?"

"You! What are you going to do for Emma?"

"Well." She blushes like a schoolgirl and gives an embarrassed little laugh. "I wasn't going to mention this; but now that you've asked, I'm going to write a book."

"Good for you! When do you start? What's the book about?"

"I haven't started it yet. It will probably take years to do. It's about the Holy Grail, the cup or the dish – it varies, you see – that Christ used at the Last Supper. It is also said – the legend is very complicated – that Joseph of Arimathea used it to catch Christ's blood at the crucifixion and then later carried it to Glastonbury in England. After that it was lost and the Knights of the Round Table set out to find it.

375

The legend is everywhere in Europe. There are even versions in the East."

"It sounds fascinating, but why you?"

"Promise you won't laugh!"

"I promise."

"According to the legend, the Grail search goes on in every generation. It's a very profound symbol of our common search for happiness and contentment and inner peace. Well, I know now that my life is never going to turn out the way I dreamed it would when I was a girl. Carl is always going to be the wanderer. There will always be a Toni in his life. So, I need a hope to keep me going. I need my own Grail search, a real one but a symbolic one too! I know it sounds silly, but . . ."

I take her in my arms and hold her to me, trying to pour into her all the love I have left, trying to call back all the wasted love and pour that in too, because I know that none of it will ever be enough for the journey she has to make. Finally, To break the tension that threatens to stifle us both, I make a silly joke:

"The way we keep falling into each other's arms, you might just as well stay the night. The bed's big enough."

To my surprise, she takes me quite seriously.

"Don't think I wouldn't like it. You're not old enough to be my mother; but you could certainly be my big sister, and I'd love to lie in bed and talk to you and fall asleep in your arms. But my brood at home need me. I'm going to have one more tiny brandy and then go. What are you going to do with yourself – not just tomorrow, but afterwards?"

"God knows! But I'm not going to think about it

tonight. I'm going to curl up and remember what a simple, lovely evening we've had."

"Oh, I almost forgot!" She opens her purse and brings out an envelope with two tablets in it. "Carl gave me these as he rushed out of the house. He said you were to take them both, half an hour before bedtime, and I was to stand over you and make sure you did it. So, please, will you take them now, so I don't have to tell lies for you?"

I do as she asks. I telephone the concierge and ask him to make sure the chauffeur is standing by and that he will accompany my guest from her front gate to the front door and wait until she is safely locked inside. This done, we sit over the last of the brandy, saying little, feeling much, not wanting to open any more doors to any more caverns, because next time we may not be so lucky. Emma's last words to me are strange:

"I'll write to your daughter. I'll write to you. I won't tell Carl. You and I will never see each other again. That's probably a good thing, because nothing can get spoiled. I don't know what you've done in your life that makes you feel so unhappy. I don't care either. I've known you only one day; but I love you and I think you love me. That makes a clean start for both of us."

We embrace. We kiss. She leaves without a backward glance. I drain the last of the brandy, throw myself on the bed in a tearless rage of grief – and tumble off the edge of the world.

I awake with a dry throat and head full of cotton-wool to find Gianni di Malvasia sitting on the edge of the bed, tapping my cheeks, urging me to open my eyes and tell him my name, age and birthplace. I don't do it very well the first time; so he makes me repeat

377

the performance until he is satisfied. I ask drowsily:

"What brings you here?"

"Jung rang me last night. He thought you might try to do yourself in. When I saw you first, I thought you had. For God's sake! You know better than to mix bromides and alcohol."

"How the hell do you know what I mixed?"

"The brandy bottle's in the lounge, half empty. And Jung told me he'd sent you two sleeping tablets for bedtime."

"When did he tell you that?"

"This morning. I went straight from the train to his house. He told me all about yesterday and gave me his notes."

"Oh Christ! So you know."

"Yes."

"Jung had no right."

"He had every right. I'm the recommending physician. Don't worry! I burned the notes in your fireplace. Now you're going to bathe, dress and pack. I'm going to feed you lunch. Then we take a three o'clock train back to Paris."

"I'm not going to Paris!"

"Where are you going then?"

"I don't know. I haven't worked it out. Rome, perhaps."

"I'm your doctor. I've worked it out. You're coming to Paris. You're going to stay with me for a while."

"I am not going to Paris!"

"Then, dear girl, here is what will happen. The good Doctor Jung and I will sign a paper that declares you a suicidal depressive and gets you committed – presto! presto! to the Burgholzli Clinic, until you

378

are restored to sanity. That's all it takes, two signa-tures. Well?"

"So we go to Paris."

"Good. There's hope for you yet."

"And what am I supposed to do in Paris? How do I cope with Zaharoff?"

"You leave Zaharoff to me. At the moment he's suffering from an inflamed prostate; so he's not going to be chasing you or anyone else for a little while. As to what you do in Paris, we'll talk about that when we get there. If you're willing to gamble some money and some effort, I've got just the project for you. It will take your mind off all your other problems."

"Including murder?" I have to be sure he knows; and he does. He deals with it in a very offhand fashion.

"The murder's not the problem. It's done; but it doesn't show on the balance sheet. It's history or myth, whichever way you want to plead it; but noth-thing can be proved. The real problem is what the murder has done to you. That's what our friend Jung couldn't handle. He's given up the God of his father. Now he doesn't know whether he's deist, theist or the High Panjandrum of Ying Yang. I'm a practical fel-low whose ancestors – Florentine snobs all of them . . ."

"Oh, shut up, Gianni!"

". . . Whose ancestors made a lively art out of assassination. They dealt with the aftermath very tidily, too. The family chaplain gave you absolution. Your uncle the bishop sold you indulgences to keep you out of purgatory and, as part of the bargain, provided you with some friendly surveillance by the city watch, so that the other side didn't knife you in an alley. However, that's all water under the bridge. We're off to Paris. Get up and take a bath. There are two smells I can't stand on a woman – stale perfume and stale alcohol!"

MAGDA
Paris

The reaction hit me the day after I arrived in Paris: waves of black depression, sudden fits of weeping, rages in which I wanted to throw things and smash them, long white nights of lying awake and staring at the ceiling.

How Gianni endured me I will never know. How he navigated between his medical practice and a half crazed woman in his bachelor apartment is a mystery, too. He coaxed; he scolded; he made demands, which he rescinded only when he saw I couldn't meet them. He was doctor one minute, big brother the next, fussy and womanish, too, when it served his purpose. There were times when I wanted to run away, hide myself for ever; but Gianni seemed to have thrown a net over me, gossamer thin but strong as steel, so that I could not escape either the house or his solicitude.

He brought me books which I skimmed and laid aside. He played me Chopin in the evenings. He walked me like a lover in the parks. He encouraged me to cook for us, forced me to confer with the Brothers Ysambard about my affairs, and, one quite memorable evening, to give a dinner party with Basil Zaharoff as guest of honour. I asked Gianni what was the idea of having Zaharoff to table. The man was a horror, a cruel manipulator, a dealer in death.

"So are you, my love," Gianni reminded me tersely. "This will be an exercise in mutual tolerance, in gratitude, too, because he pays my bills on time, and in diplomacy – which touches you quite closely."

"Diplomacy?"

"Sexual and social. The man offered you employment, which you turned down. You gave him one night in bed, for which he rewarded you quite handsomely. That's his bracelet you're wearing now, isn't it? After that one night, he went away, pleasantly inflamed at the prospect of an affair with you. What happened? You fled to Zurich without so much as kiss-my-hand! The man is offended. He isn't used to that sort of treatment. He has told me so himself. I have pleaded for you – ill health, menopausal problems, the whole list! He's only half mollified. He can be a bad enemy. So you're going to put him at your right hand for dinner and you're going to eat a little humble pie, while he enjoys the saddle of lamb. *Capito*?"

Capito! It was hard not to understand Gianni and his Latin logic. The dinner party went off well. I don't remember the other guests. They were rich nobodies, but good patients of Gianni's. I do remember, most vividly, how Basil Zaharoff questioned me about my experience in analysis with Jung:

"So you sit and talk, just that?"

"Well. You sit, you move about, you stand. That's Jung's method. I understand Freud and others like the patient to lie down on a couch. I could see that one might avoid certain aggressive reactions that way."

"And you talk intimately?"

"The more intimately the better."

"Does the doctor – the analyst – take notes?"

"Jung did. He took copious notes."

381

"And presumably those go into his files?"

"In Magda's case," Gianni cuts into the dialogue without so much as a by-your-leave, "in Magda's case, Jung gave me all his hand-written notes. I burned them. But in general, yes, the analyst records the conversations for later study."

"Any such record could be highly damaging." Zaharoff is determined to pursue the argument. "Damaging not only to the patient, but to any other person mentioned in the discussions."

"It's a perennial problem in medicine," says Gianni, agreeably. "The law prevents disclosure in court. It protects the Hippocratic confidence between doctor and patient. But I agree: there is no protection – no adequate protection – against malicious or irresponsible disclosure. That's why I insisted on having Magda's notes handed to me, why I burned them in her suite at the Baur au Lac."

"Were they so damaging then?" Zaharoff asks it like a joke question: when did you stop beating your wife?

Gianni is quick to answer.

"I don't know. I didn't read them."

"Why not?"

"I have my own opinions of Magda. I did not want to pollute them with those of another man. Come, my friend! Would Basil Zaharoff accept another man's judgment of a woman? Of course not."

"But why," asks Zaharoff innocently, "why didn't you, Magda, continue with Jung?"

"For quite a serious reason. We were temperamentally incompatible. Patient and analyst alike have to repose enormous trust in each other. Jung and I were at odds the whole day."

"As the recommending physician," Gianni continues to assert himself in the talk, "I felt it wiser for her not to continue."

"But surely Jung's notes would be valuable for further treatment?"

"They might also be very confusing," says Gianni. "It's not the same as physical medicine: I could describe your symptoms to any reputable doctor and he would make the same diagnosis as I. In psychiatry it's different, much more clouded."

"Weren't you curious about Jung's notes, Magda? I can't imagine any woman not wanting to know what the man was writing about her."

Zaharoff is jocular, benign. I, on the contrary, was concerned to be serious.

"You miss the point. When you're there, as I was, anchored in the chair, you don't care what he's putting down. He's doing surgery on your psyche and it hurts like hell. For all you know, he could be writing bad verse or drawing dirty pictures. Anyway, I'm glad Gianni burned the stuff!"

"Fascinating," says Basil Zaharoff. "I can see a future for the art! It has lots of problems and some interesting uses. Just at this moment I would very much like to have a transcript of the love life of Mr. Lloyd George!"

When the evening was over, Gianni paid me a big compliment. I had done very well. I had charmed the vultures out of the trees and turned them into singing birds. I asked him:

"What was Zaharoff going on about? Why should he be interested in analytic procedures?"

"He's not," said Gianni with a grin. "He's interested in you – and how much you might have told about his business offer or his prowess in bed."

"And if I'd spilled it all?"

"Then, this week or next, next month perhaps, you'd be dead! Don't laugh! It's true. He's made a huge fortune. He's achieved enormous power. Now he has to be respectable. That was the whole point of the dinner party. I want you in Paris. I can't keep you here if Basil Zaharoff is unhappy about you."

"I don't believe this!"

"Believe it, my dear!" says Gianni curtly. "We live in a jungle, and Basil Zaharoff is king of the beasts."

Two mornings later Gianni knocked on my bedroom door and commanded me to get dressed:

"Old clothes, stout shoes. The dowdier you can look, the better. We leave in thirty minutes."

"Where are we going?"

"La Ruelle des Anges – Angel Lane."

"It's a pretty name."

"That's the only pretty thing about it. It's a couple of blocks behind the Boul 'Mich', a rough quarter – hence the sober clothes."

"Why are we going there?"

"Business."

"What sort of business?"

"Possess your soul in patience."

"I don't have a soul."

"Then possess your body in patience."

"What the hell do you think I've been doing? It seems years since I've had any sex."

"Good! Then you'll have a clear head and a pure mind."

"I don't have a mind either, at this hour of the morning."

"Then we'll have to make do with whatever's left,

won't we? Hurry please! It's five past eight; we leave at eight-thirty."

La Ruelle des Anges belied its name. It was a grimy cobbled alley with an open gutter down the centre and rows of bedraggled old dwellings on either side. At the far end was a big wooden coach gate with a smaller door cut into it. Gianni explained that the name Angel Lane was an irony. The angels in question were the prostitutes who used to live there but who had left long since for better accommodation. When we approached the coach gate, Gianni pointed to a newly lettered sign: "Hospice des Anges". He pushed open the wicket gate and ushered me into what had once been the stable yard of an imposing mansion. The stables were now in an advanced stage of reconstruction. The yard was busy with workmen. Gianni threw out his arms in an expansive gesture.

"Well, this is it!"

"This is what?"

"The business, the investment we talked about. We should be able to open in about six weeks."

"Doing what? Bringing the angels back?"

"In a way, yes. That's what the name on the gate signifies. It's a hospice for women or girls who've been on the game and fallen victims to it, one way or another. It's a place where they can come when they get out of gaol, or when they've been beaten up or fallen pregnant. There'll be lodgings, a kitchen and dining room, an infirmary. The commune of Paris has promised a small subsidy on the basis that we'll help to keep down the V.D. rate."

"And who's going to run all this?"

"There's a small group of women in Paris – widows mostly – who are experimenting with an old Christian concept of common life and service. They call themselves 'Les Filles du San Graal'. They don't wear religious dress. They don't make vows, just pledge themselves to service for as long as they can offer it. They've taken up this idea and they're going to staff the place for us. I've undertaken to supply medical service and try to raise the funds we'll need to keep going. It's a simple idea. A place for women to go when things get too much, a place to be when they're sick and friendless. We've got a motto. We're printing it on the cards which will be passed out around the quarter: 'Hospice des Anges. Here we make no judgments. We offer only friendship and service.' Well, what do you think?"

"What am I supposed to think?"

He tells me – tic-tac! – in a swift rattle of words.

"That it's a good idea! That you'll give us a lot of money and that you'll come and work here as a doctor!"

I simply do not believe what I am hearing. It is all too cliché for words. I round on him.

"If this is your idea of a joke, Gianni."

"No joke."

"You're out of your mind! I'm known on the circuit the girls come from! You'll make yourself and this place a laughing stock."

"Change your name then! Call yourself Sister Mary of the Angels. I don't give a damn! But I want you here."

"The money you can have, but . . ."

"To hell with your money! I want you. And you, by God, need this!"

"Like the plague I need it."

"You are the plague!" He is cold and utterly con-

386

temptuous. "You're the Black Death! You kill everything you touch – because you've never in all your life thought of anyone but yourself. This place is a refuge for the casualties you and your kind have created and will go on creating. I read Jung's notes on you very carefully. I understand you better than he does. I'm an odd one, like you. I'm also an old fashioned absolutist; and so – God damn it! – are you! You want to kill yourself. And you will one day; because you're a defaulting debtor and you don't want to face the accounting. I'm giving you a chance to do just that: pay life for life, child for child, love for hate. Jung wrote something about you that hit me like a hammer. 'She expects too much. She demands a god I can't reveal to her, an absolution she hasn't earned and probably never will!' How right he was! The only time you were close to God was at your husband's bedside and you ran away from Him. You couldn't face what He meant. The moment our first girl walks through our gate, with a broken nose and a dose of clap, He's going to be here again, and you're going to miss Him again – and again and again until you can't bear the solitude any more and you blow what's left of your brains out! Oh hell! What's the use! Come on, I'll get you a cab."

"Gianni!" He is halfway to the gate before I find my voice, a small unsteady voice that I hardly recognise as my own. "Gianni, wait a minute, please!"

"What is it?"

"Suppose. Just suppose I said yes."

"I'm supposing. Go on."

"How could it possibly work? You know everything about me now. I can't trust myself too far. You've said yourself I'm the Black Death. I know I

387

am. In a place like this I'm very close to old memories and not-so-old associations. I don't know what that's going to do to me."

"Frankly, I don't either. I'm gambling."

"Not on me, please! I'm a bad risk."

"There was something else in Jung's notes: 'She is much taken with the inscription over my door.' "

"I was impressed by it, yes. But I really did feel something should have happened: a puff of blue flame, divine fireworks. I don't know."

"I believe something did happen."

"What, for God's sake?"

"That day in Jung's house, you died a little."

"A little! Oh, Gianni, Gianni, so much of me died that the rest hardly matters!"

"That's what I'm gambling on: 'Si le grain ne meurt.' "

"Say that again."

" 'Si le grain ne meurt. Unless the seed dies it remains for ever solitary and sterile.' It's a quotation from the gospels."

"I've never read them."

"No matter. In this place you'll be living them, with the blind, the halt, the maimed – and the spirochete as well. Come on! Let me show you round. I need some suggestions."

"Gianni."

"Yes?"

"What are you doing to me?"

"Just what you asked Jung to do – except he didn't know how. This is a breech presentation, maximum risk, high-forceps delivery. You're being born again – into Angel Lane!"

"You're a bastard!"

"No, my darling, you have it wrong. You're the one born on the wrong side of the blanket. I'm a high born, totally legitimate Florentine snob!"

[FRAGMENTS IN EPILOGUE]

Undated letter from Emma Jung to Magda Kardoss von Gamsfeld

My dear one,
I cannot tell you how sorry I am that Anna Sibilla
has responded negatively to my letter; but at least
she has responded and I think we both understand
her answer. Sometimes it is best to leave things the
way they are, because the effort to change them is
too painful . . . Carl is vigorous. His fame grows, as
does his entourage. There is still love between us, of
a strange and thorny kind. He has never mentioned
you once since you left. I, of course, have said
nothing. I am content to enjoy our friendship in
secret.

Much, much love,
Emma.

Letter from Magda Kardoss von Gamsfeld to Emma Jung, probably written in January 1914:

I still do not know what holds me at the Hospice
des Anges. It is all so sordid and futile. The girls
come; the girls go. I clean up their infections, patch
up their injuries, dole out medicine, money and
useless advice – then wait for them to come back in
worse condition than before. I feel their pain. I rail
at their stupidity. I carry on a running battle with
the pimps and brothel touts who batten on them
like parasites. I change nothing. I am like a blind

donkey harnessed to the millstone, plodding around the same circle, day after day.

Why do I endure it? Perhaps it is because I am in the same state as your Carl, who needs an architecture, a structure to hold him together. Perhaps it is only because Gianni goads me and coaxes me and makes it seem that I am important in the scheme of things. He has no desire for me as a woman; yet he loves me and protects me against myself. When I am most deeply depressed, he insists on the point of honour: I am repaying a debt. When I ask to whom I am repaying it he grins and tells me: "To yourself of course. You cheated yourself of so much."

Sometimes – only sometimes – it makes a little sense. Even as I write, there is a girl child sleeping in a crib beside me. She would have died if I had not been here to deliver her. I wish I had the courage to adopt her. Gianni counsels against it. The Daughters of the San Graal will find a home for her . . . Well, my dear Emma, a New Year for both of us! I wonder . . .

Fragment of a holograph memo from the files of the Ministry of the Interior, with pencilled date 19 March 1914:

. . . The Minister met with Zed-Zed. Among matters discussed was the security of the houses of appointment on the Selected List. There is a danger that this security may be damaged by subversion or defection of the girls. Zed-Zed points out that some girls, who defect from the life in Paris, now find their way to the Hospice des Anges, where the principal medical officer is a woman of Austrian nationality, but of mixed parentage (Hungarian and English) who has herself a long record of sexual delinquencies. The situation is sufficiently anomalous to merit attention, especially in view of possible hostilities this year. You are requested to investigate and recommend appropriate action . . .

Letter to Frau Magda Liliane Kardoss von Gamsfeld, from the Vicarage, Bibury, England, dated 23 March 1914:

Dear Madam,

It is with great regret that I inform you of the death of Miss Lily Mostyn on the eighteenth day of this month. She passed, very peacefully, in her sleep. I had been to visit her the day before and found her most chatty and tranquil.

As one of the executors of her will, I am charged with the disposal of her effects. She has bequeathed directly to you a package of papers which turns out to be a translation of *The Scented Garden* in the handwriting of the late Sir Richard Burton.

This is, as you know, a valuable, if rather exotic item. May I ask whether you have any special instructions about its disposal? One would not want to run the risk of contravening regulations regarding the transmission of obscene material through His Majesty's mails.

I am remembering Miss Mostyn in our Sunday Service. You may wish to join your prayers with those of our congregation here.

Yours in the Communion of Saints,

(Signature illegible)

Vicar

Extract from an unpublished notebook of Carl Gustav Jung, inscribed Obiter Dicta, undated:

It has taken me a long time to come to terms with my failure in the case of Magda von G. I still cannot discuss it even with Toni; but at least I can contemplate it in meditation. One day I shall try to make clinical sense of it, although I shall never be able to publish it in literal form. It touches the living; it touches the dead; it is, for me, a numinous event, rich in mystery, heavy with terror. It raises questions to which I have still no adequate answers: the nature of evil, the complicated logic of guilt, man's absolute need of pardon as a condition of psychic health, the authority – or is it simply the love? – which makes the pardon acceptable and potent. Have I forgiven myself for what I did to Magda von G? Not yet, I think. Has she forgiven me? I shall never know. I have not found the courage to enquire whether she is alive, or dead . . .

Letter from Gianni di Malvasia to Arnaldo Orsini dated 26 April 1914:

. . . I am heartbroken over what has happened. I have lost a dear, dear friend. The hospice has lost a gallant and loving collaborator. At the same time I am so enraged, I could, myself, commit murder. The whole affair is so calculated, so brutal.

It was about eight in the evening. Magda had handed over the keys of the dispensary to the night nurse and was walking down the Ruelle des Anges to pick up a cab on the main road. A man was seen to step out of the shadows and speak to her. He

393

stabbed her once and then ran. Nobody stopped him. Passers-by picked Magda up and carried her back into the hospice. She was already dead.

The post mortem, which I performed myself, revealed a puncture that ran from the sternum upwards into the heart. The wound was obviously made by a cheese needle or a very fine stiletto. The police think it may have been a professional job. I know it was.

We have always had occasional trouble with pimps whose girls ran away from them and came to us; but this was something different. The hand that struck the blow was Corsican: thumb on the blade and strike upwards! The man who bought the service? Boh! I can never prove it. It is too dangerous even to set it down on paper. My house was burgled the other night. Little of value was taken but my papers were in disarray. What does that tell you?

I am leaving here and coming home to Italy. I have handed the hospice and the funds Magda left for its maintenance, to the Daughters of the San Graal. There will be war before the summer is out. I am told so on the best authority: Basil Zaharoff. He sent flowers to the graveside and wrote a most tender note about Magda and her work! I hope he rots in hell!

The Poor Clares were kind. They let me bury Magda in the convent cemetery. I had to be honest and tell the Mother Superior she was an unbeliever. The old girl was marvellous. She's eighty if she's a day; but she still has all of her wits about her. She told me: "Gianni, my boy, it doesn't matter what we believe about God. It's what He knows about us. Your Magda will be very welcome here."

I've left money for the headstone. I can't for the life of me think of an epitaph. How do you describe a woman like that? She was all of us, good and bad, rolled into one package – except she had the courage that most of us lack! I still haven't found the words; but they'll come. There is time. The ground hasn't sunk yet. The flowers have hardly withered on the grave. *"Il pleure dans mon coeur. . ."* I am lonely tonight. I never thought I could miss a woman so much . . .

MORRIS WEST

McCREARY MOVES IN

Mike McCreary was an oil man out of a job. His only possessions were a plane ticket to Singapore, a month's pay in Indonesian rupiahs, and the luck of the Irish. So when the mysterious Mr Rubensohn approached him with the offer of a breathtaking salary for a drilling operation on a remote island – no questions asked – he thought that luck was running with him once more.

But then he met Lisette, and within twenty-four hours he was involved in murder, intrigue and an international fraud of frightening proportions . . .

'A great writer'   *Daily Mirror*

POST A LITTLE HAPPINESS

Post·A·Book

A Royal Mail service in association with the Book Marketing Council & The Booksellers Association.
Post-A-Book is a Post Office trademark.

MORRIS WEST

THE SECOND VICTORY

NO SURRENDER ... The jeep skidded perilously on the icy surface and Sergeant Willis stopped to put on the chains. While he fitted them, Major Mark Hanlon stepped out into the road and looked up through his field-glasses at the mountains.

Then he saw the skier, a tiny black puppet, motionless. A moment later he began to move, gathering speed, in a flurry of snow – a wild, suicidal plunge down the dazzling hillside.

Hanlon watched him; breathless, waiting for the fall. But he came onward faster and faster, until they could see the grey of his uniform and the green flashes of the Alpenjäger regiment and the rifle slung between his shoulder-blades and the gleam of his polished pistol-belt.

An Austrian soldier, armed and in battledress. Yet the war had been over for months now ...

'Action and insight'

New York Times

HODDER AND STOUGHTON PAPERBACKS

MORRIS WEST

THE SHOES OF THE FISHERMAN

THE THRONE OF ST PETER

The Pope is dead – but the papacy lives on. Already, from all the corners of the globe, grizzled, scarlet-suited cardinals are gathering to elect a successor. Within the hushed confines of the Vatican, the air is alive with intrigue. Then in the midst of the most frenzied canvassing, comes a surprise result. The new Pope, Kiril I, is the youngest cardinal – and a Russian, recently released from seventeen years in the labour camps . . .

'A great writer'

Daily Mirror

'High drama . . . beautifully executed'

Sunday Times

'Tough, spare, and wholly unsentimental: a brilliant, vitally committed novel of our age'

Bookman

HODDER AND STOUGHTON PAPERBACKS

MORRIS WEST

THE NAKED COUNTRY

While riding to a lonely water-hole in the rugged heartland of Australia's Northern Territory, cattle-station owner Lance Dillon discovers aborigines killing his £3,000 stud bull in a ritual slaughter. In a desperate effort to save his bull and his livelihood Dillon attacks the aborigines. Badly wounded, he only just manages to escape to the bush with his life ebbing away.

But at the Dillon homestead, his city-born wife Mary and Neil Adams, the tough, handsome, local police-man, set out together to search for the lost man. Inevitably, the gruelling journey and the lonely, nightmarish bush bring them together and it is not long before each is secretly hoping that Dillon is never found alive . . .

HODDER AND STOUGHTON PAPERBACKS

MORE TITLES AVAILABLE FROM
HODDER AND STOUGHTON PAPERBACKS